Getting It Real

Selina Rosen

Getting It Real
Selina Rosen
First Edition Copyright © Selina Rosen, 2017

Published under "Just Cause," an imprint of Yard Dog Press at Create Space

ISBN 978-1-945941-04-7
Getting It Real
First Edition Copyright © Selina Rosen, 2017

Yard Dog Press
710 W. Redbud Lane
Alma, AR 72921-7247

http://www.yarddogpress.com

Edited by Tina Black
Copy and Technical Editor Lynn Rosen
Cover art by Melanie Fletcher

First Edition June 1, 2017
First EEdition 2017
Printed in the United States of America
0 9 8 7 6 5 4 3 2 1

Dedication

For my aunt, Mary Jean Gibbs, for always having my
back and for her love and support.

Chapter 1

There were days when Jerri forced herself to get out of bed, when she had to work to quiet her mind before she could even think to put her feet on the floor. It could be nearly impossible to do if there was nothing that needed her immediate attention. The—you have to get up NOW—factor was just one of the many reasons Jerri kept livestock on her farm. When you had things to feed, eggs to gather, and goats to milk... Well, animals didn't care whether you were depressed or sick or just didn't feel like getting up. All the things they needed still had to get done, and they couldn't do it themselves. So, because of the animals Jerri had to get up. She didn't have a choice.

As if to remind her of this fact one of the roosters picked that moment to crow from somewhere right outside her window. Since she didn't remember leaving them out the night before that added a little extra urgency to the getting up process.

She sat on the side of her bed running her hands through her hair and over her face trying to return some sense of feeling. It had been over a week since she had slept more than three hours in a night; it was starting to take its toll. When she looked at her hands they were shaking. She knew from experience that it had as much to do with fatigue as the nightmare she'd had in the short time she had slept.

The phone rang and Jerri jumped. She wasn't expecting it, but when she wasn't deep in the middle of an "episode" there wasn't much in the waking world that could startle her.

She took the phone off its cradle and put it to her head. "Hello."

"Jerri?"

"Yeah." Normally she knew who it was before she even answered but there was nothing remotely normal about her in that moment. Jerri didn't have any idea who it was until the other person laughed. "Janice?"

"Yes. It's nine. I thought you lived on a farm. That you had to get up with the chickens."

"I have them on a ten AM/ten PM feeding and milking

schedule because I still work from about nine in the evening to one in the morning." Jerri started doing the math in her head. When was the last time she'd heard from Janice? Hell it had to be years. "What's up?"

There was that signature laugh again then Janice said, "Everyone knows what's going on with us, but then I guess you don't do anything as mundane as watch TV up there in hippie land."

"A little, but I don't watch reality TV—which I consider to be neither—nothing personal. I see the commercials. The girls have certainly grown up." Jerri knew she shouldn't ask, knew it was just going to make Janice jump to the wrong conclusions, but she had to ask anyway. "How's Rhonda?"

"So I'm guessing you watch enough TV to know she's in the weeds again. I probably don't know much more than you do. She doesn't come over to just hang out much these days. She's out grown me—as a friend not as a client." Janice was hesitating, which meant two things. First, she knew a lot more about what was going on with Rhonda than she was saying and second would be the reason she had called in the first place. Janice wanted something from her but Jerri couldn't imagine what it might be.

"Ah..." Jerri tried to hold the phone and dress. In that moment she wished she had one of those fancy-shmancy phones she could have put on speaker, or even something without a cord. "...is there something I can do for you, Janice? I do have to do my chores."

Janice laughed again. "Your chores. You know someday I'd like to get up there to see that farm of yours."

"Well come on. I'm just a couple of hours up the coast tops." She sat down on the bed and started to pull her work boots on. Being focused on getting dressed it took a second for her to realize that Janice wasn't answering. "You still there?"

"Yeah. Listen, I have a favor."

Jerri smiled. She couldn't even work up surprised. "What?"

"Do you remember Tara?"

"The oldest one? She just got divorced, her husband was a dog. Now he's had a drug overdose."

"I thought you didn't watch the show."

"I don't but you know they show all the best crap in the commercials, and though I don't watch much news when I do there is nearly always something about one of you."

"And now I finally hear the, oh-so-familiar sound of disapproving Jerri.

'I just don't see how anyone can live a fulfilling life with a camera shoved up their ass.'"

"Well that would be pretty uncomfortable," Janice said, then sighed. "Tara divorced Fred and she was having a hard enough time but now the jackass damn near killed himself. He's in rehab and telling everyone that will listen that he can't cope without Tara. In other words he's blaming her for a problem that is only his. I know you know first-hand what that's like."

"Yes I do."

"He's saying that her leaving him was what drove him to drugs. That he just needs her back. His doing drugs is only one of a list of reasons Tara left him. She doesn't want to even talk to him, the media is having a feeding frenzy, and the tide of public opinion is against her. She needs... something."

"You need to hide her out here on the farm? That's fine but no camera crews, not here, not ever."

"She's been writing a book..."

"Ah come on, Janice! What did I ever do to you?!"

"I think it's actually a pretty good story it just needs something. I think the writing is helping her and if she focuses on it..."

"Come on, Janice!"

"Isn't that how you dealt with all your crap, Jerri?"

"Yes, but I had real crap, Janice..."

"So does Tara. She needs a distraction."

"Yes and God knows my life's work is a great 'distraction.' How about you try removing the three to six cameras that follow her everywhere she goes."

"That's a whole different argument and I don't want to argue with you because no one can win an argument with Jerri Blue." Janice let out an audible sigh. "I'm an agent. I know all sorts of models, actresses and rock stars, but the only actual writer I know is you. I don't want to play the, 'You owe me card,' but I will if I have to."

Because of course Janice had gotten her the agent that had made her career.

"Shiiit! Alright what exactly do you want?"

"Well I thought a nice drive in the country might do Tara

some good. If we should happen to wind up at your farm you could bring up writing, get her talking and..."

"You want me to make it look like you didn't talk to me about it at all." Jerri sighed.

"Don't act like you aren't at least that good an actress. Come on, Jerri. Tara isn't like my other two girls. They are all about letting me get them everything, but Tara... Well she wants to do things on her own. I don't think she likes being on camera any more than you think she should. She needs to do something right now that has nothing to do with the rest of us. She's been dabbling in writing since she was a teenager, she absolutely adores your body of work..."

"First the 'you owe me' card and now the flattery card, what's next, 'If you love me you will'?" Jerri finished lacing her boots and looked at the phone as if Janice was sitting there. "And what does Gary think about all this?"

"You don't by any chance think I give a damn what Gary thinks... Oh that's right you don't watch our show. Gary and I are barely speaking these days."

"So nothing really new," Jerri said with a grin.

"Believe it or not it's gotten worse, you know like everything else since the election. The truth is you and he agree on exactly two things: one being that the girls shouldn't be on TV, but that's mostly because no one's remotely interested in him unless he's screaming which is all he seems to do these days. Frankly I don't know what's eating him. Maybe the fact the kids are all grown now and way more famous than he ever was."

"You know he wouldn't want any of his girls talking to—much less working with—me."

"And see right now that only makes it sound like that much better an idea."

Some days it was nearly impossible to even get out of bed. Tara reached over and turned the phone off without bothering to look at the texts. After all it was a more or less constant stream of judgement twenty-four hours a day.

Today she hated that stinking smart phone and all the Twitter followers who were all weighing in on what she should do regarding her ex-husband's drug overdose. Most of them thought she should run to his bedside, be there for him, help him out of his dark pit of despair. Millions of people all thinking they knew what was best for her liberally dabbled with psychopaths who hated her—just because they had nothing better to do—saying things they wouldn't normally say to anyone they actually knew. They all had an opinion on how she should conduct her life, and she always had a way of knowing what they thought right at her fingertips thanks to technology. Most days she wished she lived alone somewhere, connected to no one. She needed some quiet, some real honest-to-God-I-can't-hear-anything *silence*.

She didn't have to log on. There was no part of her that wanted to so much as *touch* her smart phone.

She had been done with her husband way before he gave her an excuse to divorce him that her parents and the general public could get behind. Her followers and family had been all about hating him when he had been cheating on her. Suddenly now since he had nearly killed himself smoking crack she was supposed to go running back to "save him." Why did they think that? Because of course he just kept yelling into any camera that came near him how very, very sorry he was and how much he loved her; that he needed her.

It was all for show. What he'd done had nothing at all to do with her. Hell he'd been on drugs ever since she first knew him. He certainly wasn't doing them now because he was pining away for her. He was doing more of them now because she wasn't there to tell him not to so that he could then lie and tell her he wasn't. He was doing more drugs now because he didn't have to sneak around to do it. Tara refused to own any part of his overdose.

While she hoped he got the help he needed she didn't really care whether he lived or died and didn't have the need to go hold his hand on any level. She liked his family; they were nice people. They didn't deserve to have to deal with his addiction.

She was just so over all of it. In the last ten years she had gotten really used to having cameras following her three months on and two months off. Her wedding was televised, her marriage, the break up. Every minute of it, every doctor appointment, every pimple, every period for the last ten years was public knowledge. In fact if they were on hiatus and something of importance happened the camera crews showed up out of the blue because....

Their family's lives had become all about the ratings.

She lived her life in a fish bowl even when they weren't being filmed. Everywhere she went the press was right there. If Tara wasn't posting on Twitter or Instagram every three minutes her followers all started to write their own stories about what she was doing and thinking.

How bored was the American public? Her mother and two sisters had lots more social media followers than she did. Only her father had fewer followers than Tara did, and she still had millions.

She didn't really want Fred to die, did she? When they had been married, yes, no doubt because she hated being married to him and if he died that would have caused less crap than a divorce. She'd have much rather been Tara the grieved widow than poor, poor Tara whose husband had cheated on her, no doubt because she was fat.

During her brief marriage Tara had been more unhappy than she had in the rest of her life. The fact that people assumed her marriage had been all about ratings didn't help. She didn't get married for the ratings. She did, however, get married for all the wrong reasons though she didn't know that when she was doing it. At least she hadn't admitted to herself that she knew it was a huge mistake till she'd already made it.

The comedians all called Tara "the fat one". The rest of the world sometimes called her "the funny one" or "the smart one" but most of them called her "the fat one" too. She was taller and broader shouldered than her sisters and she had a flat ass—at least that was what her sisters told her. They were always suggesting liposuction from her stomach and sticking it on her ass. Irva was a model and Lori... Well Lori was famous mostly for being famous.

Tara helped her mother run her agency. Tara dealt with the "talent" especially if they were being difficult. She ran errands for her mother her sisters and the clients; mostly she handled the books and made sure everyone was where they were supposed to be when they were supposed to be there. Tara had a title, but most days she didn't remember what it was. The truth was she was mostly nothing more than her mother's glorified assistant. But she was a Darting girl which made her reality TV royalty.

Being a Darting meant that more people knew who she was and details of every aspect of her life than knew who the vice president was or what role he played in government. At least that's what had been decided on an E-entertainment poll. It had been like that for the last ten years. There was nowhere she could go where people didn't know her. Even when she went to another country she was still followed by the press with their cameras. Everyone knew her, so she couldn't walk out of the house without dressing to the nines. When she thought about it she was just like her sister Lori. Tara was mostly famous for being famous.

She was sick of the whole thing. Tired of strangers pretending they knew her—how could anyone possibly know her when she didn't even know herself? Millions wanted her to go hold Fred's hand and she was just glad he wasn't her problem anymore. Tara was damned if she was going to let herself be guilted into making him her problem again.

Fred had been a pro football player so Tara's father, "the most gifted quarterback to ever play the game," liked him and she'd realized way too late in the game that the only reason she'd been attracted to him at all was because her father approved of him.

Which he didn't anymore. Her dad didn't like cheaters, he didn't like drugs, and he was an all-black or all-white kind of guy; gray wasn't in his color spectrum.

Her mother kept telling Tara what she should tweet. Things like she wished Fred well but thought he needed his space. She didn't do it, so her mother had Lori tweet that Tara was heart-broken and couldn't stand to even talk about all that Fred was going through. That Tara couldn't bear to see him in this state, and wished him nothing but goodness, light and fairies flying out of his ass... Well maybe that wasn't exactly what she posted, but it was damn close.

Tara wasn't allowed to have her own feelings unless they were closely monitored for content. She had a role to play; she was supposed to be the funny one, the smart one, the laid-back one... the fat one.

The fat one. She'd lost the weight they had all said made her look fat and she was still "the fat one." So at the end of the day why had she bothered to kill herself to lose the weight? So that she could fit into a dress her mother had talked her into buying two sizes to small so she could have a goal? That wedding dress cost more than most people made in a year, and the wedding cost more than most people made in a lifetime.

The marriage had lasted less than a year, but felt like it had lasted ten. All such a huge waste, mostly of life.

Tara made herself sit up. In doing so she knocked a book off her nightstand. She looked at it lying on the floor. It was a stupid-assed Harlequin romance novel, the kind she hadn't read since she was a teenager. Tara couldn't imagine why she had dug it out now. She'd been reading a lot lately but certainly this was scraping the bottom of the barrel. She'd probably grabbed it in a stack of other books. She picked the book up off the floor, and when she did something fell out of it. She looked down and saw it was a four leaf clover. Curious, she picked it up and looked at it. When she finally remembered why it was there she started to throw it and the book away, but something made her put it back between the pages then carry the book over and put it back on her bookshelves.

She went to the bathroom, and when she walked back in her room she couldn't think of one single reason to get up, so she went back to bed.

Chapter 2

Tara's mother suggested they leave the city and drive into the country, no camera crew just the two of them. Janice said maybe a day communing with nature away from the city would do them both good. When she told Tara she could drive Tara was more than happy to dress casually as her mother—who never did—suggested she do and get the hell out of there.

Now they were driving her navy blue SUV on a dirt road which was mostly mud, and far from being pissed off she was excited that she finally got to put her car into four-wheel drive. Her mother said they were just going for a drive in the country with no destination in mind, but Janice kept looking at her phone. It was obvious she had a GPS helping "fate" tell her when to have Tara turn, so Janice was up to something.

They were in rolling hill country and had been climbing for the last fifteen minutes. The woods were occasionally broken by small funky little farms.

"Did we travel back to the sixties when we hit that big mud puddle?" Tara laughed. She was almost shocked. That was real laughter; she couldn't remember the last time she'd done that, just laughed without working at it. Her mother was right; just being in the woods away from the city was making her feel better about everything.

Suddenly the road just stopped at a wooden gate. Beyond the gate was a short driveway that ended at a small clapboard-sided house. It looked like something out of a fairy tale. On the gate in six-inch high hand-painted yellow letters it said, "Don't let dogs in or goats or chickens out."

Tara started to turn around but then Janice got out of the car and started waving.

"Jerri is that you?"

"Has to be. No one else wants to do it."

Tara heard the stranger reply, and then she watched as a tall, thin woman dressed in tattered jeans and a stain-covered white T shirt folded out of the woods and walked up to the gate. She also was like something out of a fairy tale, not quite real but amazing.

"Janice what the hell are you doing here?"

"Tara and I were just out on a drive. You remember Tara, don't you?"

"Barely."

The woman waved at her and Tara waved back though she knew she had been set up. She was so tired of her mother's constant meddling. She wondered just what the woman was. Her mother often came up with some wild-assed "healing" ideas. The woman might be a shrink, or a massage therapist, or someone who did energy work or talked to the dead. At the end of the day her mother was a new-ager. It didn't really match the business woman she was or her TV persona, but Janice was constantly contacting one psychic or another.

"Let me get the gate and you come on in. It's been too long."

Her mother was back in the car before the woman opened the gate.

Tara glared at her mother. "What the hell are you up to, Janice?"

"Nothing." She motioned for Tara to drive through, which she did. "You'll get a kick out of Jerri."

The gate was shut behind them and far from feeling trapped Tara felt... safe. She could feel the tension leave her body even before her foot actually touched the ground. As she shut the car door she took in a deep breath and looked around. The house had a small footprint, but was tall—two storied— so that it looked like something out of a Tim Burton movie. It had a porch that went across the front and wrapped around the east side. It had a tin roof, and the rails and the posts of the porch were made of twisted driftwood. The roof of the house was covered in solar panels, and there was a windmill behind it that was spinning in the gentle breeze that blew through the pines. She was aware of her mother and the other woman talking, but she didn't hear what they were saying.

She heard running water. When she turned towards the sound through the trees she could just make out a small creek, and she had the oddest sense of *deja vu*. Not like she'd been there before but more like this was something she had wanted to see her whole life. Yet it was all very simple, natural, clean.

"Tara, are you alright?" her mother asked.

"Yeah." She turned to look at the woman and smiled. "You have a fabulous place." She looked hard at the woman; she might have been forty. She looked familiar, but Tara couldn't place her.

"Thanks. I'd love to show you around."

"Tara, don't you remember Jerri at all?"

Tara started to lie but then felt like to do so would somehow foul the pureness of the earth there. "Not really."

Janice reached out and grabbed the long black braid the other woman wore and shook it. "You know I have to say I hardly recognized you with this. Last I saw you your hair was cut in a flat top."

"I got tired of paying for haircuts and when I tried to cut my own it looked like ass. Plus I read an article that said Native Americans lose their intuition when they cut their hair. Since my great grandfather was a Cherokee chief I thought why tempt fate. So I let it grow. Does it make me look too much like a girl?"

"Not at all." Janice grinned. "Do you have better intuition?"

"Not so as I've noticed."

"That's probably a good thing. You have always been way too spooky as it is."

Jerri pointed to the house. "Come on in and I'll get you something to drink."

The inside of the house was small with very little furniture but what was there was amazing—antiques that had been reclaimed just enough to make them functional but not enough to lose their history. It was the kind of stuff Tara always loved and that her mother had never let her have even in her own house. The walls were made of the same unpainted wood siding as the outside but inside everywhere she looked there were quotes painted on the walls in every color you could imagine and in every style. Some were even painted so that the words took on the shapes of different animals or plants.

Some quotes were attributed to different writers and scholars but some didn't have the author's name and among these was one she knew very well because it was from one of her favorite books. "If you have to lie to make a point the point you have made is that you're wrong." The minute she read it and saw it didn't have the author's name with it, she knew exactly who her mother's friend was.

"Jerri" was none other than Jerri Blue. Tara didn't

remember meeting her before, but then teens never pay any attention to their parent's friends and that was way before Tara had found Jerri's work—no doubt when she was reading all those crappy Harlequin romance novels. Her mother knew she wanted to write and she had brought her to meet Jerri Blue. Tara was no longer mad about her mother's meddling at all.

"Didn't your mother teach you not to write on the walls?" Janice asked.

"My mother abandoned us when I was three so if she did I don't remember. My dad was always all about us shutting up and sitting down. I buy up odds and ends of paints at yard sales and that's what I use–it stops it from going to landfills and then into the ground water."

Jerri could see that Janice was nervous and couldn't imagine why. Maybe she just wasn't used to doing anything without a half a dozen cameras running. Or maybe she saw the way Jerri was living and decided that Jerri had finally gone all the way to Madville. She wouldn't be the first one of Jerri's friends from her old life to think that. But the truth was the farm was the only thing that had kept her from going insane. Living wild had made it possible for her to finally find peace. She didn't have it right that second, but she knew she would again and that made even the worst things in her head bearable.

"It's my house I can write on my walls if I want to."

Jerri really was off her game because as she looked at Janice now she realized she wasn't nervous at all, she was worried. When Jerri looked at the kid she could see why. The girl was raw. Jerri was a little surprised. She knew all about being raw, but she didn't expect to feel it coming off in waves from this girl who had basically everything, who as far as Jerri knew had never been through an actual trauma. She turned her attention back to Janice.

"So how long has it been?"

"At least three years. I was thinking about it on the way… from the car."

Janice obviously caught herself about to step on her own lie. From the half grin on the kid's face, Jerri was pretty sure she wasn't fooled at all.

"I think it was Pat's party."

"Ah, yes. Pat's party." Jerri took in a breath and let it out.

"Yes, that's what she told me." Janice grinned. "Seriously, that was huge step backwards for both of you, wasn't it?"

"The sex in Pat's closet or the giant public fight afterwards?"

"Both I'm thinking," Janice said, with an understanding smile.

And Janice did get it. Janice was not only Rhonda's friend but also her agent, and at the time of Rhonda and Jerri's very public breakup Rhonda was by far Janice's most important client, but when they broke up Janice told Rhonda just exactly what she thought. Janice also told Jerri she was always going to be her friend, making Janice absolutely the only one of Rhonda's friends to do so. So even though Jerri didn't consider Janice a close friend, she considered her a really good one.

Seeing the chagrined look on the girl's face, Jerri smiled and said, "It was a really, really big closet."

"Yes as big as your whole house," Janice teased.

"Ha, ha. You can sit down if you like," Jerri said. "You want something to drink? I have about a dozen different kinds of herb tea, or I have some kick-ass grape wine."

"I have read all your books," the young woman blurted out like she was having a bout of Tourette's. No doubt she had just figured out who Jerri was.

"Thanks." Jerri smiled back. The last time she'd seen Tara—except for on TV in commercials—was about ten years ago. She wasn't lying—about not watching much TV and NO reality TV. She wrote fiction. As far as she was concerned TV kept people from reading books and reality TV meant there wasn't even script work. Not that she didn't make enough money; just that she knew a lot of authors who didn't.

"I want wine," Janice said.

"I'd have a little, too. I'm driving though," Tara said.

Jerri laughed. "No doubt because you want to live." She walked into her kitchen. The house was small on purpose, less area to heat, less area to cool. But her kitchen was the largest room in the house because... Well this was a working farm.

She poured the wine and brought it to them. When she walked in her guests were having an excited, whispered conversation that stopped as soon as they saw her. She handed them glasses, keeping the one she had poured for herself.

She sat in her chair—an old leather rocking recliner with just the right amount of wear.

"This is good, whose is it?" Janice asked after taking an experimental sip.

"Mine," Jerri answered.

"I know that, smart ass…"

Jerri laughed. "I am a grade-A smart ass, but I meant I made the wine. If I don't raise it and make it right here or get it from one of my homesteader friends I don't eat it unless I'm at a restaurant."

"You gave up coffee?" Janice said, knowing Jerri's extreme addiction to the brown liquid.

"Well no… I had to have some vice or God would take me right up."

"But didn't they recently decide that coffee was good for us?"

"Ah, man! Now ya have ruined it for me."

"Don't tell me you haven't found some lovely hippie chick to come up here into your rustic hovel and make an honest woman of you."

Unwillingly she looked at her friend's daughter who was no longer an irritating teen not-really-grown-into her face. She was a knockout with long dark hair—with a few artificial highlights—bright blue eyes, and a body your friend's kid shouldn't have. How old would she be now? Jerri did the math in her head and smiled. Hell "the kid" was thirty now, so it didn't make her a sick-o to check her out.

"I haven't been serious about anyone since Rhonda which I guess sounds pathetic but the truth is—Pat's closet aside— I've been over her a long time. I just have no desire to repeat a mess like that. And decent hippie chicks who want to help you with your off-the-grid lifestyle all want to get really serious, really quick. Fortunately there are lots of women who will happily give me a little, no strings attached. Let's face it, I'm sort of the Mount Everest of lesbians—you know bragging rights and all. Come on I'll show you around the house and then take you on the two-bit tour of the farm."

When Tara was a kid they would go camping and she would just run in and immerse herself in nature. But somewhere in her teens—when she started seeing everything she wanted as something wrong—she had put her love of the woods, plants and animals away with everything else. In Tara's adult life everything revolved around clothes, makeup, fashion and celebrity, seeing and being seen. It was a superficial existence that had never fed her soul, yet she hadn't realized till that moment that she was spiritually starving.

She had still thought nature was pretty but had been very happy to just look at it out the car window. She once wore six-inch stilettos on a date to the beach. Fred had called her an idiot. He had accused her of not appreciating anything that didn't come off a showroom floor or a shelf, and she'd yelled back at him that wasn't true because he came off a showroom floor and she didn't give a damn about him. The fans had loved that whole fight; the cable network ran the episode during sweeps.

For years she had liked the idea of nature but the minute she was getting nature all over her shoes and clothes she was done. Not today. With every step she took on what Jerri called the Blue Homestead she felt freer more alive, more what the self-help books her mother kept making her read called being present. The person she had buried all those years ago in a bid to be popular was coming back to life with every breath she took of air that smelled like air instead of car fumes.

They all just kept saying "be present". I read it and thought I knew what they meant, but I had no idea. This is being present. I left my phone in the car; I didn't even think of taking it with me. For years I've treated it like an umbilical cord without which I couldn't breathe or function, and now it's in the car and I don't miss it at all.

Tara took a deep breath and let it out slowly. She could smell the pine trees, the earth, she swore she could even smell the water.

And this, all of this is why Jerri Blue is here. She is here because here she can be present and just create without the pressure of the outside world bearing down on her.

"Jerri... did you build all of this?" Janice asked as they walked on a small rock and concrete bridge that went over the creek.

"Mostly. I had some help, but I designed everything. I always had my hands in the building."

"You always were a creative little shit," her mother said, and Tara realized that while it hadn't been the case when they first arrived her mother seemed more relaxed by the minute. For one thing Janice just didn't cuss this much, no doubt because she was very aware that they were always being watched and everything they did was recorded.

Hearing her mother, who was all of five-six, refer to the woman who was every bit as tall as Tara's five-eleven frame as "little" made her smile. Then she knew why Janice called Jerri "little." It had nothing to do with Jerri's size; Jerri was at least ten years younger than Janice, probably younger than everyone in that group of friends... and well now she knew which Rhonda they were talking about. The woman Tara called Aunt Rhonda. Rhonda Heart, the rock star with more platinum records than she had face lifts. Who filled stadiums and sold records in staggering numbers, who had never hidden her affairs with women and had married at least three men. Rhonda was currently suing husband number three for custody of her only child; a boy of five who was such a holy terror that when Janice had once asked Tara to watch him while she had a meeting with Rhonda Tara pretended she was coming down with the flu.

She looked at Jerri, thought of Rhonda, and made a face for two reasons. First she just couldn't see those two as being together they seemed all wrong for each other and try as she might she couldn't remember seeing them together at her house. Second thinking about all that had pulled her right out of the present and being unused to being present she found she couldn't just jump right back into it.

At least not till they got to the barn and without asking if Tara wanted to hold it, before she had even seen them in the pen, Jerri handed her a tiny goat kid. Tara took it and the "present" was right back. Jerri helped her to hold it till it seemed content to let her.

"That is the cutest thing ever," Janice said, petting the goat as Tara held it.

"I like the pigmies because they'll breed at nearly any time. These are African pigmies, so they are really hearty and give good milk, but if I'm honest I mostly have them because the babies are just so damn cute," Jerri said.

Suddenly as Tara looked at the little goat in her arms she thought back over everything she had seen since she'd been there and realized something profound. "This is the farm from Walking River."

Jerri gave her a startled look. "Wow, kid, that's fucking

amazing. Do you know that no one else, not my very in-tune friends who are here all the time, not my brother, no one else has ever guessed that. You're right of course, right down to the goats."

"It's my favorite book," she said. *No wonder I feel so at peace here. When I read the book I kept picturing the place in my mind and it always made me feel better, always. I would skip the scenes most people read over and over and just read the description of this place... She knows it brings peace because she built it to do just that. It makes me wonder just how much of her work is nearly autobiographical.*

Jerri stood by Janice against the fence and watched as the girl waded through the goat berries and straw playing with the kids. Jerri had two kids at the current time. She kept three does and one buck. The buck she kept in a pen halfway across her property because he stank, but mostly because he was a bastard. He was a necessary evil, and by evil she meant *evil.*

"If you would have told me in a million years that Tara would willing walk around in goat shit to play with animals I would have told you that you were crazy. Thanks, Jerri. Even if you don't help her with her writing, thanks for today. This is the first time I've seen her smile a real smile or laugh a real laugh in months."

"The city stifles us, Janice," Jerri said simply. She stopped herself from going off about having their family paraded across the TV screen with an effort.

"I'm sorry it's been so long since I touched base with you."

"I could have called you. The truth is I hole up here for weeks at a time and see only a handful of my closest friends and the neighbors. I haven't been to LA except to work since you saw me last."

"Why not?"

"First I don't like or need the city. Second... Well you were right, and what happened at Pat's was a giant step backwards for me. I had just started to think I was ready for a real relationship and then I did that. Honestly it wasn't till just recently that I was finally ready to wade into relationship waters again and then... Something else happened. I'm beginning to think that if a healthy relationship was in my future something crappy wouldn't happen every time I'm even thinking about it."

"I won't pretend to understand Rhonda. I love her, but I don't get her."

"Yes you do, Janice. In that way you and I are exactly alike. We know what she is. She wants everything when she wants it and wants it to go away when she doesn't. That includes the kid she's fighting over right now. I have been over her a long time, but banging her again reminded me of how stupid I was when I was with her, put me back in a place where I didn't feel like I could really trust myself to ever make a good choice when it came to a woman."

Janice smiled. "So you do watch some TV."

"Actually I read about it on the web." Jerri grinned. "And before you give me a lecture I wasn't lying, I'm done with her, but I still care what happens to her. I still worry about her. As much as she used and abused me let's face it if it wasn't for Rhonda no one would even know that I write, and I sure as hell wouldn't have the awards I've won or had all the bestselling books. Rhonda's narcissism hurts no one as much as it hurts her. Being connected to her—that's the only reason I'm allowed to do the job I love and have all of this." She waved her hand around. "I wouldn't have any of it without the money those books make me. So yes, she hurt me. But the truth is that all she really did was open a wound so corrosive that it made me have to finally face all my demons which made me a much better writer and frankly a more contented person."

"You don't seem happy, Jerri."

"Most of the time I'll take peace of mind over happy any day. Happy is a lot of work. Most days I'm content. I have PTSD, I didn't know that when I was with Rhonda,"

Janice looked at her and it was obvious that she wasn't surprised.

"The constant yelling which Rhonda thinks is alright in a relationship just about killed me. So I now know that I'm so much better off without her. But you see having the trophy girlfriend, that made me feel worthy and till then I never really had. When she kicked me out the way she did it ripped that away from me. I had to fix me. Now most days my worth comes from within."

"As it should because there isn't anyone any better much less as talented as you are."

"I'm still not completely healed, maybe I never will be, but most days I'm great. I had something happen recently. To tell the truth if I didn't badly need the distraction, if I didn't hang out with a lot of very spiritual pains in the asses who believe everything happens for a reason and other such mystical crap, I probably would have told you not to come up here at all. I have to tell you one of the things I avoid like the plague is dealing with ANY want-to-be writer."

"She needs something, Jerri, something real. You're right; I hate to say it but you are. Being always in the public eye has changed all of us but the other girls... even Gary who bitches about it constantly... will shove the girls out of the way to get his camera time. Tara has never really found her place. She has body issues...."

"Are you kidding me? That kid is built like a brick shit house," Jerri said.

"That's my kid, Jerri. Could you maybe turn the perve way down?"

"You know I really can't," Jerri said with a grin. When she looked the girl was holding the other kid which she had caught on her own. She really was just a kid, thirty or not. "It would be easier if she WERE ugly."

"Can you help her, Jerri? At least look at what she's doing and set her on the right path? You know without all your usual brutal honesty about what you think is crap.'

"That's asking an awful lot," Jerri said with a smile, but then got serious. "I have yet to kick someone when they're down, and I can feel the rawness of her."

"What the hell does that mean my crunchy granola friend?"

"So she's read my books but you haven't."

"Not all of them."

"She's neither what she was nor what she will be. She feels lost and hopeless and without direction. She s looking for something but has no idea what it is. She hates what she was and fears what she will become. She's raw. She's raw and in the public eye where she can't escape to find herself because everyone has already decided what she should be. She doesn't want to let anyone down but is sure she can't help it because she doesn't fit where everyone says she belongs."

Janice nodded and took a deep breath. "I forgot how smart you are."

"Because I've always done really stupid-assed things. Besides you haven't really known me for ten years. I'm not

the same person I was any more than you are the same person
that I knew. I reached a point where I either had to fix myself
or stick a bullet in my head."

"Do you think... Is Tara suicidal?"

"No," Jerri said without hesitation. "She is in a state of
flux which is never easy anyway and even harder because of
the lifestyle you—not she—chose."

As they were walking back across the bridge Jerri said
without turning, "Your mother tells me you are writing a book."

"I am." Tara went right back to being mad at her mother
for meddling.

"Why don't you send it to me? I'll have a look at it, we can
meet later and I can give you some suggestions."

"It's really just rough; I'm not even half finished and..."

"I will take all that into account," Jerri said. "I'd like to help
you if I can. After all some writers are a lost cause... Of course
most of them sell more books than I do."

"Alright," Tara said, but she couldn't have really told anyone
how she felt about Jerri Blue looking at her work.

As they were getting into their car Jerri took hold of her
hand and she turned to look at her. "You see this place how
beautiful and green it is?"

"Yes it's wonderful just the way I pictured it."

"During the drought the creek stopped running, most of
my ponds dried up, my garden even my orchard and vineyard
were in trouble because I was so carefully rationing water.
Everything dried up; it was brown and dead looking. Just
when I thought I was going to have to give up completely on
my garden and start hauling water in just to keep myself and
my animals alive it started to rain. Soon it looked just like this
again. Remember, the rain always comes."

Tara nodded. "Thanks."

As they were driving away her mother said, "Well I have no
idea what that was about the rain and such."

"No matter how bad things get they always get better,"
Tara said, and found herself wondering for the thousandth
time how someone as smart as her mother could be so stupid.

Chapter 3

What a pile of crap, Jerri muttered as she looked at the manuscript in her hand. She had printed it off because she hated the editing program on the computer. Now she was wondering if there were enough red pens in this part of the state much less her house to mark all the mistakes. There was a knock on the door. She happily set the manuscript down and went to open it. When she did she grabbed the woman—so tall she dwarfed Jerri—who stood there and hugged her. "My God, Judy, are you a sight for sore eyes. What brings you here? I thought you were working in the holy land." She meant San Francisco of course.

"I was I just got home. I'd like to say I just came by for some free-range eggs and local honey, and I will get some before I leave or my wife will kill me, but the truth is Cyndy told me you called. Since you NEVER just call I came to check on you. So what's wrong?"

Jerri took her arm, led her into the house and pointed at the couch. Without asking she went and got them two glasses of wine, setting one on the coffee table in front of Judy. She took the other one walked over and sat in her recliner.

"It's been a hell of a couple of weeks," Jerri said, and noticed a catch in her voice that immediately pissed her off.

"You're my best friend, shithead. You know you could call my cell phone any time night or day."

"You know what? You are my best friend, and I know what it's like to get up in front of a roomful of people and talk. The last thing you needed was my meltdown. You're working for our rights. You're on the front line fighting for our community which I have done, too. It's nerve wracking; you've got to be able to focus. That was more important than dealing with my stuff."

"Not to me, Jerri. I think you forget what you did for me, everything you did for me. So what happened?" Judy asked. Judy wasn't just her best friend; she was one of the best psychiatrists in the state, so not telling her wasn't an option.

"Remember that kid I gave up for adoption twenty years

ago?"

Judy sat up very straight and tried not to gasp, which would have been funny under normal circumstances. "Yes?" Judy finally said.

"Well as you know I have kept in touch with the couple who adopted her. They called me two weeks ago—which wasn't so unusual—but then they told me that the kid turned twenty and for the first time she asked about me. The kid always knew she was adopted. The deal I had with them was that if she ever felt like she needed to meet me I would meet with her. Seriously, Judy, after the kid turned fifteen I thought I had dodged that bullet." Jerri fell silent taking a long drink of her wine.

"Are you going to meet with her?"

"I already did."

"For the love of God, Jerri, you never should have gone through that on your own."

"What makes you think that I did?"

"Because I know you; if you didn't call me you called no one. What happened?"

"Well of course Amy and Tim have always known how I got pregnant and why I didn't want the baby, but they had never told her. They said it was up to me what I told her. They had given the kid my birth name; they didn't even tell her I was Jerri Blue, so that sort of told me they would rather I didn't tell her. They flew into San Francisco, and I met them there."

"So... You literally could have driven across town and gotten me before you met them or if nothing else come to me afterwards."

"Before I didn't want to bother you with it because I really thought I could handle it and afterwards... I didn't want to be near anyone at all. I had an episode nearly as bad as the one I had when Rhonda kicked me out. I just needed to get home as soon as I could. I have to be honest; I don't remember most of that drive..."

"What was she like?"

"She was tall like me, she had my eyes, but she didn't look at all like me which immediately made my flesh crawl. Amy and Tim were the same great people they were when they took her; I was actually really glad to see them. They've done a great job with her, she seems pretty solid, but of course she had to ask why I gave her away."

"And what did you tell her?" Judy asked, a careful note to her voice knowing she was treading on dangerous ground.

"I lied out my ass. Told her I just had to see if I might be straight, that I had a one-night stand with a stranger and wasn't in a place or in a state of mind where I could raise a baby."

"How did you feel about that?"

"You are such a shrink."

Judy smiled. "Don't say it like it's a bad thing and answer my question."

"I could see by the look in Tim and Amy's eyes that they really didn't want me to tell her the truth any more than I wanted to. I couldn't tell that poor, ugly kid...."

"Was she really ugly?"

"Like a mud fence. Like I said she looked nothing like me. So I told her a lie, she seemed to buy it, and I felt pretty good about it but that didn't stop me from opening the wound, or it from bleeding anything remotely sane from my brain. I started looping pretty bad."

"But you seem like you're handling it right this minute."

"I have this really good friend who has worked really hard to teach me coping skills," Jerri said with a smile. "And I have to say that just talking to you always makes me feel better."

"How did you feel meeting your daughter?"

"The truth?"

"A lie would be a waste of both of our time."

"I was glad she was healthy that she has made Tim and Amy happy because people that want kids should have them. I would have aborted that kid if they didn't want her so badly, so they are literally the only reason she's alive. I can honestly say that I felt not one ounce of connection to her. She hugged me and I hugged her back. I thought I'd have a sense of connection and I just didn't. I didn't meet my daughter; I met Amy and Tim's daughter. I hope I answered some questions for her even though my answers were mostly lies. I maybe talked to her for all of fifteen minutes. I just couldn't stay there and talk to her. I tried; I just couldn't. I couldn't look her in the eye even for that short period of time. I felt like a heel because it was an awful long way for them to travel for nothing. I'm sure I didn't answer all of her questions, but if I had stayed I was going to lose my shit in front of her which wouldn't have helped anyone. Seeing her... It was never something I needed. Does that make me a terrible person?"

"There is not now, nor has there ever been, anything terrible about you my friend." A tear came to Judy's eye. "Can I hug you now or do you still not feel like being touched?"

"You can hug me. I think I need a good hug."

They drank a couple more glasses of wine as they talked about everything and nothing. Judy admitted she wasn't going to be safe to drive until she allowed some of the alcohol to leave her system.

"What exactly did Janice want?" Judy asked.

"For me to turn one of her camera whores into a writer," Jerri said, pointing at the pile of manuscript on her coffee table. She sighed. "And see that was just mean. She's a nice kid and so raw right now it hurt to be near her."

"That's probably going to get worse before it gets better," Judy mumbled.

"What?"

"Nothing. Well how is it?" Judy asked pointing at the manuscript.

"Every bit as terrible as you would think but... She actually has a good idea for the plot and she's built some really interesting characters. She can tell a story and there is a glimmer of magic in it. But it's a mess. She doesn't understand tense at all; she jumps viewpoints so many times without warning that you never know whose head you're in, and she absolutely does not know which "to" to use—ever."

"So all things you could fix easily."

"Yes," Jerri hissed. "Exactly. But I hate working with new writers. You know how they are—every word they have written is gold and they just don't see why you don't understand that's the way they want to tell the story. You know—wrong."

"But you'll do it anyway simply because you think you owe the kid's mother because she wasn't hateful to you at one of the lowest moments of your very traumatic life. You're going to delve into the process not because of anything the woman ever did for you but because of what she didn't do."

Knowing Judy was right, Jerri wanted to change the subject. "So what's this big deal you were talking about earlier? The one that's going to flip America on its ear when it comes to how they look at the trans community?"

"I can't say yet...."

"Not even to me?"

"No, but if things go the way I can see them going I am definately going to need you on board."

"Yet I can't know the super secret."

"No, because to tell you I would have to breach patient-doctor privilege."

Jerri let it go mostly because she wanted to believe that patient-doctor privilege really meant the things she had told her doctor would never be repeated even to their best friend.

Tara had Jerri Blue's e-mail address and after three days she seriously considered e-mailing her and asking if she'd had a chance to look at the book yet and what she thought. She really wanted to work on the book but felt sort of stupid going forward if Jerri was going to tell her it was a piece of shit or she needed to go in a totally different direction.

In the hallway she could hear the camera crew following her sister around as Lori told them how distraught Tara was over Fred. Because of course they had let Fred out of the rehab because he demanded they do so. Since he had checked himself in after he OD'd, no one could make him stay. The night before he'd gone right to one of the more popular clubs and within minutes Instagram was lighting up with pictures of Fred obviously drinking and at least drunk.

Lori started banging on her door. "Are you alright, Tara?"

"No, I'm horribly distraught," she said, mocking her sister.

Fred had been drunk texting her most of last night. She tried not to look at what he was writing but it was hard because the things he said were hurtful. What she didn't do was answer him. She'd just ignored him and deleted his texts. Unfortunately he had moved on to her Twitter account where he blew it up. He was calling her a fat cunt, talking about how bad she was in bed and other such sweet ex-husband things. To her mind he was showing his true colors. She could only hope the rest of the country saw it that way. He didn't give a damn about her and he never had. He wasn't crushed she'd kicked him out; he was mad. Mad because she didn't beg him to come back and save him from dwindling into obscurity, mad that she wasn't devastated not to be with him. Fred's football career was over and he couldn't do ANYTHING else. He was missing his fifteen minutes of fame and doing everything he could to pull her back into his life so he could get the spotlight back on him. Even if he had to literally kill himself to do it.

Tara might feel sorry for him if he wasn't chewing her to pieces on the Twitter verse, if the things he said didn't hurt, if every time he opened his mouth or keyed in a text she didn't feel like kicking her own ass for ever having anything at all to do with him—spreading her legs for much less marrying him.

Tara had convinced herself she didn't really wish Fred dead, but now she couldn't even pretend that she didn't hope the bastard popped so many pills or smoked so much crack he just keeled over.

If nothing else it was his fault the camera crews were back. They were supposed to have two more weeks without them.

So the person she was most pissed off at was her mother because Janice was the producer. She could have told the rest of the team of producers and the cable network no, but... Their whole life was about ratings, so if something horrible happened they simply must get that on tape.

She would have liked to go out with HER friends, maybe have a few drinks and a good time and just work at getting out of her funk. But Tara didn't dare step out the door because right now there was a price on her head. If the press caught her smiling or frowning—they didn't care—either way they'd use one picture to write a whole story. All because her ex was acting like the asshat that he was.

The worst part? At the end of the day she had no one to blame but herself. No one made her go out with, have sex with, or marry the bastard. She had made a really bad choice. It was an extension of the same bad choice she'd been making for years; she was trying to be what everyone else wanted her to be till she had no idea who she really was.

"Tara, at least come out and eat breakfast," her mother said from right outside her door.

"I don't want to." She pulled one of the more nasty tweets her ex had put up and read it out loud, "Tara is a fat cow. Just be glad none of you have to see her naked... That's an image I won't soon get out of my head. It almost puts me right off sex... almost."

"Tara, come on now that's enough of this."

"You know what Mom? Send the cameras away and I'll go to breakfast."

"Honey you need to be able to show your side of things...."

"Yes during sweeps no doubt."

What was her side of it? Would the truth be any easier for the general public to swallow than what they thought was true? She had never loved Fred, she had married him only because she thought it was her duty to marry, she didn't care whether he lived or died but she was leaning towards him dying. She didn't think the truth would win her any popularity contests.

After a brief moment of silence her mother started, "Your fans...."

"Are a bunch of people I don't know and who don't know me, feeding on my carcass." She got up and started dressing though she had no intention of leaving her room—at least not through the door. She'd spent the last ten years on TV; she knew how to get out of her room and out of the house without being seen on most days.

She dressed in jeans and a neon-blue spaghetti-strapped T then she slipped on matching high tops and laced them up. She grabbed her purse and threw it over her shoulder. Tara picked up her phone started to stick it in her pocket then instead turned it off and set it back on the bedside table.

"Tara, you need to come out now. This is getting ridiculous," her mother said.

"Everyone's on your side, Tara," Lori said helpfully. "Just look at Twitter."

"Bite me, Lori!"

Lori with the douche-bag live-in boyfriend and the two rug rats lived for every moment the camera turned on her. "Why don't you take them to see the shrine you made to your dead dog?" She used the yelling to cover the fact that she was opening the window. "America ate that shit up. Why don't you just do thirty more minutes of crying over a dog you had less than a week that dad ran over in the driveway because you didn't care enough about the God-dammed thing to make sure it didn't get in the road."

As Lori started screaming obscenities at her, Tara climbed out the window and started across the garage roof. When she got to the end of the roof she climbed down the downspout the way she had dozens of times before, often with one or both of her sisters with her. She saw the paparazzi outside the front gate. Ignoring them as they yelled her name she got in her car and started it as her dad ran out the front door.

"Tara where the hell do you think you're going?" he thundered.

She backed out of the twelve-car garage and headed for the gates with her father chasing after her. It was a good thing he wasn't as fast as he had once been or he might have caught her because the gates took so long to open.

"Dammit Tara, don't do anything crazy!" her father yelled as she sped out of the gates and he gave up his chase. She almost ran over a couple of paparazzi, but at the end of the day most of them were used to jumping out of the way of moving vehicles.

A couple of them tried to tail her, but she easily lost them and she just kept driving.

Chapter 4

Jerri was busy putting in potato slips when she thought she heard someone at the front gate. A few seconds later she heard a car door slam.

"Son of a bitch!" she cursed.

The cat meowed.

"No not you. I'm trying to get my potatoes in before it rains, and..."

"Hello, is anyone home?" She heard a woman yell from out front of her house.

"Son of a bitch," she said.

Again the cat meowed.

"No, I said not you. Stay here and put the potatoes in."

The cat meowed again.

"You lazy son of a bitch... That time I was talking to you."

She stood up, wiped the dirt off her hands onto her pants and started towards the house. "I'm coming."

As she walked across the bridge she recognized the car and could see the girl standing beside it, not that she was surprised at all.

"Oh great," she mumbled. "Just once I'd like to be wrong. Now I get to dash a little girl's hopes and dreams on the rocks. It's been such a really great month so far."

Tara started walking to meet Jerri, and as she got closer Jerri could tell that the girl's energy was scattered and if anything she was even rawer.

"And now I have to find some gentle way of telling her the book is a wall-eyed mess. All I wanted to do was plant my fucking potatoes." She looked skyward and muttered, "Thanks a hell of a lot God."

"Hey kiddo," Jerri said as the girl got closer.

She stopped about five foot in front of Jerri and she was leaking negative energy.

Jerri concentrated on putting her shields up. She had a big enough storm brewing on the inside; she didn't need anything coming at her from the outside.

"I wanted to..." The kid was so rattled she hadn't even

come up with an excuse to be there.

"What's wrong?" Jerri asked.

The girl broke down, crying huge, wracking sobs.

"Son of a bitch." Jerri mumbled, walked over and held the woman letting her cry on her shoulder, patting her back for several minutes before she said, "I understand just needing to be out of the city, just needing to be away from all the noise. Come on now..." She let her go. "...as long as you're here you can help me put in my potatoes. I figure we have about thirty minutes before it starts raining." She reached in her pocket, pulled out the red bandana she'd been wiping sweat on for two days, and handed it to the girl who gratefully took it. "All I did was sweat on it I swear."

The girl nodded and wiped her eyes and nose on it. If she noticed the funky smell she didn't say so. She followed Jerri to the garden more or less silently until they were there.

"It's beautiful."

It was; Jerri knew it. A terraced hillside of rich, black earth freshly turned ready to start to receive seeds and plants was one of her favorite things.

The orchard was to the left and the vineyard to the right. "You should see it when all the trees are in bloom when the grapes are leafed out and the plants are all growing."

"I'd love to." Tara smiled. "You know what surprises me? I really like the smell of the dirt."

"Me, too. That's 'too' with two o's by the way. You must have gardening in your soul. People who don't never even realize the dirt has a smell."

"When I was a girl my mother used to garden; I used to help her."

Jerri nodded. She actually remembered Janice gardening.

"I've already cut the slips." She picked one up and showed it to the girl. "I'm sorry, what's your name again? I'm shit with names."

"Tara."

"Like terra firma and you like the smell of dirt. Alright now I should remember it. Do you see the hills?" She pointed to the first of a row of them.

Tara nodded.

"Take the slips and push them into the dirt with this part up. Put about eight to a hill; these are big hills. You start at that end and we'll met somewhere in the middle hopefully just before the sky opens up." She handed the girl a spade and a bag full of slips briefly noticing her nail job that probably cost more than most women her age made in a week.

She kept an eye on Tara. Far from being afraid of getting dirty, Tara was immediately on her hands and knees digging in the dirt planting the slips. She didn't look disgusted; she looked at peace and her energy immediately quieted. Jerri dropped her shields.

They put the last slips in the hills just as it started to drizzle.

The barn is closer, Jerri said. Gathering up her tools she started booking towards it. Tara wondered why, but ran right after her. Just as they hit the barn the sky opened up. The rain on the tin roof was loud and Jerri yelled over the sound, "Perfect timing!"

Tara walked over to the stall where the goats had run in even as they had. "Can I?"

"Knock yourself out; only try not to let the big ones in here. They go right for the feed bin, and I have to wrestle them back into their pen. It's a whole thing."

Tara soon found out what she meant when the goats crowded the gate, all pushing against it. Jerri walked over and helped her in. Tara grabbed one of the kids and picked it up.

"Bring it on out here so you don't have to deal with those assholes."

Tara walked through the gate with the kid as Jerri kept the big goats in their pen. There were two lawn chairs in the barn. Jerri sat in one and indicated that Tara should sit in the other, which she did. She started to pet the kid and without looking up asked, "So what was wrong with my story?"

Jerri laughed, not a bad sound at all. "There is nothing at all wrong with your story or your characters. The only thing wrong is the way you are telling it and... Well I can teach you how to do that if you won't have a meltdown..."

"To me, you are the greatest writer who ever lived. I'd have to be an idiot not to listen to what you have to say. Though I play one on TV, I'm not really an idiot."

"I never thought you were, and for the record I have never seen the show. So what brings you here?"

"I really just want to write now because it's helping me

cope. Somehow I think you might understand that."

Jerri nodded.

"But I didn't want to just keep working on it if it's a piece of crap or if I'm going in the wrong direction."

"First off, don't let something like that stop you from writing. Write crap. Get it down; you can always fix it later. Besides I can give you a few hints and if you listen it will fix all your problems. First off you need a lesson in tense..."

So as the rain fell and she sat there holding and petting that tiny goat Jerri Blue gave Tara her very first writing lesson.

The rain had finally stopped and they'd gone back to the house where Jerri fixed them some lunch. They'd eaten and then she had started going through the manuscript with Tara page by page explaining the marks she had made. Tara asked questions but she never disagreed and seemed to be as good as her word.

When she was making dinner Tara asked if she could help. Jerri had her slice some tomatoes she had picked from the green house that morning. Tara grated the cheese while Jerri made her version of pizza crust which was really just cornmeal with a little flour in it—no leavening, so mostly it was a big tortilla. She rolled it out and spread the tomato slices on it and then the cheese. She then diced fresh oregano, basil and thyme, threw that on and slid it into the oven. Jerri poured them a couple of glasses of wine and they sat at the table as they waited for dinner to cook.

"So you really raise all of your own food?" Tara asked, sipping at the wine.

"Mostly. I buy coffee, salt, chocolate—you know important stuff. I have a neighbor I trade milk for flour and one I trade wine for beer. This is a great community for bartering because most everyone is raising something and has some skill. We trade for what we don't raise or make. I'll sometimes go weeks and not even drive my truck. Most of the time I scoot around the neighborhood in my electric golf cart. My whole place runs on solar and wind power; it's why my appliances are pretty small. I love it, all of it."

"What made you decide to live like this?"

"You mean because 'aunty' Rhonda is a material girl?"

"I didn't mean to pry...."

"If I really thought you were prying I'd bow up and tell you nothing." Jerri grinned. "You're right. When I was with Rhonda we were trying to burn our own hole in the ozone. But that lifestyle... It was never really a good fit for me. I had been poor most of my life, so I thought I wanted all the things that make other people say, 'Wow! You're so successful.' You know the things only lots and lots of money can buy. It took me awhile to understand that *stuff* wasn't going to make me happy. I had started my work life framing houses in Tennessee where I'm from. I got out of there for a lot of reasons. I came here and I got a job which had me framing one of Rhonda's houses. She saw me and had to have me. Because of Rhonda I met your mother who introduced me to my agent. I sold a book, and because I was with Rhonda the book did really well. The numbers had nothing at all to do with the merit of my work and everything to do with who I was sleeping with. When Rhonda left me—or in more accurate terms kicked my ass out—I moved into my own apartment. Long story short I had a mental breakdown. One morning I was lying in bed wondering what the point of getting up really was."

Tara's head jerked up.

"I can see you know exactly what I'm talking about. I lay there not even feeling sorry for myself because I was way past feeling and... There was so much *noise*. The more I tried not to hear it, the louder it got. So I got up, went to the window, and all I could see besides the things man had made was the smog all those things had made. The noise was deafening. I got in my car and in my head I said, 'I'm going to drive this car out of this hellhole I'm going to drive to the middle of nowhere and buy the first place that feels right to me.' And that's exactly what I did. Ten years later I'm still here and it still feels right."

"How did you learn to do... Well all the things you do?"

"Writers love to read, and we really don't believe that there is much you can't learn from a book. I already knew how to build. In a community like this one what you don't know someone else will happily teach you. We trade skills and ideas as easily as things. I had plenty of money a lot more than I needed. Because of that I could afford to buy and build just exactly what I wanted. Not having to pinch every penny makes building something like this simple, easy. In fact, if I'm not careful I could feel guilty about how much easier it is for me than it is for my neighbors."

She got up and got the "pizza" out of the oven. She left it to cool for a while and turned to face Tara. "A lot of my friends from the city think this is the craziest thing I've ever done."

"I love it here. The craziest thing you ever did was have a thing with Rhonda Heart." She made a face and Jerri laughed.

"Oddly enough that's what all of my real friends think, too. But without her I'd probably still be framing houses."

Tara shook her head. "No way. You're too talented a writer..."

"Come on, Tara, if you admit it you know as well as I do that at the end of the day talent by itself will get you nowhere. In the entertainment business luck and connections will beat out talent and hard work every day."

She cut the pizza and stuck it in the middle of the table then set out a couple of plates.

"Don't you get lonely?"

"Sometimes I miss having a woman around if that's what you mean. If I miss it too much I go find it for a few hours. Mostly living alone means I don't have to answer to anyone else, and that's what I've most needed in order to heal. I needed to be responsible for no one but myself. To be able to make all my own decisions without having to worry about how they affected anyone else. Besides, my friends are all new-age freaks who love this place. They look for excuses to come up here. I'm sure you noticed that this place has very good energy."

Tara nodded.

"To tell the truth sometimes they are up here too much."

Tara didn't say anything, no doubt not wanting to get the crazy all over her. Jerri got herself a piece of pizza and Tara followed suit. Jerri watched as Tara took an experimental bite.

"My God this is really good!" she blurted out.

"I know, right? Who would have guessed that actual real food could taste so good?"

"My mom said you looked like you'd lost about twenty pounds."

Jerri sighed. "You aren't fat."

"What?"

"Your dumbass ex's tweets were the topic of conversation on "The View" this morning. There is nothing fat about you. You don't need to go on an all-organic all-natural diet. There is nothing at all wrong with the way you look. You are drop dead gorgeous. Fuck that pencil-dicked reject and the horse he rode in on."

"How did you…"

"Know he had a tiny pecker?

Tara laughed. "He didn't really, but thanks for saying it. I was going to ask how you knew what I was thinking.'

"Do you think I've had an easy life, Tara?"

"No."

"Yet I have no visible scars, I have all my limbs, I don't walk with a limp, so how do you know looking at me, listening to me that I've had a hard life?"

"I… I don't know."

"You do because you have read all my books. You know all of that had to come from somewhere. Someone who has never had pain can't write about it and make you feel it. That's what young writers such as you aren't ready for. In order to write something deep and profound that makes people feel, you have to be willing to walk in your truth. You have to find your voice. You have to pull out the ugliest parts of yourself, the thing you buried deep in your memories, and put it on the page. For people like you and I who use writing as a form of therapy… Well just like it doesn't do any good to lie to your therapist, it doesn't do you any good to lie on the page."

It was late and they'd gone through every single thing she had written so far. Jerri had just gone to the barn to milk. Tara almost went with her but decided she should probably call her mother before her parents called in the police and the National Guard to find her.

She took Jerri's antiquated phone out of the cradle and punched in the number. She had to do it twice before she got it right. Her mother answered the phone. It was late, so obviously she was right on top of it. "Mom don't freak out. I'm alright."

She had to pull the receiver away from her ear because of course her mother did freak out. "For the love of God Tara where the hell are you? I was getting ready to call all the hospitals."

"I'm fine. The most dangerous thing I did all day was climb out my own window. Could you maybe stop being such a huge drama queen?"

"Do you need us to come get you?"

"I'm a thirty-year-old woman, mom. I can take care of myself."

"Where are you? Caller ID says unlisted."

"Good."

"When are you coming home?"

That was a good question. She couldn't just stay at Jerri's, but there were hotels between here and LA and she was not ready to go home. She looked at what was left of her nails. She didn't even have a change of clothes but she had a pocket full of plastic. "Tell you what, Mom. I'll come home when the camera crews are gone." She hung up the phone.

"Wow! That is so much more rewarding than just hitting a button." Tara picked the receiver up and hung it up again. She sat down and started to gather up her pages wishing she had thought to grab her laptop. Of course that would have been hard to carry out the window. She could always get it off the cloud with her... Well she didn't have her phone either.

She didn't really want to leave the farm. The couch looked pretty comfortable, but she guessed she had overstayed her welcome as it was.

Jerri walked in the back door into the kitchen whistling. Tara walked into the kitchen just in time to see Jerri set a bucket of milk on the counter.

"I guess I better go."

"It's really late and the roads are wet," Jerri said. "I actually have a very well-used guest room upstairs."

Tara started to say she couldn't possibly, but the part of her that didn't want to leave in the first place wound up speaking for her. "That would be great thanks."

Jerri was doing something with the milk and then she was putting bottles in the fridge. "I actually need to work. I'm behind on my deadline as it is. You know where the bathroom is. It's the only one. I run the house on a water catch system that gutters the roof water into a tank on stilts behind the house. In order to get enough pressure the bathroom had to be downstairs—which I have been told is a huge pain in the ass. There are towels in the bathroom closet."

Jerri finished cleaning up the milk bucket in the sink then she turned around. When she did Tara felt something she always pushed away. She quickly pushed it away this time, too, or at least she tried, but this time it was in no hurry to go.

"I have a couple of robes hanging by the tub. The white one is clean; the black one is only mostly so. There are extra toiletries in the top drawer including new tooth brushes. Like I said, I have a lot of company. The guest room is the first door to your left at the top of the stairs. The washer's in the bathroom. You could throw your clothes in and wash them and we could hang them on the line in the morning. There are several sets of pajamas in a drawer in the guest room. If you need anything you don't find just holler. Make yourself at home."

"Thanks, Jerri, for everything."

"You'll be alright. I know it doesn't seem like it right now, but you will be. Everything changes. Things that don't change wither and they die. Change is never easy; that place between what you were and what you're going to be is the hardest place to be of all because you feel like you're being pulled apart. See we never really want to change. Even if we're miserable it's at least something we understand. Stepping away from that into a space we don't know takes a lot of courage. Good night."

And then she walked away and Tara could hear her walking up the stairs.

My God every time she opens her mouth she either teaches me something I never knew or wisdom spills forth. She looked around the kitchen and started to read some of the quotes. She has surrounded herself with all of this not because she is sure of it all but because she isn't. It's here to remind her. Why am I shocked at all that she is so eloquent? she talks just like she writes... And now I know exactly what she means by finding my voice.

Jerri took a deep breath and pulled up the book she was working on. She started as she always did by reading the last few pages she had written the night before. She wasn't too surprised to see that darkness had seeped right into her story.

"Well fuck," she mumbled. She tried to find a way to lighten the text but she couldn't. The problem with allowing the characters to go through something so dark was that she then had to work that much harder to bring them back into the light. Jerri Blue didn't write unhappy endings. Her writing was her escape from reality, and she knew it was the same for her readers. Real life sucked. There was no reason at all for fiction to mimic real life to the point that nothing ever worked out the way you wanted it to. It was why writing was therapeutic for her. No matter what she put the characters into she could always find a way to bring them right out of it.

Real life she hadn't been so great at. She was living a pretty good life now, but she didn't kid herself into thinking it was complete. She knew her life could be fuller. She wanted that, but in order to make it happen she had to be vulnerable. Being vulnerable when you'd had the life she had led was really hard to do. Every time she thought she had successfully left her past in the past someone came and stuck a boot in her face pushing her right back into her own personal hell.

Healing was a process. Life was a process.

She asked herself all the questions she normally did when her work took an unexpected turn. Was the scene important to the story? Did it work? Was it going to help the reader define the characters? The answer was yes to all of these, so she then found herself having to finish this very dark scene in a way that would allow the light to seep back in later. She had to write it so that it drew the reader in and didn't turn them off, but she had to write it.

She wrote some of her best stuff when she was in a funk, but a PTSD episode wasn't just a funk. While she felt she was seeing the end of this particular one she still felt pretty beat up. Knowing this she was going to have to be extra careful or she'd write herself into a corner so bad she'd wind up having to do a complete rewrite. Jerri hadn't been lying to the kid just to get away from her because the way Tara had looked at her made her uncomfortable; she really was pushing her deadline.

A few minutes later she heard the door to the room next door close and admitted she always felt better when someone else was in the house. That the reason so many people stayed the night probably had less to do with them wanting to than to her insistence that they stay.

The room was small and nearly dwarfed by the queen-size bed that was set against the back wall. There was a small dresser, a closet, a bedside table and a chair. All of it—like the rest of the furniture in the house—was obviously antique and only partially restored. The bed had a headboard made out of a truck tailgate that said Chevy in letters that were raised and that the paint had come off of.

The cover on the bed was a patchwork quilt. When she looked in the top dresser drawer she found the pajamas, picked some dark blue ones in her size and traded the robe for them.

There was a knock on the door. "Tara, there is a flashlight in the drawer on the bedside table," Jerri told her.

"Thanks," she said, though she had no idea why she'd need one. Then she turned off the light and understood. It was darker than she'd ever seen. She turned the light back on, went to the bedside table and got the flashlight. Then she turned the light off again and headed for the bed. She crawled under the covers and immediately felt any remaining stress she had leave her body. She turned the flashlight off and set it on the bedside table with her watch. Complete and total darkness. She immediately realized why—there were no street lights. Apparently Jerri had even shut off the light in the hall because there was no light shining under the door, either.

She put her hand right in front of her face and could not see it. Even though she had always been afraid of the dark she was not afraid of this pitch blackness at all. In fact she felt safe in a way she couldn't ever remember feeling safe before. She shut her eyes and listened... There was nothing— pure silence—but then as she listened more carefully for any mention of sound she heard a slight clicking noise. It took her only seconds to realize what it was. The great Jerri Blue was creating magic in the room next to her. An adventure of great magnitude was being born, something people would read and if they let it in, it would change their lives. She knew Jerri's words had changed her life and they still were.

Chapter 5

"I told you Gary she didn't say where she was," Janice said, looking from her phone to her husband of thirty-three years.

"Can't you trace the call?" Gary demanded.

"Yes because we're the CIA up in here. She's fine. She said she was fine and she didn't sound drunk." Janice was used to the cameras, so used to them that a fight with her husband in front of them—even having one of the girls take off—wasn't normally a reason for her to even be aware of them. "You picked a hell of a time to do this, Gary."

"You aren't happy Janice. I'm not happy." He shoved the papers towards her.

She'd already read them three times and her lawyer had already looked at them. There really was no sense in putting it off. She quickly signed the papers in all the appropriate spots then took them and threw them in his face.

"Fine, there you go. Tell the truth, Gary, what you really want is a spinoff."

He carefully picked up the scattered divorce papers. "That's it; I'm out of here. I have had it with your crap, Janice. I just want to finally be my own person, to have the life I want to have." He stomped out of the house. Half of the crew followed him and the rest stayed with her.

"Yep, he wants his own show," Janice mumbled.

When she'd found out why he'd been in such a mood it had only been a little bit of a shock. She wished she could have acted like it had been huge but the truth was she'd always been really good at not seeing what she didn't want to see. What was going on with Gary was something she flat didn't want to know.

Right in that moment she really hated him. She wished she had listened to Tara and not let the producers talk her into letting them come in to film them midseason, because now the public had a front row seat to her own failed marriage. When it all came to light—and eventually it would—this was going to be a shit storm of huge proportions. Janice wished she knew where Tara was hiding so that she could go hide with her.

When Tara woke up light was streaming in the small window
in the room. It was still incredibly quiet, but when she listened
closely she could hear birds singing. She hadn't woken up
even once all night. It was the first decent night's sleep she'd
had in weeks and the best night's sleep she could ever
remember having.

Her watch said it was eight-thirty. She knew she had gone
to bed at about ten-thirty, so she had slept ten hours straight.
She slipped her watch onto her wrist and got up heading
directly for the bathroom which had suddenly become urgent.

She washed her hands and listened. Jerri obviously wasn't
up yet, so she remembered to move as quietly as she could.
She got her clothes out of the washer and went and hung
them on the porch rail because she didn't know what else to
do. There was a washer but no dryer. Hell, she hardly knew
how to use a washer and though she knew you could air-dry
clothes she had certainly never done it.

Tara went to the kitchen, found the coffee maker and
made some coffee. She found the cups and poured herself
some. She couldn't find sweetener or sugar and realized that
Jerri probably used the honey that was sitting by the coffee
maker, so Tara used that. She then went right out the front
door to the porch and sat down in the porch swing that hung
beside the front door. She took a deep breath and let it out,
totally relaxed. The morning sun streaking its way through
the trees made the place look almost magical. Right in front of
the porch to the left a bit was a large patch of tall, dead-
looking grass. In amongst it were dozens of brightly-colored
song birds all digging around eating something.

She tasted the coffee experimentally and found that she
really liked the honey, enough that she might start doing it at
home. But then she could almost hear her mother and sisters
telling her how fat she was going to get.

She wasn't even aware that it was cold till she was almost
chilled. So she got up and reluctantly went back in the house
to see Jerri, dressed in boxer shorts and a tank top, putting
wood in the living room stove.

"I'm going to make a small fire to take the chill off," Jerri
said. "You sleep alright?"

"Like a log. I didn't wake you up, did I?"

"Nope, this is the time I normally get up." Jerri lit a match put it in the stove and it ignited. A few seconds later she shut the door. "You mind getting me a cup of coffee? I like mine with a little honey."

"No problem." Tara went into the kitchen and got the coffee but when she returned Jerri was obviously running a tub. Tara set the cup down on the coffee table then sat down on the couch. She looked at the small TV and looked around for the remote, but when she found it she realized she didn't want the noise of the TV or to hear or see anything she didn't want to hear or see.

Jerri walked out of the bathroom—obviously freshly bathed—wearing the black robe and working at braiding her hair which she did in a few seconds. She wound a rubber band around it then sat down and took a sip of her coffee. She made a face.

"Not sweet enough?" Tara asked.

"Nope, too sweet."

"Sorry."

"It's alright. Just means I'll drink it half way and then not have to sweeten the next cup, or the next, or the next," Jerri said with a grin. She got up and messed with the stove a little. Tara couldn't even pretend to know what she was doing.

"What about you, did you sleep alright?" Tara asked

"As good as I am these days. I suffer from PTSD. Sometimes I handle episodes better than others. One of its many 'gifts' is insomnia."

Tara had heard the letters before but had no idea in that moment what they stood for. Her confusion must have been obvious because Jerri looked at her and said, "Post Traumatic Stress Disorder. It's not just for veterans."

Tara knew what she was talking about. "I'm sorry."

"What for? You didn't do anything to me."

"I'm up here whining about some pretty trivial stuff, and..."

"Let me tell you something I forgot and had to be reminded of." She turned away from the stove and when she looked at Tara her green eyes seemed to bore right through her. "Everyone's pain is the same. It might not all come from the same place, but it all feels the same when you're going through it. Is my story worse than most? Yes. Is my pain worse? No. Everyone's pain is the same."

Tara didn't know what to say. Of course the minute

someone said something like that you always wanted to know what they had been through—all that they had been through. You wanted to know their story because if it was really bad then you could look at your problem and maybe see it as trivial bull shit. Part of her already saw it that way. Jerri left the stove and went back upstairs, no doubt to get dressed. The room was already warm by the time Jerri came back downstairs dressed in tattered jeans and a black T shirt.

"I'm sorry. I woke up in a pretty crappy mood," Jerri said. "I wrote some pretty dark scenes and sometimes the stuff I wake up to do that doesn't want to go back to sleep."

Tara heard the apology and was pretty sure she had missed something. She started to mutter a half-assed "that's alright," but then just said exactly what she was thinking. "I'm sure I have no idea what you're apologizing for. I'm sorry you're having a hard time, but Jerri all you did was say how you were feeling. In my house on national TV we all scream at each other and call each other names over stupid-assed things like what we're wearing, ruining each other's clothes, saying stupid shit about each other's asses or our boyfriends. I'm in your house uninvited. All you did was tell me you have a condition."

The kid was right. So why did she suddenly feel so guilty? Because it wasn't the sort of thing she blurted out even to people she knew really well. It was the sort of thing she kept to herself until someone was going to be around enough that they probably needed to know. So why did she have this sudden feeling of guilt? Because this was only the second time she'd seen Tara yet she thought she needed to know which meant she liked having Tara around. She was enjoying her being there, and at least in part it was because of the way Tara had looked at her for just a second the night before.

So Jerri left the room without another word and started to make breakfast. Tara followed her to the kitchen. "Can I help?"

"You know how to beat an egg?" Jerri asked without looking at her.

"I do. I'm actually a good cook. Mother enrolled us all in some gourmet cooking classes when I was a teenager."

"Then grab three or four—depends on how hungry you are—eggs out of the fridge, find a bowl and whip them up. I'll run out to the garden and get some spinach." She nearly ran out the back door. Outside she stopped and took a deep breath of the chill air. "Sometimes I hate being me," she said in a hissed whisper. She took several more deep breaths then stood and worked at quieting her mind. When she felt calmer she walked to the garden and started to pick some of the baby spinach. She checked to see if the asparagus was coming up yet. It wasn't, but it shouldn't be long now. By the time she got back to the kitchen Tara had already cooked the eggs, so she didn't bother to tell her she was going to cook the spinach first and then throw the eggs into it. She just cleaned the spinach, quick fried it and put it on top of the eggs.

They ate in silence till Tara said, "Are you mad at me?"

"No. Why would I be?" Tara shrugged. "I'm not mad at anyone but maybe myself. But then I'm usually mad at that silly bitch for some stupid-assed thing she's done." Tara smiled and Jerri relaxed a little.

"These eggs are so good."

"Most people in the modern world, in the city, are always so filled with stress and angst and they don't even know why. But I know. They feel like they have NO control at all and they don't. Do you know why?"

Tara shook her head no and didn't quit eating so she wasn't just saying she liked the eggs.

"Because there are really only four things that a human needs to survive. Air which is given to us, we don't take good care of it but it's free for the breathing. That leaves three, the same three that ancient man had to constantly struggle for... water, food and shelter."

It was hard to say whether Tara looked at her then because she was extremely interested in what she had to say or because she had already scarfed up her whole plate of food.

"Most people think their water comes from twisting a faucet. They have no idea what its source is or what it takes to make the water run through the pipes. Their food comes in cans or packages, and let's face it a lot of people don't even cook at all anymore. They drive up to a window and get their food in a sack. They live in structures someone else built... Hell, they live in homes they let someone else decorate. They are completely covered up with stuff and most of it is stuff they didn't even choose. Is it any wonder that they have no sense of control? And what do they do because of it? They try to micromanage the people in their lives. They try to have control of their relationships, yet you can never control anything that involves other people because you can never control them."

"But you control your water, your food and your shelter," Tara said nodding. "It's how you took control of your life."

"Yes... and hours and hours of intensive psychotherapy."

Tara put on some of Jerri's clothes because hers were still wet and went with Jerri to milk the goats. Jerri tried to teach her to milk, but Tara didn't know what she was doing at all and the goats weren't having any part of it.

She kept waiting for Jerri to ask her when she was leaving but she didn't. Tara kept wondering when she would feel like leaving but that didn't happen either. She kept thinking she was really waiting for her clothes to dry but even when they walked from where Jerri had been working on a piece of equipment—Tara had no idea what it was—to the house for lunch her clothes were way dry and she still wasn't in any hurry to put them on and go home.

They wound up eating what was left of the pizza from the night before while talking about the difference between character-driven and plot-driven fiction. Jerri had turned on the radio. It had been playing mostly heavy metal classics till the news came on and then... She found out her parents were getting a divorce.

When the report ended she looked at Jerri. "Well I guess I HAVE to go home now."

"I guess you do," Jerri said. It was the way she said it.

"I was sure you'd be way ready to see the back of me. I was sure I was bugging the living shit out of you."

"What, are you some kind of dumbass?" Jerri laughed and slapped her hard on the shoulder. "Hot young woman wants to follow me around all day hanging on my every word? I thought I died and went to heaven."

As Tara got in her SUV to go, Jerri closed the door for her. "It gets to be too much for you, kid, you can come up here anytime. Only make damn sure the jackals with cameras don't follow you."

"Thanks Jerri, for everything."

"Don't be a stranger."

Jerri opened the gate and Tara reluctantly drove away. She started crying and she would have liked to think it was because her parents were divorcing but that just wasn't true. She was crying because she didn't want to go back to the feeding frenzy. She knew what it was going to be like—a big three-ring circus with she, her sisters and her mother as the main attraction. She wondered if Gary had thought about that. He craved the spotlight, but without all of them no one was going to give a shit about him. He'd have to do something monumental to get anyone to even snap his picture.

There was a mass of commotion at the front gate, and then Janice watched from the window as Tara's car pulled into the garage. The camera crew followed her as she went to the door that led to the garage to meet Tara. She slung it open and took Tara's appearance in at a glance. She was wearing the same clothes she had left in which were now wrinkled.

"Where the hell have you been?" Janice thundered just because she had already screamed at everyone else in her family.

Tara sighed and shifted the large cloth shopping bag she was carrying from one hand to the other. "Minding my own business till I found out my parents were getting a divorce." Tara said it, she didn't yell it, and she looked well rested in a way she hadn't been in weeks. "You need to calm down, Janice. What happened?"

"Your father filed for divorce citing unrecognizable differences."

"That's irreconcilable, Mom," Tara said and added in a mumble, "Geez it's no wonder I don't know which 'to' to use, I grew up in a house where English is a foreign language."

"Where the fuck were you?" Lori demanded sweeping into the hall. "Mom needed you. I needed you."

"Why? Because you just needed someone else to yell at?" Tara mumbled. "Seriously, where I was would make for really bad TV because what I was doing was relaxing."

Janice happened to notice the condition of Tara's nails. She grabbed Tara's hand and took a closer look. "What the hell happened to your nails?"

Tara laughed and pulled her hand away. "I actually did something, and let me tell you what you already know about the fucking French nails, you can't actually do ANYTHING in them."

"What the hell is wrong with you?" Lori yelled as if she had just admitted to joining a cult.

"Nothing is wrong with me. Nothing. And you know what?

I'm not fat. I'm hot as hell. Now if you'll excuse me..." She looked at Janice. "I mostly came home in case you might need me, but I'm not in the mood to be yelled at, so... I'm going to my room to write."

Janice watched her go and when part of the crew started to follow her she snagged the guy in front and stopped him. "No, leave her alone."

"Did you nail the window shut?" Lori asked.

"No." Janice looked in the direction Tara had gone. "She needs her space. She needs to not feel trapped like a rat in a cage." She looked at the camera crew with disgust then headed for the kitchen. Going out the window was Tara's way of getting away from the camera crew; Janice's was to run around doing nothing at all interesting till they got bored and followed someone else.

Chapter 6

Six days in a row Tara found some excuse to go all the way to Jerri's to ask her a question about her writing that she could have just as easily and probably more effectively asked in an e-mail. She had tried not to stay more than a couple of hours but had managed to get there every day just in time for dinner which she admitted—at least to herself—was no accident. She didn't want to bother Jerri when she was working on her farm. She could tell looking that it was a lot of work. She wanted to leave before nine which she knew was when Jerri started writing and mostly Jerri was a really good cook.

When she finally got home she would work on her book till she couldn't hold her eyes open and then go to bed. By doing this she was getting a solid five hours of sleep a night which was so much better than she had been getting for the last few months.

It wasn't even seven when her mother knocked on her door. "Tara, your sisters and I have a shoot this morning. I need you to take the boys." Tara rolled over and tried to go back to sleep which she should have known wasn't about to happen way before her mother shrieked, "Tara get up right now! I need you to take the boys."

She got up and stumbled to the door. She opened it and glared at her mother. "Seriously Janice you're waiting till now to tell me? I stayed up most of the night writing and..."

"I forgot Tara, alright? I forgot. Irva flew in late from France last night believe me she's no happier than you are about this. Normally you help me keep up with what I'm doing. On good days it's hard to keep up with all this crap, and with everything that's happening I flat forgot."

"I'm not part of the photo shoot?"

"Ah... No, just the two younger girls."

"So what, Mom, now I'm not just too fat I'm also too old?" She looked right at the camera men then she pulled her T shirt off over her head. "How's that look to you, huh boys? Does that look old and flabby to ya?"

"Tara, for the love of God!" Janice grabbed Tara's discarded blouse from the floor and tried to cover her up with it. Finally Janice just shoved her back through the door and shut it in the crew's face. "Tara, what the hell is wrong with you?" her mother gasped.

"Nothing. That's my point. I'm tired of everyone treating me like the ugly duckling."

"You can't just disrobe in front of the crew like that..."

"Mom we wouldn't be here today if Irva hadn't made a sex tape. All I did was flash my boobs."

Her mother seemed to calm down a little. "I need you to watch the boys. What the hell did you do to your nails? I told you to get them fixed."

"I did, this is how I fixed them." Her nail girl had been almost as appalled as her mother when she told her to remove the French tips, clean them, cut them short, and coat them with clear coat.

Her mother sighed as if Tara's nails were the least of her worries which showed Tara just how upset Janice was about her divorce. "Think of it this way, Mom, at least we won't have to be pulling the Vote for Trump signs out of our yard next election."

Janice looked at her, laughed, then started to cry and put her arms around Tara's neck. Tara held her. "Everything is such a fucking mess. You have no idea and... You've always been the only one I can count on, Tara. I just need you not to be crazy right now. I need you."

Tara held her mother and let her cry on her shoulder. "I'm fixing myself Mom. You don't really need me and you don't have to worry about me. I'm fine."

Her mother nodded against her shoulder then released her and stood up. "I really need you to watch the boys."

"Oh alright. I mean you wouldn't want me to screw up the girl's photo shoot and hey God forbid that Lori should do anything like I don't know hire a nanny or ask their douche-bag father to watch them."

"Todd actually has a job today and do you really want Todd to watch the boys?"

Tara took in a deep breath and let it out. "No." She decided she was neither the fat one nor the old one; she was the *responsible* one, which she decided in that moment sort of sucked.

Jerri was running the tiller so she had no idea anyone was
there till she looked up and saw her walking down the path to
the garden with one kid on her hip and another trailing along
beside her.

"Shit," Jerri muttered turning the tiller off. She looked
down at her watch. "It's only ten. This kid is going to get me
in trouble." She waved and walked towards them mumbling.
"I shouldn't be so damn charming, but really I just can't help
it."

"My Mom and sisters had a photo shoot so they left the
kids with me. As you might guess things at the Darting Estate
are nuts these days. I thought we could all use a break from
the camera vultures. The walking one…" who was now hiding
behind Tara's legs "…is Channing, and the curtain crawler is
Tylor."

Jerri put out her hands, clapped them and the baby went
right to her. Tara looked at her in shock and Jerri smiled.
"Don't be surprised. I love kids and they love me." She leaned
down to look at the other kid. "I don't eat babies."

She stuck the baby on her hip and started walking towards
the barn. "Where are you going?" Tara asked, walking up
beside her pulling the toddler along. When Jerri saw him
struggling to keep up she slowed her pace.

"Well unless I'm wrong you didn't bring them up here
promising that they could see an old farming dyke, so I'm
going right to the barn so they can see the baby goats."

"Goats," Channing said, looking up at her and smiling.
Apparently she was no longer scary. He wasn't much more
than two and the baby she held was probably close to a year
old.

She looked at Tara. "So… did your sister have a private
room?"

"What?"

"These boys are like ten minutes apart, so I'm thinking
she had at least a semi-private room."

Tara laughed, "I know right."

A cardinal flew down and landed right in front of them.
Jerri reached in her pocket, grabbed a fistful of millet and
threw it on the ground. The bird moved closer and started to
eat. The boy tried to go for the bird, but Tara restrained him.
Jerri hunkered down, motioned for the boy to come to her

which he did. She put some grain on her knee and the bird jumped up and started eating. The baby let out an excited sound and the bird flew quickly away.

Channing clapped, laughed and the baby followed suit.

"How did you do that?" Tara asked as Jerri stood up and resumed walking towards the barn.

"Magic."

"No, seriously?"

"Alright but it will just ruin it for you. You might have noticed that birds congregate in that patch of dead grass in front of the house. That's because it's not grass at all; it's a patch of millet and sunflowers I grow specifically for the wild birds. Feeding them means I get to watch them, they mostly leave my garden produce alone, and they stick around and eat worms and bugs out of my fruit trees and vineyard. It's one of those win, win, win things. I harvest part of the seed patch but leave most of it there. If you walk around with a pocketful of grain long enough the birds see you out walking in the woods and come hit you up for food. If you never molest them eventually they will just come right up to you," Jerri said. "But your soul has to be calm."

"And is your soul calm?" Tara asked, a worried note in her voice no doubt because Jerri had told her that she was going through a rough patch.

"It is now," Jerri said honestly. "Is your mom alright?"

"Mostly. You know mom she eats drama for breakfast and spits out chaos for lunch. I haven't heard from my dad, neither has anyone else. He's apparently gone into hiding which... I don't know why he always has to do everything I'm doing."

"No doubt all his hyper-conservative Republican friends have him locked up some place queer free."

"It wouldn't surprise me. He cited irreconcilable differences as his reason for wanting a divorce. The first thought I had was that this was an election year and that as political as he has become in the last few years he just couldn't handle the whole he's a Republican and mom is a Democrat thing anymore, though he was the one who changed parties not mother. Whatever his reason, he's apparently divorcing us, too. So it's not all bad." She gave Jerri a crooked grin. "I love my dad, but all he's done for the last six months is bitch so much that I felt like he was trying to one up Mom on her menopause. Seriously it has been the house of pain over there."

The boy was suddenly pointing and jumping up and down. Clearly he had just caught sight of the goats in their pen.

"What do you think, Channing?"

"Not babies," he said.

Jerri sat the boys together in one of the lawn chairs and went in to catch the kids. She handed one to Tara who happily took it then she caught the other and brought it to the boys. She set it on Channing's lap. He immediately started kissing the kid as Tara held a goat in one hand and took photos on her phone with the other.

Tylor at first didn't quite know what to think, but as soon as he saw that his brother wasn't afraid, neither was he. He kept touching the goat and then putting his hand in his mouth until finally he was tasting the goat.

"Tylor no!" Tara said, and moved to make him stop.

"Ah come on." Jerri laughed. "As long as he doesn't bite the kid we're alright."

"I can't promise he won't." She stuck the phone in her pocket and walked over and pushed Tylor's face away from the kid. "Don't bite." Tylor gave her a "go to hell" look. "Don't you give me that look, mister."

Jerri was just cracking up.

Tara looked at her and grinned. "You aren't helping."

"I eat goat. I'm not going to judge him," Jerri said.

Tara frowned. "You aren't going to eat these, are you?"

"Of course not; those are does. I am going to keep one and trade the other for fifty pounds of pork."

"Could I buy one?" Tara asked.

"No you cannot; I already shook on the deal. They don't stay young and cute. They turn into that." Jerri pointed to where one of the does had climbed up on the fence and was leaning over trying to chew on Tara's blouse.

"Still pretty cute." Tara grinned but moved anyway.

"The city is no place for farm animals. Hell, it's no place for human animals."

"Every day I agree with that statement a little bit more."

Jerri walked over, took the kid away from the boys and put it on the straw in the middle of the barn floor. The boys looked really unhappy till she picked them up and put them in the straw, too.

"Ah come on, Jerri, they're going to get covered..."

"In mostly straw," Jerri said. "The animals don't come in this part of the barn except to be milked. It's just a staging area."

"I'm sorry we're keeping you from working."

"Honestly that rototiller beats me to death. I needed the break."

That's what the machine was. It was a rototiller... Whatever the hell that was.

Tara put the other kid down so the boys could play with it, too. She went to stand next to Jerri. "Am I freaking you out a little? I don't want to freak you out."

"You aren't freaking me out at all," Jerri said. "I fully understand needing to get the hell out of the city and the very real draw of this place."

"Look," Channing said. When Tara looked the kid was sucking on the babies fingers.

Jerri stepped quickly over and removed the baby's fingers from the goat's mouth.

Tylor gave her his best indignant look.

Jerri glared right back at him and told him. "Baby goats have teeth in the back and if your finger gets back there they will bite you."

"Really?" Channing asked.

"They wouldn't do it on purpose and you'd have to be pretty stupid to let your fingers get in the back of their mouth, but your brother doesn't look like the sharpest crayon in the box if you know what I mean. Come on, we'll go check out the rabbits and the chickens then we'll go get some lunch."

The rabbits were just on the other side of the barn, but the chickens were in another building altogether, just down the same trail everything else was on.

"How much land do you have?"

"Twenty acres." To the blank look on Tara's face she said, "An acre is only a little smaller than a football field. The whole farm is actually only on about five acres; the rest of it I keep wooded. Though sometimes I let the goats and the chickens have the run of the woods, so the whole place is fenced."

"There are fences everywhere," Tara observed.

"On a farm fences and gates mean more options. For instance if I ran the goats in the woods all the time they would eventually kill everything off, but if I let them in there once a week they keep the poison ivy and poison oak down and keep the woods clear enough that I can walk through them easily. I don't want them in my garden when there are plants in there, but in the fall after the first freeze I shut them in there. I don't want my chickens running all the time because they would make a bigger mess than the goats, but by letting them run the whole place a couple of days a week they keep the bugs down and get lots of good minerals they wouldn't otherwise get."

The chicken house was as charming as everything else on the place and built in the same tall but narrow style "I don't really like to keep one kind of chicken, so the red ones are Production Reds, the striped ones are Barred Rocks, and all the weird colored ones... Well that's what happens when you mix the two breeds together. I keep them on such a huge run because it means I hardly have to feed them and I have two pens because corn—which I feed all of my livestock—is really rough on the soil, but chicken shit is really strong fertilizer. So I turn the soil on one side and plant it in corn one year and run the chickens on it the next. It makes sure the chickens have plenty to eat and the corn has plenty of fertilizer."

"Me go," Channing said.

Tara looked at all the chicken shit and shook her head. "Nope I don't think so."

"Ah come on, aunty, a little chicken shit will make them grow."

"Shit!" Channing laughed.

"Gee, he finally learned a new word," Tara said with a grin.

Jerri made them all lunch. She knew kids were picky because so many of her friends had kids now. In fact she drug out a toy chest full of toys she kept in the living room closet and the boys were playing in the middle of the her living room floor. Tara stood in the door way watching them.

"So what will they eat? You know, that I might have?"

"They both like scrambled eggs. I should have brought something. I shouldn't just expect you to feed me, us..."

"Yes, because I don't live on an organic farm where I wind up giving food away. Scrambled eggs it is then. What do you want?"

"I'll have whatever you're having. So... Why do you have all the toys?" Tara asked.

"Well with recent changes in the laws all of my gay friends

are either getting married and/or having babies. So I've become their token lonely lesbian friend. I've had to make the place more kid friendly. But the truth is I've always loved kids. Don't get me wrong; I never ever want to be a parent. But I like being an aunt. Lots of people seem to have it in their heads that you either have kids or you don't like them, but I love kids just don't feel the desire or the need to raise any."

"That is exactly how I feel. The minute I married that huge dumbass my parents and he were all about me right away getting pregnant." She looked away from the boys for a second to catch Jerri's eye. "I just kept taking my birth control pills and acted sad that I wasn't getting pregnant. It made for great TV. Ain't nothing real about reality TV." She looked back at the boys. "I love them, but I don't want any of my own and I don't think that makes me a terrible or selfish person. I mean there are seven billion people on this planet."

"Everything that's wrong with the world is wrong because there are too many people on it," Jerri said.

"Exactly." Then Tara let out a stern. "No!"

Jerri smiled. You also didn't have to have kids to be a good mom.

Tara's phone rang and she answered it. "What?... Don't worry they're safe... I understand you're home now but I'm not... They're having a blast that's what they're doing. They're playing without a camera crew up their ass for one thing... We are feeding them... None of your business... So they're your kids when you don't need me to watch them... I'll bring them home when I get damn good and ready to." She hung the phone up and put it back in her pocket. A few seconds later she got a text. She texted something back and then turned her phone off altogether.

Jerri was more impressed with Tara by the minute.

It was unseasonably warm and Tara watched as Jerri held the baby with his feet in the creek. He was cracking up and kicking up so much water Jerri was basically drenched. Channing was running around in his drawers playing in the water. "You might ought to take your sister's kids home before she has an apoplexy," Jerri said.

"I will in a minute. Let them sweat. Besides a few more minutes of this and they will both sleep all the way home," Tara said. "Of course I guess if we leave right now you can probably finish doing whatever that machine does."

Jerri laughed. This just made Tylor kick even more water all over her. "It turns the soil to aerate it for planting."

"And some day you will have to tell me why that is important. For right now I should gather these brats up so that you can get to it."

"I didn't mean to run you off."

"You aren't are you? Running me off I mean."

"No."

It was the way she said it. "But you want to?"

"I didn't say that at all. I don't want to which means I probably should."

"What's that mean exactly?"

"I don't 'exactly' know."

Tara nodded and stood up from where she'd been sitting on a rock. "Hand me that sopping wet baby and you grab Channing. I'll get them dried up, dressed and we'll get out of your hair."

"That's not what I meant, Tara."

"Do you know what you meant?"

"No."

"Then I need to go."

Lori made a huge deal out of hugging her kids like maybe she thought Tara had made a run for the border with them. She glared at Tara even as she asked Channing, "So what did you do?"

He was super excited and most of what he said a linguist couldn't have figured out but her sister didn't even try. No she decided it was time for her semi-weekly tell Tara off in front of the cameras moment.

"Tara in case you have forgotten these are my kids not yours."

"I didn't forget. Did you?" Tara spat back as she strong armed a camera man standing between her and the way out of the room. Of course her sister and the crew followed her.

"What's that supposed to mean?" Lori demanded.

"Just get off my back, Lori. The kids had a good time they're fine."

"When I tell you to bring my kids home I expect you to bring my kids home."

Tara turned slowly around and looked back at her much

smaller sister. "I'm not your fucking servant. I'm your God damned sister! I did you a favor watching them today. They had an awesome time, which you would know if you bothered to listen to them. They are home in one piece, they have been fed, they are clean, and what? It's not good enough because when you said 'jump' I didn't? You better get the fuck out of my face, Lori, and leave me the hell alone or I am going to beat the living shit out of you! You don't tell me what to do! You are not my boss; you aren't even mom."

Janice appeared as if out of thin air and was quickly between them. "What the hell is going on now?"

Tara used her interference as a chance to escape, went right to her room, shoved the camera crew out, shut the door and locked it. She decided to work on her book while she was mad at her sister and upset over what Jerri had almost said, to see if she could do that thing Jerri talked about doing where she tapped into her emotions to give her words power. But all she did was make an even bigger mess out of what was already a huge mess.

What the hell was she really thinking? What did she really want?

"Not this," she said out loud looking around her. "I don't want any of this."

It was almost dark when Jerri finished planting the last of her Spring garden. By the time she got her tiller back in the shop the sun had gone all the way down and... Well she was dirty and alone after days of not being alone, and she didn't like it at all. She wondered where all of her friends—who she normally had to beat away from her door with a stick to have any time to herself—were.

Then she admitted that living on the Blue Homestead was always like that when it came to visitors, feast or famine.

She had just stepped out of the tub and thrown on her robe when Judy called.

"So what's up?" Jerri asked.

"I was calling to check on you. How are you?"

"Fine why don't you and your missus come over? I was just getting ready to make dinner and..."

"I wish we could but I am up to my eyeballs with that thing I didn't tell you about."

Jerri sighed. "Oh yes the super-secret thing that's going

to knock the straight world on its ear."

"Yes that. So tell me how you really are?"

"I'm good really, just... Nothing. I'm good."

"Good just trying to figure something out or good lying out your ass so you don't have to tell me the truth?"

Jerri laughed. "The first one. I really am fine. I'm over the episode, but there is this thing I haven't quite figured out."

"Does this "thing," have legs and a pussy?"

"I believe so yes."

"Then my only advice to you is don't do anything stupid."

"Oh come on..."

"Alright don't do anything stupid you're going to regret."

"I'll try."

She was eating alone so she ate a dish of yogurt. No one was there so she went to work. "Don't do anything stupid? Hell, I probably already did but I don't know if the stupid thing was encouraging her to come over here whenever she wanted in the first place or nearly telling her to go."

She had rewritten the first three chapters and was sure she was on the right track, but it was slow going because on the one hand Jerri had told her to keep other voices out of her head, but on the other she had told her all sorts of stuff she needed to remember and all of those things were in Jerri's voice. And when she heard Jerri's voice in her head the way it made her feel was very discomforting.

She had come out of her room exactly three times in the last two days and she had neither eaten nor slept much. Her mother had demanded she let her in the middle of the second day and Tara had done so.

"Can you tell me what's wrong?" Janice had asked.

Tara had looked up at the camera crew from where she was lying in the middle of her bed. "No."

"Guys can you give us a minute?" Janice had asked.

"They're not the problem, Mom. I just don't want to talk about it. I'm fine just working on my book and working through things."

"What sort of things?"

"Just things, Mom."

"Is it because Daddy left?"

"No. Christ, Mom I'm not four. You guys have done nothing but yell at each other for months. I have *things*, Mom. Things that as an adult of thirty I'm going to deal with myself."

"You can always talk to me if you need to," Janice said, and she left the room.

Parents always said that. It was, of course, the worst load of BS. You couldn't tell them the truth because they never wanted to hear it. When you told them how you really felt they immediately told you all the reasons that wasn't the way you were feeling at all. At the best they meant well, at the worst they were trying to make you into what they needed you to be which bore only a slight resemblance to who you really were. She was tired of trying to be what they wanted her to be.

The truth was she was making herself write because all she really wanted to do was go to Jerri's farm and see Jerri. And why was that? Why? Tara knew why. She'd always known. At what point was she allowed to live her life? At what point was she going to grow a backbone and quit trying to have the approval of her parents and the rest of the free world?

Nothing matters if I can't be myself. If I always have to play a part, if I never get to relax into myself what the hell am I? What's the worst thing that will happen if I go up there? Jerri may send me away, but I'm not there now so why does that matter? At least then I'll know, right?

Jerri thought she heard a knock on the door. She looked at her clock it was eleven PM. She smiled. Judy got worried about her and came to check on her; it wouldn't be the first time. But as she walked down the stairs she knew who was at the door. She couldn't even act surprised. When she opened it Tara was standing there just sobbing. She'd obviously been crying for a while. Jerri took Tara's arm, drug her inside and shut the door. "What's wrong, Kiddo?"

"Are you going to send me away?"

"No. Why would I?"

"Because you said..."

"That I should. Not that I would or that I wanted to. Why are you so upset?"

For answer Tara threw her arms around her and kept crying on her neck occasionally uttering things unrecognizable as language.

Jerri pulled her tightly to her and held her. "You'll be fine."

"I'm really confused," Tara said, finally managing something coherent.

"I know," Jerri said.

"I only feel good when I'm here with you."

"It's a really calming place."

"It's not the place. You are this place; this place is you It's you, I need you."

Jerri took a deep breath and let it out. "You're going through a lot right now, kiddo."

"I know. I know. I'm a mess. And I'm sorry, so sorry that I keep ending up on your doorstep but I can't help myself. I can't."

"When's the last time you've had a decent meal?"

"When I was here."

"When's the last time you really slept?"

"When I was here."

"Did you bring a bag?"

Tara nodded.

"Give me your keys. Go draw yourself a tub. I'll get your things make you something to eat and you can go right to bed."

Tara didn't let go of her, but she had quit crying.

"Come on now."

"I just want you to hold me."

"You'll feel better with some food in your belly and a good night's sleep."

Tara released her and handed her the keys to her car.

"Go on, draw yourself a bath."

Tara nodded and started for the bathroom.

Jerri went outside to Tara's huge gas-guzzling SUV, all the time looking for any sign that Tara had been tailed. A distraught Tara Darting sneaking out in the middle of the night; it was a miracle she hadn't been followed. In a sudden act of pure paranoia, Jerri put a chain and lock on her front gate. Then she drove Tara's SUV to her shop, drove her truck out and put Tara's piece of shit in. It took up nearly her whole garage.

"Worthless gas guzzling..." She stopped mid mutter when Tara's phone on the dashboard made a noise. She picked it up. Jerri hated smart phones but that didn't mean she didn't know how to use one. When she had to do speaking engagements or talk shows she carried one. She thought about just taking the phone to Tara then decided if Tara had wanted the phone she would have taken it with her in the first place. She checked; it was a text from Janice.

"Where the hell are you now?" it demanded.

"I'm fine. Leave me alone." Jerri typed it in, sent it, shut the phone off and put it back on the dash.

"Fuck me, what the hell do I think I'm doing?" she grumbled as she got out of the car taking Tara's bag with her. As soon as she got back in the house she locked the doors but that was habit not paranoia. She set the bag to the side of the bathroom door and went to the kitchen to make Tara something to eat. The whole time her good side was arguing with her bad side.

What are you going to do with that girl? <Fuck her rotten that's what.> She is vulnerable and confused and she just needs you to be here for her not to use her. <She's not a girl dammit she's a thirty-year-old-woman whose already been married and divorced. If she wants me who am I to deny her? It's a civic duty.> Don't be such a turd; you keep your filthy hands off your friend's child. <She's not that good a friend.> No but the girl is and if you do anything to hurt her you're just going to feel like the world's biggest heel.

"Dammit, good Jerri, you're right," Jerri muttered as she warmed up a jar of chicken soup she pulled out of the cupboard. She didn't can; she got it in trade for one of her chickens. She handed them a fully-butchered chicken and three days later they came back with two quarts of chicken and vegetable soup. It was a good trade and now she could feed the shattered woman/child chicken soup and pretend that was going to fix everything that was wrong with her.

Tara got in the tub and suddenly felt more naked than she ever had in her life. What the hell was she doing? She wasn't at all sure, but in the meantime hadn't she just done everything but beg Jerri Blue for sex? What the hell was wrong with her?

She washed her face every time she cried and gave up when she felt like if she didn't she wasn't going to have any skin left. She got out, took the plug out of the tub, and started to dry off. She threw on the white robe and tied it tight. Tara was about to leave the bathroom wondering if it was possible to sneak back to her car and just leave when she saw the toothbrush she had used last time she spent the night still in the holder next to Jerri's.

She is super tidy, a place for everything and everything in its place. If she really didn't want me around she would have thrown that toothbrush away the minute I left. Wouldn't she? No, but she would have recycled it.

She left the bathroom stepped around her bag and walked to the kitchen. Jerri was pouring some soup into a bowl. She walked over and set it on the table then she set a glass of milk beside it. Tara just looked at it for a minute.

"Sit down and eat," Jerri said. She sat down across from Tara when Tara sat down. When she didn't immediately pick up her spoon, Jerri said again, "Eat!"

"You're kind of a bully," Tara said with a smile.

Jerri laughed. "Just eat."

Tara started to eat the soup but she knew that was goat's milk and she wasn't sure about it. As if reading her mind which she seemed to be good at Jerri said, "If you don't like it you don't have to drink it, but goat's milk is loaded with tryptophan; it will help you sleep.... And.... I don't know which one of us is crazier. You because you just want to be here with me or me because I'm just so excited you are here."

Tara felt like she could finally breathe again. "So you *do* like me."

"Of course I like you, you crazy little shit. But think about this for a minute, please. I'm ten years older than you...."

"My dad is twelve years older than my mom, so that isn't an issue for me. Rhonda is at least ten years older than you, so until right this minute age difference has never been a problem for you."

"You're on camera twenty-four/seven."

"But I don't want to be and I'm not when I'm here."

"Your father actually hates me. Did you know that?"

"He's not my favorite person right now anyway."

"I'm fucking crazy?"

"According to you so am I."

"We just met."

"No you've known me since I was a kid."

"See now that isn't a very good argument."

"I'm not trying to argue with you, Jerri, but you *do* know me, and I've read all of your books, so I know you. What you don't know is that my first crush was on a girl. My second, third and fourth, too, but my parents explained to me that wasn't right and... I always wanted them to be proud of me. I always wanted to be just like everyone else and it was easy because I liked boys well enough, they didn't repulse me, but... it never felt right. There was always something missing. I saw you in this kitchen and suddenly I knew exactly what was missing. What I always wanted."

Jerri took in a deep breath and looked at her. "You know what I don't need in my life and you don't need in yours? Another big-ass mess, anything else to have regrets about. You and I are way past a point where we could just have casual sex. Do you agree with that?"

"Yes."

"If you and I hook up it needs to be for all the right reasons. Not because I'm a handy butch dyke or you're a handy, very appealing fem. I don't want to rush into this, find out it's not right and you get hurt and I get hurt. I don't do hurt well and neither do you. And you, my friend, are in a state of flux..."

"What's that even mean?"

"It means what I've already told you. You are in the middle of a shift going from one part of your life into the next and adding 'slept with my mother's old friend' may not be a good thing to put in there. You can't play with me because that's not who I am. I can't be a testing ground."

"I don't want you to be. I have no trouble at all with taking things slow."

"Oh thank God because I have to tell you bad Jerri was not on board with the waiting."

Tara laughed. "Bad Jerri?"

"You know in the cartoons where they have a devil on one side and an angel on the other. Well both sides of my id had a huge fight right before you stepped out of the bathroom, bad Jerri lost and she was NOT happy."

"I think I like bad Jerri," Tara said with a smile. She finished eating her soup. She eyed the milk.

"Just try it," Jerri ordered.

Tara did and well it tasted like milk so she drank it down.

"You know every new thing I've tried since we met I have actually liked."

"You're killin' me, kid."

As Tara brushed her teeth and changed into her pajamas Jerri took Tara's bag to the guest room. She turned the bed down.

This is a huge mistake, huge! <Shut the fuck up weenie and bang the bitch.> *No you shut up.* Jerri's eyes went to the bed and she quickly walked into the hall just as Tara reached the top of the stairs.

"Good night," she started for her room but Tara followed her.

"Aren't you even going to kiss me good night?"

"Ah come on," Jerri said. She turned around and Tara wrapped her arms around her neck. They were exactly the same height, so it wasn't like she could avoid her. She gave her a quick peck on the cheek.

"No you come on," Tara said. "That wasn't what I wanted and you know it."

"Dammit, Tara." And then she just went ahead and kissed her. Tara's lips parted under hers then she put her tongue in Tara's mouth and came in her own pants. She moved, pushing Tara into the wall, her hand started climbing right in Tara's top. She stopped herself with an effort, removed her tongue from Tara's mouth and pushed away from her.

Tara gave her a look of immediate frustration and Jerri took another step back till she hit the other side of the hallway. "You need to go to bed." Then seeing the words Tara was about to say added, "In your own bed, not with me.'

"I'd rather not."

"What you want is to jump into bed with me before you can talk yourself out of it, but if you can talk yourself out of it then you shouldn't have sex—at least not with me. You need to take your hot ass in your room, shut and lock the door because this may come as a shock to you but I'm no saint."

Tara nodded and started towards the guest room. She turned in the door and looked at Jerri. "I'm pretty sure there is no way I can talk myself out of this. For one thing that kiss was better than any sex I've ever had, so I'll go in my room to my very lonely bed but I'm *not* locking the door."

Tara lay in the dark hoping that the door was going to open but it didn't. She went to sleep to the sound of nothing but the slight clicking of the keys on Jerri's keyboard.

When she woke up and looked at her watch it was after nine. She got up and got dressed then ran down to the bathroom. As she was brushing her teeth she could hear Jerri in the kitchen. She finished quickly and practically ran across the house. Jerri was standing at the sink doing something. Tara just walked right up behind her, wrapped her arms around her waist and laid her head against Jerri's shoulder.

"Did I not explain the whole bad Jerri thing?" Jerri asked, a hint of laughter in her voice.

"Yes," Tara said.

"Well could you get off me so that I can finish what I'm doing?"

Tara let her go reluctantly. What Jerri was doing were the dishes Tara had made the night before. "I need to learn how to clean up after myself, but as stupid as this may sound, you'll have to teach me how to do it because I have taken cooking classes so I'm a good cook but I do dishes by asking the maid to put them in the machine."

"It's not rocket science." Jerri quickly taught her how to wash dishes. She was right; it was easy.

"You want me to cook breakfast?" she asked, pouring herself a cup of coffee.

"I'm actually waiting for one of my neighbors..." There was a knock on the door, "...and there they are."

"Should I hide?"

"Why? Everyone knows I'm queer..." Jerri started and then she seemed to realize why Tara asked. "But no one knows your queer and everyone knows who you are."

Tara nodded.

"Emily won't. She doesn't have a TV because she's afraid it will rot her kids' brains."

Jerri went to get the door and Tara stayed in the kitchen. A few seconds later Jerri walked back in a bag in her hand and a woman—who looked so much like a sixties love child she could have walked off a movie set—trailing her, a baby on her hip. When Tara looked into the living room a four-year-old was pulling out the chest of toys from the closet.

The woman briefly looked at Tara and smiled before continuing the conversation she had apparently started at the front door, "...and I told him not to sell our chickens but you know Harold. He's about as handy as a stick and the chicken house he built didn't hold them. They kept tearing up our wheat field so now we have no chickens so I need both eggs and milk. That's why there are three loaves of bread instead of two." Having finished her sentence she looked at

Tara and said, "Hello."

"Hi," Tara said nodding.

Jerri looked at her and then looked at her friend. "Ah. I'm sorry. Emily this is…" It was sort of funny to watch Jerri Blue of all people suddenly have a problem with words.

"Terri."

"Terri…" Jerri made a face at the name. "…is my…" She stumbled again and Tara smiled.

"Girlfriend," Tara supplied.

"It's about time." Emily laughed and playfully punched Jerri in the shoulder with the hand that wasn't full of baby. Then she turned and offered her hand to Tara who shook it and found her handshake firm and her hands very rough. "So what's your specialty?"

"Excuse me?"

"Homesteaders have different areas they're really good at. They specialize in things," Jerri explained.

"Jerri is disgusting she can do anything. Harold grows and grinds grains. I bake bread. What's your specialty?" Emily asked again.

"Till now nails, hair and fashion," Tara said with a smile. "But I'm learning."

"And she's a writer," Jerri said.

"A want to be writer," Tara corrected.

"If you write you're a writer," Emily said with a shrug. She looked at Jerri and grinned. "There are going to be a whole lot of very sad, horny lesbians when they learn you've chosen a mate. You know that, right?"

"You can't please everyone."

"Though you have certainly tried."

"A girl's gotta do what a girl's gottah do."

When Jerri walked back into the house after loading the milk and eggs in Emily's car and helping her corral her four-year-old she went to work making French toast from the bread she'd just traded for.

"What was the look for when I told her my name was Terri? I think it's in both of our best interests that people don't know who I am."

"I know that but come on, Jerri and Terri?"

Tara laughed. "Alright. I didn't think that one through. But it will be easy for even you to remember." She was quiet then in that way that could be heard.

"What?" Jerri asked, not looking away from what she was doing.

"Are you a player?"

Of course. Emily talks for twenty minutes about sex-linked genes in chickens which bored even me, and all the bitch remembers is what she said about me laying slutty lesbians. "I told you. I'm no saint. If I get tired of taking care of business myself there are several ladies who are more than willing to help me out with my problem no strings attached."

"Oh."

Jerri sighed and turned around to face her. "Listen you little shit because I'm only going to say this once. I don't cheat. I've been with people who did; I don't ever. I haven't left this place much less gone out to get a little since I met you, so I'm guessing that tells you everything you need to know."

The smile returned to Tara's face and Jerri thought Tara's smile felt like a gift. "There would be no excuse for you to go anywhere else. I'll give you whatever you want whenever you want it."

"And again I think I have to point out that your idea of taking it slow is a lot different from mine. If it will put your mind at ease I can't even think of anyone but you right now."

"Good."

Of course since Tara was there and they were really just trying to figure out where they stood and how the hell they were going to stand there, all the people who had completely left her alone for the last three days all showed up at once. They needed eggs, or milk or herbs. They were bringing over the soap, candles or shampoo they owed her from previous barters, and of course every single one of them came mostly because they wanted to see her new girlfriend. Damn Harold for giving in and buying Emily a phone.

As yet another one pulled out of the drive she told Tara, "I have half a mind to put the chain and lock back on the gate."

"And now I'm thinking we're stuck being Terri and Jerri."

"Let that be a lesson to you, think before you come up with a fake name."

"Oh I will. So it just dawned on me... Where is my car?"

"I put it in the shop, why?"

"I'd probably better check my phone." Jerri took her hand

and they started walking towards the shop.

"There was a text from your mother demanding you tell her where you were. You told her you were fine and to leave you alone."

"Seriously? You've won like a thousand awards for writing. Could I not have come up with something more eloquent than that?" Tara squeezed her hand, and Jerri felt it all the way to her toes. She squeezed her hand right back.

"I'm thinking that's the best a girl who comes up with an alias like Terri could do."

"Ha, ha."

They got to the shop and the car and Jerri said just what she was thinking, "What the hell do you need with a huge urban assault vehicle like this?"

"My parents bought it for me as a wedding present. I wanted a Mini Cooper, but Mother said I was too big for it…"

"Ah so this is a fashion accessory?" She let go of Tara so she could get in her car.

"Yes I guess it is." Tara sounded defeated as she opened the car door and grabbed her phone. Jerri found that just like Tara's smile made her happy, her frown did not.

"What's wrong?"

"What am I? I'm a construct. I don't even drive the car I want. The house mother picked for Fred and I? I hated it and even if I didn't before I do now. What did you say? I'm in a state flux and I am but you know what I don't wonder about at all? Whether I belong here with you. I admit I don't really know what that means but I'm not scared at all."

"Well I'm scared enough for both of us," Jerri said.

"I don't think you're really afraid of anything."

"Then I'm a much better actress than I think I am."

Tara looked at the phone in silence for a while before she finally turned it on. When she did not too surprisingly she got that unhappy look on her face again, the one that hurt Jerri's heart. "Caaarap," She hissed. "Mother is threatening to have the cops look for me and Twitter is blowing up saying I've had a nervous breakdown." She looked up at Jerri and smiled. "I guess I kind of did, didn't I?"

"Baby, if that was your nervous breakdown you obviously weren't trying hard enough," Jerri said.

They were silent as Tara looked at more of her messages. "Fuck! Irva's boyfriend of the week just announced he's sure he's the messiah and Twitter is blowing up. So we are now officially a four-ring circus." She looked at Jerri and sighed. "I have to go home. You know before Mother sends the cops to look for me. The Twitter verse has me dead in a ditch somewhere or I miss how mine and Mother's divorces are going to be all about Irva."

"You know what would help?"

"If you had banged me rotten last night like I wanted you to?"

"I was going to say if you had your own house."

"I do."

"I mean one you could live in. I get why you don't want to live in that one."

"I sort of want to live with you, Jerri. I sort of want to just stay right here."

"But that's further away than the banging," Jerri said with a smile, "because you aren't just any girl you're one of the Darting girls."

"I wish I weren't."

"Really? Because if you weren't you never would have ended up here. Believe me I have tried a million times to cherry pick the items I don't like from my life. Every single time I do I'm not here. I lose all the stuff I do want right along with the stuff I don't. It's not going to be easy, kid, but we'll figure it out."

Tara moved to wrap her arms around Jerri's neck and Jerri held her. "God you feel so good."

"And you aren't even touching the good spots," Tara breathed against her lips and then she was kissing her and Jerri was kissing her right back. When they finally parted Tara looked right in her eyes and in that moment she didn't wonder at all whether Tara wanted her as badly as she wanted Tara. "Do me a favor."

"Anything," Jerri choked out.

"Oh, you would say that when I have to go."

"What do you want?"

"Well you could start by not calling me kid anymore."

Chapter 7

Janice looked at the proposal in front of her. "Come on, Janice. You know this will be huge," her agent said. "You're going to want a piece of this."

Did she, did she really? She could let him take it to another producer and let them take the risk. Except when she thought of it she knew it wasn't a financial risk at all. Reality TV fans loved a train wreck. Irva was dating some rap star who thought he was the second coming. Todd and Lori were fighting like cats and dogs. She had just divorced her husband and God alone knew where Tara disappeared to for hours at a time. Tara was under contract to be on camera five hours a day six days a week and she did it in shifts disappearing for most of every day. The crew had tried to follow her a couple of times and Tara had lost them. The second time she came home mad as a hornet and swore to Janice—and everyone else in the LA basin area—that if they did it again she would walk off the show. They could just go ahead and sue her for breach of contract.

Whatever she was doing she wasn't going to tell Janice. Tara had learned what Janice had known for years—that if she was really boring the camera crew would stop following her. So when she was available to be shot she spent most of her five hours a day writing.

And all of it, every bit of it, had increased their ratings even though none of it had been shown on TV yet. *We're internet people. If we fart it's heard across the globe.* "Give me a pen." He did and she signed. "You tell that douche bag I'm not doing his dirty work. He's going to have to tell the kids what he's doing."

"I will. This is a good decision, Janice. Lots of money..."

"Yeah, great it's all about the money. At the end of the day that's all that matters to anyone—the fucking money."

As she drove up in the driveway Tara was on her way out.

Janice parked and got out.

Tara started to pull out of the garage, but she stopped.

There was something about the way her mother was moving. Tara turn her car off and got out. "Mom... you alright?"

Her mother turned to look at her and shook her head. "No. And I just did something that I hope... I hope it doesn't make it worse for all of us. I'm second guessing everything I've done and everything I'm doing. I trust no one and maybe especially not myself."

Tara walked, over hugged her mother and tried to remember the really deep thing Jerri had told her. "You know what, Mom? If you change anything everything else goes away."

"What?" her mom asked with a sniffle.

"Who knows where we'd all be if you didn't put us on TV, Mom? Dad was already famous, you were a successful agent, we still would have grown up right here. Maybe it would have been worse. Maybe it would have been a lot worse. Irva's a giant pain in everyone's ass but she's happy. Lori is stuck to toad boy but she's mostly happy. My only bitch right now is the cameras, but if it weren't for them maybe I wouldn't be happy at all."

"And are you happy, Tara?"

"Mostly yes."

"And can you tell me why, Tara?"

"No I cannot." Tara laughed and hugged her mother. "Now I have to go."

"To your secret place?"

"No, not today. The realtor called and said she's pretty sure she's got someone to buy the house. She says if I go over there she can get them to make an offer today. If so she'll have paper work she'll need me to sign. If I sell I'm going to rent something, maybe on the beach."

Janice pushed away from her and looked up at her. "The beach? I thought you hated the beach."

"Me too, but I don't."

Because of course Jerri loved the ocean. Jerri had taken her on a day trip up the coast to a secluded section of beach. They'd sat together covered with a blanket watching the waves come in talking about everything and nothing. Now she understood completely why people all wanted to go to the ocean. The sound, the smell, the taste of it fulfilled a primal need to be close to the earth. Turned out it wasn't the beach she hated it was the millions of people that had crowded every beach she'd ever been to.

"Can I... Can I go with you to show the house?"

"Ah sure," Tara said, not understanding why her mother wanted to do something so boring.

"I don't really want to be alone right now, Tara." Then she whispered, "And I sure as hell don't want to be on camera."

They drove in near silence. Janice looked around the car trying to see something that would tell her where Tara kept going, but there wasn't a clue.

"Do you have a boyfriend?" Janice asked.

Tara sighed. "No, I do not have a boyfriend." Then she reached over and turned on the radio.

"What the hell are you doing, Tara?" Janice asked. She wanted to be cool mom and leave it alone, but she just couldn't.

"I'm writing, alright? I've found a quiet place where no one knows me and I go there and I write."

It was a bold-faced lie. Janice knew when her kids were lying, but she didn't dare call Tara on it because Tara was about ten seconds from telling them all to go to hell. At least for the moment Tara seemed to be doing pretty well, disappearing for hours of the day aside.

"Are you finished with the book yet?"

"No, not even close."

"Did Jerri help you?"

"Yes and no," Tara said with a grin. "She red inked the shit out of my manuscript which basically made me have to start all over from the beginning but it taught me more about writing than I ever would have figured out on my own."

"Rhonda is suddenly single again and every other word out of her mouth is Jerri. She's asked me half a dozen times for Jerri's phone number and I have half a mind to give it to her just to shut her up."

"No don't!" Tara snapped then said in a calmer voice. "You can't do that, Mom. You know Jerri wouldn't want her to have it."

"I said I had a half a mind to and so far I still have more than half a mind. Geez." Janice laughed. "I'm not stupid, Rhonda and Jerri that never made any sense to me. If you look at how Jerri lives right now..." She laughed. "...could you see Rhonda living that *Little House on the Prairie* lifestyle?"

No she couldn't, which was why she should have just kept her big mouth shut. She was starting to wish she hadn't taken her mother with her at all. She wasn't going to Jerri's today because Jerri was having some sort of giant weenie roost with a bunch of her friends. It seemed that once a year they got together, built a bonfire in the woods, roasted hot dogs, drank beer and threw things they hated into the fire. Jerri told her most of these people *did* watch TV, so Tara had opted out.

But now she wasn't going up there at all and Rhonda wanted Jerri. She and Jerri still hadn't consummated their relationship which she was way ready to do but apparently "good" Jerri kept winning those arguments.

And what the hell was wrong with Rhonda Heart that the minute she didn't have some man in her bed she was all about Jerri? She decided she hated Rhonda—in part because she knew one of the reasons Jerri was so gun shy about having an actual relationship instead of just easy sex was because of all the shit Rhonda had put her through. Why would you ever treat someone like that unless you were done with them?

Beside her Janice laughed. "Where the hell did you just go?"

"Nowhere." She was glad they had reached the house. The realtor was already there and had already shown the couple around the property again. Tara was glad they had missed having to do that. Of course the prospective buyers were super psyched to meet her and her mother. Meeting the celebrities who had lived in the house was probably what would make them decide they just had to have it which... Tara didn't care why they were buying it as long as they did.

Tara felt almost sick to her stomach. She didn't want to be at this house, and though she hadn't known why before she did now. She didn't want to remember that she had willingly married Fred. It made her feel stupid. But more than that Fred had come in stoned one night and he wanted sex. She never really did, but she was sure she was supposed to, so most of the time she put on a good show of wanting it. That night she made it crystal clear that she didn't. He made it just as clear that he didn't care what she wanted. He was persistent, at one point making it obvious she didn't really have a choice. She gave in to him because it was better than the alternative. When she had told Jerri about it she had been really upset and told Tara, "That's rape."

"Not really…"

"Yes really. You wouldn't have remembered it if it didn't feel like a violation. The worst part is that he got you to help him do it. If you don't want something and someone gives it to you anyway it's not a gift it's a curse." And then her very spiritual very philosophical, enlightened girlfriend said, "I hope that fucker kills himself with his drugs."

So she couldn't stand this house because it reminded her of that moment when she could either give in to him or get the crap beaten out of herself and have him take what he wanted anyway. What had Jerri said? *He took my power. She said in that moment he took my power but that he could only keep it if I let him. I'm not going to let him, but I never liked this fucking house anyway and now it's just a monument to the stupidest thing I ever did trying to make everyone else happy. When it's gone, for me the whole thing will be over.*

They wanted to buy the house furnished. She said fine. She accepted their first offer, ignoring the realtor's eye roll and her mother's rather loudly-voiced opinion that the house was worth three times what they offered. Janice had even told the prospective buyers that their offer was an insult. Tara signed the paper work and then she got the hell out of there.

"You didn't make a penny on that house," Janice said as they were on the way home. "Worse than that you spent a fortune furnishing that house and you gave it all away. You lost a fortune, Tara. What you spent on drapes alone…"

"I didn't decorate that house, Mom you did. Hell, you didn't even do it you hired that interior decorator who had shit taste to do it because he was who all the 'in' people where using. I don't care about anything in it. That whole thing was like an albatross around my neck. Peace of mind is priceless to me right now." Tara paused and took a deep breath. "Mother, I love you, but please, please I beg of you, don't make any more decisions for me. I'm way beyond just signing papers when you hand them to me. I'm going to read them, and if I don't like what they say I'm going to rip them in half. I'm not one of your clients, Janice, I'm your daughter. You have to let me have my own life whether I chose something you like or not."

When they got back to the house she tried to call Jerri and wasn't too surprised when no one answered. Jerri said they were going to the woods, and when Jerri said she was going to do something that's what she did. It was one of the things Tara loved most about her. Most of Tara's life she'd been surrounded by people who said they were going to do something or other and then never did anything or did something that was close... not at all.

She put her phone back in her pocket and toyed with the idea of going to Jerri's anyway, but then the part of her that wasn't ready to be outed—especially when she hadn't done more than kiss a woman—decided she needed to stay home. Besides there was something more than a little intimidating about meeting all Jerri's friends at once. What if they didn't like her? If they knew who she was they sure as hell weren't going to think she was a good match for Jerri. Yet Tara no longer had even a shred of doubt that she was. Tara had realized just that afternoon as she was signing the papers to sell her house that one of the reason Jerri had kept putting her off was she needed Tara to be as sure as she was now.

The film crew was on hand as they sat down to have a "family" meal cooked by the maid. It tasted worse than it smelled, and it smelled terrible. Irva had been to and come back from Europe again already. She was going on, and on, and ever on about her most recent trip—though why she was bothering to rehash it for the cameras Tara couldn't imagine since there had been a crew with her at every fashion show she did. As Irva started to talk about the rap star boyfriend, Tara was way beyond being able to even pretend to be interested. She hadn't met him yet and she already liked Todd better which was saying a lot. Todd might be a human slug, but at least Todd didn't think he was God.

Tylor threw more food on Lori and the floor than he ate then demanded he be taken out of the highchair, so of course Lori let him down. Tara grabbed him and quickly wiped his face and hands. Of course as soon as Tylor was down Channing got down, too. Then they were both running around hollering like animals and throwing things. They never ate; she didn't know why they hadn't starved to death. *They ate at Jerri's and they didn't act like this.*

Her mother was talking about some shoot she had to do with Irva the next day. Irva was saying she felt too fat for it. Lori and Todd started fighting on Twitter. Tara knew they were because they were quiet but glaring at each other and their fingers were flying across the screens of their smart phones.

Then there was one of those inexplicably quiet moments and into that the entertainment anchor of the show on the TV none of them were watching very clearly said. "Fred Summers was rushed to the hospital after what appears to be another accidental overdose. We expect his doctors to make a press statement within the hour. Summers, who recently divorced Tara Darting, has been observed over the last few months drunk, high and clearly out of control. A family member released this statement to the press, 'It looks grim. Fred is unconscious, unresponsive, and on life support. Please pray for him. He is in God's hands now."

"Crap, don't piss off Jerri Blue," Tara muttered under her breath.

"What?" Irva asked her.

Tara ignored her and stood up. She took her phone and texted Todd.

"Quit fighting with Lori for a minute and get me your car keys, one of your hoodies, and some sunglasses. Meet me in the garage in ten minutes."

She watched as he texted her back. "All right." But it was obvious by the look on his face that he had no idea why.

"Just do it. Don't say anything to anyone, and don't let anyone follow you," she texted.

"Alright," he texted back.

"I'm going to my room!" Tara yelled, whipped up some tears and headed for the stairs. The camera crew followed her to her room where she slammed the door in their faces and pushed her chest of drawers in front of it. She turned her TV on to the same station they'd been not watching downstairs, turned the volume on high and then... She went out the window again.

"I'm going to have to get my own house because this is probably the last time this is going to work," she muttered.

Janice knew exactly what Tara was up to. She knew Tara didn't give a damn what happened to Fred because she had told her so. Janice had also seen the quick looks between Todd and Tara. Now Todd had gotten up, yelled something incoherent at Lori and left. Tara was making a run for it before their currently un-papparized gate would be hanging with them again. She was going wherever she was going these days, and in that moment Janice was in one hundred percent agreement with Tara's plan. But Tara was going to need help. It wasn't going to take the camera crew that long to realize Tara wasn't in her room or that she had crawled out the window again. Janice knew for a fact that one of those bastards called the vultures in whenever anything of interest happened at their house.

"This is all your fault!" Janice screamed at Irva as she jumped to her feet.

"My fault? How the hell is this my fault?"

"You introduced Tara to Fred, dumbass," Lori supplied, always quick to point the finger of blame for... Well anything at Irva.

"How horrible of me. I just wanted my poor, fat sister to have a little love in her life!" Irva yelled.

Janice's plan worked because the camera men left the hall outside Tara's door and soon were right back in the dining room. But just to be on the safe side Janice picked up a plate and tossed it like a Frisbee into the far wall. Not near her kids or her grandkids, but nearly hitting one of the boom guys. It wasn't hard to put on a show of rage; she had enough to go around. She was going through menopause which was bad enough, but now she was in the big middle of a family and media circus of grand proportions. So Janice proceeded to throw the fit of her life as the cameras rolled and Tara made her escape.

It turned out Todd was a really good accomplice and she remembered something she had forgotten. Todd was actually a pretty decent guy just maybe not cut out to be Lori's husband or a father to anyone.

He handed her the keys, a hoodie and the sunglasses. "I texted Lori and told her I was tired of fighting and that I was going out for a couple of hours which... Well she was already pissed off at me so it doesn't matter. I'll try to stay out of the line of sight for the next couple of hours and then... Hopefully they'll think you're in your room. That I'm out and... I figure you want my car because you know no one ever follows me."

"Thanks Todd," she hugged him and kissed his cheek.

"Be careful. For what it's worth I never liked that douche."

As she donned her disguise and drove right out of the gates completely unmolested she decided she was going to have to cut Todd some serious slack in the future.

When she got to Jerri's it was obvious that when Jerri said "a bunch of people" she meant a *bunch*. There were cars parked all the way down the road, but the driveway was clear. Tara was able to get all the way to the shop where she parked in front of it. The house looked empty, but the lights were on so she decided to go there. After all they were in the woods. How was she going to find them? But when she stepped out of the car she could hear music blaring and when she turned her head towards the sound she could actually see the huge fire through the woods. It looked to be at least a quarter of a mile away.

She went to the house anyway. No one was there. She went to the bathroom and when she was washing her hands realized she looked rough. She went ahead and washed her face. She wondered what she should do. Probably the wisest thing would be to just go up to the guest room, climb in the bed and go to sleep. It was nearly ten, and it had been a hell of a day. But she really needed to see Jerri, and she couldn't lie to herself; part of her wanted to meet Jerri's friends. She was afraid to, but she still wanted to.

She applied minimum makeup, opting for no lipstick just because she didn't like it when she smeared it all over Jerri's face. She kept the hoodie and the sunglasses. She was about to leave the house heading in the direction of the noise and the fire light when she remembered she was going to need a flashlight. She had one on her phone, but she didn't have her phone. She went up to the guest room found someone's luggage already there and smiled.

So the guest room is full. She went to the bedside table and got the flashlight out of the drawer. She left her purse on the living room couch but not before extracting a paper wading it up and stuffing it in her pocket. She looked at the couch. *I'm pretty sure that all Jerri needed was for me to be sure, and I know exactly what I want so... I'm not sleeping on that couch.*

The band was playing, she'd had a hot dog and a couple of beers, she was surrounded by her best friends, and this was their favorite party of the year. Jerri was enjoying it, but she no longer felt single which meant she had to completely ignore women she would have normally been hitting on. Yet she was alone.

She, Judy and her wife were all sitting on the same section of log bench. "You've done it again haven't you?" Judy said with a sigh.

"Done what?" Jerri asked and took a sip of her beer.

"You've fallen hard for someone whose got at least as many problems as you do."

"Not even close." Jerri laughed.

"Leave her alone, Judy," Cyndy said. "Quit analyzing Jerri and everyone else. It's a party. For once stop being Dr. Willis."

"I don't analyze everyone," Judy defended.

"What's that thing you always tell me? There is no point in lying," Jerri said. Then she felt her, Jerri smiled and stood up. "Here hold my beer."

"Nothing good ever comes of me holding your beer," Judy said with a laugh, but took it from her anyway.

Jerri took off into the woods.

"Where are you going?" Judy yelled after her.

Jerri ignored her. When she saw the light bobbing through the woods towards her she knew she was right.

Tara could hear the party and see the fire but that didn't make her feel any less afraid of walking in the woods alone at night. Though she had to admit that knowing she was on the homestead and Jerri was close by made what would have normally had her immobilized by fear something only mildly uncomfortable. Her light caught on something moving towards her at a quick pace and she nearly screamed before she stopped herself, but she did jump about a foot in the air.

"Dammit, Jerri, you scarred the living shit out of me. How did you know I was here?"

"I felt you," Jerri said and then she walked over and took Tara in her arms. "I did spook you. I can feel your heart pounding." Then Jerri was kissing her and Tara's heart didn't slow down at all. She could taste the beer Jerri had obviously been drinking and no part of her wanted to go to that stinking party now. When they parted they said together as if they had planned it. "I love you." Then they were kissing again and Tara knew Jerri wouldn't let her sleep on that couch even if she wanted to.

"You look ridiculous," Jerri said with a laugh when they got close to the clearing and Tara put the sunglasses back on.

"It's worse than that; I look like Todd."

Jerri gave her an odd look and Tara smiled at her and shrugged. "It's a long story I will gladly tell you later. For right now I'm all about meeting your friends—but more than I don't want them to figure out who I am because then it might leak back to the press, I don't want them to know who I am because then they won't like me. They'll judge me on who they think I am."

"I'd like to think my friends are more enlightened than that but they probably aren't, for one thing most of them are buzzed right now."

"What about you?" Tara said, knowing Jerri had been drinking.

"I don't get drunk, ever, and I don't smoke pot. But while I don't allow them to bring hard drugs to my place, and most of my friends don't do them in the first place, I do let them smoke pot—just not where I can see them. I won't judge you if at some point you want to head into the woods and take a quick toke."

"I don't want to do that. I want to be with you."

"You just need me to be sober?"

Tara nodded.

"Don't worry; I will be."

Tara's attention was suddenly drawn to the area across the fire where a band was playing on a small wooden stage. "Is that..."

"Black Rage? No it's just Gene and Aggy; they're friends. You know how it is; all gay people know each other," Jerri said with a wild grin.

"So funny." Tara looked around her and even in the dim light clearly saw half a dozen A-listers. *Because, dumbass, your girlfriend is an extremely famous writer who used to live with an even more famous rock star. She only lives in the woods like a hermit because she wants to. The last time I saw this many gay people in one place was when me and my sisters went to a gay club because the dancing is always better there. Now... Well now I'm one of them. I don't want anything as badly as I want Jerri and I can't pretend I'm not a lesbian and have a girlfriend.*

There were a half dozen wooden picnic tables set at intervals around the fire and long benches had been made by cutting logs in half and setting each end of the ten-foot sections on a short log with a saddle cut into it.

There had to be well over fifty people there. They were an odd mix: celebrities, new agers, writers and homesteaders. Most she knew were gay but a lot of them were straights. Everyone was just walking around drinking beer, eating hot dogs they were roasting on sticks on the fire, listening to the music and talking. Some were dancing. No one looked like they were seconds from starting a fight over someone looking at someone else or any other such obvious club-type bullshit. They were completely comfortable in each-others' company. They all waited on themselves and it was clear they were all having a blast.

"Come on." Jerri started pulling her along again. "I want you to meet my best friend."

Tara followed, but when she saw where they were headed she tugged on Jerri's arm till she stopped and whispered, "Is your best friend a man?"

"No. She used to be a woman trapped in a man's body," Jerri said with a grin. "She's all woman now."

Tara remembered her talking about Judy before. "But she's married to a woman."

"So she's a lesbian. Baby, all women are either bisexual or gay and now Judy is a woman, soooo."

"I'm finally normal!" Tara laughed.

"Judy has that effect on people. Relax, she's going to love you even in your bad Eminem disguise."

As they reached them Judy held up a beer and Jerri took it. "You were gone long enough your beer got almost as warm as you did." She looked up at Tara. "So you must be the reason all the single lesbian women are crying tonight." Judy offered her hand and Tara shook it. "I'm Judy this is the light of my heart, Cyndy."

"I'm Terri," Tara said.

"Did you come up with that or did she?" Judy asked Jerri.

"Don't start with me, old woman," Jerri growled. "And she made up the name not me... For once in your life just be my friend and don't pry. Just let her be Terri."

"You're as famous as anyone here aren't you?" Judy said, looking at her through squinted eyes.

"Maybe I better go back to the house," Tara whispered in Jerri's ear.

"No," Jerri said loudly, glaring at Judy, "because no one but Judy just has to know everything about everyone and she's going to shut her fucking mouth right now."

Judy held up her hands. "Absolutely."

"Good come on I'll make you a hot dog." Jerri took Tara's hand and led her away. "Don't pay any attention to Judy. She thinks she has to protect me from... Well mostly from me. Just blow her off."

"Maybe I should just go back to the house."

"No, this is my place, you're my girlfriend. When you go back to the house I'm going with you..."

"Cyndy tells me that I'm very, very sorry," Judy said.

Tara turned to look at her.

"Jerri really is my very best friend. More than that she's my hero, my savior. I'm afraid I'm a little over protective."

Judy was near tears, and suddenly Tara just loved her. She hugged Judy's neck and whispered in her ear, "She's all those things to me, too. I have no intention of hurting her."

Jerri threw up her hands. "Girls!" she exclaimed and walked away.

Judy released Tara and looked after Jerri. "She doesn't look or act it, but she's fragile."

Tara nodded. She did know that.

Jerri taught her how to roast a hot dog on the fire, and it was by far the best dog she'd ever eaten.

It was Jerri's party so it made a certain amount of sense but every time she thought they could just sit and enjoy being together someone grabbed Jerri to do something or to talk to her. Even though Jerri kept dragging her with her they kept getting separated. They certainly weren't anywhere near alone. Everyone was super nice to her and very welcoming even the women who were telling her how lucky she was in a way that told her that they knew Jerri if not better, then at least more intimately than she did.

She went to get a beer and there was Aggy Long doing the same thing. When she looked at Tara she smiled and said, "You're a lucky girl."

Tara took in a deep breath nodded and felt like banging her head against the ice chest. *I wouldn't know!*

Gene and Aggy had quit playing and then Lisa Freely did a couple of songs. After that anyone who could play or sing at all got up and did something. Tara didn't even know Dana Sinclair the author was there till she got up half drunk and sang a filthy song that had them all cracking up. They were certainly an extremely talented bunch, but Tara was sort of jaded she guessed. After all her mother was a talent agent. Tara had been to so many red-carpet events over the last ten years she had lost count years ago.

Right at midnight Jerri and Judy took the stage. It was then that Tara first realized that Jerri and Judy did this party together. Everyone got quiet. "So the time has come to burn those things we hate most," Jerri announced.

"A cleansing ritual to purify our souls. I will start, then we will go around the circle." Judy reached into a bag pulled out a picture and held it up. "A copy of the picture my mother refuses to take down of me." She walked off the stage and threw it in the fire. Everyone cheered.

Jerri pulled a book from behind her back. "*Burning Rain*, the worst book I ever wrote." When Jerri threw it into the fire Tara actually gasped. She turned to Cyndy, who was sitting beside her.

"I love that book," Tara said indignantly.

"You and fifty bazillion other people in forty-five different languages, but Jerri is a perfectionist when it comes to her work, and she was never happy with the book. Every year everyone else brings something different, but my wife and your girlfriend always burn the same thing. Judy burns the picture of herself pre-surgery that her mother won't take down, and Jerri burns another copy of *Burning Rain*. I wouldn't worry; she's never going to get all of them."

"Well she's certainly not getting her hands on my copy." Jerri walked right over to her and sat down beside her. "I love that book, asshole."

"It is and was a total cop out."

Judy who was now sitting on the other side of Jerri looked around Jerri and said, "The real reason she hates the book is because of when she wrote it."

"Shut up Judy!" Jerri said. She pushed Judy till she almost knocked her off the log bench which just made Judy laugh. Jerri was really rough with Judy and Tara realized something, *Jerri was friends with Judy before her transformation; that's what Judy meant. Jerri helped her through it, and Judy has helped Jerri with whatever her problem is. It's why they're so close.* "I don't understand why your Hippocratic Oath applies to everyone else but not me."

"You aren't my client; you're my friend."

Jerri dismissed Judy with a wave of her hand.

"If you watch carefully and listen you can tell a lot about people by what they burn," Jerri told Tara as she put her arm around her and drew her close. Tara laid her head on Jerri's shoulder.

"Well then I'm wondering about what I brought," Tara said, dragging it out of her pocket.

"What did you bring?"

"My marriage license."

When the burning ceremony ended people told each other good bye and started working their way back to their cars with only a few people still hanging out. When the stream of people coming to tell Jerri good bye and tell her it was nice to meet her had finally died down, Tara took Jerri's hand and dragged her away from the firelight into the darkness of the woods where she wrapped herself around her. Jerri pulled her close and kissed her. Tara untucked Jerri's—just as stained as any other day—T shirt and ran her hands over Jerri's back. She caught Jerri's eyes and held them.

"So someone asked me if I was a top or a bottom or a switch and I quickly changed the subject because I had no idea what they were talking about."

"I'm thinking you're a switch, but that might be wishful thinking."

They kissed again and this time when they parted Tara gasped. "Take me to the house and fuck me right now or I'm going to die."

Jerri laughed and pulled her against her hard. "Now there is one I haven't heard before."

"Half a dozen women at this damn party have made a point of telling me how lucky I am. I would just like to find out if they're all full of shit before I die. I don't understand why I have to wait for something that you obviously give to everyone who lies still long enough."

"Well if it's a matter of life or death..." Jerri took her hand and started pulling her through the woods to the house.

Chapter 8

When they got to the door of Jerri's room Jerri opened it dragged her in then slammed it and locked it. Then she grabbed the tail of the hoodie and pulled it off over Tara's head in one fluid motion. She shoved Tara against the wall. Tara could feel Jerri undoing the snap on her pants. Jerri's tongue was in her mouth, and Tara felt Jerri's hands working on pulling her pants down. Then Jerri was touching her and she felt like she was going to crawl the wall at her back.

Tara had no doubt at all that this was what she wanted and who she wanted it with. That made everything that happened afterward so much better. Tara made a note to thank "good Jerri" for not letting "bad Jerri" or even Tara rush the process.

The bedside lamp was on. Jerri looked down at the woman in her arms, smiled and held her tighter. Tara was beautiful. As Jerri held her she had no doubt about the way she felt or that she'd made the best choice. She moved her head and kissed Tara's cheek. Tara started running her left hand over Jerri's right hip.

"You alright?" Jerri asked, realizing that Tara hadn't said anything since they—well for lack of a better word—finished.

"I feel amazing."

"Then what's wrong?"

"I don't know what I'm doing, Jerri. I'm just flying by the seat of my pants and... I should have at least read some books, looked it up on the internet."

"I came till I damn near passed out what else do you want, Tara?" Jerri laughed and kissed Tara's cheek again. "You were amazing."

"I was trying... I mean I wanted to. I wasn't thinking anything stupid or doubting myself at all the whole time we were having sex; I was completely present. Then after I was just sort of basking in the after-glow of the best sex I've ever had and actually feeling pretty smug because I was sure I gave you a mind blowing orgasm. But then as the blood started to return to my brain so did all my self-doubts and I remembered you have slept with Rhonda and Aggy Long and half the models on the west coast. How could I ever stand up to all of that?"

"I am crazy in love with you, Tara. You should never doubt yourself because you are amazing, but never *ever* doubt how I feel about you or how you make me feel. Being with someone you feel connected to in your soul..." Jerri actually felt a little choked up. "I love you, but beyond that I trust that you love me, and that makes you different from anyone else I've ever been with."

Tara looked up at her and smiled. "So can we do it again?"

For answer Jerri grabbed Tara, threw her on her back, jumped on top of her and started kissing her. When their lips parted Tara grinned and said, "Oh, now I get it. Top."

When Tara woke up she had a death grip on Jerri who was still sound asleep. Here was the thing—with any of the men she had been with she couldn't get away from them quick enough. She never could have slept on a tiny bed like this one with any of them. It wasn't even a queen size, it was just a full, and they were both sleeping on less than half of it.

She smiled and looked around because until the night before she'd never been in Jerri's bedroom, and she certainly hadn't looked at it last night. There were bookshelves completely filled to the right of the bedroom door that covered the entire wall from floor to ceiling. On the other wall were two small windows. Between them was Jerri's desk with her computer. The bed sat with the head against the front wall and had another tailgate—this one from an old ford truck—for a headboard. There was no TV, but there was a stereo. There were doors on either side of the bed which she assumed went to closets, so the bed wasn't really against the outside wall.

Like in every other room of the house there were quotes painted on all the walls. The one right across from her said, "The journey of a thousand miles starts with you getting your lazy ass out of bed." It had no author which meant it was Jerri's. Tara smiled and thought seriously of waking Jerri up, but then she had to go to the bathroom so she got up, threw on her robe, and went downstairs thinking, *Her friends are right. Having no bathroom upstairs is a pain in the ass.*

She did her business, brushed her teeth, cleaned up a

little bit and decided to go right upstairs and wake Jerri up. When she walked in the room Jerri must have heard the door because she flopped over in bed and the covers landed in the floor. *My God there isn't an ounce of flab on her. She is all muscle. How could I have ever deluded myself that I could be happy with anything but this?*

She threw her robe in the floor and nearly jumped on Jerri. Jerri laughed, grabbed and held her. Then when Tara made her intentions clear Jerri pushed her away saying. "I need to go to the bathroom." Then to the look on Tara's face, "I will be right back and I will have brushed my teeth so that's a huge plus." She pushed her quickly off of her and got up. She grabbed the robe Tara had just thrown in the floor, and as she was putting it on she said, "You should probably call your mother while I'm gone."

"Caarap," Tara said and watched as Jerri left. She got up went to Jerri's desk and there sat another of the old phones, this one with an actual rotary dial. She picked it up and dialed her mother's number.

"You alright, Tara?" Her mother asked in a groggy voice. Tara looked at the phone and cringed it was already nine if her mother wasn't already up she hated to find out when she'd gone to bed the night before.

"I'm fantastic. What about you?"

"I'm fine. I was just up till the butt crack of dawn because everyone and their dog was calling. Last we heard Fred was still unconscious. It doesn't look good. One doctor said his brain hemorrhaged. They have no idea how much brain damage he may have and won't until he becomes conscious again—if he ever does."

Jerri walked back in the room, closed the door, threw off the robe, then walked right over to her and started rubbing her hands all over Tara's body.

"Get this—Todd went in the window, turned the TV off and opened the channel to the intercom in your room. Periodically Lori gets on it in her room when the camera crew isn't looking, cries and says how she wants to be left alone. So far no one has figured out that you aren't in your room. So if you could, just lay low for a couple of days till this calms down."

Jerri took her into her arms and held her, kissing her neck.

"If I had my way I'd just stay where I am."

"Forever," Jerri whispered in her ear. "You can stay here forever."

"Where are you, Tara?" her mother asked.

"Someplace safe. That should be all that matters, Mom. I'm not drinking or drugging myself into a comma, and no one is here asking me about a dumbass that did. I don't have to put on a show; I can just be me." She hung up and then practically tackled Jerri till they were back in bed.

When they had finished making love, Jerri asked, "So can you tell me what happened yesterday?"

So Tara told her, finishing with, "So that's why I was wearing Todd's clothes and driving his car."

Jerri got up and got dressed.

Tara just threw the robe back on because the only clean clothes she had here were in the chest of drawers in the guest room.

"I don't see why anyone thinks you should care. Not only did you divorce the turd for cheating on you but then he got on Twitter shitter and trashed you out. The stupid bastard." Jerri walked over to her, untied the robe Tara had just carefully closed, pulled it open and looked her up and down. "This is the most rocking body I've ever seen and touched and tasted and..."

"You're dressed," Tara said, closing the robe. "I'm pretty sure your friends are up and your goats need to be milked."

Jerri nodded her head, kissed Tara and started for the door. She opened it and turned. "But I heard right. You get to stay for a few days?"

Tara smiled. "Yes, at least a few. I may be able to milk it for more."

And then her very spiritual, enlightened, girlfriend hissed in a way that told her that Jerri was filled with hidden rage, "I hope that fucker dies."

"Shut up Judy!" Jerri said looking across the kitchen table at her.

"You've been saying that so much you could tape it and play it on loop." Judy laughed.

"She wouldn't have to if you'd just shut up, love," Cyndy said with a giggle. Then she sipped at her coffee when Judy cut her a look.

"I wouldn't have to keep asking if she would just tell me who her girlfriend is."

"I'll tell you what, asshat. I'll tell you if you tell me your big, secret, straight-world crushing thing."

"I can't," Judy said.

"Really?"

"I told you it involves a client, so... that Hippocratic oath thing that doesn't apply to you does to them." Judy was obviously listening to see if Tara was still in the bathroom, which she was. "When I saw her this morning without her disguise—well she's hotter than hell but more than that she looked familiar. I just can't place her at all, which means I've seen but don't know her. So she's famous, and if she wouldn't let herself be seen at our party last night it means she's closeted. You and I both know the closet is no place to grow people."

"It's complicated, Judy, alright? I'm her first lesbian relationship. She needs time to grow into it."

"And she's got plenty of time for growing because she's about ten." This came not from Judy but Cyndy.

"*Et tu*, Cyndy?" Jerri said with a mock frown. "She's thirty."

"Besides the fact she's got a great rack and ass, can you tell me why you love her, Jerri?"

"She's sharp as a tack. Not only does she not mind that I live like this, but she loves it here. She has a great sense of humor, and mostly when I'm with her I don't feel broken at all."

"Is that because she needs you?" Judy asked carefully.

Jerri thought about that for a minute. "Why would that automatically be a bad thing?"

"Jerri, being with someone because they *need* you means you still don't feel like you deserve to have someone just because they add something to your life, just because you want them and they want you. What happens when she no longer needs you?

"Then I'll still want her. I'll still love her." Tara walked into the kitchen drying her hair with a towel and proving she was bright because, first she figured out how to wash her hair in the tub all by herself, and second she figured out they were talking about her and cut her bath short. Tara handed the towel to Jerri and tied her robe a little better. "She needs me, too." She looked at Jerri for confirmation.

Jerri didn't even have to think about it. She nodded her head. "She's right I do," Jerri said.

"I'm not some stupid kid. I know what I'm doing, who I'm doing it with, and what that makes me," Tara said to Judy, and then walked right back to the bathroom.

"Now see what you did?" Jerri hissed at Judy then got up and went after Tara. She didn't knock on the bathroom door, just walked in.

Tara was standing at the mirror, angrily combing her hair.

Jerri took the comb from Tara's hand and started combing Tara's hair for her.

Tara looked a little weepy. "What's wrong?"

"I wanted your friends to like me."

"They do."

"No, they don't they think I'm using you."

"No, they absolutely don't. If she didn't like you believe me most of the state would already know it. Judy's just incapable of not being a shrink for five seconds. She's curious about everything and everyone, and if she's afraid of anything regarding us it's that I'm using you to make me feel better about being me."

"Which is what you did with Rhonda?"

"Mostly. Look at you, and look at me." She pointed at the mirror and was about to point out why other people might think they didn't belong together because they didn't look like they did, but then Jerri really saw them together and they glowed with a single aura. "My God, we even look like we belong together." She put the comb down on the sink, moved Tara's hair and kissed the side of her neck. "I love you, Tara, I don't care what anyone else says, I don't care what they think, and I know it's not going to be easy but all we have to remember is not to blame each other. If we take on the rest of the world together, we will win."

Tara caught her eyes in the mirror, smiled a smile just for her, and Jerri felt whole and loved and... Judy just needed to shut up.

Apparently it was tradition for Judy, Jerri and Cyndy to go back to the bonfire site the morning after what they all called "the burn." Unfortunately without breakfast which didn't make Tara happy because she was suddenly starving.

"Is 'Terri,' going?" Judy said, putting emphasis on Tara's fake name.

"Yes she's going. Of course she's going. Why wouldn't she be?" Jerri was still obviously pissed at her friend, which made Tara feel really good but she couldn't have told anyone why.

"My name is Tara," she said. When there was no sign of recognition from Judy she damn near sighed with relief.

Judy laughed looked at Jerri and said, "Well at least now I understand how she came up with Terri. Come on let's go, and yes Jerri, I will leave it alone now."

When they got to the bonfire Jerri took a long piece of metal with a hook on it and started sifting through the ash and coals. Tara was some surprised to feel that the fire was still very hot.

At her shoulder Judy explained, "Life should be full of ritual. Not the religious trappings of the old world but things that have meaning for us. A personal religion if you will. Last night we gathered together as a community and burned the things which have caused us pain. The things we didn't like, sometimes the things from that year, sometimes things from years ago, each are only a representation of the real pain. Watching it burn as it becomes a fragment of what it once was allows us to start clean."

Tara remembered the night before when it had been her turn. She'd walked to the fire and said, "I married a man to make my parents happy and I divorced him to make me happy. This is my marriage license," and then she tossed it into the fire as everyone cheered. She watched it burn and when it had been consumed she did feel like a chapter of her life had closed. Now as she looked over at Jerri's ass as she was bent over messing with the fire she thought. *A new chapter has started and this time I'm writing it, no one else just me.*

Judy kept talking, "Not everything people throw in burns entirely so Jerri digs all those things out..."

"I'll never forget the year Jessy threw her stinking wheel chair in. That was a giant pain in the ass," Jerri said looking briefly at Tara.

"And the toxic smoke plume from it no doubt polluted the air in three states," Cyndy said with a laugh. She was looking through the ice chest. And pulled out a bottle of water and opened it.

"But very cleansing," Judy added. "Any way Jerri sifts

through the ash... because let's face it that's no job for us girls. She mixes it with concrete, makes blocks, and then she adds it to the wall around the bonfire pit."

Till then Tara had hardly paid any attention at all to the block wall around the fire pit. Now she noticed each one had a year marked onto it.

"She transforms the things we all hate into something useful everyone can enjoy," Tara said.

Judy looked over at Jerri with wide eyes.

Jerri grinned back at Judy. "I told you; she's sharp as a tack."

"That didn't surprise me; that I could tell. She's very spiritual."

Tara didn't know about all that.

"We never clean the ash from the pit. Why do you think that is?" Judy asked.

Cyndy looked at Tara, rolled her eyes and said, "Bet you didn't know there was going to be a test."

"With Judy there is always some test," Jerri growled out.

Tara only had to think about it for a second then she said, "The piling up of the ash reminds you of how far you've come in your lives."

Judy then looked from Tara to Jerri and a tear came to her eye as she told Jerri, "She's perfect."

"I already knew that, Judy," Jerri said.

Tara wondered if she would have been able to figure all that out before she met Jerri and knew she never would have in a thousand years. Every minute she spent with Jerri she learned something else about the universe and about her true self.

Jerri was throwing pieces of metal she was pulling out of the fire into a metal bucket and grumbling, "The year of the wheel chair I had to cut the metal down and... five blocks from that year." She turned to look at Judy, "Where the hell were they this year anyway?"

"Their little one had a cold so they didn't want to leave him with a sitter."

"Everyone and their baby thing," Jerri muttered, and just kept sifting through the ash.

Judy gave Tara a questioning look and Tara just smiled and said, "We have already had the baby talk, and neither of us wants one."

Judy nodded her head approvingly.

"I think that's got it... Son of a bitch." She carefully lifted something from the ash that her last turn exposed. It was the spine of the copy of *Burning Rain* she had thrown in the night before. Judy laughed, and they all watched as Jerri threw it and a bunch of wood onto the red hot coals she had exposed in the middle of the fire. There was smoke and then in seconds flames.

"And now we eat... You know if anything is left," Judy said and looked at Cyndy.

"There are five sausages left, no buns, no condements. Two waters, five cokes, and about ten beers."

Judy and Jerri ran up to each other, high-fived and yelled out, "Perfect!"

"That's part of their ritual, too," Cyndy told Tara. "Even if there is so much left over we couldn't eat it by ourselves in a week, or nothing at all so that we have to go back to the house and eat, they always exclaim that it's perfect."

Tara smiled because she knew why. "It's perfect because it always tells them exactly what they are doing next."

"Of course," Cyndy said, nodding. "You really are very spiritual."

"I'm not even sure what that means."

"Which just makes you all that much more spiritual."

They roasted the rest of the sausages, ate them, and drank up the last of the beer. They were sitting at one of the tables, just bullshitting mostly about the party the night before— which was also more or less ritual—and then Tara asked, "Those hot dogs were really good. What were they?"

Jerri was having such a good time she started not to answer, but then with a sigh she said, "Pork and goat. Kert had a pig he wanted butchered. I had a goat. We butchered them together, made them into sausages, and he took half and I took half."

Tara made a face but didn't say anything.

"What?"

"I can't imagine killing much less cutting something up."

"Oh, now you're in for it. The fifteen-minute speech about modern society's hypocrisy," Judy muttered. She was of course right.

"Tara, you eat meat. Hell, you eat the meat I butcher all

the time, you just hadn't thought about it till right this minute. If you were a vegan than I'd let you sit there all day and tell me how wrong and awful I am for killing my animals. But you aren't. Like me you are a meat eater. The only difference between you and me is that you are more than happy to let someone else do your dirty work…"

"I wasn't judging you, Jerri. I was just saying I don't think I could do it," Tara said quickly.

"Oh," Jerri said.

Judy laughed and shook her head. "Geez, Tara, she didn't even get into all the horrors of the way corporate farms raise their animals, all the toxins they're fed, the tiny little pens they are kept in. How kindly, very kindly, she slaughters her animals."

Jerri laughed and kicked Judy under the table. "Fuck you, Judy."

"I think that ship has already sailed," Cyndy said with a grin.

Tara was then glaring at Jerri.

"What?" Jerri asked.

"Is there absolutely anyone you haven't screwed?" Tara accused.

Jerri leaned over and whispered in Tara's ear. "You. I never screwed you. I made love to you."

Tara turned her head, kissed her, and Jerri happily kissed her back.

"Ah my friend does have a silver tongue," Judy said.

"That's what all the girls say," Cyndy laughed.

Jerri shot her a look. "What the hell has gotten into you today, Cyndy?" Because of course Cyndy wasn't normally the one to ride her high.

Judy pointed to the beer bottles in front of her wife. "There were ten beers. She drank four of them, and you know what a light weight she is."

Jerri went off to milk as Tara stayed to help Judy and Cyndy pick up the area. Tara had wanted to go with Jerri, but Judy had suggested if Jerri was actually going to make it back in time to help them with clean up Tara probably shouldn't go with her which was true because the main reason she wanted to go with Jerri was so she could talk her into sex.

The bonfire site was actually pretty cool. It was a small

clearing in the trees. She'd seen the benches and tables last night, but there was also a building which housed two toilets, two sinks, and two shower stalls. Apparently they often had other parties where people brought tents and camped out. There were six fifty-five gallon metal drums set out at intervals for trash. The stage was small and centrally located so that you could see it from all parts of the area, and there was a curved wall behind it made of wood planks—no doubt for acoustics—on which the words "The Burn" were written in huge yellow block letters. There were what looked like Christmas lights in the trees that Judy told her were run on small solar panels.

"Were they on last night?" Tara asked.

"Yes." Judy smiled at her knowingly and said, "I doubt you really saw anything last night. Your eyes were on Jerri every time I looked at you. The glasses didn't hide that."

Then Judy was looking at her, obviously trying to figure out just who she was. Tara quickly got busy picking up beer bottles and putting them in a bucket so that they could be taken back to the guy who made the beer in the first place and recycled. There was really very little mess to clean up which made sense. They weren't a bunch of twenty-something idiots getting shit-faced drunk and just seeing how much damage they could do. They had all come to be together and celebrate their freedom from the things they hated.

She smiled remembering one of the homesteaders throwing something into the fire and yelling, "I hate this fucking trowel and all it stands for!" She'd asked Jerri what that was all about and Jerri had told her.

"Alvin built a root cellar this year. He dug the hole by hand, mixed all the cement by hand, and laid all the rock by hand. He thought it was going to take him about a week; it took him about three months. He said if he never did rock work again it would be too soon."

Tara had watched Jerri pull the metal part of the tool from the fire that morning.

They were almost done when Judy started dumping the contents of the trash barrels onto the ground.

"What the hell?"

Cyndy laughed, obviously knowing exactly what was going through Tara's mind. They were almost finished cleaning it up.

"We have to separate the trash—plastic in one bucket, paper on the fire. Any food stays on the ground and the bottles go with the rest of the bottles."

Tara followed Cyndy to one of the piles of trash and started pulling the bottles out with two fingers and putting them into the bucket.

"So are you going to her lecture at UCLA next week?"

"Whose?"

"Jerri's. She's slated to speak at the university next Friday. Judy and I are going."

"I don't know. I didn't know anything about it till right this minute. I'd like to." She would, too, but could she and would it be a good thing? If she went a camera crew would no doubt be following her, and in the college crowd everyone was going to know just who she was. "I don't think I can."

"That's too bad; she's a brilliant speaker."

"I have no doubt. It sucks," Tara said.

"Maybe Tara Darting could just be a fan of Jerri Blue's work. Go and sit in the back."

"You... You know who I am."

"I did as soon as I saw you this morning. Those assholes don't watch much TV, but I do. It will take Judy some time to figure it out because she is completely preoccupied with her current project, but she will eventually."

"You aren't going to tell her?"

"No, and I'm not going to tell anyone else. In our community we don't out each other in any way, shape, or form; it's kind of an unwritten law. Everyone needs to come out how they want, when they want, and to who they want. Most of us come out in stages."

Tara nodded.

"But Judy would never go to the press. Judy would never do anything that might hurt Jerri. You have to know that."

Tara nodded. "But if she knows who I am she's going to hate me. She's going to think I'm all wrong for Jerri."

"Yesterday I would have agreed with you. But now she can see that Jerri loves you. More importantly, it's obvious that you love Jerri. For Jerri to trust anyone enough to actually love them is huge. With their back and forth it may not sound like it, but Judy trusts no one's judgement—except maybe her own—as much as she does Jerri's. Jerri knows Judy would never tell anyone who you are, but she will never tell anything you don't want told. You need to know that about Jerri if you don't already. Jerri is beyond trustworthy. "

Tara nodded. she did already know that. She looked up and looked around till she saw Judy separating trash in the barrel across from them. She took a deep breath, tried not to think about the catsup on her hands, and walked over to Judy.

Judy looked up at her.

"I'm Tara Darting." Judy obviously still didn't knew who she was, so she just smiled and said, *Daring with the Dartings.* As recognition crossed Judy's face she looked momentarily like she had been punched in the gut.

"You're one of Janice and Gary's kids?"

Tara nodded.

"Crap, the marriage license. I should have known." She took in a deep breath and let it out. "Your secret is safe with me, but... You do know that if this thing is going to work with Jerri eventually you're going to have to come out."

Tara nodded. "I will, but right now isn't a good time."

"Honey, I could not agree with you more."

Tara got the feeling there was a lot more that Judy wasn't saying than what she was.

Suddenly a sea of chickens surrounded them and started right away eating every piece of food trash they saw. Then she saw Jerri heading for them in a golf cart dragging a small trailer behind it. Jerri parked, and the minute she got out Judy yelled at her.

"Seriously, Jerri? One of the Darting girls?"

Jerri looked at Tara, and she shrugged with a half grin. Jerri turned towards Judy. "Don't give me any more shit, Judy."

Then Jerri walked over to Tara and handed her a wet towel which she gladly wiped her hands on. "What? Could she just not leave it alone, or did she just figure it out?"

"Cyndy figured it out. She said she wouldn't tell, and... Well I wouldn't want to know anything I couldn't tell you, so I just told Judy. She's not going to tell anyone, so it doesn't matter anyway. As things with my family return to a three-ring circus instead of the six it is now I'm coming out because truthfully I'm way ready to start my life with you, Jerri Blue, and leave all that crap for the rest of them."

Chapter 9

She had been at Jerri's for three full days and nights. Tara didn't want to, but she was going to have to go back to LA tomorrow.

Fred was still in a coma, but that was mostly old news and things had calmed down a little. Her mother had told her that morning that she needed her to come home and actually do her job. Tara would... tomorrow morning.

They had left the farm and were driving up the coast because Jerri had an appointment to look at a goat. Tara smiled. *An appointment to look at a goat. Who in a million years would have thought that would be a thing?* She looked across the small cab of the ancient Chevy love pickup at the side of Jerri's face. A stray strand of hair had blown out of Jerri's braid. Tara reached over and pushed it back behind her ear. *I never thought I could feel like this about anyone but she's not just anyone she's Jerri Blue.*

Jerri looked quickly at her smiled then looked back at the road. "I had no idea this was so far from the house.'

"Why are we getting a goat?"

"Because our billy goat is evil. That's why. You weren't there, but a week ago he ripped a hole in his pen and damn near tore me a new asshole before I could get him shut up again. The bastard tore through cattle panel."

To the blank look on Tara's face Jerri said, "It's really, really strong metal fencing."

"It's a beautiful day," Tara said. "I'm kind of enjoying just riding around with you. For one thing you can't get away from me."

"I'm never trying to get away from you." Jerry laughed, reached over put her hand on Tara's knee and left it there. Now normally if someone so much as took their hand off the wheel for a second and she was a passenger Tara would flip completely out, but Jerry didn't drive like a moron. She drove neither too fast nor too slow, and the minute Jerri felt like she needed both hands on the wheel Tara had no doubt that she would move her hand. Which she did all too soon. "What would make you think I'm trying to get away from you?"

"Well for one thing you can't sit still for more than ten minutes without getting up to do SOMETHING," Tara said.

"That..." Jerri laughed. "That's not true."

"It absolutely is."

"Well, I'm not trying to get away from you."

"Maybe not, but in order to be with you I have to run around after you. The only time I ever have all your attention for more than ten minutes at a time is in bed. You act like the entire world as we know it will fall completely to shit if you aren't doing something constructive every waking moment of the day. I know the homestead takes a lot of work, and there's the writing, but I want to learn to help you do everything... except the butchering... and then I want you to learn to actually sit and relax."

"That's a lot to ask." Jerri sighed. "Are we ever going to make it to this fucking place?"

"How about we start that relaxing thing right now, Jerri?"

"Stupid GPS," Jerri said, picking her smart phone up off the dash and shaking it. Till they'd left that morning Tara hadn't even known that Jerri owned a smart phone.

Jerri set the phone down again and Tara picked it up and looked at it. "Alright. According to this you missed the turn about..." She messed with it. "...five miles back."

Jerri muttered a bunch of choice words and turned the truck around in a drive way. A huge Rottweiler hit the fence barking, and Jerri actually jumped.

"Could you..." Jerri pointed to the phone.

"I will gladly navigate," Tara said.

They had passed the church before. This time she actually saw what the marquee outside said, which was good because otherwise Tara would have had no idea what Jerri was talking about when she said, "Then we're all fucking screwed." The sign said, "Jesus is the only hope."

"Do you not believe in God?" Tara asked carefully.

"I believe in God. What I don't believe is a story about some guy who became a sacrifice for our sins. That's absurd. I don't believe in a God that watches over, cares for, and protects us—at least not in the way most people understand those things. I believe people want to think of God as a helicopter parent who follows them around making sure they don't fall or cry, that comes undone when they scrape their knee. They want to believe in a God that will come to their rescue and save them from the darkness. That is not the God I know.

"The God I know is more like my own father was. They have the kids and then just let them raise themselves. To believe that God watches over and protects us puts us right on a path of unworthiness. Because where is God when we most need God? Why does God not come and save us, show us the light, help us when we most need it? If we need help and none comes from this God who cares so much for every tiny sparrow, it must be because we aren't worthy. If I found my worth in God's protection I would be dead now many times over because I have never felt it.

"The whole point of being a human is to learn things, and we rarely learn things of real value from the good things. No, we learn all our most important lessons from the bad things that happen. If we're always in the light we never have to climb any higher, but if we're in the bottom of the pit we climb or we die in the dark." Jerri sounded highly agitated.

"Are you alright?"

Jerri had to think about that a minute. She had been fine just a few minutes ago. She admitted she wasn't now. What happened? *The dog barked at me. Dammit, the dog barked at me.*

The road was narrow and winding, and there was a dirt pull off on the right side of the road so that you could get over and let other cars pass. No one was behind them, but she pulled over anyway and parked. She turned the truck off, took her seat belt off, and then turned to look at Tara. "I'm not alright." She took a deep breath then let it out. "Why do you suppose I don't have a dog on the farm?"

"I guess... I hadn't given it much thought," Tara said in a way that let Jerri know Tara knew Jerri was telling the truth when she said she wasn't alright.

Jerri took her hand off the wheel and it was shaking. "Because a barking dog is one of my triggers. Probably my biggest trigger if I'm honest. I want us to live together at some point in the future; do you want that, too?"

Tara didn't hesitate. "Of course I do. I'd do it right now if it was possible. In fact, in my mind we already live together."

"Then I have to tell you because you're going to find out at some point and I'd rather be the one to tell you." She took a deep breath and collected her thoughts. "When I was nineteen years old I was physically and sexually assaulted. I was walking home from work. A beat-up white sedan pulled up and someone yelled, "Hey butch want to party?" I took off running because I was walking through a half mile stretch of the walk home where there were no houses, and I guess I instinctively knew I was in trouble. The driver purposely hit me with the car. I was dazed and beat up. There were three of them. They drug me into the car. They all raped me and when they got done with me they threw me out of the moving vehicle about five miles out of town. I have no idea how fast the car was going, but I'm pretty sure their intention wasn't that I'd live to tell. I wound up falling to the bottom of a ravine about twenty feet down from the road surface. I was in pain, it was dark, and it was cold. I had no idea where I was or how badly I was broken up. And I prayed. I prayed like I never had before and haven't since and there was NO help. No light to show me the way. No angel to carry my tattered body to the road surface."

"You don't have to tell me any more, Jerri."

"Yes I do, Tara, because I own no part of the shame in what happened to me, but I can't pretend that it didn't happen nor should I. You can't live with me and not know."

Jerri took a deep breath let it out and continued. "There was nothing but pain and shame in the bottom of that ravine, just what was left of me. You know what did show up that night? A great big black dog that barked and barked and barked all night long. Now that I'm older and wiser I know the dog was just barking because I was something different in his space, but at the time I was sure it was going to come down and kill me. Some of my spiritual friends have suggested the dog was what the universe sent to help me. Maybe they're right. Maybe it was the dog's barking that kept me from falling into unconsciousness. Maybe that black dog barking like he was going to finish me off was the only help the universe thought I needed. But to this day if a dog barks at me I still jump, and I've been mostly well for many years.

"I lay there all night dazed and in pain. Spiritually, emotionally and physically destroyed, and no help came. When the sun finally started to come up in the morning I couldn't get up, but I could tell which way the road was. I remember wondering how much longer it would take me to die, if maybe

I wouldn't be better off dead. I didn't know how I was ever going to be able to live with what had happened to me. It wasn't divine providence or even hope for something better in the future that made me drag my mangled body up that embankment. No it was the need for vengeance, the idea that I would make my attackers pay. I knew what they looked like, I knew their license plate number, and I had beaten the living shit out of them so there was loads of evidence all over me.

I drug myself up to the road. Three cars went right past before a fourth stopped and called 911. My right wrist was broken in two places—that's what these scars are, they had to pin it." She showed them to Tara "They broke my right femur, three of my fingers, and I had cuts and contusions everywhere. I have a five-inch gnarly scar on the right side of my head that couldn't even be stitched because of the length of time the injury stayed open. I had a concussion. They collected all the evidence. I gave them descriptions and the license plate number... No one was ever punished for the crime against me. The cops somehow lost all the evidence the hospital collected. They put out the sketches, but they were half assed. They said they put out a bolo on the license plate number, but I don't think they did a damn thing. The truth is that because this was over twenty years ago in the south and I was an obvious queer, all those cops thought I got just what I deserved. They didn't think their sisters or daughters had anything to worry about from those 'boys.' Since they had yelled, 'hey butch' at me obviously that was the only reason they attacked me. In the cop's minds I was attacked only because I was a blatant pervert who had it coming. In their eyes I was the danger to the community not those men. After a couple of weeks they told me that the boys were obviously, 'Not from around here,' and they might not have been because I looked for them myself for months and never found them. So no one paid for what was done to me, and I still can't stand a barking dog. I don't believe at all in a God who actually cares about me in a way that humans understand caring because if I do then I go right back to a place where it's all my fault. And I can't live there."

Tara had no idea what to say or do. Her instinct was to hug Jerri and tell her how sorry she was that she had to go through that, how angry she was for her. Her heart hurt for her. But all of that seemed like it was more about how uncomfortable she was with this knowledge and not about Jerri's real pain at all. She had guessed—because she did know Jerri's work so well—that Jerri's PTSD stemmed from some form of sexual assault, but she never would have guessed the extent of it. Tara realized she was crying her eyes out but when she looked at Jerri, she wasn't crying at all. Her mouth was set in a snarl. Tara dug around in her purse, found a tissue and dried her eyes. Then she looked at Jerri.

"What do you need me to do now, Jerri? What do you need from me?"

Jerri's whole body language changed and when she spoke this time there was a catch in her throat. "What did you say?"

"What do you need me to do?"

Jerri grabbed her and pulled her to her, then Jerri was crying and Tara held her.

"I always knew, Jerri. I always knew you were the most amazing person, but to have gone through that and to become Jerri Blue...."

"How did you know I changed my name?" Jerri cried out.

"I didn't. I just meant everything that you have become."

"I changed my name when me and my brother moved from there because I just wanted to bury Ann Bourough as deeply as I could. When I did then it was like it happened to someone else. I buried it, Tara. I buried it so deeply I never thought about it, but it was always there like a shadow in the corner of my eye. One I didn't dare turn to see because if I did it would be real again. But then when the shit hit the fan with Rhonda, all the stuff I buried rose from its grave and consumed me. I dealt with it, I went to a therapist, I went to the woods, I healed myself. But I still can't stand it when a dog barks at me."

"What can I do for you, Jerri? How can I help?"

"You're doing it right now."

Tara didn't know what the hell she was doing, but in minutes Jerri appeared completely back in control. She buckled her belt, started the truck, and put it back on the road as if nothing had just happened. She must have noticed the confused look Tara was giving her because she said, "I knew I had to tell you at some point. I've been dreading it, putting it off. Now it's done so I never have to do it again. Please don't think you have to tiptoe around me. I don't want you to dwell on it; I don't. I don't want you to think you have to handle me with kid gloves."

"What are your triggers?" Tara asked.

"Mostly barking dogs. I don't like to have disparaging things yelled at me especially if the person yelling is male." She paused looking briefly at Tara. "So is this too much for you, Tara? Am I too crazy?"

"I love you, Jerri. You aren't crazy at all. Real crazy people never seem to know they have a problem."

They wound up getting the goat. He was just a kid and when Jerri tried to put him in a cage in the back of the truck Tara had protested so Jerri let Tara hold him in her lap all the way home. That he didn't pee all over her was a small miracle except that goats usually didn't pee till they stood up.

Jerri expected to feel really raw, exposed and uncomfortable with Tara for a few days, but it hadn't even lasted a few minutes. The second Tara asked what Jerri needed it was like the whole horrid ordeal was lifted right off of her. In the past the people she had told—except for Judy who was a trained psychologist—all of them wanted to hold her and say how sorry they were. They all spouted advice and told her things she had already told herself a thousand times. But Tara just cried for her, looked at her, admitted she had no idea how to help Jerri and asked what Jerri needed her to do.

Jerri covertly watched as Tara fed their new arrival a bottle. She was doing it wrong and he was spilling as much as he was eating, but Jerri didn't care. The kid was still getting plenty of milk; she could teach Tara how to do it right later. In that moment all she wanted to do was watch Tara and think about how incredibly lucky she was to have her.

She makes all my pain go completely away. She needs me, but she was right when she told Judy I need her, too. I didn't even feel like anything was missing from my life when she walked into it and now... Well the idea she has to leave in the morning... If I'm not careful it could actually make me panic.

"I'm going to go to your lecture at UCLA. Is that alright?"

"Of course."

"I've been gone for four days, so I probably won't be able to go to the can without a camera crew. But I can sit in the back..."

"When can you come back up here?"

"It depends on how crazy things are. We don't want the paparazzi or the camera crew up here. You aren't under contract, so they can't put your face on film without your permission, but the rest of you they can. They can't come on the property unless you let them but I'm thinking our neighbors aren't going to be too happy with a bunch of morons crowding the road and the gate throwing their crap everywhere."

"The college is paying for a hotel room for me for two nights. We could meet there."

"What about all our babies?" Tara said, motioning with her head towards their new goat.

"Tate is watching the place." She grinned at Tara. "I could go in tomorrow evening and you could meet me at the hotel late. Then you could meet me again Friday night and maybe by then they will have gotten enough film of you that you could at least come home on Saturday for a few hours."

"The dumb asses might try to follow me to the hotel." The bottle was empty and Tara stood up.

"Ah, but you're forgetting I'm a big deal and the hotel staff isn't going to let them into the room block," Jerri said. "I'll tell them only you're allowed."

"You know someone is going to tell someone who tells someone who tells someone that I was in your room all night."

"How worried are you about that?"

"Not enough to not meet you in your hotel room."

They put the new goat in with the others and after she assured Tara that the adult goats were just trying to show him his place in the herd and not trying to kill him they walked back towards the house hand in hand. "So you know nearly everything about me, tell me something about you that I don't know."

Tara looked over at her and seemed to think for a moment because of course they had done nothing but talk for weeks. Tara finally grinned and said, "I'm super fast."

"Super fast, huh?"

"Yep. I ran track every year of high school and college. One year I even qualified and ran in the preliminary tryouts for the Olympics."

"Imagine a lesbian who liked to play sports."

"I know, right? But I probably loose points because I mostly started running in an effort to lose weight."

"You were never fat."

Tara laughed then said, "I'll race you to the house." Then she pulled her hand out of Jerri's and took off running.

Jerri tried, but Tara wasn't lying. She really was "super fast." By the time Jerri got to the house Tara was sitting in Jerri's recliner with her feet up and she wasn't even winded. Jerri was a little, so she made a big show of trying to catch her breath then falling in the floor, lying there spread-eagled.

Showing how quick she really was, Tara was on the floor with her in seconds wrapping herself around her. Then she was kissing her. They peeled each other's clothes off and had sex right there in the floor which turned out to be the best sex Jerri had ever had. She told Tara that when afterward they were just wrapped all around each other on the floor.

"Really?" Tara said. "You aren't just saying that?"

"Really, Baby, why would I just say it?" Jerri laughed and kissed the top of Tara's head.

"If I don't go back... How long do you think it would take them to find me here?"

"Probably not as long as we'd like to think. Your mother is preoccupied right now, but she isn't stupid. Eventually she'll figure it out. After all she's the one who brought you up here. Hell, the goat guy recognized you today and you had on your Todd disguise. Seriously, Baby if you never went back to the city your friends, your family, you'd probably get pretty restless up here in the woods."

"I don't think so, Jerri." Tara moved to lay her head on Jerri's chest. "I love it here with you."

There was a knock on the door and they both moved to look at each other. "If we're very quiet maybe they will go away," Jerri whispered.

"Hey Jerri are you home? I need to use your welder. I broke the head off my plow." It was Jim.

"Ah... just go ahead and use it. My truck keys are in the glovebox if you need to move it."

"So what are you up to, Jerri?" Jim asked, a hint of laughter in his voice.

"What do you think I'm up to, asshole? Now just go work on your plow." Jerri laughed and then grabbed Tara and flipped her onto her back. "I can see why you love it here so much. All the privacy, the peace and the quiet..."

"And I think you've forgotten what it's really like in the

city, worse yet in the public eye, and worse still in my life. Hell we didn't even have to see Jim and I can tell looking you didn't lock the door when you came in. He didn't just walk in and catch us in the floor naked which... If I had a dime for every time I've had my naughty bits black barred or blurred in the last ten years... Well I'd have a jar full of dimes..." She slapped Jerri on the shoulder. "We're fucking idiots!"

"I thought we were both geniuses," Jerri said, because of course in one of their many conversations they had discovered that they had the exact same IQ.

"We both have more money than we need. We can rent a house between my mother's house and this one..."

"Then we don't have to worry about getting caught in a hotel and any time you can't lose them you can go there wait for them to get bored and leave then I can meet you there or you can go ahead and drive up here. Alright get up and get dressed we're going to go rent a house."

Jerri got off Tara and she looked rejected.

"Right now?"

"Look, you little shit, I can't stand the idea of spending even one day without seeing you. You're right; we have indecent amounts of money. I have a friend who is a very discrete realtor who I bet can find us something by the time we can get our shoes on." Jerri went to the phone and called before she even bothered with clothes. "Raymond... This is Jerri... I need to rent a house, not huge and ostentatious, but something some pampered princes might rent..."

Tara cut her a look.

Jerri covered the phone with her hand. "It's a front, Tara. It has to look like something a Darting would rent."

Tara nodded.

"I need it to be far enough out of LA to miss most of the traffic if you're coming to my house."

"Thank you God," Tara said, and started to put her clothes back on which was a very nice show.

"On the beach would be great especially if the beach is private or semi-private, and I need it by tonight."

She knew Jerri was watching her, so Tara put her pants on nice and slow.

"Do you have something or not, Raymond?... How expensive?... That's not a problem. Give me the address and we'll meet you there in thirty minutes with the deposit.... No

I'm not kidding... Well I trust you, Raymond. Is there some reason I shouldn't?"

Jerri hung up, grabbed a phone book, and flipped through it.

"What are you doing now?"

"Just keep doing what you're doing." Jerri dialed another number. "Yeah... My name is Jerri Blue. My card number ends in 5726 I need a bed... What size?" she asked Tara.

"A king it will give us more room to play on."

"A king... I don't know is that the biggest one?... Then give us one of those... Do you care what style?" she asked Tara.

"A light wood would be nice. I like every single thing in this house so I think it's fair to say we have the same taste so get something you would like," Tara said, pulling on her blouse.

"Something rustic in a knotted pine... I don't know, a mattress is a mattress..." Jerri looked at her. "Do you care what kind of mattress?"

"Not really."

"Give us something mid-priced, and we'll need a couple of pillows and a set of sheets... Do you care what color, Tara?"

"No." The truth was she didn't care about anything but the fact that Jerri obviously wanted her as much as she wanted Jerri.

"It's got appliances but it's not furnished. Do we need anything else?"

"Nothing I can think of. I don't even know if we need the bed after all you apparently prefer to do it on the floor."

"Deliver them to..." And then Jerri was giving them what was really Tara's new address, but as far as Tara was concerned she was already home.

It was a beautiful house on a fantastic stretch of coast and the bed arrived before the realtor had even finished showing them the whole house. Raymond was a very nice energetic, obviously gay man, and when the truck showed up to deliver the bed he had looked right at Jerri and said, "What the hell is the hurry, Jerri?"

Jerri laughed and handed Tara the rental agreement to sign even as she wrote him a check. Tara signed the document and handed it to Jerri. Jerri handed the check and the paperwork to Raymond. When he saw the name on the document he looked at Tara with sudden recognition and shock.

Jerri grinned. "If anyone asks Tara rented this house alone. You got me, Raymond?"

He looked right at Tara then back at Jerri then back at Tara.

Tara smiled and shrugged.

"Jerri, are you and she..."

"Yes, so please go have the people deliver the bed to the master bedroom. The fewer people who see us together the better," Jerri said.

Raymond nodded and walked away muttering something to the effect of knowing something so juicy he couldn't tell anyone about and the ninth level of gay hell.

Tara had walked over to the huge bank of windows that allowed her to see a gorgeous sunset over the ocean.

Jerri walked up behind her and wrapped her arms around her. "I like the house," Jerri said. "It has good energy."

"Which is good because if there was a dark, hate-filled ghost residing here, or the ceiling had fallen in, you would have rented it anyway."

"I wouldn't, but then I would have had to deal with Raymond and the freight deliverers."

"It's beautiful but I don't want to live here."

"We won't, but things are going to be crazy till we figure everything out. This house is going to let us be together more than we would otherwise be able to which makes it wonderful."

"I've got some stuff at mother's, enough to make it look like I'm living here. For one thing the closet is almost big enough to hold all my clothes unlike that tiny thing at your house." Because of course Jerri had already emptied one side of the closet in her room for Tara to use, but it was a small closet.

"We might ought to just rent this house indefinitely so that you can have a place for your clothes and accessories."

At their back they could hear the men bringing the bed in and assembling it. Tara had no desire to run and look at it; she just wanted to stand there watching the sunset wrapped in Jerri's arms. Jerri started to go, no doubt to help them. Tara grabbed her hands and held them.

"No, let them do it, Jerri. Stay with me; you don't always have to be working."

"Okay, baby." Jerri rested her chin on Tara's shoulder. "Is

something wrong?"

She chuckled. "Nothing has to be wrong for me to want all your attention."

They stayed there just long enough to break in the new bed and then they went back to the homestead.

Chapter 10

Janice watched as Tara drove up the driveway in Todd's car. The camera crew had figured out two days earlier that Tara wasn't in her room. The cable network had insisted Janice tell them where Tara was, so Janice had just been glad she really didn't know. The tide of public opinion wanted Tara to rush to Fred's bedside. Janice felt like she had forgotten how to do damage control or maybe she just no longer cared. Really what was the point when the worse they acted the higher their ratings were?

She met Tara, camera crew in tow, in the garage as Tara stepped out of Todd's car. Tara looked well rested, her skin had a healthy glow to it, and her eyes were bright. In short she looked like she had been at a spa for four days. There was even a spring in her step. She embraced Janice and kissed her cheek; Janice hugged her back. How was Janice going to encourage her daughter to look and act distraught when Tara obviously wasn't at all? Wherever she went and whatever she was doing when she was there was making Tara happy in a way that Tara had never been happy before. When had the happiness of her children taken a back seat to public image?

"Do you have a boyfriend?" she asked in a whisper.

Tara boomed out laughing. "No, Mother. I do NOT have a boyfriend."

"Are you even going to ask about Fred?" Tara had been mostly incommunicado for days and the few moments she had talked to Janice Tara had never once asked about Fred. Of course she could have gotten any information she wanted from the TV.

Tara looked at her and said with a grin on her face that Janice hoped the "director" would see fit to edit out later, "Is he dead yet?"

"Jesus Christ, Tara," Janice said, and followed her long-legged daughter towards the house. "I know he cheated, I know he did drugs…"

"Did you know he forced me to have sex with him one night when I didn't want to?"

"No." The first thing Janice felt was shocked, and then a little sick. This was Tara. Unlike Irva and Lori—who never seemed to have a private thought—Tara usually played her cards close to her chest. She didn't just blurt out things like this. Janice felt guilty and sad about what Tara had been through. She now knew exactly why Tara didn't care what happened to Fred. Some men thought just because you were married to them they could have whatever they wanted whenever they wanted it. Her first husband had been like that. It was why she had divorced him, and she should have warned her daughters about men like that but she hadn't because of her own embarrassment. Gary had never been like that but he hadn't been much easier to live with.

"I'm so sorry, Tara."

"He's a creep. I don't care what happens to him," Tara said. Then she turned right around and started for the gate where the paparazzi were two and three thick—no doubt because some rat in her employ had told them Tara was coming home this morning.

Janice found herself running after Tara. "Tara, for the love of God."

"You know what I've learned after ten years of this shit, Mother? Give the bastards what they want and they will leave you alone."

"Tara, don't say anything you're going to regret."

"I said 'I do' to a walking turd," Tara said, throwing her hands wide and continuing to stride down the driveway. "I'm never going to say anything I'm going to regret that badly again. I want this to go away."

Janice held her breath as Tara reached the gate. The cameras flashed with a blinding multitude of light.

"Can you answer some questions?" one of them yelled out.

"No, but I can tell you what you want to know. Yes, I know Fred is in a coma and most likely going to die or be a vegetable for the rest of his life. No, I do not feel guilty for his condition. No, I don't give a crap what happens to him. He treated me badly in ways that you know and in ways that are none of your business. I'm tired of people telling me what I should do and how I should feel. I divorced that man for a reason. It was a good one. What he has done to himself since is NOT my fault and it is NOT my problem. I feel sorry for his family; they are great people, but I felt sorry for them way before he did this."

Then she turned around smiled at Janice and started back towards the house.

Janice ran to catch up wondering if what Tara had just done was going to make things better or worse.

As if knowing what Janice was thinking Tara said without turning, "I don't really care, Mom. It's the truth. If they are going to vilify me in the press at least let them do it for the truth."

Her nephews had been happy to see her and Tara had missed them. Irva was working, Lori and Todd had gone for couple's therapy, and the maid had been trying to keep an eye on the boys which she wasn't really good at. And why didn't the boys have a nanny? Because too many celebrities' husbands were having affairs with their kid's nannies and Lori wasn't having any of that. When Tara had suggested she get an old, ugly nanny, Lori had said that would make her look insecure.

When Tara got to her room to start packing Tylor was on her hip and Channing was running behind her telling her everything he had done every second that she had been gone in a language far, far different from her own. Her manuscript and lap top were still in the big middle of her bed. She hadn't even thought about the book in days. She realized Jerri hadn't worked on her book at all, either. She grinned; there was no way Jerri was going to make her deadline, but Tara didn't feel at all guilty about that, either.

"Where go?" Channing asked as she put Tylor down went to her closet and got a suitcase.

"I was at the farm. Do you remember the farm?"

"Goats," he said.

"That's right."

"I go to farm?"

Tara thought about that for a second and grinned at him. "You know what, baby? Real soon."

Tylor started to put one of her manuscript pages in his mouth and she took it out of his grubby little paw. She realized the camera crew was in her room with them. She went over what she had just said sighing with relief because she hadn't said anything that would tell them where she had been. She wondered why her playing with the kids while she packed was a TV moment. She had become so used to them always being there over the years that she was going to have to be a lot more careful about what she said in front of them.

Her mother walked in. "What are you doing?"

"I rented a house on the beach. I'm going to pack a bunch of my stuff and take it over there." When she looked up at her mother Janice looked a little panicked. "What's wrong, Mom?"

"You... You didn't even take time to really think about it, Tara, and you didn't ask my opinion."

"We don't have to ask you about everything we do, Janice."

"We?" Janice asked.

Dammit in just a few days my vocabulary has changed. "There are three of us, you know."

"I'd at least liked to have seen it before you took on the expense... I don't know why you can't stay here with us till you get things sorted out."

"I have things sorted out, Mom. I know what I want. This is me doing what I want. You didn't have any problem with me moving out to go live with the turd in the huge ugly nouveau-house you picked out for us."

"I just don't think it's safe for a woman to be alone...."

"First off, I should be so lucky as to be actually alone." She looked with meaning at the film crew. "Second... What century do you live in where I will only be safe if I'm with a man or living with my mommy?"

"Well can I at least go with you now to see the house?"

She thought about it for a second. Jerri wasn't going to even try to come in till after ten. If her mother went with her most if not all of the camera crew would likely as not follow Janice back home. "Yeah, sure."

So her mom and the boys helped her pack till Lori and Todd came home fighting worse than ever. Then they took their boys—no doubt so that they could learn that the only way to converse with your partner was in a scream. Tara and her mother loaded everything that would fit into Tara's SUV and her mother took her car. Some of the camera men went with Janice, some followed in their own van, and... Tara was so tired of being on camera.

As Janice helped her carry in her suitcases, boxes, an end table and lamp, she looked at the huge bed that looked like it had obviously been slept in—which of course they hadn't slept in it yet—and asked Tara again, "Do you have a boyfriend?"

"No, Mother, I don't have a boyfriend."

"Swear to God, Tara?"

Tara laughed. "I swear to God, Mother, that I do not have a boyfriend."

"Well this is a nice house and the price is right. The view is outstanding but isn't it a little small?"

Tara smiled to herself. Jerri's only real bitch about the house was that it was so big, and her mother's only real bitch was that it was too small. "How much room do I need? It's just me; I don't even have a pet."

"That's what you need, Tara, a huge dog to protect you."

"No," Tara said, probably a little quicker than she should have. Her mother looked at her. "I don't want a dog, Mother. I don't want anything I have to clean up after or take care of. I just want to sit here in my really cool beach house and write." *Or you know be at the farm with Jerri and a whole list of animals which very specifically doesn't include a dog.*

As expected half the crew left when her mother did. The other half left when she sat at the bar in the kitchen with her manuscript pages spread all over just pecking away at her laptop being lousy TV fodder. She was all alone by eight and called to tell Jerri so.

"I could come home," Tara said.

"Tate is already here and I have two lectures tomorrow, one starting at ten AM, so it actually makes more sense for me to come down there. The university is already having kittens over me not staying at the hotel."

"Why should they care where you stay?"

"Because they have sold out their auditorium for both lectures. Having me in the hotel means they know exactly where I am. They can come get me and make sure I'll arrive on time. I imagine not being able to meet with me tonight and remind me where I'm supposed to be and what I'm supposed to be doing has someone's ass puckering up about now."

"Sold out. Does that mean I can't come?"

"No. I got you a seat in the back for both lectures since I didn't know which you'd want to attend. I explained that I was doing a favor for your mother. I'll go ahead and milk early and come on. See you in a little while. I love you."

"I love you, Jerri. I can't wait to see you and other things."

"Ah yes... the 'other things' I'm going to do to you."

When Tara woke up in the morning she realized that she could hear the waves of the ocean; that they in fact mostly canceled out the noise from the central heat and air unit. Tara had never even been aware of all the noise a modern house made until she had spent the night at Jerri's were there was real quiet—at least until the animals got up and started to make a racket. She looked over and saw Jerri was mostly dressed and she frowned knowing she wouldn't be getting any this morning. She rubbed at her eyes.

"Did you sleep?"

"Surprisingly well. Actually a lot better than I would have in a stinking hotel. What about you?"

"Like a rock though it's obvious we don't really need the huge bed since I find I want to sleep right against you."

"But it's fun to play on," Jerri said with a gleam in her eye.

Tara walked over and wrapped herself around Jerri making it more or less impossible for her to get dressed. "Should I go to the first lecture or the second?"

"Well I have more energy for the first one but usually do a better job with the second one."

"So." Tara smiled and kissed her quickly on the lips. "Just like sex."

"What's that supposed to mean?" Jerri asked, pushing Tara off of her so that she could finish dressing.

"Just what I said." Her smart phone rang and she frowned. "And see, in this reality I have that electronic umbilical cord which holds me to a virtual world." She walked over picked it up and answered. Seeing it was Lori she said a curt, "What?"

"Half the crew just took off. I think they are heading for your place, so...."

"Thanks, Lori. I owe you one." She hung up.

"The camera crew is on their way," Tara said in a panic.

Jerri nodded and finished dressing. She was wearing a black suit coat with skinny jeans and a red cotton shirt and Tara gasped.

"What?" Jerri asked.

"God, Jerri you look really good."

"And normally?"

"You look really good but sort of like an unmade bed."

"In other words I clean up nice."

Tara nodded silently because Jerri needed to go, but all she really wanted to do was strip her clothes off her.

"So which one are you going to? You know so that I don't look up, see you and lose my cool."

"I doubt seriously that you would lose your cool." Tara thought about it a minute then smiled and said, "While I appreciate the first one I really prefer the second one."

She kissed Jerri goodbye and Jerri left mere seconds before the camera crew got there. They of course reminded her that they were going to need a key to her house which pissed her off so she was a total bitch to them till she got dressed and left so they thought everything was normal.

"Why?" Tara asked looking at her Mother.

"Because Irva wants to go to the lecture."

"Why?" Tara said again this time more slowly.

"She just does," Janice said.

"Irva wants to go to a lecture on writing the hero's journey for a new generation. Does she even know what the hero's journey refers to?"

"I doubt it. Maybe that's why she wants to go, to learn something. Or maybe she just wants to spend some time with her big sister."

"Yes because we've always been so close. Maybe she wants to go because you want her to spy on me." Her mother put on her very best hurt look and Tara mumbled, "Yeah, that's what I thought."

"What crappy seats you got us," Irva said.

"I didn't get you a seat, dumbass I got me one. I purposely sat in the back so the stupid camera crew wouldn't distract from the lecture. Now I'm the one sitting on a God-damned metal folding chair because you wouldn't shut the fuck up about it so now... Shut the fuck up."

Tara had never been more aware of people looking at them—or the camera crew for that matter. At least most of these people were just looking not running up mobbing them asking for autographs. They were mostly college students here for the lecture. That alone made them more intelligent than ninety-nine percent of the *Daring with the Dartings'* audience.

The lights went down on them and came up on the stage. The university president walked to the middle of the stage, introduced himself, thanked them all for attending, then said simply, "Please welcome to the UCLA stage the author of *Burning Rain, Just Fire* and *More Rain* just to name a few, Ms. Jerri Blue.

Jerri walked out on the stage and Tara could almost feel the quiet excitement that ran through the crowd. Jerri walked right up to the mike, immediately saw Tara and locked eyes with her, though Tara had no idea how she did such things. She smiled just for Tara then she started talking.

"Thank you for having me. In his definitive work on mythology, Joseph Campbell wrote at length about the hero's journey. The hero's journey is a story that has been told over and over again since people first started to scratch letters onto rocks."

"Isn't that Aunt Rhonda's old girlfriend?" Irva asked. Tara gave her a seething look wondering why Irva remembered that when Tara hadn't. "Alright geez," Irva fell silent again.

"...The hero's journey is always the same formula. First the hero gets the call, then he runs from the call, then something happens that forces him to heed the call, he finds people to help him, he goes through a series of trials and finally he fights the big fight and is victorious. The hero's journey is always our favorite tale. It's important because it makes us fight our own demons and slay our own dragons. It's a hopeful tale about what happens when you don't run away, when you don't give up. It's a story about the reward of fighting for what's right.

"But until very recently only men were the protagonists of the hero's journey. Campbell went so far as to say that women didn't need to go on the journey because they already created life. That was their heroic quest—to have babies.

"Here's a fact. Not all women will have babies, not all women *want* them, and not all women will find fulfillment in raising children, cooking and cleaning for their spouse. They may love them, nurture them, be all about them, and still have another call."

Tara noticed that beside her Irva had not only gotten very quiet but she was actually listening. *Ah the magical charisma of Jerri Blue. Even the stupid can't help but listen to her.*

"Women are taught from an early age to put their call away. In the hero's journey remember that he gets the call and at first he runs from it? At that time in any story do we all root for him? No. When God tells Moses to go to Pharaoh and he runs to hide in the desert, do we identify him as a hero? When Luke Skywalker is called to fight the Empire and runs back to the farm, do we find his actions heroic? No. It is only when the protagonist stops running and dives into the quest that we see him as the hero. Only when he starts to fight for his destiny that we start to root for him.

"But women are taught to always put their calling second— even third—if they are encouraged to have one at all. There were no stories where a woman went on the hero's journey. Women are encouraged to douse the light of their purpose, to help their husband to go on his journey, and to help their children to go on theirs.

"I am a feminist, so some may not believe it, but I understand and appreciate that some women will happily find their hero's journey in the raising of their children and in helping their mate. There is nothing wrong with that. There is also nothing at all wrong with a woman wanting more from her life and more for herself.

"The truth is that there have always been women who went on a hero's journey; they just never wrote stories about them. Until the last thirty-some-odd years, a woman was never the protagonist in a hero's journey story, and they are still like rare, book-bound gems.

"When you are young and growing up, reading the hero's journey can help you find your way. It has been told over and over again in many different ways in every language in every age because at its essence is the lesson we all need to understand to have a fuller, richer life. For our physical, emotional, and spiritual health we all have to follow our calling. It's never easy, but at the end we find our authentic self.

"For most of history this story has been told and over half the population never had a starring role. Women were the lovers, wives, mothers of the heroes—or worse yet—the victims the hero had to risk life and limb to save as they sat on their hands and did nothing more heroic than cry. In the hero's journey women had never been more than secondary characters. The hero's journey didn't belong to women, and it sure as hell didn't belong to women like me.

"Where is a gay woman to find her worth in the hero's journey of old? She is not even part of the supporting cast. Not even the villain or the victim."

Beside her Irva said smuggly, "So she *is* Rhonda's ex."

Tara wanted to smack her, but was mostly just glad that she didn't keep talking.

"I had been writing all my life and unwittingly writing the hero's journey with women protagonists—even gay and transgendered protagonists—since I was eleven years old. It was how I escaped from a world I never felt part of. But when I was nineteen I was physically and sexually assaulted. Writing had always been my escape, and there was no part of me that wanted to be a woman..."

And that is why she told me that she wanted to be the one to tell me because every time she has a live audience she tells them... Because it's how she takes her power back, by telling her story so that it might help someone going through the same thing. It's how she makes her pain have meaning, becomes a survivor instead of a victim.

"...in the ten months after my attack I wrote the first draft of what would become my first published novel, *Burning Rain,* which is a hero's journey tale with a male protagonist. Every time someone tells me they love that book..." She looked right at Tara then. "...I just cringe because I know I took the path always traveled. I in fact did *not* take MY hero's journey. I got the calling and I ran from it. It wasn't till my next book, *Just Rain,* that I wrote my hero's journey with a lesbian protagonist.

"I have been accused of always writing the hero's journey, and I admit it, I do. But within that formula are a billion very different stories. My hope is to write that important story with a protagonist that lets everyone at least once be the hero of their own story. That I open that door for someone who never before read a book where someone *just like them* was the hero."

"She's fucking brilliant," Tara muttered.

"Shsush," Irva hissed, and Tara had to stifle a giggle.

Jerri kept talking for about thirty more minutes, and then she had them turn the house lights up and she took questions from the audience.

Irva's hand shot up and Tara sighed and whispered, "Please for the love of God don't ask if she used to screw Rhonda Heart."

"I'm not stupid, Tara," Irva said.

Jerri called on a guy from the middle of the audience who stood up and asked, "Where do you get your ideas?"

From the look on Jerri's face as she looked at her, Tara

knew this was a question Jerri was asked all the time.

"I don't get ideas. Ideas get me and then I have to write the book or it's all I think about."

She then took a question from an older woman on the front row who stood up and asked. "How do you know when you have a calling?"

"Sadly it's not as easy as a phone ringing and all you have to do is pick it up. Usually a calling comes in the form of a loss, a failure, an all-time low. A moment when you can keep doing what you have always done or listen to the voice of your spirit as it whispers to your heart, follow your curiosity, your passion, get in touch with your soul. Now I know it may sound like it's easy for me to say because I did that and I wound up rich, but I didn't start rich and believe me I don't live a rich lifestyle. Stuff, having stuff... At the end of the day it will never make you happy or even content. In fact I'm just going to go out on a limb and say that having a bunch of material sh:t will do nothing but cause you stress if you aren't on the road to your purpose. I only enjoy fame because I get to try it on, wear it for the day, then go home hang it up and do what I really want to do. What we have to do is change what we see as success. You already know what your calling is. The problem is that the journey is unsure and not everyone is going to wind up with shiny pots of gold. But if you never go on your journey no matter what you acquire it will never be enough."

Jerri then pointed at Irva. Irva stood up and Tara cringed, more than a little afraid of what her stupid sister was going to ask.

"When you say women have got to start listening to their calling and following their heart instead of believing all the noise, what exactly do you mean?"

Tara was shocked. That was actually an intelligent question.

"I don't believe there is a person alive of any sex that doesn't know exactly what they should be doing. But they allow what society, their spouses, their parents, their peers tell them keep them from following their true calling. Women have been taught almost from birth that if you don't fit into this particular pattern there is something inherently wrong with you. Women are worse about blowing other women's dreams apart than men are. For instance, a woman who works in the corporate world will feel compelled to make women who have a family feel like they are wasting their time. A woman who is a stay-at-home mom might try to make a female corporate executive feel like *she* is wasting *her* time. Both do so in an effort to make themselves feel better—not about the path they're on, but about the path they didn't take. I think it's harder for women to even hear their calling because there is so much noise telling them it's selfish and self-centered to follow their bliss."

Irva nodded, obviously happy with the answer and sat down. She turned to Tara and whispered, "That does it. I'm kicking that shithead to the curb."

Tara couldn't say she wasn't happy about this. For one thing it meant she never had to meet the creep but she still had to ask.

"Why?"

"Douche bag thinks he's Jesus. Everything always has to be what he wants when he wants and... What about *my* hero's journey? I'll never get to do what I want if I'm with him... Besides. he has a tiny penis."

"Wow! I wouldn't have thought that of God," Tara whispered.

"I know right," Irva said, then shushed Tara again to listen to Jerri.

Jerri continued to answer questions for another thirty minutes and then she moved into a hall where she had a scheduled signing.

"Give me a second," Tara said to her sister and the crew. She walked over to try to go behind the table but security stopped her.

"Let her through, for God's sake," Jerri ordered impatiently. She held up her hand to the person who had just laid his book down and said, "Give me a second."

Tara knelt beside Jerri and Jerri smiled at her. "I thought you were coming to the afternoon session?"

"I was but..." She nodded her head towards her sister. "...Irva had to tag along, and she has something 'important' to do later. Pretty sure Mother has her spying on me. You were amazing."

"Thanks, but as you know I do better with the second one." Jerri smiled.

Tara moved up till she was whispering in her ear, "I love you."

Jerri then whispered in her ear, "I love you, too. I'll see you later."

Tara wanted to kiss her but she couldn't, and she was immediately frustrated as she got up and moved back to where her sister and the film crew were waiting. Irva gave her an odd look. Because she was pissed off about the situation anyway she looked right at her and said, "She's a friend, alright?"

"I didn't say shit." Irva actually laughed at her, and for some reason this calmed Tara right down. "The woman is brilliant. She's your favorite author and you want to be a writer. It's alright if you have a little hero worship going on. Hell, I was impressed, and I've been sleeping with god."

Tara thought they were going to be able to get away clean, but they didn't. As soon as they walked outside they were hit by a wave of fans wanting autographs. She tried to do it with a smile on her face, but she really wasn't feeling it. She was glad when they made it to their car and could get away.

"So…" Irva started from the seat next to her as Tara drove. There were two camera men in the back of the car and a dash camera. "Do you have a boyfriend?"

"Key-rist, Irva I knew mother had you spying on me."

"You're so suspicious. I just wondered."

"I do not have a boyfriend!" she said looking right at the dash cam. "Are you really going to break up with god?"

"Yep. I'm done with jumping through Frappy's hoops."

That wasn't too surprising. Irva changed boyfriends the way most women changed shoes.

"So if you don't have a boyfriend where have you been hiding out?"

"I rented a house on the beach. I've been working on my book."

"Your book and your computer were lying on your bed at mother's house last time I saw them."

Well she had her there but, "I have another computer and my manuscript is stored in the cloud."

"And you don't have a boyfriend?"

"No, I don't have a boyfriend!"

Judy and Cyndy sat towards the middle with some other transgendered woman that Jerri didn't recognize. Jerri looked at Judy before she stared her lecture and grinned.

As always she did a lot better job with her second lecture

than she did the first and she wished Tara could have been there for the second one so that she could have seen Jerri at her most magnificent. When she had signed so many books her hand was sore she jumped in her pickup and headed for the restaurant where she was to meet Judy and Cyndy and their friend. She had that little moment of intense pleasure that she always had when she went to a five-star restaurant and saw the look on the valet's face as he got in her beat-up old truck to park it. She grinned then she went inside. She was immediately shown right to their table. She liked this, too. She liked to live in the deep woods on her homestead then every once in a while come out and bask in the glory of being Jerri Blue. She hugged Judy and Cyndy, and then Judy was introducing Jerri to her new friend.

"Jerri Blue, I'd like you to meet Georgia Darting."

Jerri took in a deep breath, looked from the hand she was already shaking into the woman's face and said, "Son of a bitch!"

Chapter 11

Jerri sat down hard and looked from her best friend to "Georgia" and cringed again. The thing was with all the work he'd obviously already had done, Georgia looked like an ugly version of Tara.

"This is your secret weapon, Judy? *This* is the thing that's going to help the transgendered community? Have you gone completely insane?"

"Jerri, I know we've never really gotten along, but think of all the good I could do for the transgendered community," Georgia said with Gary's voice.

"Fuck me!" Jerri said, as her brain down loaded the far-reaching ramifications of Gary Darting having had sexual reassignment surgery. She glared at Judy. "You've got to be kidding me, Judy. You already know why Gary and I have never gotten along..."

"Georgia," Judy corrected.

"Bullshit, Judy. I call bullshit!"

"Excuse us a minute," Judy said. She got up took Jerri by the arm and started to propel her towards the ladies' room. Once inside the powder room area she stopped and said, "Now Jerri I know this is complicated..."

"Complicated!" Jerri said in a harsh whisper. "That's not just any ultra-conservative, ex-football-hero reality TV star. That's my girlfriend's fucking father, and... Shit! Tara said he was super bitchy the last six months before he left, so he was already on hormones, which means Janice had to know."

"Janice knows, but Georgia hasn't gotten around to telling her kids."

"I sort of know that, Judy." She took hold of Judy's shoulders and shook her. "What the hell were you thinking Judy?"

"That if someone as public and seemingly masculine as Gary Darting comes out, it's going to be huge for our community, especially my part of the community."

"That douche bag can't be a voice for our community. Judy, he can't be..."

"*She* can."

"Do you remember me telling you about the last argument he and I got into? He's a fucking right-wing, conservative Republican. That guy…"

"Woman."

"He's not a woman yet, I don't care what surgeries he's had and you know that. There is a transformation period. You don't just cut off someone's dick, turn it inside out or give him boobs, hormones and *poof!* he's a girl. He's in the big pink cloud where nothing matters but him."

"*Her*. I can't believe that you of all people Jerri won't use the right pronouns, that you are denying Georgia her womanhood. Aren't you the one who said all the worst homophobes always turn out to be gay?"

"No that was Dana Sinclair."

"Oh, so it was, but you have to admit there is truth in the statement."

"Did he have the whole thing done or just the top?"

"Now, Jerri, you know that's a very private matter…"

"She's my girlfriend's fucking father, Judy…"

"Yes, he's made a full surgical transformation."

"Fucking beautiful! Have you talked politics with HER yet?"

"No, but I know how she used to feel…"

"Used to my ass, Judy. Gary Darting with tits in a dress can't be a spokesperson for our community. And notice he does not call it *his* community. He's not brave. Brave is you stepping into who you are in your thirties when you had so little money you were looking at having to do it in stages…"

"But I didn't have to because you gave me the money to do it right. For that and a billion other things I love you."

A woman walked out of the stall room and looked at them. Jerri had to fight the urge to yell, "What the hell are you looking at!" Because the truth was anyone was going to look at that point.

"Having Georgia on board could be huge for the trans community, Jerri. I love you with all my heart, but I think you forget that it's still harder for transgendered people than it is for gays. Georgia is willing to let herself be filmed going through this process."

"Oh, crap! Reality TV jackpot! Judy, do you have any idea what this is going to do to me personally?"

"Well it wouldn't have been a problem if you weren't

shagging one of Georgia's daughters," Judy said with a smile.

"Not as big a one, but it still would have been a problem for me because his politics are going to be a huge issue. He votes... Hell, he has *campaigned* for people who have done nothing but try to make it impossible for us to have any rights. But you're right, all I can really worry about right now is how this is going to affect Tara. Tara went and told you who she was the minute Cyndy said she knew because she didn't want Cyndy to know something she couldn't tell you. Now what? I either break what I think is a sacred rule and tell Tara about her dad or I just keep it from her."

Judy put her hands on Jerri's shoulder and looked into her eyes. "We need this, Jerri. We need someone this public to speak for our community, but you're right. She doesn't really get it. I need you to order some food... When's the last time you ate?"

"I had a bunch of crap in the greenroom and they brought me lunch, so I'm not just being difficult because I'm hungry. I'm being difficult because this is the worst position you have ever put me in, which makes it monumental because you are always and forever sticking me right in the middle of some huge crapfest."

"Because you're Jerri Blue, and no one is as brilliant as you are. You're right about her, though. Unless we handle this right she will do our cause more harm than good I realize that. But Jerri, it's a calling."

"Dammit."

"I need you to be centered, enthralling, spiritual, Jerri Blue, not all angry gonna-kick-someone's-ass Jerri Blue."

They ordered in near silence and as the waiter walked away Georgia said, "I know this is a shock, Jerri, and I know you and I have had our differences in the past..."

"Differences, GARY? You campaigned for a man who wanted to pass an amendment to the constitution to...' She made air quotes. She knew it was wrong, but she did it anyway. "...*Protect marriage.* But if that wasn't bad enough, I'd bet money you campaigned for Trump."

"My name is Georgia," she said with meaning.

"Jerri, please refrain from using male pronouns and Georgia's pre-surgery name when speaking to her." Judy glared at her.

Jerri ran her hand down her face then kept her hand on her face looking at "Gerogia" through a couple of her fingers.

"Alright, let me try for a minute to wrap my head around it."

Jerri took a deep breath and let it out. Even if she weren't in a relationship with Tara this would have been hard for her because she had never liked Gary. He was, in fact, exactly the kind of person she had always hated most. Cocky, self-aggrandizing, and... *Every bit of it a front because he was always hiding his desire to be a woman. And I have been with people before and after their transformation; they change. It takes time, but they do.* "Do you realize that you can't be a transgendered woman and a right-winged Republican?"

"Why should being a woman change my political views?" Georgia asked, with no understanding.

"Because you aren't a ciswoman; you are a transgendered woman. The world as a whole will not embrace you as a woman. That's the world you have entered, and I'm pretty sure Judy has already explained this to you because she is a damn good therapist. Just like I'm supposed to address you as Georgia and use the right pronouns when I speak to you, *you* have to stop addressing the LGBT community as *them*. *You* have to stop saying *the transgendered community, the LGBT community*, and start saying *us, we and ours*. Like it or not, sister, you are now in the same boat as I am. As long as you are voting the way you have always voted, what you are saying is that you expect to be exempt from the kind of crap all of us have gone through."

"I don't believe the Republicans are against the LGBT community."

"*Our* community," Jerri reminded.

"Bullshit, Georgia," Judy said. "Did you or did you not have an argument with Jerri about gays' right to marry?"

"I... Well I don't see why gays need special rights. I mean marriage is a religious thing between men and women. I have no trouble with them being together, but I don't understand why they have to call it a marriage."

"Wow, did you just step in it," Cyndy mumbled.

Jerri had already had this argument with Georgia when Georgia was a man. Jerri looked at Judy and rolled her eyes. The waiter brought her salad and Jerri decided to eat it and let Judy handle her pet tranny's idiocy.

"So you enjoy being the same but different?" Judy said. Now Judy was hot. After all she was sitting at the table with her wife who she couldn't have married before the laws changed, because of course she was now legally a woman.

"What?" Georgia asked, and moved to let the waiter set her soup in front of her.

"You have no problem with being the same but being treated as different?"

"I'm not sure what you mean."

"We all want the same rights. No one is asking for special rights. We just want the same rights. You don't get it because money is never an issue for you, but without the right to marry we had to jump through hoops to do even the simplest things—like being able to sign off on each other's medical care. We couldn't even start to jump through those hoops without buckets of money." Judy said. "The same but different has never worked for us."

"It's never worked for anyone," Jerri said.

"I guess I didn't know."

"You can't judge us and find us wanting anymore," Jerri said, pushing her salad away. "You changed your body and your face to match what you saw in your head. Now like it or not you are part of OUR community. You're about to find out how hateful the world can be when you're different. Money and fame will help you only so far, then you're going to have to wade through it with the rest of us. And you are going to do it on camera the way you have done everything else for the last ten years. What about Janice? Better than that, what about your kids? You haven't even told your kids yet."

"I was going to get them all together at my new house this weekend..."

"Are you nuts!" Jerri yelled, then lowered her voice when Judy looked at her. "You can't just invite them over and walk out like this. This is possibly the one time that you need to do something this monumental over the phone. You need to explain to them exactly what you've done and why you did it then let them come to you in their own time. Don't you understand? Without asking them you changed who you are and in doing so you killed the father they have always known."

It was obvious by the look on her face that she hadn't taken anyone else's feelings into consideration.

"You, who have always been a huge homophobe, gave your

children two mothers—one of the things you have always said was evil—and now you want to do what? Have a Sunday dinner and invite them all to meet New Mommy? You need to tell them on the phone preferably without them being filmed which I guess is probably impossible."

Jerri turned to look at Judy. "You need to convince *Georgia* that she needs to call her kids tonight, and sooner is better than later. Before you run around with her in front of cameras you need to think good and hard about whether having a super right-winged transsexual woman on your team is really going to help your cause. And me..." she stood up. "...I have to leave before I become angry, ass-kicking Jerri."

As Judy watched her friend walk away Georgia said, "Well that went better than I thought it would."

Judy got up and went after Jerri. Jerri looked over at her as she stood waiting for her truck. Judy could see her friend was mad at her.

"Dammit, Judy, you put me in a terrible position," Jerri said, not looking at her.

"In my defense until a few days ago I didn't know you were in love with Georgia's daughter, and I can't do this without your help. You helped me through what she's going through now, and I'm trying to help her..."

"...on camera for the whole world to see. I have no idea how this is going to affect Tara. No idea whether I need to tell her or let Georgia do it herself. Gary was always such a chicken shit. He has been holding out waiting for Janice to do his dirty work, but just like I wouldn't be able to think of how to tell Tara, she has no idea how to tell her daughters that their daddy is now a woman."

"Will you help me or not, Jerri?"

"Help you what, Judy? Do what exactly?"

"Do what you did tonight..."

"Get mad and throw a fit?"

Judy laughed. "You didn't really. Everything you said was something she needed to hear. I've put together a group of mostly trans women to lead Georgia through this process, but you have a presence that none of us have. I think you alone have the voice to put her in her place when she needs to be put there."

"Judy, for the tenth time, she's my girlfriend's father. Wow, who would have ever thought that sentence would leave my lips? I have no idea what this is going to do to Tara."

"All the more reason you should want this to go as smocthly as possible."

"What I want is for it to be this afternoon before I knew this. I'm so mad at you right now, Judy... I didn't ask to be put in the big middle of the circus."

The valet brought her truck. As he got out and handed Jerri her keys, Jerri looked at Judy and said, "Help you? I don't know if I'm even talking to you. If you can't get that turd to call Tara tonight and tell her what she's done I may never talk to you again." Jerri walked around and got in her truck.

"Ah come on Jerri, come on." But Jerri roared out of the parking lot. "Georgia's right. That did go better than I thought it would." She walked back into the restaurant where their entrées had just been served. She decided she liked the steak Jerri had ordered better than the pasta she'd ordered, so she just sat in the seat Jerri had vacated.

"Is Jerri alright?" Cyndy asked carefully.

"She will be. She's mad as hell." Judy looked at Georgia. "But she's right. You need to tell your daughters, and it had better be tonight."

"What do I say to them?" Georgia asked, near tears.

"You tell them the truth. I will sit right with you and help you through it."

Jerri immediately called Tara.

"Listen to me very carefully. Am I on speaker phone?"

"Of course not, are you alright?" She would never put Jerri on speaker phone because she was the one who had told Jerri that she was pretty sure any place they lived was bugged.

"I'm fine, just extremely pissed off." Jerri took a deep breath and let it out. "Where are you?"

"At the beach house, why?"

"Is the camera crew there?"

"No. I bored them to tears and they left about two hours ago."

"Get the hell out of there. Get your things and get to our place as quick as you can."

"Alright, but why what happened?"

"It's not what happened. It's what's about to happen. I

need you to be with me away from all the crap."

"I'm halfway to the door. I love you; drive carefully."

"I love you, too, and you drive carefully. There is no reason to freak out, Tara. Everything is alright. I just really don't want you in the middle of the media shit storm that is about to erupt."

"Did someone find out about us?" Tara asked.

Jerri found her sense of humor where it usually was—in a box in the back of her brain behind a jar of irony. She laughed. "Oh sugar, that would be nothing compared to this."

When she got off the phone with Tara she immediately called Pat. "Pat?"

"Yeah."

"Pat this is Jerri Blue."

"Jerri... I haven't heard from you in ages. What's up?"

"I need you to call Janice Darting and tell her that Georgia is about to have a coming-out party."

Pat laughed. "What the hell, Jerri?"

"I'm serious as a heart attack, Pat. Write it down—Georgia's about to have a coming-out party. You call Janice and tell her, and do *not* tell her I had you call."

"Seriously, Jerri, what's going on?" he asked.

"You know what Pat, you'll know *exactly* what it's all about shortly, and you will have been part of it. I swear to you it is the most magnificent scandal of our generation."

They were having yet another barely-edible meal. Irva had been telling them all about the lecture she and Tara had attended, how it made her decided to break up with Frappy— which she had apparently already done by text of all things. Lori and Todd were Twitter fighting again, and the kids were running around like wild animals. All of that was normal. What she didn't like at all was that ten minutes ago the film crew had all been whispering and milling around and then part of them left. She imagined they were on their way to Tara's house. She wondered if they knew more about what was going on with Tara than she did.

Her phone rang and she answered it. "Hello, Pat. What's up?"

"An anonymous caller told me to call you and tell you that Georgia is about to have a coming-out party."

"Well crap."

Janice knew now why the crew was so jumpy. Gary's producer had called hers. It was about to be the big reveal. No one had bothered to tell her—no doubt so they could catch her and the girls' reactions on camera. She looked over at Irva who was still talking and Lori who was still Twitter fighting with Todd. She wondered again about signing those papers making this an even bigger public spectacle than it would have been, about being part of the wheel that put this into motion.

"Thanks a million, Pat. I owe you one."

She hung up and called Tara. "Tara where are you?"

"On the road, Mom."

"Look, wherever you've been going, go there. A crew is on their way to your new house right now."

"What the hell is going on, Mom?"

"Leave your phone on; I'm sure you'll find out very soon. I love you, Baby."

"I love you, too, Mom."

Janice hung up and turned to look at Irva and Lori in turn. How she was feeling must have shown on her face because neither of them spoke or Twittered. They just looked at her. Was there anything she could do to prepare them? It wasn't her place to tell them and she didn't want to. The whole thing was ripe and it stank.

"Your father is going to call with some news in a while. Whatever he says I want you to remember it doesn't reflect on any of you at all."

Tara walked into the house. Jerri was obviously in the kitchen cooking which Tara was glad about because she was starving. When Jerri heard her she nearly ran from the kitchen, ran over, hugged her, then she fished into Tara's pocket got her phone and made damn sure the tracking device was off—which Tara had already done. Jerri looked jumpy as hell. Tara wondered if maybe she was having an episode but then she remembered the strange call from her mother.

Jerri walked back in the kitchen to check on what she was cooking and Tara followed.

"Can you tell me what's going on?"

"No, I can't. That's why I'm so pissed off at Judy. She put me between a rock and a hard place. Now we have to wait and see if your phone is going to ring and an asshole is going to tell you, or if it doesn't ring and I wind up having to break what for me is like a sacred oath."

"My mother called and ordered me to go into hiding."

"Good for Janice," Jerri said, but didn't elaborate. "I'm hungry; are you hungry?"

"Yes. What can I do to help?"

"Toast us up a couple of pieces of bread. I just heated up the rest of that minestrone we had on Wednesday."

"So we aren't going to talk about whatever it is?"

"No, we're going to not even think about it or worry about it. We're going to eat our dinner."

Tara knew—she could tell by what little her mother said and the way Jerri was acting that whatever this was, it was huge. But all she could think about was that she didn't really care because it meant she had permission to come home which is where she wanted to be anyway.

"Did Fred die?" Tara asked.

"Am I doing this?" Jerri did a little dance and Tara laughed. "Well I am now, but I wasn't. If I'm not doing a dance like that then you know Fred isn't dead yet."

"You're awful." Tara had sliced the bread and it wasn't till she went to put it in the toaster that she realized she had sliced them too thick. She made them fit anyway and then pulled them out with a fork when they were done.

They sat down to eat and Jerri kept looking at her covertly as if trying to see if she was alright.

"Jerri, I'm fine. After all I don't even know what it is yet. I'm just so glad to be home with you that it's going to have to be something God awful to break my happy. Until all the 'run for the hills' stuff I was having a great day. I woke up to the sound of the ocean, looked over and you were dressing. I got to see you in clothes that weren't either torn or stained or three sizes too big. Most of the paparazzi were gone before Irva and I left for your lecture. I got to hear and see you speak and now know you are every bit as amazing as I think you are. Irva and I actually had a good day together. Your lecture made her break up with the dumbass rapper she's been dating, and she also said he had a tiny penis."

"Humph. You'd expect more from god."

"That's exactly what I said. As soon as I dropped Irva off at Mother's I went back to the beach house took a walk on the beach—next time I want to do it with you—then I went back and wrote. Absolutely the only thing that sucked all day was the cameras, and now I'm here with you and no cameras."

After they finished eating and cleaning up the kitchen, Jerri poured them a couple of glasses of wine and they went to the living room. She set the wine on the coffee table

Jerri started to turn the TV on then thought better of it. Who knew when the news was going to break, and if it didn't then she was going to have to tell Tara about her father—which just sucked. Jerri sat on her recliner and patted her lap till Tara came over and sat all over her. She laid her head on Jerri's shoulder, and Jerri put her arms around her.

"You know we're going to break this chair if we keep doing this," Tara said. She was probably right. The chair made a horrible creaking sound every time they did it.

"Then we'll buy another one. It's no good to us if it won't do what we need it to do."

Tara's phone rang. Jerri could tell because she could feel it vibrate.

Tara got off of her and answered the phone, but not before she put it on speaker.

"Tara, this is Daddy."

Tara knew this was the call she was waiting for when Jerri took her by the shoulders and more or less forced her to sit on the couch. Then sat beside her, picked up her glass of wine and downed it in one swallow.

"The daddy that hasn't talked to me at all in months?" Tara asked carefully.

"Yes. Well, I'm sorry about that, Baby. I've had a lot on my plate."

Tara watched as Jerri grabbed her glass of wine and downed it, too.

"What the hell is going on, Dad?" Tara ordered

"There is no easy way to say this, Tara."

"Just spit it out, Dad. Do you have cancer?"

"No." Her dad laughed nervously, "I... I never really felt right, Tara. When I looked in the mirror I never saw me. I was never happy. None of that was you girls fault or your mother's I love you girls with all my heart. But I was never happy being Gary, so I'm not Gary anymore. I'm Georgia."

Jerri poured two more glasses of wine. She handed one to

Tara and mouthed the word "drink."

Tara downed the glass and indicated to Jerri that she needed to fill it again, which she did.

"Dad... What exactly does that mean?"

"I never felt like a man, Tara. I was never happy being a man. I always wanted to be a woman. I've been cross dressing since I was a child."

Tara sighed with relief. "So what, Dad? Big deal."

Then she saw Jerri drink half of her third glass of wine.

"What are you really saying, Dad?"

"I'm a woman now, Tara. I've had a complete sexual-reassignment surgery."

Tara downed her second glass of wine.

"Did mother know?"

She saw Jerri nodding her head before her father could answer.

"Yes she knew. She didn't know when I first started taking the hormones, but she knew when I had the first few surgeries to start reshaping my face. When I started letting my hair grow out I couldn't hide it."

Her parents were always having something lifted or tucked, and when her father's most recent face lift had left him looking more feminine she just assumed his next TV appearance—besides their show—would be on *Botched*. She thought he let his hair grow out to help cover the bad surgery.

"So your irreconcilable differences were that you wanted to be a woman?"

"Now Tara you know that wasn't the only problem your mother and I had."

"Yeah, but that's a huge one. So what, Dad, your whole life has been a gargantuan lie? We're all part of your lie and now what? What are we to you now?"

"You'll always be my daughters. I love you. How do you feel, Tara?"

"Dad... Is someone prompting you?" Because her dad had never been the touchy-feely type which you would think if he was really a woman all this time he would have been.

Jerri got her attention and mouthed the word "Judy."

Tara nodded. It was all starting to make sense except the part where her father had a sex-change operation.

"I have help. Let's face it; I've never had to tell my kids that I'm a woman before. I didn't do this to hurt you, Tara. How are you feeling?"

"Pissed off, alright, Dad? I feel pissed off. All the crap you always told me, all the stupid crap. Always telling me how to live my life... What a hypocrite you are, Dad. Did you already talk to Irva and Lori?"

"Yes."

"And how did they take it?"

"They were confused, a little hurt."

It was obvious he—or was it she—didn't understand at all why Tara was pissed off, but it was all his fault that she hadn't spent her life till now chasing girl tail and now... Well how could she sling her gayness in her mother's face after this? Now the ropes were going to tighten, the troops were going to move in, and none of them were going to be able to move a muscle without some camera in their face.

"You know why I'm so pissed off, Dad? Because you have no idea how badly you just screwed up my life and frankly you don't give a good rat's ass. Have fun with your new life." She hung up on him.

She looked at Jerri. "It's worse than I think, isn't it?"

"He's got his own show. They are going to film his coming out, his real transformation... everything. Judy's been working with him. She thinks 'Georgia' is the answer to bringing legitimacy to the transgendered community. Judy wants me to help, but frankly your dad—though he's obviously had a bazillion dollars in surgery to make him look like a woman—still acts just like a man. I'm so mad at Judy right now I could gladly pinch off her head and tell God she died."

"So... You've seen him/her. What does she look like?"

"Like you if you were older, bigger and ugly," Jerri said.

Tara finished another glass of wine and then called her mother.

"Tara?"

"Mother, are you alright?" Tara asked.

Her mother started to cry and was obviously being comforted by Tara's sisters. "I was about to ask you the same thing."

"I'm fine, just pissed as hell."

Jerri took her hand and held it, and Tara immediately felt the rage start to leave her body.

"How are you Mom?"

"I think I'm mostly relieved. I didn't want to tell you and he just kept putting it off. I'm glad it's over. Maybe this will take some of the heat off of you, Tara. Maybe they'll be so busy going after Daddy they'll leave you alone. He's doing a press conference first thing in the morning."

"Will you think I'm the world's biggest chicken shit if I just lay low for a few days?"

"Kid, if I had some place to hide right now I'd be there. Are you alone, Tara?"

"No."

"But you don't have a boyfriend."

"No, Mom. I do not have a boyfriend."

Tara had just finished talking to her mother when Jerri's phone rang. Jerri answered it. "Hello..."

"Jerri I..."

"Judy you traitor! You Benedict Arnold...."

"I got him to call them tonight. I thought you were only going to be mad at me forever if I didn't."

"Well I'm going to be mad a lot longer than this."

"I need you to write Georgia a speech to read tomorrow. She's nervous as a cat and..."

"I'm not writing that asshole a speech," Jerri said.

Across the room a now crying Tara yelled, "You write my daddy a speech! One that makes him look like less of an asshole and us like more than his victims."

Jerri could damn near see Judy smiling through the phone. "You are going to owe me forever, Judy."

"I already do."

Chapter 12

Judy looked down at the sea of reporters. They hadn't gotten much sleep the night before.

Georgia'd had no idea what to say. Judy drew a complete blank because of course she was sure Jerri was going to come through for her. After all she always did. But until they got the speech at one in the morning Judy, Georgia, and the five other transgendered women who were helping her teach Georgia how to be a woman kept trying to write a speech just in case. Thank God Jerri wrote the statement and a list of answers to questions she expected the press would ask because everything "the team" had come up with was pure crap.

Judy didn't know whether the speech was just that hard for Jerri to write or she was just making Judy sweat because she was pissed off. Of course Jerri wasn't the only one who was pissed off. Cyndy stormed off after dinner, took their car home, and hadn't accepted any of her texts or calls. Apparently being right about how mad Jerri was going to be wasn't good enough for Cyndy.

Georgia stood in the wings and she looked back at Judy. "Maybe this is a huge mistake." She looked from the statement she'd practiced reading a dozen times out to the sea of reporters. "I didn't listen when you told me how the girls were going to feel, and maybe going public..."

Judy pointed to the film crew that had showed up at Georgia's. "It's a little late for second thoughts, Georgia." Then added in a much bitchier tone—no doubt because her wife and her best friend were both pissed off at her and every minute she was a little more sure that Jerri was right about Georgia being all wrong as a spokesperson for their cause—she snapped, "What are you going to do? Have them turn your dick around again and sew it back on?"

Georgia gave her a hurt look, no doubt because this was the harshest thing Judy had said to her.

"I didn't come looking for you. You came looking for me. This is too important a cause to me to let you screw it up. You walk out there proudly with your head held high and you read that brilliant statement Jerri wrote as if you wrote it yourself. You own who you are now, and you own those words."

Georgia nodded took a deep breath and walked to the center of the stage behind the podium.

Judy could tell the exact moment at which the reporters realized that this woman they were looking at had once been one of the greatest quarterbacks in football history because flash bulbs went off with a blinding light and their combined gasps and whisperings rose to an ear-piercing level. Georgia looked back at Judy for support; Judy smiled and nodded.

Georgia looked at the papers in her hands, and then cleared her throat. When she did you could have heard a pin drop, the pool of reporters got that quiet.

"I'm going to read this because I'm far too emotional and this is far too important for me to stumble around through the tangled, nervous, even fearful thoughts in my head..." And of course Jerri had even written that. "I don't stand before you today to shock, or scare, or make anyone uncomfortable. I know first-hand what all of those things feel like because for nearly sixty years I felt that way every time I looked in the mirror and saw a stranger. I have had sexual-reassignment surgery. I am no longer Gary Darting; I am now Georgia Darting. This was not a decision I made quickly or without thought. It is something I have wanted to do since the first moment I learned such a thing existed. I know people will judge me, call me sick, misguided and perverse. Again these are things I have called myself. But today I finally stand before you in the body that matches my brain and my spirit.

"This does not in any way diminish the years I spent with my ex-wife Janice or our three girls. Those girls..." She got choked up now, and even that Jerri had written into the script though Judy could tell looking that Georgia wasn't faking the emotion. "My daughters are the light of my heart. I never meant to hurt them or cause them any pain. I can only hope and pray that they will find a way to have a relationship with who I am now. That they know no matter what I will always be their daddy and that my love for them hasn't changed except that now that I can love myself I can love them with a fuller heart." Georgia had finished the statement. She gave herself a few moments to compose herself and then said, "I will take a few questions."

They all put their hands up at once. Georgia called on a man somewhere in the middle, and now was when all the years Georgia had lived in the spotlight was going to pay off. She knew how to work a crowd.

"Are you going to date men now?"

Judy hoped she was the only one who saw Georgia looking at her notes. "Why, are you asking me out?" She let the laugher die down before she answered. "Truthfully, at this time sex is the furthest thing from my mind. Think about how you were when you were going through puberty. That's where I am except at my age I know puberty isn't a good time to date anyone."

She took another question from a female reporter this time. "How do your ex-wife and your daughters feel?"

Again Georgia looked at her notes, which was so obvious to Judy that she started to sweat. "Janice knew about the cross-dressing—which I have done for years—but she didn't know I wanted a sex change till about a year ago. She was, needless to say, shocked but has taken it surprisingly well. In fact, her production company will be filming my transformation for a TV show which is currently untitled. I just told my girls last night and they are in different states of shock, but I understand that completely."

"I will take one more question," Georgia said, and called on a man sitting right upfront who had been jumping around like he had ants in his pants.

"How do you expect the general public will react?"

Again she looked at her notes, and Judy cringed. "I hope that they will react with compassion. I am not the only transsexual person in the world. My hope is that my story might shed some light on the injustices and prejudices my community has and still does face. We are not trying to tear down the world; we just need a place for us in it. Thank you very much."

Georgia walked off the stage. By the time she reached Judy she was just bawling.

Judy held her, patted her back and thought, *Thank God Jerri Blue is a genius.*

They woke up just in time to throw on their robes and get downstairs to watch her father's press conference. They sat down on the couch and got comfortable. Tara made a face the

minute her father came on screen and said, "It's creepy. He/
she does look like me."

"If you were older, bigger and ugly. Shush. I want to see if
the dumbass can stay on script," Jerri said.

Tara listened to his speech and even though she knew
every word he said Jerri had written for him—or was it her?
She didn't think she was ever going to get used to that—she
actually got choked up. "I wish that was the way he... she."

"Honey, you're her daughter I think you're allowed to use
the pronouns that spring to mind till you wrap your head
around it. It hasn't even been twenty-four hours yet."

"I wish he really felt that way."

"You don't know that she doesn't."

"I know he has stayed completely on script."

"Shut up and listen. I'm brilliant."

So she did and even though she knew for a fact her father
hadn't written a word of it she did feel herself start to soften
towards him until she remembered that it was all his fault she
had hidden who she really was, and all his fault that they
were about to be in the middle of a giant media tornado that
was going to make it even harder for her to spend any real
time with Jerri. Then she was mad all over again.

They were having breakfast when her phone rang. When
she saw it was her dad she started to just shut her phone off.

"You're going to have to talk to her sometime," Jerri said.

Tara grudgingly answered the phone, this time not putting
it on speaker because if Jerri made noise or talked she didn't
want to explain it.

"What?"

Jerri grinned at her and kept eating.

"Did you see my press conference, Tara?"

"Yes."

"Are you still mad at me?"

"Yes."

"Tara I can't stand it that I hurt you." Then Georgia was
crying. "I want you to come visit me at my new house on
Sunday. I'm going to grill. Your sisters are coming up, and I'd
like us all to be together."

"Is a camera crew going to be there?"

"Yeah, but..."

"No, Dad. No. I have my own stuff going on. It's been going
on a while, and where have you been? You've been doing your

own thing. And that's fine, I get it. You finally get to be who you really are, but when is it going to be my turn? Between my divorce and Fred trying to kill himself, you and mom's divorce and now this… I need to take care of me, and that's what I'm doing. I want to do what I want to do. You know what I don't want to do? Sit with my dad with a woman's body and face, and my sisters and talk fashion while a camera crew rolls film. I'm allowed to have some time to try to wrap my head around what you have done. If I can, maybe we can have a relationship then."

"Wow, that's kind of harsh," Jerri mumbled across from her.

"Well maybe I feel like being harsh," Tara told Jerri.

"Who… Tara, who are you with?"

"Why don't you ask your new bestie, Judy?"

To the stunned look on Jerri's face she said, "Relax. I hung up on him before I said that."

"You're going to have to try to meet her somewhere in the middle, Tara."

"Why? You don't even like him/her, so why do you care whether I have a relationship with them?"

"My dad was only a dad because of his sperm count. For our birthdays every year he gave us a card with five dollars in it, and that was a huge deal because he never really did anything with or for us. He spent the entire Christmas season being so mean that to this day I still dread December coming around and my brother Bob buys the biggest tree he can find and buys his kids more crap than he can afford or they need to make up for what we didn't have. Nothing I ever did was right. Nothing Bob ever did was enough. He whipped us with a belt for everything from getting in trouble at school to smacking when we ate. He yelled, he screamed, and he married three different women after our mom left—all of whom just loved Bob and couldn't stand me because I was so 'wrong'. He kicked me out of the house when I was sixteen because I was an obvious queer, which I wasn't even a hundred percent sure about at that time. As soon as I got a place Bob moved in with me because we were really all each other had. My dad was one of those men about which people will say, 'he's a good guy,' when what they really mean is he isn't a bad guy. And there is a huge difference between being a good guy and just not being a bad guy. Good people do good things; my dad never did anything good. He was a mean drunk and he was drunk most of the time he wasn't at work.

"He died three years ago. I hadn't seen him in eight years. I had talked on the phone to him maybe four times in all that time. He died without ever telling either Bob or I he was sorry for anything, and I really wanted—maybe even *needed*—that apology. When he was dead I cried like a baby, and I find that I still miss him."

"Why?"

"Because he was my dad. I never really knew my mom, and poor Bob didn't know her at all, so he tried to replace her with every woman Dad brought home. Every time they left it was like Bob was losing his mother all over again. Everyone has a story, Tara. My dad's was that when he was in his mid-twenties and working two jobs to pay the bills, his wife ran off with his best friend leaving him with a three-year-old and an infant that wasn't one yet. He could have left us, too, but he didn't. Maybe we would have been better off in the system, but I doubt that seriously. My dad did the best he could with what he knew. He didn't know better, and that included how to raise a gay kid in the middle of the Bible belt. He didn't reach out to me, so I never reached out to him. I never told him how what he had done and didn't do made me feel. I disengaged because it hurt too much to try to have anything approaching a real relationship with him. Now I'll never know if he was actually sorry for the way he raised us, for kicking me out of the house, for all the terrible things he said to me because I was different, or if he really was just a shithead."

"Where's your brother now?"

"Bob moved out here with me, went to community college got a degree in business and moved to Phoenix for work. He manages a chain of grocery stores there. He met a nice girl, got married, and had two kids—a boy and a girl. They're 11 and 13 now. We were always really close till our fucking mother found me about five years ago. Guess someone told her that I'd changed my name and who I was. One day she e-mails me. This may be shocking to you since you're hiding here, but I'm not hiding, and I'm not that hard to find. Long story short she wanted money. I tell her I not only am not going to give her any money, but I have no desire to have any kind of relationship with her. But I have to tell my brother that she contacted me and how he can get in touch with her because not doing so would be 'wrong.' So I tell Bob, but I also tell him just what she is and that I don't think he should contact her at all. But he has this stupid mother thing so he contacts her. She winds up moving to Phoenix and she is now a part of his life. Since I don't want her in mine... Well I don't go there for holidays or birthdays anymore, and he and I have sort of grown apart."

"Jerri, do you have a single story from your past that isn't awful?"

Jerri grinned. "Lots but they aren't all that interesting except one. A friend brought her bright, beautiful daughter to my homestead so I could teach her to write, and I fell in love with her. Everything would have been perfect if her turd of an ex-husband didn't nearly kill himself with an overdose, her parents didn't get divorced, and then her father came out and was instantly the most famous transsexual in the world... And all on TV..."

"Oh crap!" Tara hissed.

"What? I'm sure it will have a happy ending. All Jerri Blue novels do."

"I just realized my mother is going to blame herself for us being together."

"I like that better than her blaming me," Jerri mumbled.

"Why does she have to blame anyone? We belong together; we're happy. I don't see why she can't be happy for us," Tara said, feeling super pissed off.

"I think I need to remind you that A) You aren't done being mad at your father yet, and B) Your mother doesn't even know about us so she sure as hell hasn't said anything disparaging about our union. Far from placing blame when someone brings two people together who ought to be together... Well she should be really proud of herself."

That reminded Tara that she was mad at her father. "I don't know but... Couldn't he just dress up like a girl? Did he have to get all that surgery?"

"You mean the way I dress like a boy?" Jerri asked with a smile.

Yes, that was exactly what she meant. Tara's silence must have been all the answer Jerri needed.

"But you see I don't feel like I have the wrong body. I don't feel like I'm a man, but I can't honestly say I feel like a woman either. I dress in men's clothing because I like to. I have no need or desire to change my body. People color their hair; you have highlights right now. You wear makeup, and spend a fortune on clothes and accessories. People get piercings and tattoos, all in an effort to make their outside show the world at the best how they see themselves and at the worst how they want the world to see them. Now me I can't imagine poking holes in myself much less getting surgery. But to me getting sexual reassignment surgery isn't any different than getting a nose or boob job. Certainly it's no different to me than weight-loss surgery."

"I've never had a nose or boob job, and I don't think having a few highlights put in my hair is the same as my dad having a boob job."

"But it really is. We are all just trying to make what other people see when they look at us either what we see or what we want to see. And with trans people no one really talks about what's down below."

"What do you mean?"

"Lots of them choose not to change that which can't be seen and it's considered rude to ask what they have and have not had done. I'm kind of rude; your dad has had it all done."

Tara made a face and Jerri grinned and shrugged. "People want to be seen the way they want to be seen."

Tara took a deep breath and let it out. She understood what Jerri was saying, but she really just didn't feel like even trying to understand. In fact, what she felt most like doing was just screaming to hear herself scream. Tara did the math in her head.

"You know I think I may be premenstrual."

"So glad I didn't ask."

As they worked on the homestead Tara realized the animals weren't nearly as time-consuming to care for as the plants. The garden was already lush and green, the trees had already bloomed and now they were fully-leafed out, and the orchard was starting to set fruit.

It was noon and she was bottle feeding the new baby while Jerri was catching the other babies—now nearly half the size of their mother—and separating them to wean them off. When they were in the separate pen they and their mother all started bawling like something was killing them.

To the panicked look on Tara's face Jerri said, "They will

do that for the rest of the day and a big part of tomorrow until they get used to it."

"Poor babies," Tara said.

"Don't make me have to give you my meat and milk-eater speech again. They can still see their mother and their mother can still see them. They are just in different pens. No kid has ever died during the weaning process," Jerri assured her, but Jerri was glad the barn was a good walk from the house because listening to them cry was heart-wrenching even for her.

When they got back to the house Harold was waiting for them with bread, ready to get his milk and eggs. He smiled at Tara and she smiled back. There was something so freeing about him just seeing her as a person not being caught up in who she was or anything that was going on in her crazy family.

"Emily said for me to tell you…" He started as he followed them into the house. "…that I will help you butcher that crazy-assed goat if you help me build a proper chicken house and run."

"You know what? That sounds like a hell of a deal to me. What about Monday we whack the goat and Tuesday I help you build your chicken house and run?"

Tara didn't want to think about Jerri killing a goat, even the evil one. She made a face as she went to the sink, washed out the bottle, and washed her hands. She heard a noise behind her. When she turned Harold was stumbling and laughing. It was obvious that Jerri had just shoved him.

"I was just looking," Harold said with an unashamed shrug.

Tara realized he had been checking out her ass. The ass her sisters said was both too big and too flat and she should maybe get either liposuction or implants depending on what day of the week it was. Her ass that was currently clothed in a pair of Jerri's baggy-assed tattered work jeans.

Jerri looked at Tara and rolled her eyes, and Tara grinned back.

When I'm here everything makes sense. I feel important, cherished and beautiful. I don't doubt myself or my place in the world. Jerri is wrong. If I never had to leave this place again I think I'd be perfectly, amazingly happy. I feel like I'm part of reality. I help make the food I eat. It's not all lights and hype and people yelling your name—not because they care about you or anything you've done—but so you'll turn so they can get their money shot.

Then she realized something profound. *I'm not embarrassed at all about my relationship with Jerri, and if I'm honest I don't really care how it would affect my mom, my dad or my sisters. I don't care at all how they would feel about us. I'm actually proud to be with her. Being with her makes me feel amazing. I don't want the press to catch us together because right now our relationship is just that—ours. If we get caught on film it will be just like everything else in my life; it will belong to the bank of public opinion. People will start deciding what we should do, how we should be. They will start running their Twittering mouths about us as if they know anything at all about us and our relationship. That scares the shit out of me because the more they hold me under a microscope and pick me apart the more unsure I am about myself. I don't want them to do that to me and Jerri. I don't want to have any doubts about us. But it's unrealistic to think we can hide our relationship forever. So I just need to get in a place where what other people say doesn't really matter to me no matter how nasty and hateful they get.*

They spent the rest of the day just walking around the property, holding hands, exploring nature, talking about mostly her dad's transition and what Tara had discovered about the real reason she didn't want to get caught with Jerri.

They had made their way back to the porch and were sitting on the swing drinking some wine.

"I'm right there with you, Tara. I know it will happen eventually because the only way we could really stop it is to just not see each other till you're contract runs out. I'd rather get caught and have to cover from the media fallout than not be with you for days maybe weeks at a time."

Tara took in a deep breath and let it out, mostly just relieved to hear they were on the same page. "It won't be the end of the world if we get caught. Who knows maybe now would be perfect timing because Daddy's thing sort of trumps I'm gay."

"I've been wondering about that, too," Jerri said. "We don't have to look at the shitty things people say about us. I never read reviews of my books because I really don't care what people have to say about them. I'm happy with them so what other people say doesn't matter. Tara, I have never loved *anything...*" She grinned wildly. "...not even one of my books, as much as I love you. I have never been as sure of anything as I am of you, of us. So when—not if but when, because let's just admit we know it's going to happen—when the shit hits the fan let's turn the phone, the Twitter and the TV off and not read or listen to or see any of the shit people are going to say about us because they don't know us at all."

"Do you ever get tired of saying deep and profound things every time you open your mouth?"

"You know that I do not... either always say deep and profound things or get tired of saying them when I do."

Tara took her phone out of her pocket. She'd had it off all day but had been checking periodically to make sure none of her family was trying to get in touch with her. "I don't want to even tell you how many texts and tweets I have. Deleting them all." She sighed. "Lori has tried to call three times." She went ahead and called Lori back.

"Are you alright, Lori?" Tara said when she heard Lori answer.

"Are you?" Lori said in a near shriek. "Our dad's a woman. How do you think I'm doing, Tara? I'm freaked out. Aren't you freaked out?"

"I'm too busy being really pissed off to be freaked out."

"Are you going to his/her thing tomorrow?" Lori asked.

"No."

"Then could you watch the boys? I just think it would be too confusing for them."

"You mean the whole 'their grandpa is now their grandma' thing? I think you're probably right."

"Besides, Tara, it's going to be hard enough for me to try to wrap my head around without having the boys there hollering and tearing shit up. Could you take them?"

"I'm hiding, Lori. I'm not coming out of hiding."

"I get that, but I could meet you somewhere? You know they don't usually follow me when I have the boys besides which I fully expect most of them will head for Dad's bright and early to make sure they get our reactions. Before you say no, you did say you owed me."

Tara turned to Jerri covering her phone. "Do you care if we watch the boys tomorrow?"

"Not at all," Jerri said.

Tara kissed her on the cheek then told Lori, "Alright. I'll meet you in the parking lot of the McDonalds where you always get the kids Happy Meals. What time?"

"Is ten too early?"

"No. I should miss most of the traffic. I'll see you tomorrow."

Jerri stood and started doing some sort of interpretive dance.

Tara covered the receiver on the phone again, "What?"

"Tell her you love her. She's obviously really upset. She needs to talk, and you said she fights with her husband all the time. Tell her you're all in this together. That this isn't your problem; it's your dad's."

Tara rolled her eyes.

"Just do it."

Tara took her hand off the phone and held it back to her ear. "Lori, I love you. We're in this together," she said as if she were reading a script poorly.

To her surprise Lori said, obviously crying, "You're the best sister ever. I cannot tell you how much I needed to hear that. It will be alright won't it, Tara?"

"At the end of the day, Lori, this is Dad's problem, not ours," Tara said experimentally.

"I know, right?"

Then Lori just wanted to talk in a way they hadn't really talked in years. Tara looked at Jerri and mouthed the words, "You're a witch."

Jerri chuckled and went in the house no doubt to start dinner.

And why hadn't they really talked like sisters in years? Because they became part of a television family and when they did they stopped being a real family. They were always fighting for camera time. They became hyper competitive with one another so they couldn't just be sisters. It became a battle over who could command the most attention from the press, get the most Twitter followers—which was always Irva and then Lori—Tara was always at the bottom of the list which had left her with a bitter feeling of never being good enough. Now she flat couldn't care less about any of it.

By the time she finally got her sister off the phone her battery was low, so she went in and put it on the charger before joining Jerri in the kitchen to help with dinner.

"How did you know she needed to hear that I loved her and that she just needed to talk?"

"I know when I'm freaked out that's what I need. Isn't it

what you need? To know you aren't alone in your pain. I think..." She pointed to a quote on the wall and read it without looking at it. "We forget that we are not that different from anyone else, that all people are looking for connection, that we all need love. What I would need in a situation is what I should give to another. If they do not want it? That is not my fault."

"Very good, but you actually *know* things. You aren't just guessing, you *know*. The night of The Burn you met me in the middle of the woods. You said you felt me."

"Do you have any scars?"

"How is that an answer to my question? What the hell does that have to do with anything?" Tara laughed.

"It's a simple question... Never mind. I know because I've paid much more attention to your body than you ever have. You have a small scar at the base of your right thumb and another one on your left knee."

"Field hockey and high hurdles respectively," Tara said with a smile.

"Are you sure it's going to surprise anyone that you're gay?"

Tara shrugged.

"Take your other hand and explore the scar tissue on your thumb and tell me what you feel."

I swear sometimes it's like living in a college classroom, Tara thought, but did it anyway. "The skin there is harder, rougher, thicker."

"It's still skin but now it's stronger right?"

Tara nodded.

"We all have intuition, but we're taught not to trust it when the people in our lives tell us how unworthy we are. How can we trust what we feel when we're dumbasses? Intuition doesn't quite seem real: we don't see it, smell it, hear it, touch it. It's just a tingling in the back of our brain. Remember I told you I ran because I knew I was in trouble?"

Tara nodded again.

"What I didn't tell you was that when I was leaving work that day one of the guys offered to take me home, but it was out of his way, so even though something was telling me to accept his ride I turned him down. After what happened scar tissue started to grow on my intuition, building it up making it stronger, but I still didn't always listen to it. I still didn't embrace it because I wasn't ready to trust myself. I stayed a victim for a long time. I thought I was a survivor, I told myself I was but I wasn't. I wasn't a survivor till I embraced my trauma, admitted it happened to me, all that happened to me, and really dealt with it. I moved out here and then for the first time I took my place in the universe. I became a piece of a vast living organism where I could finally see that being so different was just part of the plan. Ever since then I trust my intuition. It isn't that I'm doing something anyone can't do or that I've trained myself for. All I did was learn to trust myself."

Chapter 13

Tara met Lori, picked up the boys and got home all without any trouble. After they took care of all the animals Jerri took them to the ponds to fish.

Right above the gardens there were three concrete troughs, each fifty feet long, twelve feet wide and eight feet at their deepest. They caught the rain that Jerri told her would otherwise occasionally run down the hill and wash out their garden. The over flow from the last pond ran through a huge pipe into the creek. The ponds were stocked with tilapia and crawdads. Jerri had made each of the boys a pole from a bamboo patch on the property and then they'd dug worms from their worm bed. Now they were fishing, which Tara couldn't remember doing since she was a kid. Her dad used to take her fishing with him and... Jerri was right. Why would anyone be shocked that Tara was gay?

As Tara threw the line in for Tylor she had a momentary twinge thinking about the fact that the father she knew was gone. She wondered why he had stopped taking her fishing with him then she remembered that it was about the same time she had expressed an interest in girls. *He quit fishing with me because he wanted me to act more like a girl so that I wouldn't want one. Yet he just wants all of us, me, to embrace what he has done.*

Tylor had started walking, so he wasn't happy to sit on the bank and fish. No, he wanted to get up and run around with the pole with the hook, and... What was Jerri thinking giving the baby an actual hook?

Jerri caught four fish pretty quick. Then she put her pole down to help Channing—who was rattling a mile a minute saying nothing remotely like a word most of the time. Both the barn cats were there and Tara didn't know what was funnier—listening to Jerri talk to the cats as if they were talking or pretending like she could understand even half of what Channing was saying.

"No, you can't have my fish," she told the yellow-striped cat. "You can maybe have a tail... I think that's more than fair... Well what have you done for me lately?... All right, you did catch that mouse. I'll let you have a couple of heads for your troubles."

Then she turned to Channing. "That is, too, what he said... How the hell would you know? Do you speak Cat?... No, you don't, I think you speak Russian."

Then she got all excited. "Pull the line, Channing, pull the line!"

He had a fish on his line but he panicked and handed the pole to Jerri who gave it right back to him then helped him pull the fish out of the water.

"I have fish!" he yelled, jumping around.

Tylor pulled his line out of the water and made unhappy noises.

"That does suck," Jerri told him.

She pulled the fish off the line and put it on the stringer.

"Trade me babies, Tara."

So she helped Channing fish while Jerri went to help Tylor. Tara watched as Jerri sat down on the bank, set the baby in front of her and cast the line, then helped him hold the pole.

"No," she told him. "Let me help... Well they will bite if you will just hold your britches."

Tylor laughed.

Tara put another worm on the hook and cast it then handed it to Channing.

He looked at her with a frown.

"What?"

"Fish with him," he said pointing at Jerri.

Tara started to correct him, but Jerri quickly said, "At this age they use the pronoun that fits in their minds. You will only confuse him and make it that much harder when he meets his new grandma."

Tara thought that was odd but shrugged it off. She watched as the cats got up to move to where Jerri was.

"I know how to fish," Tara told Channing.

Tylor got a bite and Jerri helped him get it out of the water. The baby started jumping around, blabbering a mile a minute.

Jerri said to him, "Yes it is a huge fish... No it isn't a shark... It isn't... Oh now you're just being ridiculous."

As she was trying to get the fish off the hook and keep Tylor out of the water at the same time she said to the yellow cat, "No you can't eat him... He isn't a really big rat... He's a child."

"Fish with him," Channing said again.

"Why because we haven't caught a fish yet?" Tara laughed then they caught another fish and she helped him bring it in, but as she was putting it on the stringer she looked up and Channing had taken his pole and moved over to sit by Jerri.

"Doesn't anyone like me better?" Tara asked from where she stood alone by the water.

Jerri looked up at her and smiled. "I do."

When they had caught about a dozen fish Jerri went to clean them.

Wanting no part of that, Tara took Tylor to the house to put him down for a nap while Channing went with Jerri. Tylor had fussed but she gave him some milk in a sippy cup, sat down in the recliner and rocked him, and in minutes he was fast asleep. She laid him down on the couch and covered him up. She looked at the clock; it was nearly one. She checked her phone, but none of her family had called and at that point in time she didn't want to talk to anyone else. Once again she deleted all her Twitter texts without reading them.

Part of her was wishing she'd gone to her dad's dinner with her sisters. Maybe it would be better to just get it over with. But she didn't want to go back into the lion's den right now, and she really thought she needed to be over being so mad at him before she saw him. Which probably wasn't going to happen until she was a hundred percent sure that this whole thing wasn't going to ruin what she had with Jerri.

I need to get to a place where I can accept what he's done or how can I expect anyone to accept me and what I'm doing? It's the same but different, and what does it say? She looked around till she found the quote. *"The same but different doesn't work for anyone." Who wrote it? Dr. Judy Willis. If my dad says anything about me and Jerri, I'm going to make him look in a full-length mirror and... God I hope that's not what I'm going to look like when I hit sixty."*

Channing hit the back door first and came running into where she was, already talking. It made Tylor jump, but he didn't wake up, having been raised by screaming parents. Once Lori's boys went to sleep you had to shake them to wake them up, except for the three or four times a night they got up for reasons known only to them.

"Cats ate heads and tails," Channing told her.

"They did?"

He nodded. "Chickens ate guts. We eat the rest; nothing wasted."

"Well that's the way we do things here on the Blue Homestead," Tara said, smiling at Jerri as she walked in from putting the fish in the fridge. "Come on. Let's clean you up and then you need to take a nap."

"No."

"Yes." She took him by the hand and led him into the bathroom.

Jerri was about to sit down when the phone rang. She grumbled walked over and answered it. "Hello."

"Could you not talk Tara into coming to Georgia's today?" Judy asked.

"I didn't try, why would I? I want her here with me till some of this crap dies down."

"This has been a very hard day for Georgia. You know those other girls take their lead from Tara."

"Judy. I'm hardly talking to you. You aren't in a good position to tell me what I should or should not do right now especially concerning Tara. Aren't you the one who told me that some things shouldn't be easy? Georgia decided to go on this journey. She didn't ask their permission to do it; she didn't even tell them she was doing it till it was done. They all have the right to feel what they're feeling."

"She said Tara is very angry."

"She is."

"Why? She didn't seem to have a problem with me at all."

"First, Judy, you aren't her father. Second, whose fault do you think it is that Tara didn't come out till she was thirty?"

"Oh."

"Yes, oh. Judy, your new bestie…" She said remembering what Tara had not told her dad. "…guilted Tara into the closet, but now he wants her to accept his decision with open arms."

"In Georgia's defense she doesn't know Tara is gay."

"Because she thinks she cured Tara by ordering her not to be gay. In society's defense, they didn't know Gary Darting was a woman."

"God, I hate arguing with you Jerri," Judy said, sounding

exhausted. "Not just because you're my best friend but because you are so good at it. The arguing that is."

"I understand that the cause has always come before everything else for you, Judy. It's your calling; I get that. But you have stuck me in the middle of something..."

"You already would have been in the big middle of. I didn't pick your mate, Jerri, you did. You'd both still be in the big middle of this."

"Yes, but I wouldn't be writing speeches for the jackass, would I, Judy?"

"I would have wanted you to."

"But I wouldn't have had any trouble telling you no. I sure as hell wouldn't have known before Tara did—which sucked. Need I remind you that what Georgia really needs to be a good spokesperson for our community is a brain transplant because the dumbass is still a right-winged Republican."

"I didn't call to rehash things we've already talked about."

"No, you called me to try to get me to tell Tara to give her dad a break."

"She is really upset. The other girls were very distant. They didn't really hug her; they played everything very cool. Tara didn't show up at all, and I guess Georgia really thought that even though she said she wasn't coming that she would. If you could have Tara call her."

"Are you fucking kidding me right now, Judy?"

"Tara hung up on her; Georgia is very hurt."

"I hate repeating myself but seriously are you fucking kidding me?" Jerri hissed. "Are you listening to me at all? Tara is hurt and confused and pissed off. That's all I care about. I don't give a flying fuck about Gary Darting."

Tara walked out of the bathroom then, Channing in tow, and gave her a confused look.

Jerri shrugged went in the bathroom and closed the door on the cord. "You know what, Judy? This is what you always do. You get tunnel vision and then you can't see anyone's side but your own."

"What is that supposed to mean?"

"You know exactly what it means, Judy. You get something in your sights, you put blinders on, put your head down, run forward and damn whoever gets in your way. You are so sure that you are right that you just plow through figuring that when you are proven right all of those you hurt will forgive you because after all you were right and everything is better. You know who it's not better for, Judy? It's not better for the people along the way who find out they aren't as important to you as your stinking cause."

"Damn, Jerri, you are really pissed off. Where is all this hostility coming from?"

"Where really where? I am in the first good relationship I have ever had in my whole stinking, screwed-up life and you are willing to jeopardize what I have to help someone who has never done a damn thing for you in the hopes that they can jump-start your cause. And what did you tell me not that long ago? You said, 'So you're helping someone not because of what they did for you but because of what they didn't do,' and now who's doing the same but very different thing, Judy?"

"Well, look at how well that worked out for you, Jerri." Judy sighed so loudly Jerri could hear it over the phone. "You're right I do get tunnel vision. And I have used you in ways that I shouldn't, but Jerri if your relationship can't handle something external like this it's not meant to be anyway."

"I don't know how external this is, Judy. You are trying to use me to manipulate Tara so that she can make Georgia feel better only so you can more easily bend Georgia to your will. If I did that I'd deserve to lose Tara, but I'm not going to do it."

She walked out of the bathroom and hung up the phone loud enough that the sleeping boys both jumped. She looked at Tara where she sat in the recliner.

"Fucking Judy," she said for answer to Tara's look. "I'm going to need a minute."

Tara watched as Jerri walked out the front door closing it quietly behind her. A few seconds later Tara heard yelling. She looked out the window and Jerri was picking up a huge stump throwing it and cussing a blue streak. Tara didn't really know what to think but it didn't look like she was going to hurt herself and... Well she said she needed a minute. The phone rang and Tara answered it. "Hello."

"What's Jerri doing?" Judy's voice asked.

"Chunking a stump around in the front yard and yelling," Tara said. She moved so that she could watch Jerri out the window and make sure she wasn't going to hurt herself. "Is she having an episode?"

"No, she's that pissed off at me. It's how she copes with

her rage by abusing the stump. When she calms down will you tell her that she's right and I'm sorry?"

"I will. What happened?"

"I did something a friend shouldn't do. All my fault."

"Should I go out and try to talk to her?"

"No. She'll get tired of throwing the stump and yelling and calm down in a minute. Right now she needs to get her mad on."

Jerri threw the stump down hard yelled, "Mother Fucker!" one last time and finally she could calm down and think.

Why am I so mad at Judy? I question her loyalty. But I know Judy is only trying to support her cause. She over stepped, but it isn't the first time she's done that, and I don't think I've ever been this mad at Judy. What am I really feeling? I'm scared. I'm actually sick to my stomach, scared in a way I haven't been in years. Why? Because I love Tara, and I'm afraid I'll lose her. I'm afraid this is going to be too much for us to get through and I'll lose her. And that's been building for a while because I'm happy and being happy makes me feel very vulnerable.

As always, knowing what was wrong helped her to calm right down. She walked over and sat on the porch swing.

Tara came out with a glass of ice tea, handed it to her and sat beside her. She took Tara's hand, wound their fingers together and didn't say anything.

Jerri took a huge drink then sat the glass on the piece of stump that served as an end table—not the one she had just thrown all over the yard. She took in a deep, cleansing breath and let it out.

Tara kissed her on the cheek.

"Judy called and said to tell you that you were right and that she's sorry."

"Am I too crazy for you, Tara?"

"I told you before, honey, crazy people never say they're crazy."

"It's a lot of shit isn't it?"

"But we're alright. As long as we're alright I have it on good authority that we can take on the world."

"What happens if we aren't alright? I'm scared shitless that I'm going to lose you, Tara."

"I was worried about the same thing earlier today, but I

think as long as we both care at least enough to throw a stump around the yard, it isn't ever going to happen. You've already dealt with all your baggage. You're coming to this relationship clean. This is all my baggage, and I'm really sorry. Frankly, if I'm not afraid you're about to kick my ass to the curb—and I'm not. I don't know why I'm not, but I'm not—then why should you be worried that I'd ever leave you? So was Judy being a huge ass?"

"Yes she was." Jerri unlaced her fingers from Tara's put her arm around Tara's shoulders and pulled her close. "But I was mostly mad because I just want us to be together. I know this mess is going to make that hard. I guess I've been more worried than I thought I was about how we're going to get through it."

"I'm not worried, Jerri, and what does your intuition tell you?"

Jerri grinned. "To stop worrying."

The girls came back from their father's—or was she their other mother now—looking spent. They were really quiet. They went to separate parts of the house, and Janice didn't see either of them till Lori came downstairs having changed and went to get the boys.

Janice didn't know how she was supposed to feel about all of this. She was sick to death of trying to wrap her head around the fact that the man she had once loved, that she'd been married to for over thirty years and was the father of her children was now a woman. It made her feel like she must be the biggest idiot in the entire world, the worst sort of failure. Her friends kept Emailing and calling, telling her it wasn't her fault, but no matter how many times she heard it, it still felt like it was.

Most of the press and the public at large were handling "Georgia" with kid gloves. There were more positive reports than negative ones on social media. Janice didn't know how she felt about that, either.

She was in the middle of menopause with its mood swings, depression, hot flashes, and just the whole not feeling like a human being thing. That all by itself would have been more than enough to deal with, but on top of that she had this swirling chasm of crap to try to swim through—all on camera—and at least for that she had no one to blame but herself.

But actually when she thought about it there was more than enough blame to go around. Gary had to retire from football because his right shoulder was gone. The timing couldn't have been worse because the girls were just hitting their teens.

He got work as a commentator but he wasn't making a fraction of what he'd been making playing ball and the endorsements didn't slowly fizzle out; they were gone practically overnight. At the same time the girls hit an age where they needed more time and more money. Janice had been stretched thin. Several of her more prominent, high-maintenance clients had bailed on her saying between her kids and Rhonda they felt they weren't getting the attention they deserved. Janice told Gary he was going to have to step up and do more with the kids. His answer was to quit his job as a sports anchor—which he hated anyway—to stay home and cart the kids around.

There was less and less money all the time and the girls spent more and more. The Dartings were used to a certain lifestyle, one that couldn't be kept up on chump change. Irva started modeling which in the beginning always cost more than a model could make. Tara was in college taking business classes. Lori had just crashed her third car. The bills just kept piling up. Just when Janice was afraid her nervous breakdown was going to run right into their bankruptcy there was the scandal of Irva's sex tape.

Irva had been barely legal when she made it with some dumbass boy she'd been dating at the time. She broke up with him and within weeks the video was all over the internet. They could barely wade through the paparazzi to get in and out of their house, and that gave Janice an idea. She pitched the reality show they were all still part of, and the rest was TV history.

Her family could point the finger of blame at her all they wanted, but the truth was without the show they never could have continued to live the life to which they had all become accustomed.

But this new chapter—the one she'd signed off on; the one her production company was producing—was giving Gary a platform for his "cause" and leaving them all open to... What? She'd done it without asking the girls how they felt, without them even knowing what Gary had done.

One of the late-night talk show hosts for which they had always been comic fodder had said in his monologue the night before, "So Gary Darting came out as a transgendered woman. What was more surprising is that it turns out Janice Darting isn't a man. All these years I thought Gary was gay. Oh, but I guess she is."

It was just a stupid joke. She should have blown it off like she had hundreds of other stupid things that had been said about her and her family over the years. The problem was she just wasn't in the mood. Janice was just so tired of being the butt of everyone's joke, and this felt so much more personal.

Lori came home with the boys and for once they weren't shouting and running around. "Where were they?" Janice asked. Then before Lori could answer added, "You know I could have watched them."

"You have enough on your plate, Mom. They were with Tara," Lori said with a shrug.

"And Harry," Channing said.

"Harry? Who's Harry?" Janice asked Lori as Channing went to go play with whatever Tylor was playing with as was his habit.

"I have no idea," Lori said. "But all the way home Channing was talking about Harry."

"Your sister swore she didn't have a boyfriend," Janice said.

"Channing's three, Mom. He also said something about a talking cat. Tara said she took them fishing. Who knows? He could have named a fish. I can only understand about one in ten words he says."

Tara had hoped to stay at the farm longer, but her mother needed her help with the clients, and Jerri was bound and determined to kill that evil goat. So Tara had gone to her mother's on Monday shortly after Jerri returned from the goat pen doing the dance that she said she'd do if Fred died. Apparently Jerri did a happy dance if someone she didn't like died or she killed something evil.

When Tara got to her mother's house she realized she really did do more for her mother's business than she thought because everything was a mess. Janice was mostly out of it and forgetting not just unimportant appointments but major commitments.

For the next three weeks Tara worked on helping her mother get caught up. If she could lose the camera crew early enough she went to the farm. If she couldn't she went to the beach house. Sometimes Jerri would meet her there really late after the camera crew was gone, and then Lori would call way too early to warn her the camera crew was coming. Jerri would have to run out and right back home again with about three hours sleep.

Three weeks seemed more like three years.

She didn't really know why Lori kept warning her Tara was just glad that she did. It was pretty obvious that the crew was sure she was hooking up with someone and was trying to catch her which she almost wished they would and just have it all over with.

Jerri had finally finished her book but had missed the deadline which she insisted was no big deal. They were mostly handling everything pretty well, still there were times when they had to admit the running around was killing them and they just needed sleep. There had been several days, and even a couple together, when they hadn't seen each other at all. Tara had stayed at the beach house alone, and Jerri had stayed at home. Saying good night on the phone wasn't the same at all.

And now she was doing it for the second night in a row. "Mom has an early call with a client in the morning, so there is just no way I can get up there, and the camera crew just left. As much as I want her to get someone else to do my job and just bail, now wouldn't be a good time. I have to go to this thing with mother tomorrow night. I have no idea what time I'll get out of there, so I may not be able to see you tomorrow either and... I really need to see you. I miss you and I realize it's only been two days..."

"It seems longer. I miss you, too. Turns out I have a party I have to go to in the city tomorrow night. Tate is already watching the farm, so I'll just go from the party straight to the beach house and meet you there."

"They may follow me; they've been tailing me pretty hard," Tara said with mounting frustration.

"I'll park in the garage. If they follow you, park in front of the garage door and walk in the front door yelling something like, 'I don't know why you dumb fucks have to follow me.' I'll hide in the den and read a book till they leave."

"I feel like this is worse for you, Jerry. Like you're having to leave everything you care about..."

"*You're* what I care about most, and this is only for a little while. We're going to have a life time together; this is all going to be over in a few months."

"I'm worried; you're getting so little sleep."

"Because you are getting so much? Tell you what, next time you get up here just stay a few days."

"You know what? I've got most of mother's crap sorted out. I could do most of it with a phone and a computer anyway, so that's exactly what we're going to do."

She had to make herself get off the phone and then she had to make herself go to bed because she didn't want to. Part of her wanted to make the trip to Jerri's, but she knew that was silly. She'd get there just in time to go to bed then have to get up at the butt crack of dawn to get to her mother's in time. Tomorrow was going to be a long day. If she was really going to see Jerri tomorrow night it didn't really make sense. If she went to bed she might actually fall asleep in the next hour and get some real rest. Lying there she really wished now that she hadn't had Jerri get the huge bed. Turned out they just didn't need that much room for sex. She was sleeping in it alone too many nights and the size of it just made her feel lonelier.

Her phone rang and when she looked it was Georgia. She checked the time. Nine right on the nose. Georgia had called her every night at nine since her dad had broken her news. Why? Because her dad had her call every night at nine the first year she was in college. Tara didn't answer; she just let it go to voice mail knowing the message would be for her to please call. Tara just wasn't ready yet, and how did she explain to Georgia that reminding her of something she and her dad had shared wasn't helping her accept his transition? It was just reminding her that all of that had been sort of a lie.

Her dad had done half a dozen appearances and given wonderful speeches, every single one of them written by Jerri. Though Jerri was hardly speaking to Judy she told Tara she couldn't abandon her in the middle of this because if Georgia got this wrong a lot of people who weren't Georgia were going to pay for it. The transgendered community had always been an easy target for haters. Her dad could actually either bring enlightenment to the masses or make them think they were right to fear, even hate, transsexuals in the first place.

Tara had never actually lived alone and she was mostly living with Jerri now except for the few solo nights she was stuck at the beach house. The first night she'd stayed there by herself she had started to get a little scared and then she remembered she had a top-notch alarm system and neighbors so close that when the rain ran off her roof it ran onto theirs. If that wasn't enough, Jerri had given her a gun. Tara had already known how to use one because of course her father, the conservative, was a gun nut. Tara wondered how Georgia was accessorizing her daddy's extensive gun collection now.

When Jerri first suggested the gun Tara had started to protest that she didn't want it. She was more than a little shocked that Jerri was insisting she have it till she remembered Jerri's history. Jerri swore she wasn't afraid of anyone then quickly added with a grin, "Because I pack heat nearly anytime I leave the farm."

The gun was in a locked box on the night stand. Before Tara went to sleep she made sure her keyring was right on top of that. Alone and trying to sleep without Jerri her mind went all sorts of places she didn't want it to go until she finally went to sleep.

When her alarm went off she could already hear that the crew was in the house. That was so fucked up. She stretched and rubbed her eyes then just lay there a minute looking at the ceiling. *Those dumbasses. This time Lori didn't even have time to warn me because of course Lori won't be up for hours. Why are they here so early, and what have I done or said that makes them so sure I'm hooking up—which I am—but how do they know that? What makes the dumbasses think that not giving me any breathing room at all is the way to catch me? All they are really doing is frustrating the living hell out of me. They're lucky I didn't wake up grab my gun and shoot one of them... Hey, I wonder if I could shoot one of them by "accident." I bet then they'd think twice about running around with their cameras up my ass. How safe am I when the film crew has a key to our house and the security codes? This fucking sucks ass.*

She looked at her bedroom door and was glad to see that she had remembered to lock it. When her alarm went off again she sat up on the edge of the bed and yelled at the closed door, "What the hell are you dumb fucks after?"

"Tara it's me. I thought I'd pick you up," her mother said from outside her door.

She couldn't imagine why her mother would come to pick her up so early unless she was trying to catch her with someone, too, but Tara actually felt some better that the crew hadn't come alone and walked into her house before she was even awake.

By the time she got dressed and walked out of her room her mother had already made a pot of coffee. Janice was standing looking out the windows at the ocean sipping at a cup of the steaming liquid. The film crew had all run around knocking themselves and each other out to film Tara as she'd walked out of her room. She'd wondered why until she realized they were trying to see inside her bedroom. She sighed and opened the door wide.

"Knock yourselves out, assholes."

She got herself a cup of coffee and joined her mother at the window. There were storm clouds gathering just off the coast. Jerri had told her last night that it was supposed to rain. Until she'd spent serious time with Jerri she had never paid that much attention to the weather, but apparently when you farmed nothing was quite as interesting or as important as the weather. She grinned a little. Her mother looked up at her.

"The view is just spectacular. I'm liking this house more and more. You're right; it isn't that small." She turned to look at Tara and smiled. "I don't know who's more disappointed that he's not here, me or the crew."

"I told you I don't have a boyfriend."

"Are you ever going to get furniture?"

"I have furniture."

"This is a wonderful room. It might be nice if there were a place to sit," Janice said with a smile.

"Don't buy me furniture, Mom. We'll get furniture if and when we want."

"We?"

"Yes, me and the fucking film crew."

"Have you... Have you talked to your father yet, Tara?"

And here was the thing about having the cameras rolling. Did Janice come over there to get her just to do something different, or did she do it for the footage of catching Tara in bed with someone, or perhaps the shot of Janice gazing sadly out to sea? Did she ask Tara about her father because she really wanted to know or because the tie-in drama would increase the ratings for both shows? What was real?

In front of those things nothing is real.

"I haven't."

"Why not?"

"I'm just not ready to, Mom."

"He wants to talk to me. He... She... dammit I don't know what to call him."

"A friend of mine said I shouldn't worry about the pronouns I use till I've had time to process it. I'd say that goes double for you, Mom. It's a shock."

"I don't think I'm ready to see him yet either, Tara. Does that make me a terrible person?"

"If you're only having this conversation for the cameras then yes, but otherwise all it makes you is honest," Her mother gave her an odd look and Tara shrugged. "Sorry, Mom, but that's the way I feel right now. I'm so tired of them and all the half-truths and lies they bring to our life." She swung her arm around at the camera crew. "When my contract runs out I am not signing for another season. You can go on without me. I am done. I was going through one of the worst times in my life and there they were for every fucking minute. Now we have this whole thing with dad and that's entertainment? I'm doing something; they don't know what it is, so they are doing their damndest to catch me doing it as if I'm doing something criminal. I am just so done with all of it."

Tara fully expected her mother to blow a gasket or at least question her about the thing she was doing, but Janice just kept looking at the ocean and said, "If I don't just live like they aren't there I have no life at all."

Tara locked the door as they left the house. When she turned her mother was pulling a weed out of one of the flower beds that lined the walkway. Tara got a very clear picture in her mind of helping her mother with her flower garden. Her mother had loved plants. Tara hated to admit that she couldn't remember when Janice had quit gardening.

"Mom, why did you stop gardening?" Tara asked as they walked down the walkway towards her mother's car.

Janice shrugged. "I didn't have time and you girls weren't interested in doing it with me anymore, so I just stopped. Let's face it; it's easier to just pay someone to do it."

"But didn't you love it, Mom?"

She shrugged again. "I suppose, but when would I do it, Tara, and why would I?"

"You'd do it because you like to. You find the time to do the things you love to do, Mom. You don't just stop doing them because you can hire a guy. Maybe you should think about taking up gardening again."

"Yes, your father is a woman, I'm all alone and going through menopause—which by the way doesn't feel natural and just part of a woman's life cycle it feels like the beginning of death—and planting some flowers is going to fix everything." Janice didn't even sound angry.

"Nothing is going to fix everything all at once, Mom, but you have to start taking your life back a piece at a time."

"Is that what you're doing, Tara?"

"Yes, that's exactly what I'm doing."

The day had been busy, hectic even, but Tara would have had trouble telling anyone what they had actually done. To her it seemed like a whole lot of running around to accomplish next to nothing. On the homestead when they did something you always knew exactly what you'd done, why you'd done it, and you always felt good about having achieved something.

Now they all had to dress for some fund raiser they were supposed to attend. Hollywood Feeds the Homeless or something like that. Tara was too rushed and frazzled to remember. Most of her clothes were still at her mother's, but though she didn't think she had lost any weight, apparently she had. She had firmed up in places, too, because all of her clothes were way too loose—a problem that a few months ago would have made her ecstatic. Now it was just a huge pain in the ass because she hadn't been shopping—or missed it at all—in months, and nothing she had fit her right.

She went to her bedroom door and yelled down the hall, "How formal is this thing?"

"Evening wear but not formal," Irva yelled from her room.

"What color are you wearing?" Tara asked.

"Wear blue, Tara, you look best in blue," Lori answered.

"I'm wearing green," Irva said. "So yeah go with blue."

Janice smiled as she put her earrings on. She didn't know why but something about their father no longer being a man had caused her girls to band together in a way they rarely did, and they had stopped fighting. Which was good because Janice didn't think she could have handled them sniping at each other at this point. She got a twinge of nostalgia thinking about when they'd all been younger and more like real sisters than feuding costars fighting over who stepped on who's line.

As they all started to load into the limo to go, the girls laughing at each other's jokes and kidding each other instead of passive aggressive back biting, it felt just like old times till she realized she was going to the party without a man on her arm.

Chapter 14

Jerri went because it was hosted by Pat who she hadn't seen in years. She'd felt sort of bad when he had said as much when she called to ask him to do a favor for her, so she decided at the time that she wouldn't blow him off the next time he invited her to one of his things. Plus it was a charity she supported any way. There were a lot of kids homeless on the streets of Hollywood; the money raised at this event would go to build a safe shelter for some of those kids.

Pat was hosting the event at his huge ostentatious house. It was hard for Jerri not to dwell on the fact that Pat could just donate his house to the cause and house hundreds of homeless kids. The people who came in their limos dressed to the nines would donate huge amounts of cash and feel good about themselves as they pocketed the tax deductions. The truth was that if they drove normal cars, wore normal clothes, and paid the taxes they dodged there would probably be a hell of a lot less people on the street to begin with, and...

And I'm guessing this would be that thing I do that makes Judy accuse me of being super judgey... Stupid Judy!

She looked at the huge buffet table piled with thousands of dollars' worth of food and thought, *But seriously, you could feed a hundred homeless people for a month for what they paid for that food. Why not just call or e-mail us all and have us send money? I'd be more than happy to do that, and then I could just sit on my nice little off-the-grid homestead that probably cost less than Pat's pool and not judge people for doing the stupid-assed, rich, "look at me I'm so generous" thing... I should just enjoy it for what it is and visit with people I hardly ever get to see anymore. Then get the fuck out of here as soon as I can, go to the beach house and jump Tara's bones as soon as she gets there.*

Just thinking about seeing Tara later put everything else in perspective.

Tara walked in with her mother and her sisters, and all eyes were on them because they were of course the Darting girls. *Gee if, Dad was here there would be five of us "girls" now.*

Suddenly Tara knew just what Jerri meant when she had said she "felt" her because Tara swore she could feel Jerri. When she turned quickly around, she saw Jerri across the room. She was wearing jeans and a long-sleeve, dark-blue shirt exactly the same color as the dress she was wearing, and Jerri stood there looking at her and smiling. Jerri was talking to a fat, middle-aged, bald man who was wearing a chartreus jump suit and holding a tiny dog. Tara wanted to just go to her, but her mother took her elbow and started steering her in the opposite direction to meet someone Tara didn't care about meeting.

For the next half hour every time Tara tried to go talk to Jerri, one of her "friends" —whom she hadn't seen in "forever" —stopped her and wanted to either ask about her divorce, her father, Fred's coma or other stupid-assed shit that she didn't know if she had ever cared about and sure as hell didn't now.

I don't actually have any real friends, she realized with a little bit of shock and hurt. *They're all like co-stars. Not one of them would give me the time of day if it didn't get them camera time, and I find I haven't missed a single one of them. Not one. I like Emily the bread lady better. Why? Because she's real. When she smiles at me she feels it. She doesn't say things she doesn't mean or mean things she didn't say. And now I know what they mean when they say someone is authentic. I thought I knew before, but I really didn't. It means there is no pretense. It's why I fell in love with Jerri because with Jerri there is no pretense. She is always exactly who she is and she fell in love with me because I was so burned out from always playing a part that for the first time I was just me.*

She hadn't seen Jerri in days. She just wanted to go to Jerri and people kept getting in her way but she was handling it pretty well till Rhonda Heart showed up with her entourage. The bitch looked fantastic for *anyone,* not just someone "her age." Rhonda hadn't been there five minutes when she started to make a B-line for Jerri.

Tara probably would have handled it a lot cooler if someone didn't pick that moment to exclaim, "Pat! You throw the most amazing parties." When Tara remembered what had happened the last time Rhonda and Jerri were both at one of Pat's, "amazing" parties, Tara's jealousy suddenly had a will all its own. She headed straight for Jerri. When Irva and a half a dozen other people tried to stop her along the way Tara pretended not to notice. She just kept going till she was as close to running as she could get in heels.

"You really are super-fast." Jerri smiled at her. No doubt seeing the look on Tara's face she added in a whisper, "I didn't know you were going to be here. I sure as hell didn't know *she* was going to be here. But even if you weren't here I would *not* wind up in the closet with her. You look amazing. If I go into a closet with anyone tonight it will be you "

"I want to hold you, Jerri, to have you hold me," Tara said in a frustrated whisper. She turned to glare at Rhonda where she had stopped across the room and was talking to someone and occasionally turning to glare at Tara. "You look great, you smell so good, I have really missed you and... I hate the way she is looking at you."

"But I am not looking at her at all, Tara. Ever since I saw you all I've thought about is all the fun I'm going to have taking all those clothes off you. It will be like unwrapping a gift."

"I felt you, Jerri. I actually felt you," Tara whispered.

"Tara!" Lori called from across the room.

Tara sighed.

"I'm getting out of here as soon as I can. Meet me at the beach house... Leave the dress on. I want to take it off."

Tara nodded and went to where her rude sister was standing across the room with two glasses of wine. She was alone, so Tara had no idea why she had called her over.

"What?" Tara asked.

Lori handed her one of the glasses of wine. "If you don't want everyone..." Lori took a sip of her wine and then talked into her glass. "...to know what you're doing and with who, I suggest you might stop standing mostly on Jerri Blue looking at her with wanton lust in your eyes."

Tara looked at her in disbelief.

Lori moved the glass from her mouth and turned so that her face wasn't on camera. "What's that you always say, Tara? I'm not a dumbass; I just play one on TV. I was there. I remember when you crushed on girls. When you were obviously having some kind of hot fling and you just kept insisting you didn't have a boyfriend, I figured you had a girlfriend. Then Irva said she thought you had a girl crush on Jerri Blue."

"Irva knows, too?"

"No, Irva IS a huge dumbass. She'd have to quit looking in the mirror long enough to notice anyone but herself. I wasn't sure you were with Jerri till Channing just kept talking about Harry. Then a Tom and Jerry cartoon was on, and guess what Channing called the show? Tom and Harry."

"Are you... mad at me?"

"For what, Tara? Hell, our dad is a woman. You're a lesbian sort of doesn't even hit the radar. I can tell by the way she is even now looking at you... No, don't look at her, Tara. that she's crazy about you."

"You rock, Lori."

As Tara looked discreetly across the room she saw Rhonda once again making her way towards Jerri. Tara made a face and started to move.

Lori took her arm and said, "I don't think you have anything to worry about, but I'll cut Auntie Rhonda off at the pass."

It would have been funny if Tara wasn't so obviously distraught. Rhonda tried to come talk to her a half dozen times. Jerri kept narrowly escaping her company by finding somewhere else to be and someone else to talk to, but mostly because Tara just seemed to keep magically appearing every time Rhonda got remotely close to her.

Jerri was more than ready to go when Tara slid up behind her and said, "I'm pretty sure I can slip the camera crew by making a fake run to the can. Then I'll go get in your truck."

"It's parked near the middle on the right," Jerri said. Tara's breath on her neck was making Jerri hot, and she had to admit—if only to herself—that Tara's obvious jealousy was a complete turn on.

"Let's get the hell out of here away from all of it. Let's just get home, and when I get you home I'm going to fuck you rotten," Tara said.

Jerri nodded unable to speak her pulse racing.

"Let me get out and then you leave and meet me in the truck."

The first time Janice saw it she really thought it was just a coincidence. Jerri had helped Tara with her book, so it made sense that Tara wanted to go say hello. The fact that she cut Rhonda off to do so just seemed like something that was bound to happen because Rhonda had never been able to stay away from Jerri anytime they were in the same space.

But when Janice had gone to talk to Jerri, Jerri hadn't been able to look her in the eye. It seemed very unlike Jerri, but Janice thought it was for the same reason no one else could. No one knew any better than Janice did how to handle the fact that Gary was a woman, and talking to most people since Gary came out had been difficult both for Janice and for them. It made polite conversation anything but polite.

But that had all been wishful thinking. As the evening progressed it was clear that Jerri was avoiding Rhonda which was understandable, but it became increasingly obvious that Tara was doing everything in her power to keep Rhonda away from Jerri. Why would she do that? For the same reason Jerri couldn't look her in the eye.

Every time she saw them together Tara and Jerri's body language seemed intimate, she was sure of it. A hundred different things Janice hadn't really paid attention to suddenly started to make sense. Tara was disappearing, sometimes for days at a time, and when she came back she always looked super healthy, relaxed, and happy. Where did Jerri live? Off the grid on a fucking organic farm in the middle of a forest twenty miles from the nearest nothing. Then there was that other thing. Tara who had always been at least as self-centered as Janice's other daughters and who had never once used "we" or "us" or "our" when she was married to Fred, was suddenly slipping and using them all the time.

Even more unlike her sisters, Tara had never told her a bold-faced lie. She swore she didn't have a boyfriend, but it was obvious—even to the crew—that Tara was having really good sex. Tara's whole demeanor was different. And what did Janice know about Jerri Blue? *That Rhonda wouldn't have stayed with her as long as she did or keep chasing her now if she wasn't really good in bed because Rhonda can't stand most people longer than it takes for them to put their clothes back on.*

Janice watched with renewed interest as Rhonda headed for Jerri and then like magic there was Tara.

A few minutes later Rhonda came stomping over to Janice. "Janice, are you aware that Tara has been crotch blocking me all night?" she asked in an angry whisper.

"That's what it looks like to me," Janice said with a sigh.

"Is my Jerri banging your little girl, Janice?"

Janice was instantly pissed off at most likely the entire world. She was tired of everyone being able to pull the wool over her eyes and tired of looking stupid. "You know what, Rhonda? I'd like to be able to tell you one way or the other, but the truth is my life has been such a fucking mess I just don't know what the girls are doing anymore. But I'm about to find out."

Of course when she went looking for Tara she was nowhere to be found—and neither was Jerri Blue.

They met in the parking lot without being seen or picking up a tail, made their way to the pickup truck and were gone. Tara sighed with relief, looked across the cab at Jerri, and then they both cracked up laughing.

Tara took her phone and sent a text to her mom. "Had a headache. Took a cab home." Then she turned her phone off and threw it on the dash. *I do have a headache. Of course five minutes away from all that shit and I won't.*

"You know that was sort of fun. Like the Great Escape."

"What the fuck is wrong with your ex?" Tara said then, and stopped laughing. "Seriously, what the fuck is wrong with her?"

"I don't think even she knows," Jerri said with a sigh. "She's always been unhappy with everything. No matter what she does or has it's never enough. The minute she gets what she thought she wanted it immediately becomes the essence of all her misery, and yes that included me. I guarantee she knew you were going out of your way to keep her away from me and—because for all her other faults she isn't an idiot— she knows why."

"I don't care what that bitch knows as long as she leaves you alone. Lori knows about us." Tara told her how.

"So that's why Lori has been calling to warn you when the camera crew is coming."

"I had forgotten about that. You know what, Lori isn't just a better sister than I thought, she is a lot better friend than I gave her credit for." She looked across the cab at Jerri and grinned. "Did you notice we're wearing the same color?"

"I didn't." Jerri turned the wipers on high. It had been

raining off and on all day, but now it was really coming down. "I want to get home before the roads turn to soup."

Tara had noticed the dirt roads tended to do that when they got wet.

"I just want to get home and be alone with you." Tara put her hand on Jerri's upper thigh and started kneading the flesh there. "I want to make sure you forget all about Rhonda."

"Rhonda who?" Jerri laughed.

Tara let her hand slide further up Jerri's thigh.

"You do know you aren't helping me pay attention to the road, don't you sugar?"

The ride home was filled with Lori and Irva talking a mile a minute.

Janice looked at them each covertly in turn then at the camera crew. She was pretty sure Lori knew exactly what Tara was doing. Irva probably didn't, but she couldn't grill them in the car because the stinking crew was there. Janice kept texting Tara but there was no response which meant she just wasn't answering or more likely she had turned the phone off.

Tara's millions of Twitter followers were mostly talking to each other these days. Janice couldn't remember the last time Tara had engaged in social media, and she wouldn't if she was off the grid wrapped all around Jerri.

Janice looked at Lori covertly. She had caught Lori a week ago calling to warn her sister that the crew was heading to her house. When Janice questioned Lori she insisted she was just calling Tara to give her a heads up. That she had no idea what, if anything, Tara was doing. She had been lying. If Janice asked Lori if Tara was sleeping with Jerri Lori was just going to insist she knew nothing then immediately call and tell Tara that Janice was on to her.

The rain was pouring by the time they got home, and the camera crew left for the day. Janice really wanted to drive straight to Tara's beach house, but she knew she'd had too many drinks to be safe even if the rain wasn't coming down in sheets.

By the time she *didn't* wake up—because she would have had to be asleep to wake up—she had nearly talked herself out of the idea that Tara was having an affair with Jerri. Almost. She dressed quickly, hoping to be long gone before the crew got there for the day. It was still drizzling, but the roads weren't hazardous to drive on, so she went right to Tara's beach house.

She wished she could have been surprised when Tara wasn't there.

Jerri woke to the strangest sound—like whale song if the gentle giants were really pissed off. Tara was wrapped all around her, so she listened to see if the sound was real or something she had dreamt.

"Jerri Blue, you fucking horny piece of shit! Open this God-damned door right this minute!"

Tara woke up and their eyes met.

"Damn you, Jerri, you open this door or I swear I will call the police!"

"Shit!" Tara and Jerri said together.

Jerri jumped up and threw her robe on. She started for the door then stopped and looked back at Tara who was throwing on her own robe. "Your mom wouldn't shoot me, would she?"

"No." Jerri was halfway down the stairs when Tara ran past her explaining, "Maybe I'd better go first."

Jerri caught up with her near the bottom of the stairs.

"But if I answer the door I can say I have no idea what she's talking about," Jerri said.

"I swear I'm calling the police!" Janice yelled banging on the door again.

"What the hell for?" Jerri yelled back.

"I...I... I'll think of something!"

"I'm answering the door," Tara insisted. "She's here. She knows, and as much fun as it has been, I'm tired of sneaking around."

Jerri nodded and hung back as Tara opened the door.

Her mother took one look at her and started yelling at Jerri.

"I knew it! I knew she'd be here. And why did I know that? Because you have always fucked any woman who stood still long enough! How could you do this, Jerri? She's just a girl."

"I'm not a girl, Mother. For the love of God I'm a thirty-year-old divorcee." Tara looked at Jerri. Jerri looked guilty as if she really had done something wrong. Tara rolled her eyes at her and Jerri shrugged.

"I brought her up here so you could help her with her writing."

"And I did," Jerri defended.

"And yourself into her pants."

"Why is it my fault, Janice? Tara kept coming up here. I didn't beg her to. I didn't put a spell on her. She came up here for weeks and rubbed her nubile young body all over me begging for it. I didn't do anything till she as much as told me I was killing her. It took a lot of restraint on my part to wait as long as I did, and you know what you already know about me, Janice? I'm not a fucking saint."

"Thanks a lot for throwing me under the bus, honey," Tara said, looking at Jerri in disbelief.

Then to her mother. "It's true I had to nearly beg her."

She turned to Jerri again. "Though why I had to wait when you normally just gave it away I will never understand."

"Because she cares about you." Janice sighed, walked over, and flopped onto Jerri's recliner looking completely done in. "She obviously loves you, Tara."

"I do," Jerri said carefully, no doubt understanding that her mother was in a fragile state even though she certainly wasn't acting or sounding like it.

Janice caught Tara's eyes and held them. "And you love her, don't you? Probably from the very minute you saw her."

Tara nodded, suddenly finding a lump in her throat.

Janice had found exactly what she expected to find when she got to Jerri's house, but after the hollering and calling Jerri names Janice didn't really have a plan. What could she actually do about it? Tara really was a grown woman, and Jerri... If Jerri loved Tara there wasn't anything that was going to get rid of her. After all, this was the woman who had lived and put up with Rhonda Heart for years. If she loved Tara, nothing Janice could say or do was going to make Jerri back off.

Tara was looking at her with an expression Janice couldn't read for a second, and then with crushing guilt Janice realized what it was. Tara was afraid Janice was about to reject her, that she was going to judge her, and why did Tara think that? *Because she came to us when she was twelve and told us she had a crush on a girl and we told her she was wrong. She came to us again when she was thirteen and told us she thought she was a lesbian and we as much as forbid it. Then she started dating boys. We thought the whole gay thing was just a phase she had grown out of, but this is who she always was, and if I'm honest with myself I always knew. Jerri's not the experiment; the boys were the experiment. Tara is as much a lesbian as Jerri is, and she needs me to finally be alright with it… You are really pushing this accepting thing, God!*

Janice needed to calm down, but maybe this was it. Maybe this was that one thing that was too much. Her husband was a woman; maybe adding a gay daughter was the straw that broke the camel's back. She was exhausted and couldn't remember the last time she had really felt like she had any control of anything.

Jerri walked over, took Tara's hand then let it go and went in the kitchen.

"I don't see why you're blaming Jerri. I don't see why you have to blame *anyone*, Mom. There is nothing at all wrong with us being together so it's no one's 'fault'. We aren't trying to hurt anyone we just want to be together, to be left alone," Tara said in a voice barely above a whisper as she sat on the couch.

"We should have left *you* alone, Tara. We should have let you love who you wanted to love. My only excuse is that I wanted to protect you from the sort of crap gay people have to go through. But I guess the worst thing a lesbian has to go through is having parents who want to make her be something she isn't, and…. Oh my God that's the real reason you won't talk to your father."

"He wants us to embrace his differentness, but he didn't embrace mine. He hates Jerri, but he has no problem at all letting her write all his/her speeches."

"Well I knew there was no way Gary was writing his own speeches, but how in hell did he get Jerri to do it?"

"Dr. Judy Willis is Jerri's best friend. Jerri's helping Daddy mostly to keep him from blasting a huge whole into our community."

"You've been with Jerri longer than your father has been out?"

Tara nodded.

"And you already know he hates Jerri. So you're sure even if he could accept that you're gay he's going to freak out when he finds out the two of you are together. So you can't accept what he's done because you have already decided that he's going to judge you and that being the case you're going to judge him first?"

"Mostly... Though when you say it out loud like that it does seem petty." Tara forced a smile and shrugged.

"You know he mostly hated Jerri because she was a feminist and her politics so maybe now he's a she..."

"Georgia's politics haven't changed at all."

"I know she's your father, but he was always a fucking idiot... So much wrong with that sentence I don't even know where to start." Janice looked at Tara and shook her head. "Oh, honey, I'm so sorry for so many things. I didn't sleep at all last night, not because I was worried but because I was so mad that you were sneaking around behind my back. But why would you think you could tell me? Right now I'm mostly completely consumed with worrying about myself. Honestly I'm so mad at me... When did I completely lose myself, Tara?"

"When Gary stopped making the big bucks but you all still wanted to spend the big bucks," Jerri said. She walked in with two cups of coffee, handed one to Tara and the other to Janice. "When he wanted to sneak around wearing dresses and told you it was just his thing and didn't mean anything. Yet somewhere in the back of your mind you knew all along that what she has done is what he always wanted to do—and where did that put you? Your girls were growing up and didn't really need you except for money. You created Janice the persona to protect Janice the mother and wife whose life was blowing up around her." Then Jerri turned on her heel and went to the bathroom, closing the door behind her.

To the dumbfounded look on Janice's face Tara grinned and said, "That's what she does. Spout profound things and then walk away." She added loud enough she obviously wanted Jerri to hear it, "She never sits still. She is incapable of just relaxing."

Janice heard Jerri laugh then Tara looked at her. "Are you going to be alright with us, Mom?"

"I hope she gets all your make-up off her face. It looked ridiculous. By the way, dear, your makeup smeared all over your face doesn't look much better."

Tara was obviously waiting for an answer to her question.

Janice thought about it a minute. "Yes. Daddy is the one who doesn't like Jerri. I love Jerri. Not crazy about her sleeping with my little girl, but... Well the truth is that I know that she will always treat you right... Even when you don't deserve it." She went to take a sip and realized it wasn't coffee. "This is hot chocolate."

"I have coffee, so I assume she thinks what you really need right now is some sleep."

Janice sipped at it. "This is really good. Do you know how she made it?"

"You know what, Mom? You'll enjoy the food here more if you just don't ask any questions."

Chapter 15

"...*But most of the really* negative stuff all talks about how it's the fault of left-winged liberals. I think if I explained that my sex changed, not my politics, that I could win those people over."

"Talk to her, Judy, because I'm sick of talking to this tired-assed boy in a dress." All three-hundred gorgeous pounds of Selma Brown jumped out of her chair and stormed out of the room, making her the last of Judy's friends to bail on this conversation and leaving her alone with Georgia.

Her team was falling apart. Georgia was unfortunately just what Selma accused her of being; she was a boy in a dress. Georgia had the resources to do her reconstruction in a way that none of them had. Judy had brought this team together because none of them had it as easy as Georgia. They'd all had to work and risk to earn their womanhood. They'd all thought long and hard about which surgeries they did and did not need to be the women that they were. Judy was hoping their back stories and humanity would make Georgia see the light. The problem was that Georgia's pampered rich life left her with nothing in common with someone like Selma Brown who had paid for her transformation working in the sex trade. Georgia would be moved to tears one moment hearing how hard they had all fought for their right to be women, then turn right around and insist that they could have found other ways, worked a little harder, a little smarter.

Rich people never really understood hardship. Vast wealth was like magic. Georgia waved her magic wand of money around and *poof!* she was a woman expecting that she would be treated like a ciswoman and not knowing there was a difference.

"You're a conservative idiot!" One of the women yelled from the other room. It wasn't helpful; it was unfortunately true.

"That was very hurtful. I don't know why I have to watch the way I talk to them, but they can say whatever they like to me," Georgia whined. "I'm a woman, too..."

"No you're not!" Judy couldn't take it anymore. "And you certainly do *not* watch what you say to them. My best friend and my wife are barely speaking to me, I have put my entire community in jeopardy, and you just don't get it at all. You say you're like us, that you're a transgendered woman. It took weeks of work, but you finally got comfortable with saying you're the same as us. The problem is you aren't. You want us to embrace you as a sister, but you still act just like a man. If we say something you don't agree with you don't even hear us out; you talk over us. You have no idea at all what it's like to make the journey without the connections and the help that you've had. Jerri said the best thing to do with you is to take you to the middle of the south in a bad dress with no money where your right-winged political friends are everywhere, dump you there and see how you feel by the time you get back to civilization if you live that long."

"Jerri Blue is a brilliant writer, but she's a left-wing idiot."

"No, dumbass, you're the idiot, and I'm an idiot for thinking that you could ever be anything but a liability to our community. I thought you were finally embracing being a trans woman..."

"I have."

"No you haven't!" Judy couldn't remember the last time she was this mad, this much out of control, which of course just made her madder. "A transgendered woman does *not* support a conservative Republican agenda because there is no way to do that and be who we are. It just doesn't match."

"Now you sound like Jerri. Republicans don't want to persecute women..."

"They have never supported woman's issues, ever. Certainly they have never supported rights for our community. They have, in fact, tried to discriminate against us at every turn. I'm not making this shit up, Georgia. It's in the public record; look it up. Their fight to discriminate against trans people isn't their *hidden* agenda they *brag* about it. Look at who is writing, trying to vote in, leading the charge against our community—it's always a conservative Republican, always."

"So to be a woman I can't have my own opinion. Isn't that what the whole feminist movement has been about? Women having the right to have their own thoughts. You want me to never take initiative, to just roll over and play dead..."

"That's exactly what you want all of us to do. You want us to follow you blindly, to become Hitler youth, and you have no idea why we are so outraged. You have been living this life for ten minutes with more money than God and constant help from all of us. You've had the best surgeons money can buy to do your transformation and top-notch spas to heal in. You've got a team of security to stand between you and those that would do you harm. Hell, you've got an award-winning, bestselling author writing every word that leaves your ungrateful mouth. Yet you are arrogant and closed-minded enough to think that we made our own journeys hard. That it didn't have to be that way. You have judged each and every one of us as we told you our stories and decided it was all our fault that the road we traveled was so hard.

"You think you are brave because you have come out to the world on TV, but again, you have security. As much as you will deny it you missed having everyone looking at you. You missed the attention of the masses and now you have everything you've ever had and then some. Hell, you have your own show! And when did you come out, Georgia? When your fancy football career was already over, your kids were grown, and you were tired of being married. You decided to come out when you had nothing to lose. That's not brave; that's calculated.

"Women *listen* to other women when they talk. When we're all sitting talking, as long as it's all fun and games or all about you then you're great just one of the girls. But the minute we start to talk about the heavy stuff, the real stuff, the real problems our community faces at the hands of bigots, then you yell over us and try to put us in our place. You take over, and honey when you do that, you're all male. You want to hold court. You have to learn to be a transwoman. We're here trying to help you. I don't think you have any idea how painful the things you say are. Your political views aren't just ignorant for society as a whole, but they are damaging to our community, a community you have never had to live in before and aren't really living in now because you have butt loads of money. You want to yell over us and tell us we're wrong, but all of us—not *you* but us—have had to live through conservative Republican policies.

"You have no idea how much it hurts when you see signs go up in your neighbor's yards to pass laws to make sure you never get the rights you already don't have. To have strangers walk up to you on the street and tell you you're going to hell. You've never been spit on just because you were holding your partner's hand in public. You are not having the traditional

LBGTQ experience, and maybe that was my biggest mistake—thinking that you could ever help our cause when you have never had to suffer with things the way they are right now much less what they were five, ten, fifteen, twenty years ago. If your Republican buddies had always won, you can bet your twenty-thousand dollar ass that you would never be able to leave your house after a public announcement that you're a woman now. If the guy you helped put in office doesn't leave this country a smoldering hole and chase LBGTQ rights back into the Stone Age, it will be a small miracle. Frankly, Georgia, I don't want to believe you're this fucking stupid..."

"Now wait just a minute..."

"And there's your big man voice again, the one you say you wish you could lose so that you would sound more like you look and feel. Yet you use it every single time you feel like you might be losing an argument. You can't win this argument, jackass, because trans women do *not* support politicians that clearly don't think we should have the same rights as other people. What *we* think isn't the problem; your top one percent logic is the problem. Don't sit there and demand the world see you as a woman and then act like a man. This is your new life, the life you choose without considering how it affected anyone else, the life you said you wanted. It's not an easy road, not at all. You have to be all in or get the hell out."

"I know that. I'm suffering, too. My male friends want nothing to do with me, my son-in-law Todd couldn't even look at much less talk to me. Two of my daughters barely speak to me and one of them won't talk to me at all..."

"Have you heard nothing any of us have said? It's not all about you, Georgia. Have you even wondered once what this is like for them? They have lost their father, the father they know is gone. It can't always be about you." Judy took a deep breath and let it out. "Me, these other women, we have our own lives. We have put them on hold to help you through this, but it's clear that this is all about us giving and you taking."

"What you want me to give is my country to a bunch of bleeding-heart doves who want to steal from the rich and give to the poor..."

"You are wasting my time. I'm going to talk to the others and we're going. You need to decide what exactly it is that you want." Judy looked at the camera crew and shook her head. "This isn't just about us and this very uncomfortable conversation caught on camera. This is about all the other people in our community who are fighting for their right to be who they are. What you are doing is either going to help us or destroy us. I can't be part of bringing harm to my own community, and I won't be."

Judy stomped outside where the other women were all hanging out around the pool. They all started talking at once. Judy put up her hand and said, "I know."

They all got quiet. She took a deep breath and reached down to find her calm place. When she saw part of the camera crew had followed her she simply said, "Everyone into the van. That's about all any of us can take tonight."

They all beat her to the van. She got in the driver's seat and closed the door.

"What the hell are we going to do about that... thing?" Joey asked, flipping her long blond hair over her shoulder and hitting Selma in the face. "Sorry."

"Please child," Selma said. "That's not by far the worst thing that's happened to me today. Georgia stepped on my toe."

"I think Georgia managed to step on everyone's toes,' Betty said.

"Not just metaphorically." Selma laughed. "Bitch stepped right on my toe with her huge size twenty-seven feet."

Georgia did have huge feet, big feet for a man so huge feet for a woman. Judy remembered the four-hour conversation they'd all had with her to teach her what clothes, colors and styles to use to down-play her size. Georgia's huge feet were the answer! As Judy started the car and put it in gear she knew just exactly what to do to Ms. Georgia to make her see the light.

"We have to do what Jerri said."

"What! We can't take Georgia Darting and dump her in the south in a bad dress," Selma exclaimed.

"We don't have to. All we have to do is abandon her. Let her try to do it without us, without our help, our support or our knowledge. The problem is we've made it way too easy for her. She no doubt thinks she doesn't really need us. Let her learn how wrong she is."

Tara had shown her to a bedroom. She opened a drawer

with dozens of pairs of pajamas in it. Janice had assured her that there was just no way she could go to sleep, but Tara insisted so she put on the pajamas Tara handed her and promised to give it a try. Janice had crawled into bed, made herself comfortable, and didn't wake up till the sun was starting to go down outside and Tara came to get her telling her that dinner was ready.

"I texted Lori and told her you were with us," Tara said.

"So Lori does know about you and Jerri," Janice said, working at sitting up.

Tara nodded.

"You could tell her but you couldn't tell me?"

"I didn't tell her. She guessed," Tara said with a smile.

"And now I just feel stupid," Janice mumbled.

"You've had so much on your plate, Mom."

"And that's why you're sneaking around with Jerri? Not because you care who knows but because you didn't want to add any stress for me?"

"In part." Tara handed Janice her clothes. "I'm not ashamed of what I am, not anymore, and I don't want to add any stress for you. But mostly I don't want our relationship beat on by the press. I'm not sleeping with just any woman, Mom. I'm in a relationship with Jerri Blue. No one is going to think the talented, iconic, Jerri Blue and the least-interesting of the Darting girls is a good match. They're all going to talk shit."

Janice nodded; she understood that. Because of the circles she ran in she took meeting the rich and famous for granted because after all she was one. She forgot Jerri Blue was sort of a huge deal. *If I admit my daughter is gay—and I think I have to—then Jerri's a hell of a catch.* She started to get dressed. When Janice thought about it for more than ten seconds, Tara and Jerri together made a certain amount of sense. Jerri had already found what Tara was looking for—peace of mind, solace, a place away from all the noise.

"She's really good in bed, isn't she?"

"Jesus Christ, Mom!"

"Well is she?"

"Yes, Mom she's excellent in bed," Tara said, looking some embarrassed but with a grin you couldn't have sanded off her face.

Janice found that she was really happy for her daughter, but that it only made her own loneliness more tangible. No one thought she was allowed to feel lonely; after all there was never a time when she was alone. Janice missed having someone around who really knew her. She and Gary hadn't been perfect—certainly their marriage had slowly eroded into nothing—but they mostly understood each other. He had been a warm body in bed.

"Your father was a good lover which makes sense. They say only a woman knows what a woman really wants."

"Crap, Mom! I'm pretty sure that wasn't on my need-to-know list."

Janice shrugged and got dressed. "I have to tell you that was the best I've slept in months. You don't just love *her* do you? You love this place, too."

"I loved this place when it was nothing but a description I read in a book. But mostly I like who I am when I'm here. I'm more thoughtful, more connected, more sure of my place in the world. I seem to know exactly who I am and I don't question myself."

"And that's why you thought I should start gardening again because then I could feel more thoughtful and connected?" Janice smiled and shook her head. "Trying to have it all I lost everything that was important. I put us on TV till we have no private life, and..."

"Don't blame yourself, Mom. We were all into it. None of us said hell no we don't want to do that. Lori and Todd eat the attention, and Irva sure as hell does. Dad—for all the bitching he's done about it—obviously likes being on TV, and you know what I loved it for a long time. The celebrity, the getting into any club without waiting in line, signing autographs, it was a huge rush. Boxes of clothes sent from all the greatest designers, walking the red carpet, going on talk shows, the whole shebang. I can't say I really would have been able to fully appreciate this place or Jerri if I hadn't done all that. I'm just so tired of it now. It was fun but now I'm done with it and ready to move on."

Janice nodded realizing that more than just Jerri's body fluids were rubbing off on Tara. Jerri thought in circles, so she easily made sense of things that made no sense. She had the unique ability to prove that your biggest mistake was in fact the hinge point to your greatest accomplishment. It was the reason universities paid top dollar to have her speak. The reason her books which touched on very controversial subjects—were read by nearly everyone who read.

So Tara was at the lowest, most confused moment in her life and Jerri talked her right out of her funk. Of course Jerri didn't have to sleep with my daughter to help her. Except I know Tara. I have no problem at all believing that once Tara had it in her mind to have Jerri she wasn't going to quit until she did. Jerri's right; I know she's no saint, though she is damn close. The fact she didn't kill Rhonda proves that.

"So I'm curious, what made you decide you just had to have Jerri?" Janice quickly added, "And if you'll remember I asked you the same thing about Fred though I guess the whole, he's really, really clean, answer you gave me should have been my first clue that you weren't really into him."

That was a good question, one Tara hadn't really thought about, but she found she didn't need to. She knew the exact moment without giving it more than a minute's thought. She smiled and told her mother, "The second time I saw her I was an even bigger mess than I was when you first brought me here. I climbed out my window and drove straight here with no plan at all. She didn't ask for any explanation, she just made me a part of her day. I planted potatoes... That's what happened to my nails. The new potatoes we're eating tonight in fact. She sat with me and went through my book page-by-page, telling me exactly what I'd done wrong and never once did she make me feel like an idiot. She is amazing yet not once did she say or do anything that made me feel like she was judging me and finding me wanting. She treated me like an equal. I felt good for the first time in months and I didn't want to go home at all. It was really late; she knew I didn't want to go, but she made it her idea that I stay. She made me comfortable. She took care of me. She didn't even try to hit on me, just let me be here. I felt like my heart just opened up and she filled it completely. Jerri made me feel good about being me. I had to have her because from then on I only felt like me when I was with her."

"That's amazing. I'm really happy for you, Tara."

"Come on chicks, dinner's getting cold!" Jerri yelled up the stairs.

"So why do you call it evil goat chili?" Janice asked.

Jerri started to answer her, but Tara quickly said, "I told

you, Mom, don't ask; just eat it."

Janice laughed a real laugh, not a made-for-prime-time laugh, and she didn't have to ask why Tara didn't want to leave here. Janice felt more at ease than she had in years. "Whatever it is, it's very good, and..." She looked at Jerri. "Tara is probably right that I don't want to know what it is. So Jerri..."

"Oh here it comes," Jerri said, throwing up her hands.

Janice smiled because Jerri really did know her well. "...is Tara like the anti-Rhonda? I mean unless I'm missing a couple in the middle, the last woman you loved was Rhonda Heart, and Tara and Rhonda are opposite ends of the spectrum."

"For the love of God, Mom," Tara said. Then she grumbled, "There were way more than a couple in the middle."

"Not that I loved," Jerri said to Tara with an unashamed smile.

She turned to Janice. "I was damaged and broken when I was with Rhonda. Living with her bipolar, mood-swinging ass I was either being treated like a queen or like crap. I was willing to put up with the crap because I thought I deserved that. When she treated me good she treated me really good and that made me feel worthy in a way I never had before. While I still have head problems and probably always will, I think I deserve someone as amazing and decent as Tara. Spiritually Tara is perfect for me, and if the truth be told when it comes to looks Tara is exactly what I like. I settled for what I could get instead of what I wanted my whole life till Rhonda kicked me out..."

"And almost immediately cried and begged you to come back," Janice reminded.

"And still chases you around years later," Tara mumbled.

"Yes, well once I got up here I was never going to settle again. It's why I haven't been serious about anyone since then till now. Tara adds to my life, she doesn't take anything away." Now Jerri wasn't having any trouble at all looking Janice in the eyes. "I never doubt that she loves me, and I love her, so you can't have her back."

When Janice stole a look at her daughter, Tara was near glowing. Janice spoke the truth. "Even if I could pry her away from you I wouldn't try. She is obviously happy. I haven't been happy or even content in so long I can't remember what it felt like."

The phone rang and Jerri went in the living room to answer it.

"What's with the five hundred year old cord phone?" Janice asked her daughter.

Tara shrugged. "The phone line was the only way Jerri could get internet access or I doubt she'd have it at all. Cell phones get half-assed reception up here at best. A cordless has to be plugged in all the time and that uses power that we can't spare because we run off a battery bank. Frankly I love the old phones because when you hang up when you're pissed off at someone it's really rewarding."

Janice nodded her head. She remembered that. "So... You're super jealous."

"I'm not."

Janice laughed. "You most certainly are. How do you think I figured it out? I spent all night last night watching you nearly killing yourself to get between Rhonda and Jerri. Every time Rhonda even looked like she was moving towards Jerri you all but ran to get between them. Rhonda knew exactly what you were doing."

Tara sighed. "That's what Jerri said. But Mom... What the hell is wrong with Rhonda that every time she's even partly single she has to chase after Jerri?"

"Jerri is really good in bed," Janice reminded, and laughed at the look on Tara's face. "Calm down. I know Jerri. Jerri loves you. She's an absolute slut when she's single, but she doesn't cheat."

"I know but... Well not every woman's lover has Rhonda Heart for an ex. It's a little intimidating."

"Did you not hear what Jerri just said?"

Tara smiled. "I did."

"Rhonda was as happy as she's ever been when she was with Jerri. That's why she chases after her every chance she gets. Jerri was miserable with Rhonda. Do you really think Jerri wants any part of her old life?"

"I do not."

From the other room Jerri boomed, "If you're out, I'm out. Dammit, Judy, why do you get to bail and I can't? Fuck'em!"

To the confused look on Janice's face Tara supplied, "Must be something to do with Daddy. Have you seen him since..."

"Only on TV." Janice went back to eating. She didn't want to think about her ex at all. She still had nowhere to put the hurt and abandonment she felt not to mention the humiliation.

Jerri came back a few minutes later mumbling things that weren't coherent and sat down to finish eating.

"Well?" Tara asked.

The phone rang again and Jerri got up. "Is it too much to ask that I be left alone to eat in peace?" She stomped into the living room and answered the phone with a, "What!" so loud it made Janice jump.

Tara sighed. "Something tells me the stump is going to get tossed around tonight."

"Quit crying. For the love of God, maybe you should cut back on your hormones," Jerri said to a wailing Georgia. She cringed a little because of course "for the love of God," was something she'd picked up since she had been living with Georgia's daughter.

"They just *left* me. I have to dress and I need a speech, Jerri. I'm addressing transgendered youth and I don't know what to say. It's in less than two hours. Judy said I'd have to talk to you myself. That she's done with me."

"And how long did it take you to actually pick up the fucking phone and call me, Georgia, since we both know you have nothing but total disdain for me and all I stand for?"

"I don't have disdain for you, Jerri, I just hate your politics and the way you're so self-righteous about... Well everything."

"Geez, that's the same way I feel about you." Jerri took a deep breath, let it out, and said to the still-sobbing woman on the other end of the phone, "And some people would say we have nothing in common." She got a laugh out of Georgia.

"Can you help a girl out, Jerri?"

"I can try, but you're sort of asking me to pull a rabbit right out of my ass. About how long do they expect you to speak?"

"Only about ten minutes."

"Ten minutes isn't an *only*, Georgia. Ten minutes equals ten pages, which is about five-thousand words."

"And I'll need answers for their questions."

"I'm going to have to use pieces of stuff I already wrote. As for the answers, get them off your other speeches."

"I owe you, Jerri."

"I'll take your first born."

"What?"

"Nothing. I'll get to work on the speech. You find your

answers, and for the love of God..." *Dammit I did it again.* "...*memorize* them." She hung up and started upstairs mumbling. "Don't even have time to finish my damn dinner."

"What's going on?" Tara asked from the bottom of the stairs.

"Well they didn't dump her in the south in a bad dress, but they did the next best thing. Judy and the whole team walked out on Georgia. They think she needs some tough love, but of course Judy called to tell me that if Georgia called I should write her speech for her because we still don't want her stupidity to blast a crater in the trans community. I figured your dad wouldn't call, but he did. So now I have about ten minutes to write her a speech."

"You want me to bring your plate to you?"

"Yes if you could please."

Tara walked up the steps to meet her and kissed her gently on the lips.

"What's that for?"

"Just because you're wonderful and I love you." She turned and walked back down the stairs.

Jerri watched her till she was gone. A second before that Jerri had been wondering whether she should write the speech or throw her stump around, but now she no longer felt agitated at all. "Good thing I'm not writing a book right now. It would just be all sweetness, light and love. The conflict would be not being able to share a toothbrush or some such shit. That girl may have ruined me," Jerri mumbled and went upstairs to save Georgia's ass.

She pulled up the file of past speeches that she usually used just to keep each speech from sounding the same. Then she started mining them for ten minutes worth of content. Tara set her plate and her wine down on her desk beside her, kissed her on the cheek, then left without saying a word.

"She's fucking perfect."

"So what was all that?" her mother asked as she walked back in the kitchen.

"Daddy pissed off all the transwomen who were helping her and they walked off, but they still want Jerri to write the speeches. The second call was Dad begging for Jerri's help. So now she has to write a speech for Georgia in only a few minutes, and... He/she is a fucking mess that none of us asked for." Tara sighed. "You know what I did the other day when I was stuck at the beach house alone? I was flipping through the channels and they were showing reruns of our show. Dad was just Dad, and he just seems like a normal guy, not like a woman trapped in a man's body just a normal mostly-happy guy."

"And that was all just for the show. Even before we were on TV he was putting on a show. He got married and had a family for the same reason you married Fred, to hide in plain sight. He was always just playing a part. He was no more happy being a man than you were being straight. Jerri was right. When Gary was dressing up like a woman and sneaking out to go into public..."

"What?" Tara was more than a little shocked. "How did he get past the cameras?"

"He would go to a hotel, rent a room in an assumed name, dress up and go out as a woman. And, yes, he's been doing it most of our married life. Even when he was doing it more and more, when he kept his eyebrows plucked and his body waxed, I told myself it was just a strange fetish at most. But in the back of my mind I knew that what he really wanted—probably always had—was to be a woman. It wasn't so much that I didn't know as that I didn't *want* to know. It's a lot to swallow, and..." There was a catch in her mother's throat that Janice denied as she cleared it and went on. "...I miss him, even bitchy effeminate-face him. When he told me that he was going to have the surgery I still thought we'd be together. I don't know why I thought that or how I thought that was ever going to work, but I just did. I was more shocked that he wanted a divorce than that he wanted a sex change."

"I'm so sorry, Mom." Tara walked over bent down and hugged her. "I've been so worried about my own stuff that I haven't really been there for you."

"And I've been so worried about mine that I haven't been there for you or anyone else." Her mother patted her back which was Janice's way of saying she wasn't comfortable with the closeness and it should end.

Tara released her and started to clear the table and put the food away. It was a minute or two before she realized her mother hadn't said anything. She turned and Janice was just watching her.

"What?" Tara asked with a nervous smile.

"You've become very domestic," her mother said. Tara couldn't tell from her expression or her tone whether she thought this was a good or bad thing.

"I take care of my own needs here. We take care of each other, the land, the plants, the animals. It's one of the things I love about being here. I don't snap my fingers and someone puts a glass of wine in my hand. I know now that wine starts with planting a seed, growing a vine, fertilizing, nurturing, and tying it to a trellis sometimes for years before you ever harvest the fruit. Then it's stealing honey from the beehives, mixing the ingredients with yeast, letting it ferment, clear, and then bottling it. It's a whole process. Out there you wave money around and people give you stuff that is genetically-modified, grown and sprayed with chemical crap..."

"Oh come on honey you know as well as I do that if you wave enough money around you can get organically-grown crap," Janice said with a grin.

"But you still aren't a part of sustaining yourself, of fulfilling your own basic needs as a human." Tara started doing the dishes.

Her mother got up and started to help her and Tara looked down at her.

"Don't look so shocked. I haven't completely forgotten how to run a kitchen."

They wound up having a conversation about gardening that turned into a conversation about Lori's parenting skills—or lack thereof—as they cleaned the kitchen. Tara couldn't remember the last time she had felt that close to her mother.

They had moved to the living room with more wine.

"...you should have seen Jerri fishing with the boys and those stinking barn cats. The whole time she's just carrying on this whole conversation with all of them. It was too cute."

"So are you and Jerri going to adopt some little brown babies?"

"For the love of God, Mom," Tara said. "First off, that's a little racist."

"No it's not. That's what lesbians do; they adopt underprivileged third-world children."

"And that is... Just a horrible stereotype, Mom."

Janice shrugged. "I don't see why. I think it's good to give needy children a good, solid home. So can I expect chocolate grandbabies?"

"Jerri and I don't want kids, Mom."

"But... You love kids."

"And so does Jerri, but we don't want to raise any."

Her mom looked thoughtful like maybe she was going to start a whole new Battle of the Baby, but then she said, "You know what it's probably for the best. The whole I have two mothers and two grandmothers may be a little much for a third-world orphan to handle. Besides, you'll most likely wind up mostly raising Channing and Tylor. Can we watch TV?"

"You just can't stand the quiet," Tara said, shaking her head. She threw the remote at her mother who caught it and turned the TV on in one move.

"I can't stand having no idea what's going on in the outside world." She found CNN and gasped in mock horror. "You mean there is cable in the middle of the utopian forest."

"No there isn't. Jerri has a dish."

"Jerri Blue the wine-making, organic-garden growing, goat-butchering, solar-power using hippie watches enough TV that she needs a dish?"

Tara laughed. "No, she watches next to no TV, but she's rich so she got a dish because when she does watch TV she wants to be able to watch something she actually wants to watch. She told me she never watches reality TV, but that's a lie. If it has anything at all to do with Alaska she watches it. She insists that what she watches is educational TV, but her favorite show follows a bunch of Alaskan homesteaders around. It's mostly a frontier version of our show."

"No because they build things and raise their own food," Jerri said as she came downstairs and went into the bathroom.

"It is pretty informative," Tara admitted. She could hear Jerri grumbling and knew it had nothing to do with TV. "Daddy gets on her last nerve. She once spent a huge block of time writing him a speech that started, 'I want to apologize to the gay, lesbian, bisexual, and transgender community. You have enough problems without an idiot like me deciding to join your ranks'."

Her mother laughed.

"It got worse but funnier after that. I'll see if I can find it and send you a copy."

The commercial ended and the announcer said, "This just in; Fred Summers has just been declared dead. His family took him off life support this morning. It looked for a while like he was going to breathe on his own, but he died suddenly just minutes ago."

The bathroom door opened and Tara turned just in time to see Jerri walk out and start doing her dance.

Tara was only momentarily shocked.

Her mother looked from the TV to Jerri and finally to Tara, so Tara shrugged and explained, "That's the dance she does when something she doesn't like dies."

"I believe in showing how you really feel," Jerri said.

Janice looked from her daughter's dancing girl-friend back to the screen and listened.

"Fred Summers had been married to Tara Darting." Because of course until he married Tara the only people who had any idea who he was were football fans. "They divorced several months ago apparently because of Fred's extramarital affairs and drug use. His drug use escalated after the two divorced and he overdosed in March, left treatment early and immediately started drinking and doing drugs again. His next overdose did major brain damage that he wasn't able to recover from. He has been in a coma for weeks and his family came to the difficult decision to remove him from life support systems this morning after being told he was brain dead. Attempts to reach Tara Darting for comment have been unsuccessful. We do have Georgia Darting on the phone…"

"Oh for the love of God!" Jerri said. She stomped upstairs saying, "Dammit all! I did it again."

Tara listened as her dad's voice said, "Fred was a very troubled young man. He had a really good thing but he tossed that out to do what he wanted to do. He was a talented athlete and it is a crying shame that he couldn't get his act together. His family are good people, and my heart goes out to them."

"Do you know where Tara is? How she feels?"

"Tara has been having problems of her own; a divorce isn't easy for anyone. I should know. I know that Tara wished only the best for Fred and that her thoughts are with his family now."

"See, Tara? Daddy's good for something."

"Yeah lying. I don't care that Fred's dead."

"And obviously it makes Jerri happy." Janice couldn't pretend that she didn't know why. She knew Jerri's history. If Tara had told Jerri what she'd told Janice it was no wonder Jerri hated Fred. "I suppose I better get my ass home."

"Why? I'm not leaving here. He won't be any less dead in the morning. Stay and get a good night's sleep, eat another good meal, and you can leave in the morning if you think it's necessary."

"You know I really think I need to go home, but there is no part of me that wants to do that. You think I could get another cup of that hot chocolate?"

"So what's in the hot chocolate?" Tara wanted to know, wondering if Jerri had used some medicinal sleeping herb on her mother.

"Organic chocolate, goat's milk, honey and fresh-crushed chocolate mint." Jerri wrapped her arms around Tara and Tara pressed her back against Jerri's front. "So are you upset?"

"I can go without sex for one night I suppose."

Jerri laughed. "I was talking about Fred, but I guess that answered my question."

"I'm a lot more upset about not getting any than I am about Fred being dead," Tara said honestly. "I guess I don't wish death on anyone, but I didn't. He did it to himself, and I'd have to pretend that I care because I just don't. It's sad for his family. I feel bad for them, except let's face it his death means he isn't their problem anymore, either. I was kind of surprised my dad had my back."

"I wasn't. She loves you, Tara. I never got along with Gary, and he couldn't stand me, but I never thought he was a crappy Dad. He wasn't was he?"

"No, except for wanting me to be straight—and I guess most parents do that—he was a pretty good Dad. I can't blame my parents for my lack of backbone."

"Just like you were in a state of flux so are they, your mom and your dad. They have to make changes. Some they want to make and some they don't. I have to say I felt a lot less pissed off about having to write that last minute speech when I heard her trying to make it sound like you actually gave a shit about your ex to save you from the negative twist of public opinion."

"Don't be mad, Jerri but I've thought about it all day and my main problem with my dad is that I don't like that my dad is a woman."

"Why would I be mad, honey?"

"Because you get the transgendered thing and I thought I did until it was my dad and now I don't get it at all. If I'm honest it makes me feel like a bit of a freak."

"Why would anything your parents do make you a freak? There is nothing at all wrong with you. Let me tell you a secret. When my best friend Jason told me he wanted to be a woman, my first reaction was to call bullshit. He was my buddy; we met framing houses. He was a man's man. We did guy stuff together. He went to college to be a shrink. I was with Rhonda and running all over the world with her and my writing, but we stayed tight. When Jason told me he wanted to be a woman I had to work to be cool about it. I must have asked Judy a thousand times if she was sure, even as I held her hand through her many surgeries. It took me months to switch pronouns, and the truth is sometimes when we're doing something like we used to do and I'm caught up in the moment I will slip and call her Jason.

"It's what they want to do, what they need to do, but it's not easy for us. I got used to the new reality pretty quick, but Judy isn't my dad. It's a process to accept that a person is a different sex than what biology assigned them. It's a process for the transgendered person, and it's a process for everyone who knew them pre-surgery."

"Why did you sleep with Judy?" Tara asked, because of course she'd wanted to know ever since she found out.

"Crap." Jerri hissed. "I knew this was coming."

"Well?"

Jerri sighed, and Tara felt the air against the back of her head and got a little warm in spite of the topic of conversation.

"So Judy did all the hormone therapy, had all the surgeries, top and bottom. She changed all her legal papers. She knew how to use clothes and makeup to their best benefit. Jason was gone; Judy was born. Rhonda and I had broken up a few months earlier, and I was already living here on the land in a teepee which I still have. Judy came over and we were talking. I had this bottle of raspberry wine that Garret had made. It was, by the way, amazing stuff. We were both pretty depressed and neither of us are really big drinkers, so we were more than a little buzzed. Not drunk, but that kind of buzzed where you say things you don't have the balls to say sober.

Judy gets to talking and… Christ, Tara, I can't believe you are making me do this. You aren't going to tell anyone what I say, are you?"

"Of course not."

"You could say you don't really care to know."

"But that would be a lie."

"Judy gets a little maudlin. Says that after all she's done she still doesn't really feel like a woman. It turns out she'd been hitting every gay club she could find trying to pick up anything that breathed and hadn't managed to even spark interest in anyone of either sex. She tells me she's not going to really feel like a woman until she is made love to as a woman. I told her that I wasn't a man but I was pretty butch and it might be fun to make love with a transwoman. So I did, and it was, and Judy finally felt all woman. She also decided she was a lesbian. For some reason having slept with me, the one-time live-in lover of Rhonda Heart just made her super confident. As we all know nothing is quite as sexy as confidence. Within six months she had hooked up with Cyndy—who is all lesbian and has never seen Judy as anything but female—and they've been together ever since."

"You are a really good friend," Tara said. She grabbed Jerri's hand and laced their fingers together. "Mother said she is going to use Fred's death as a reason to pull the crew's key to the beach house. She's also going to tell them it's off limits. She has certain contractual obligations with the network, but she wields a lot of power as producer. At the end of the day the crew works for her, which is why we're all so pissed that one of them calls the press every time one of us farts. If she finds out who's doing it, they will not only be fired but she'll make sure they never work again. Frankly, I think it's the skinny camera guy because he always looks past but never at us."

"How long can you stay before you have to go back?" Jerri asked. It was clear from her tone that she didn't want Tara to go any more than Tara wanted to.

"A couple of days, but we'll be safe at the beach house at least for now."

Jerri's hold on her tightened. "I sort of enjoy it there. I've always loved the ocean. Being there with you, especially if I don't have to get up at the butt crack of dawn pulling my pants on as I run for the truck, will be great."

"Now my mother and Lori know... I don't really care who else knows about us, but..."

"Right after Fred died would be sort of crappy timing."

"Yes." Tara grinned then said, "I'm going to need you to

write me a statement for the press so that I don't sound like a heartless bitch."

"You're a writer; you can come up with something brilliant," Jerri said with a laugh.

"Come on. You write Daddy's shit for him."

"Yes well first off I couldn't write shit if I tried. Second, your dad can barely read much less write. And third, you aren't likely to say something so insensitive it would cause a riot. Just remember that the shithead had friends and family. Think about their feelings and you'll say the right thing. You don't have to hold him up as a martyr for any cause or make him into an angel, just say as little as you can about it, remember the living and piss on the dead."

Chapter 16

Georgia looked into the mirror. Her face was a complete mess. She looked back at the phone; Judy had just hung up on her again. Judy wanted her to change political parties or she and the others weren't going to help her anymore.

It was a lot to ask, but the more she checked out what Judy and the others had told her about, the more clear it became that her party was against her new community. The thing was she was a woman now, and she couldn't help being a woman born in a man's body; it was a medical condition. But she still thought being gay was a choice. Georgia didn't really feel like it was her place to fight for the rights of anyone but the transgender community. She looked at the newspaper article and cringed. Some Republican senator had just said he didn't want transgender women to use the women's restroom because they might molest his daughters. A Republican governor had just passed a "Freedom of Religion law" that allowed businesses in their state to discriminate against LBGT people.

If I'm honest, I know the Republicans will never support who I am now. And who am I now? Do I really believe that being gay is any more a choice than being trans? I think the new me knows that any form of discrimination is wrong, but .. Gary Darting wasn't such a bad guy. I feel like if I let myself be bullied into changing political parties I am neither honoring who I was nor being the person I want to be now.

Georgia looked at her face; she'd done her own make up. *I did my own make up for years and I thought I looked good, but those girls taught me stuff I never knew. Even though I'm trying to do just what they told me... I just don't look as good without their help. Besides, I miss them. I walked away from my family to follow the path I always wanted to walk and was too afraid to. Irva and Lori hardly speak to me; Tara won't talk to me at all. They would know just what to do with this mess,* she thought, looking at her face. She didn't look away the way she had done most of her life because she was seeing just what she wanted to see... except for the half-assed make up job.

God help me, was Jerri always right? Am I blind to how most people live because I've always had so much? Am I the one who doesn't understand how things really work? Are the people I vote for and support making things harder for the LBGT community? The working class? Are they really trashing the planet for personal gain? I know they are. Crap. Do I really believe the liberals would tax the job makers into oblivion and hand our country over to the terrorists? Yes! I'm sick of hearing people bitch about the top one percent. I'm the top one percent; my kind keep the world running. Why should I have to fork over my hard-earned money to some crack whore and her three illegitimate kids?

And just like that Georgia talked herself out of apologizing to Judy and the others. She was a transgendered woman and a Republican. What she needed to do was make her party see the light.

The garden was producing massive amounts of vegetables and fruit. Tara was eating like a pig and losing weight, so the trick to dieting was not to diet at all, but to eat actual, real food.

"It's all the added sugar and crap they put in the food that makes everyone fat," Jerri said when Tara said something about it. Jerri looked up from where she was digging potatoes and smiled at her. "You've got dirt on your right cheek."

Tara rubbed it off on her sleeve.

"You were never fat."

Tara laughed and turned the shovel again unearthing a bunch more potatoes. "If I wasn't fat before am I too thin now?"

Jerri mumbled something.

"What?"

"That's one of those questions, honey," Jerri said, pulling the spuds out of the earth and slinging them into a bucket.

"What?"

"Well a normal human couldn't answer that without getting in trouble, which means it takes me more than sixty seconds to answer."

"You're sort of arrogant."

"I'm not arrogant; I'm Jerri Blue." She looked up at Tara and her smile reached her eyes. "You were neither too fat then nor too thin now because in my eyes you are always perfect."

It wasn't just what she said but the way she said it. Tara just wanted to jump on her right there in the dirt. Of course there were potatoes to dig but that alone wouldn't have stopped her—Tara heard a car pulling into the driveway.

"That's probably Carol coming to catch the swarm," Tara said. Because Jerri had six bee hives, but a woman who lived down the road and had a huge apiary took care of Jerri's bees and split the honey and wax with Jerri in exchange for caring for them. Jerri said she didn't have the temperament to tend the hives, but she loved honey, used the wax, and needed the bees for their garden.

"Nope it's your mother," Jerri said, not looking up from where she had gone back to pulling potatoes out of the dirt.

"Again?" Tara sighed. She didn't for a second think Jerri was wrong; she never was. Whether the phone rang or a car door slammed she always knew who it was. "She's been here three times in five days."

"She likes it here." Jerri laughed at the sigh that escaped Tara's mouth.

"I love my mother, and I know she's going through a really hard time, but for the love of God I'm going back tomorrow and I just want it to be us."

"Because digging potatoes is so romantic?"

"Well it almost was," Tara mumbled. When she looked up the road her mother was walking down it, but when she saw who was with her she got over her mad. "She brought the boys." She put the shovel down and went to meet them.

Channing came running towards her and she got down to get a hug from him but he made a b-line around her and headed for Jerri. Tara stood up feeling a little rejected. She walked over to her mom bent down and picked Tylor up.

"You still love me best, right?"

He gave her a sloppy kiss on the cheek and hugged her neck.

Tara gave her mother a half a hug. She realized she'd gotten dirt all over Tylor and her mother, but then she noticed they were all dressed for it. Because of course Janice had been there the day before and knew they were digging potatoes today.

Before Jerri really had time to realize what was happening she had a whole crew digging and pulling.

She was working with both of the little boys, so it was easy to pretend like she wasn't listening to the conversation Tara was having with her.

"I know I have to go, Mother," Tara said. "But I'm not getting my nails done for a funeral. I don't think that's appropriate and my nails won't last ten minutes here."

"They would if you'd wear gloves." Janice held up her gloved hand. "You should really wear gloves."

Jerri didn't want Tara to go to the funeral. Not because it was for Tara's ex-husband, but because Jerri hated the entire idea of funerals and everything about them. The sadness, the despair was tangible. It wasn't the dead that would radiate the sorrow of a life cut stupidly short, only the living would. Tara didn't care about her ex-husband's death, so she didn't think it would affect her to go, but she was going for his family which meant she still cared for them. that being the case she would feel their grief; it would trail after her.

The barn cat came over and sniffed at the fresh earth.

"No NOT a cat box!" Jerri said, shaking her finger in his face.

He meowed because after all he was very vocal.

"No, cats don't eat potatoes."

He meowed again and by now Channing was cracking up and Tylor started laughing because his brother was.

"No, I don't think either of them ride the short bus. Although the little one does crap his pants."

The cat meowed again.

"Well it's a damn sight better than shitting in the potatoes. You need to be less judgey. People who live in glass houses and all."

"Oh my God you're right. That is the cutest thing ever," Janice said, watching and listening.

"Don't eat a dirty potato," Jerri said, pulling it out of Tylor's hand and sticking it in the bucket. "No, you can't eat the cat... No, that isn't what Daddy meant."

Jerri then looked at Channing who was laughing and clapping his hands. "No, he doesn't think you're crazy yet, but he will if you keep laughing like that. You need to get to work; these spuds aren't going to pull themselves."

"Are you sure you two don't want to adopt at least one underprivileged brown baby? You'd be such good parents."

"Geez, Mom, I told you no and that really is... It's horrible, Mom," Tara said, but grinned and shook her head.

"Why don't you want kids?"

"There are seven billion people on this planet, Mom. I want to do what I want to do when I want to do it. I love these guys, but I don't have any desire to have any of my own."

"No doubt Jerri is afraid of the environmental impact but if you adopt."

"Mom... I like our life the way it is or at least I will when my contract runs out and I can just stay with Jerri."

"You say that, but if you're stuck with her twenty-four/ seven? You're going to get bored."

"Yes as if *that* could ever be boring," she said

Tara nodded to where Jerri was holding a potato up looking at it like it was a gem stone and saying, "I believe it just might be the cursed diamond of the Zombie queen of Burbank."

"It's a potato." Channing giggled.

"Are you sure?" Jerri asked.

Channing nodded.

Jerri turned to the cat. "See if I ever listen to you again!"

"You have a point. You know, Tara, if we could get Jerri to sign on you guys could have your own show. People would eat up all this organic gardening crap, and..."

"No, Mom!" Tara shook her head violently. "I want *out*. I don't want to drag Jerri in."

"But look at her. She's TV gold. When you come ou... Well everyone would watch. It would take a ninety share in its time slot."

"No, Janice," Jerri said, proving she could talk to the kids, the cat, dig potatoes, and still listen to their conversation at the same time. "You cannot turn on the TV any moment of any day that someone in your family isn't on screen in some capacity, so... No. I know you don't hear that much, but what it means is NO."

"So I'm guessing that's no," her mother said to her. It was pretty clear that her mother was happy about it, which was a little surprising. Janice looked at Tara and smiled. "If I could talk her into something I know she would hate and that you don't want, she sure as hell wouldn't be right for you." She added in a whisper, "Jerri used to let Rhonda walk all over her, and you don't need that, either."

"I'm a lot healthier than I used to be, Janice. I don't let people take advantage of me anymore," Jerri said, defending herself.

Janice looked embarrassed and shocked.

Tara smiled and whispered, "She has really good hearing."

Janice suddenly got really busy pulling potatoes and throwing them in a bucket.

Jerri stood up with a full bucket and the boys followed her to the golf cart. Tara watched as Jerri put the bucket in then set both boys on the front seat climbed in and took off for the barn where Jerri would lay the spuds out to dry before putting them in the root cellar.

Janice sighed and didn't look at Tara. "I'm sorry if I made her mad or uncomfortable. It wasn't my intention."

"She didn't seem either to me, Mom. I think she just wanted to take the boys on a ride to keep them from getting bored."

"Well then I'm sorry I've been up here nearly every day, but... In case you forgot I usually spend most of my day with you."

It was true, and with a sudden uncomfortable feeling Tara realized that for most of her adult life her mother had been the substitute for a girlfriend. She was glad when her mother started talking again.

"You know what I realized when the shit hit the fan? I don't have real friends just people who want to ride on my coattails to get their fifteen minutes of fame..."

"That's exactly what I realized at that charity event the other night. I've made better friends here in a few months than I have made in the rest of my life."

Janice nodded. "And you were right. I need to do something real, and this place... I think I'd willingly sleep with Jerri to be able to stay right here."

"Mom, first off... gross... and second, I'm not with Jerri just so I can stay here."

"I know that. The press doesn't give a gnat's ass what I'm doing on a good day and they sure don't now for which I'm glad. Irva's dating another rap star. This one is fighting with the one who thinks he's God and just blowing up Twitter with stupid shit. They mostly want you right now so they can grill you about Fred, and Dad because right now he's more interesting than the rest of us lumped together. Honestly, honey, I know I don't have a right to be because it was my idea, but I'm sick to death of having the disaster which is my life paraded for the world to see. I'm having a nervous breakdown, going through menopause, and my husband had a sex-change operation... I sort of asked the crew to be disinterested in me. Even though they often forget it, at the end of the day they work for me. It's been easy for me to get away and... I just want to get *completely* away. I think I understand more than I want to why you just want to be here all the time."

"Mostly I just want to be with Jerri. In fact she lived here alone for ten years and she kind of likes her space, so I sometimes get worried that she's going to get tired of me in her face all the time. I keep telling myself I won't be so clingy, but I haven't managed to do it yet. Being with Jerri has been like finding something that I didn't know was even missing."

"I was so pissed off when I realized what you were doing and with who. Mainly because I thought, what the hell besides sex could you possibly have in common? But the more I think about it the more I realize you really have everything important in common. A lot more in common than say your father and I ever had. Hell, since he became a Republican we don't even agree on politics. When I see you together, far from being uncomfortable, I feel like you have made a really good choice and will be happy. I think that's maybe the bigger reason that I have been up here every day. My marriage imploded, Irva is a shallow piece of work, and Lori and Todd are a train wreck waiting to happen. I have no idea what in the hell I'm going to do with the rest of my life, but it can't be what I've been doing. My life is a huge mess, but when I see you and Jerri I think, that one isn't a fucking mess. I'm very proud and happy for you Tara, and when I see the life you are making for yourself I don't feel like every single breath I've taken was a waste of time."

"Your life hasn't been a waste at all, Mom, but thanks." Tara felt a little bad about resenting her mom being there every day now, and something else... Any residual shame she had been harboring because she was a lesbian just went right away.

Jerri came back with the boys and this time Tylor was on her lap and she was letting him "drive." He wasn't of course, but from the look of concentration on his face he obviously believed he was. As soon as she stopped Channing jumped off and ran over to them.

"I drove first," he told them. He giggled and looked at Janice. "Harry named the little goat Flower, but he's a boy."

Her mother looked at Tara. "The last one was named T-Rex and he tried to kill Jerri, so this time she wanted to name it something less threatening."

Jerri looked at Tara. "And for the record I didn't name him, Tara did."

"He likes to smell flowers," Tara said with a shrug. "...and then eat them."

Janice's head suddenly turned so quickly Tara was reminded of the exorcist. "You should write children's books."

The minute she said it Tara knew that was exactly what she wanted to do even before Jerri yelled out. "Oh my God, Tara, she's right!"

Janice glared at Jerri. "Well you don't have to sound so surprised!"

Chapter 17

"Please, Judy, I feel like I should go to the funeral but I look awful," Georgia begged.

Judy looked at Cyndy and rolled her eyes wanting to just drop her phone.

"Do you really think you should go to that funeral, Georgia?"

"The man was once my son-in-law. I should go to support my daughter."

"The daughter who isn't speaking to you?"

"Well... maybe if I go to support her..."

"She'll have to talk to you? You should NOT go to that funeral." Judy was already way tired of this conversation. "If all you need is help with your make up, hair and clothes, why not call one of the two daughters that are talking to you and ask for their help."

"They aren't transwomen, Judy. You know it's not the same, and... I don't want to ask my daughters to help dress their dad. I know it would be weird for them."

"I'm a doctor. Believe it or not, Georgia, it is not my goal in life to be the dresser of the first ultra-right-winged transgendered woman in the world." Judy started to end the conversation.

"I need you, Judy. I need my friends," Georgia said quickly.

Judy didn't end the call.

Georgia started to cry. "I'm lonely. I miss you girls. I'm sorry that I hurt your feelings. I can just not talk politics and ignore it when you do..."

"Can you really?"

"I can try and... Well I have been checking, and I do now understand what you're talking about. Republicans have a bad record when it comes to trans issues."

"That is actually a huge, giant step in the right direction. It shows growth, Georgia."

"I think my purpose might be to enlighten the Republican Party about trans issues."

Judy sighed and started to just give up, but then... Well

that might be the best plan ever, *Talk about killing two birds with one stone.* "What exactly are you saying, Georgia?"

"That I'd like to write a letter—well for Jerri to—and send it to that governor who just signed that so-called freedom of religion act into law and that Senator that said we might molest his daughters if we were allowed to use the woman's room."

Yes this just might be perfect. "We'll be there as soon as we can."

She was already sorry she'd come when she'd had to wade through the rows of paparazzi to get into the funeral parlor. She, her mother, and her sisters had barely expressed their condolences to his family when there was a commotion at the door. She knew before she turned that it was her father, and when Tara saw her she couldn't help what she felt. There stood the woman who had killed her father. The look on her mother's face was something Tara wasn't going to soon forget.

Tara turned to Fred's mother. "I am so sorry. Would you like for us to go?"

She smiled at Tara. "No, you know Fred. He would have loved all this mess at his funeral."

Tara smiled back and said, "You know what? You're right."

"I'm sorry for the way he treated you, Tara. You always were such a lovely girl."

"You once said—in regard to what I don't remember—but you said God has a plan for us all. I would have missed what I was supposed to do if Fred hadn't done what he did. Again I am very sorry for your loss." She remembered what Jerri told her and found the words just flowed. "He didn't deserve to have the problems he had. Now he's at peace, and we don't cry for him we cry for ourselves." His mother hugged her and thanked her for her words.

Tara took Janice's arm and led her away. She didn't look at her father but knew her mother was.

"That was really pretty," Lori said in a whisper. Then she added, "Did you have Jerri write it?"

"No, geez Lori." She looked at Irva with meaning, but Irva was busy tweeting something on her phone.

"For the love of God, Irva, put your fucking phone away. We're at a funeral."

Irva quickly finished her text and then put her phone away.

Their father was headed their way and Tara said quickly, "Irva and Lori, please go get Daddy and steer her to another part of the room away from me and Mom."

"Tara, Daddy just wants to be here for you, for the love of God," Lori said.

"Please, girls," Janice said in a voice so unlike her own that she immediately had all her girls' attention.

Without another word Irva and Lori went to intercept Georgia and easily pulled her to the other side of the funeral home away from them. Tara found a place towards the rear, vowing to leave as soon as they could, and just bullcoze their way through the press. She looked at her dad, and Georgia was looking at her.

She looked quickly away, even closed her eyes before whispering, "Are you alright, Mom?"

"Not really. I knew I was going to have to see her. I even knew there was a good chance she'd be here today, and I thought... I thought I was ready, but I'm really not."

"Because it's like Dad died," Tara said. And the tears she wasn't crying for Fred started to fall. "Jerri told me that, and I don't really think I understood exactly what she meant until right this minute. He's dead, and she isn't him at all."

Her mother looked at her nodded, and then they both just started sobbing, hanging on each other. Of course everyone there and all the idiots snapping pictures and taking footage were touched by the depth of sorrow they felt for Fred. As the service started they cried at all the right moments because their grief was real. By the time the funeral was over Tara felt like maybe she was ready to heal concerning her father, and she had forgiven Fred for everything... Which was easy—mostly because he was dead.

As they were getting in their car Georgia tried to approach them, but Tara pulled her mother along quickly, practically shoving her in the car.

Lori and Irva had come with them, so as she ordered the car to leave. She sent a text, *"Lori, Mom is in a state. Please get a ride with Georgia or if you want I can have another car sent."*

Lori texted back in seconds. *"I saw the look on Mom's, face and know she wasn't that fond of Fred. Is she alright?"*

"She will be, but neither of us were thrilled to see Georgia," she texted.

"*I get that Mom is that upset, but you're gay. I don't get why you're so mad at Dad.*"

"*I'm not really mad, Lori, I'm upset.*" And she didn't want to explain that to her their dad was dead because after all she didn't really know what that meant till she saw Georgia in the flesh. If Lori did understand what she meant it might make her as sad as it made Tara. Lori was uncomfortable with what their father had become, but she wasn't actually sad about it. "*Mom's not mad, either, just upset. Please don't tell Dad; there is no sense in upsetting her.*"

"*Again I have to say how fucked up is it that we have to use female pronouns with our Dad? If you were really worried about upsetting her you wouldn't refuse to talk to her.*"

"*I'm just not ready, Lori.*"

"*And see… I guess the only difference between us is that you aren't lying about how you feel.*"

Georgia was crying her eyes out and Judy worked on patience by remembering how emotional she had been right after her sexual reassignment surgery and trying to get used to the female hormones. "Are you this upset about Fred?"

"No," she whimpered out.

"Well you looked great till you started crying," Selma said. Judy glared at her and Selma shrugged.

"You should have seen the look on Janice and Tara's faces."

"Disgust?" Selma said. Judy cut her another look. "What?"

"Did you visit the all-male island of insensitivity today?" Judy asked, but managed a smile.

Selma smiled back and shrugged.

Georgia had started crying the moment she walked in the door. That was more than a few minutes ago, and it seemed that Selma didn't have much more patience than Judy did.

Judy handed Georgia a box of tissues. She blew her nose loudly several times and dried her face off. "They weren't disgusted; I could have handled that. They were hurt… No, Janice was devastated and Tara… She could hardly look at me. When she did she looked like I'd just run over her dog." She started to cry again. "And I *did* run over Lori's dog, I *did*."

"They have to come to terms with your transition in their own time, Georgia. I told you not to go to the funeral. You're trying to force them to accept you as you are. You need to give them time to come to you, to figure out what place you are going to hold in their lives. In the meantime Janice no longer has a husband and your girls no longer have a father."

"I'm still their Daddy! I'm always going to be their Daddy. I want them to be proud of me." Georgia cried. "Tara hates me, she hates me. I know it's wrong to have favorites, but she was always mine. She had her sisters intercept me to keep me from being able to comfort her. She left them there and took off with her mother so that she wouldn't have to talk to me."

Yep, Georgia was really miserable.

"I should just get her address, go to her house and talk it out."

"No," Judy said too quickly. Once again wanting to strangle Jerri because this would have been so much easier if Jerri wasn't boffing Georgia's oldest daughter. Then she remembered that she didn't exactly tell Jerri what she was doing regarding Georgia. "She isn't ready to talk about it yet, and showing up at the funeral today didn't help, if anything it pushed her further away."

Selma opened a box of chocolate ice cream. They drank some red wine and pretty soon Georgia forgot that she was sad but remembered that she was Republican, so before they could get in a fight Judy and Selma had their driver take them to their respective homes.

She and Jerri were barefooted walking down by the water in front of their beach house. Tate was watching their farm for the night.

"Is your mom going to be alright?" Jerri asked.

"She was doing a lot better before I left. Lori and Irva are there, so she's not alone but... I thought I knew what you meant when you said my father was dead, but when I saw her in the flesh it suddenly hit me. It was worse for Mom."

"It's funny how you can think you understand something. Then something happens and you realize there is an entire dimension to it that you hadn't even thought of."

"Exactly. I thought you were being metaphorical. You know metaphorically my father is dead because after all he's Georgia now. But he isn't; he really is dead, and now there is a woman living in the very-altered body that once was his. He's dead." There was a catch in her throat, and Jerri reached out and took her hand.

"And yet he's not. Georgia has all his memories and all his same loves. If she didn't she wouldn't still be a fucking Republican and... Dammit that's why she clings to it like a dog with a bone. It's how she's trying to keep him alive." Jerri seemed to store that idea for later so that she could make the point she was working on now, and Tara grinned because Jerri did that a lot. "She still loves you, but it's going to be a process. She's going to have to try to relate to you as a woman, and you're going to have to get to know someone completely new who still knows you in a way few people do." Jerri stopped, sat down in the sand and tried to drag Tara into the sand with her.

"Honey, I don't want to get all sandy," Tara complained.

"Yes because we don't have a ginormous shower to clean off in. There is no camera crew here." Jerri laughed and pulled Tara into her lap.

Tara wrapped her arms around Jerri's neck. "You know there could be paparazzi damn near anywhere."

"I don't care; do you care?"

"Obviously not as much as I just want to do what I want to do, or I wouldn't have suggested you come out here with me in the first place." She released Jerri and crawled out of her lap to sit beside her. Then she looked out at the orange and red sunset over a calm ocean. "It's beautiful and way too pretty to stay in the house, but it's easy to not care when we aren't being beaten to death by the press and every ass hat with an opinion. If they get even a half-assed picture of us together that's what's going to happen."

"You know who never has anyone say unkind or crappy things about them?" Jerri didn't give her time to answer. "...people who live in a fucking box of perfect and never do anything the least bit different or interesting. The ones who are so afraid of being vulnerable that they never once say what they really think or show how they really feel. Those that are never just exactly who they are. Mean people are going to say hateful things about us, but we are just going to keep the TV off and stay away from social media. We aren't going to look at it, listen to it, or read it because we know it's all bullshit."

"I have to admit the less I am plugged into that crap the happier I am. For years I couldn't go more than a few seconds without looking at my phone or getting on the internet. Now

I'll go days without even looking at any of it. I can't remember the last time I insta-grammed or tweeted anything. My Facebook page has become a vast tumbleweed-filled virtual wasteland."

"I like this beach house and we ought to enjoy it while we have it because as soon as your contract is up we're going to the farm and we're staying there. I know you'll still have things you have to do with your mom and your family, and I'll have to go here and speak there, but I think it will be enough for you. Don't you think it will be enough for you?"

Tara replayed that in her head and still didn't understand which was rare, because Jerri could normally explain clearly things that Tara had never before understood. She suddenly realized something odd; Jerri was nervous.

"Did something happen today? Are you alright?"

"I am but... Well, I was alone at the farm today. I was working and I was thinking about you because I love you and you had to go to that funeral and I hate funerals. I know it makes me sound pathetic because this started when you had only been gone a couple of hours, but I missed you." Jerri took her hand. "Then I started to worry. What if when your contract is done and you are living with me on the homestead all the time you're bored— or worse yet you decide you hate it there and you hate me..."

"That isn't ever going to happen." She squeezed Jerri's hand. Suddenly she knew what Jerri had meant with her earlier statement and she quickly kissed Jerri's cheek. "I think it's more likely that when I have to go do something with my family or you have to go somewhere that neither of us will want to leave. We'll have a good time when we get there but always be super glad to be home." She thought for a moment and then added, "But we are not moving to Alaska even though it is the last frontier."

Jerri laughed and then returned her quick kiss on the cheek and whispered in her ear, "You really are perfect."

Tara sighed. "I hope you keep thinking that when we become the topic of the week. Jerri... I really don't care what they say about me, but I can't stand it that anyone might say anything crappy about you."

"And see, baby, I feel the same way. Like I said, we just won't pay any attention to it."

"It will be harder than you think."

"And now you are forgetting I used to live with Rhonda."

"Yes, I do it on purpose." Tara chuckled. Jerri was right they weren't going to say anything to or about her that she hadn't already heard in spades. "I hate to admit it, but the minute Mother said write children's books, that's what I knew I wanted to do. Did you know that I'm a decent artist?"

"I didn't, but it doesn't surprise me at all."

"It's one of those things I stopped doing because it seemed pointless."

"And that is the biggest mistake people make. We stop doing the things we love to do because they don't turn a profit or no one applauds. We let negativity run in a circle around our brain till we have no idea what we really want or who we really are."

"Exactly," Tara said. "I haven't even thought about the book I was working on in weeks. I was kind of over it... When I first started writing in junior high my intention was to write and illustrate books for kids. When Mom said that and you agreed I realized it was why the novel wasn't doing it for me. I was writing it because it's what I thought I could sell, not because it was my passion. I've already got about a half dozen ideas most of which revolve around that thing you do where you talk to the cat as if he were talking..."

"You mean... the cat doesn't talk?"

Tara laughed. "If he does, I don't hear him. The truth is that right now I can't even start on anything creative. I know we're supposed to live in the present, but I need this part of my life—the one coming up that I'm trying not to think about— I need it to be over. I won't mind being on camera when I go to help my mother with something or go somewhere or do something with my sisters, but I'm sick to death of the whole I must be on camera at least six hours a day shit. I was at that funeral and the whole time I'm on camera crying like a baby, but it had nothing at all to do with Fred it was all about Dad. But every moron with a TV is going to think that I'm torn up over my ex-husband which... well I was able to forgive him which was a good thing."

"It is," Jerri said.

"I realized something today. You've said it before. You can't turn on the TV any time of the day and not see one of us doing something. Everyone thinks they know us and they don't know us at all. Because all these years I bet NO ONE knew I was gay or Dad wanted to be a woman, and today they thought I was all torn up over Fred and that's not why I was crying at all. So I'm in someone's living room every minute of every day, and the only person who really knows me at all is you because when I'm with you I'm not playing a part; I'm just me."

A guy was walking down the beach. Before Tara even saw the camera around the guy's neck, Jerri had jumped up and put down her hand to help her up. They started to walk back up the beach to the path that led to the staircase they had to climb to get to the house. As the guy got closer he looked at them.

Tara tried not to let it bother her or at least not to show it, but her hand must have tightened on Jerri's because Jerri whispered in her ear, "It doesn't matter Tara."

But Jerri wasn't nearly as alright with the whole getting caught thing as she was saying because when the guy stopped short and said, "Aren't you…" Jerri didn't let him get finished before she snapped, "Yes she's Tara Darting."

The man looked confused and looked from her to Jerri. "Tara Darting?" he said as if it was a name that he recognized but didn't know from where. "I was going to ask if you are Jerri Blue."

Jerri made some really uncomfortable noises then and Tara didn't know why but for some reason that was just the funniest thing that had ever happened. Tara started laughing.

Jerri gave her an odd grin and said to the man. "Yes, I am. I'm sorry." She pointed at the camera and said, "We were afraid you were the press."

He laughed. "No, I came to take pictures of the sunset which I already did. It's just so pretty I thought I'd go for a walk on the beach. I'm sorry to have bothered you, but I am a huge fan of your work. I went to a talk you did on sexual diversity in fiction at the University of Phoenix. I thought I recognized you. I just moved into the condo down there…" He pointed down the beach. "Coming from the desert I'm still pretty fascinated with the ocean. My wife tells me I have taken way too many pictures."

He looked at Tara who was still laughing.

"She's easily amused," Jerri explained, which just made Tara laugh more. "See what I mean?" Which was even funnier.

The guy started to laugh which proved that laughter is contagious.

"What's your name?"

"Bill, Bill Porter." He shook Jerri's outstretched hand and Tara almost—but not quite—quit laughing.

"Seriously, honey," Jerri said to her, which got her laughing all over again.

Tara shrugged and laughed still harder.

Jerri sighed and said to Bill. "The truth is she is much more famous than I am. I guess that's what's so funny?" She looked at Tara.

Unable to stop laughing, Tara just shrugged again.

Now Bill was laughing again only because she was.

Tara took a couple of deep breaths and tried to stop laughing, but when she looked at Jerri, Jerri rolled her eyes in mock embarrassment which just made her laugh even more.

"Well, Bill, it was very nice to meet you. I'd better get Tara home before she passes out." She laughed, took Tara's hand and started pulling her towards the house.

"I'm sorry," Tara croaked out as they passed Bill.

"It was a pleasure to meet you," he said at their departing backs.

Jerri looked at her and smiled. "Do you feel better?"

Tara nodded, still laughing, and realized instantly why Jerri asked. Tara had been tense and grieving most of the day. When she had thought they were about to be caught by the paparazzi it had brought all that up. Then when it turned out to be nothing but one of Jerri's fans taking pictures of the sunset it had just been such an amazing release. By the time they reached the bottom of the steps she had stopped laughing. She pulled her hand away from Jerri's, wrapped her arms around her neck and kissed her on the mouth. In that moment she was completely over getting caught by anyone.

Irva had gone off to meet the new rapper, and before they could get in the club they were swamped by paparazzi who brought them to the attention of a bunch of Frappy's fans. They started to scream insults, and the new boyfriend's fans started to yell the same shit back. Then someone shoved someone and it went from bad to worse. Club security had to intervene because it turned out their personal security sucked ass. The new boyfriend had popped one of the paparazzi in the face during the near riot. Irva had been hurt; it was minor but uncalled for. Janice was looking around the room at the crew, not just the ones that followed her and the girls, but some of the ones following Georgia around as well. It was time for a show down. This crap had to stop.

"One of you," Janice accused, "is leaking stuff to the press. What happened last night never would have happened if the paparazzi hadn't been waiting for Irva when she got there. Irva was damn near mauled last night. She actually panicked, and Irva doesn't panic over things like that unless it's clear she's five seconds from being trampled to death. Now her stupid boyfriend is being accused of aggravated assault because he was trying to get them off her, and we're all over the damn news. Come clean right now and I will just fire you. Keep doing this shit and when—not if but when—I find out who it is I will sue you for breach of contract so that you will be paying me for the rest of your natural life! You will have to go work for the tabloids you love so much because I will make damn sure you never get decent work again."

None of them stood up. None of them even looked at someone else like they all secretly knew who it was.

"I swear, if you are doing this or you know who is... I will burn you and spread your ashes at Gorman's Chinese Theater."

Nothing. Crickets. It made her wonder if they were all equally dirty, and she told them so as she got rid of months of frustration by cussing them out for the next thirty minutes.

"Is she hurt?" Tara asked looking over Jerri at the clock. She made a face when she saw it was only seven.

"Not really, just shook up," Lori answered. "Mom called a huge meeting with all the crew members she could pull together. She's still yelling at them now. We've all been up since the middle of last night because of course that's when Irva and Fats..."

"Seriously, can our sister not date someone with a normal name?"

"I know, right? Anyway it was like one in the morning when they got to the club and the paparazzi made it nearly impossible for them to get out of their car. The press had obviously already stirred up the crowd. You know, to make news so they could get pictures." It wouldn't be the first time they had done that to them. "Fats popped one of the paparazzi, though I have to tell you seeing the tapes, they had it coming.

We're just lucky there wasn't a complete instant riot because there for a minute that was what it looked like."

Tara was silent, looking at Jerri.

"You still there?"

"Yes." She got out of bed, went to the bathroom and closed the door. "What the hell is happening, Lori? What's with all the crazy?"

"Mom thinks whoever the leak is he's calling every single publication and telling them—maybe even charging them extra for position—you know on who he calls first. Besides the obvious, what's wrong?"

"God Lori, I know everyone is going to find out and then we're going to have to deal with that. I'm used to it and yes even though I don't like to think about it I know Jerri was with Rhonda Heart and she should be used to it, too. But you and I both know it has gotten so much worse in the last ten years."

"And Rhonda has a team of huge security guys. I sometimes look at our security and think Channing could take them. After last night I think Mom pays them way too much to mostly yell at people to get back. I'm telling you Tara I have seen the footage three times now, and it's scary. If the club security hadn't stepped in and taken care of things I don't know what would have happened."

"You aren't helping me feel any better, Lori. I'm really worried about Jerri."

"I think Jerri can take care of herself, honey..."

"Lori, Jerri has PTSD."

"I know I should know what that is."

"Post-traumatic stress disorder."

"Like vets."

Tara sighed. "Yes. I still don't know what all her triggers are, but my guess would be that having a bunch of idiots with cameras crowding her space is going to be a nightmare at the least."

Now Lori was quiet.

"You still there?"

"Well this isn't going to be very helpful, either, but it just dawned on me that Jerri might be the reason Rhonda hired all the beefy security guards in the first place."

"You're right. That isn't helpful," Tara said with a sigh. "You know I may rethink Alaska."

"What?" Lori asked with a giggle.

"Nothing. Look, I'm going back to sleep. I suggest you try to get some sleep yourself."

Jerri was staying the whole day and another night before going back to the farm. She had planned to anyway just to make sure Tara was alright with everything that happened the day before. At least that was what she told herself. The truth was dealing with all the negative energy Tara dragged home with her had left her feeling a little sketchy. Jerri just wanted—maybe needed—to be close to Tara, which was actually huge if she thought about it because usually when she felt raw she just needed to be home alone.

Tara was in the kitchen cooking; they had brought real food from the farm.

Jerri threw on her robe and went in and sat at the bar. "So what's wrong? I mean besides your sister nearly being caught in a riot?"

"Nothing."

"Well that was an obvious lie," Jerri said with a laugh.

"They are going to find out about us and then... I'm worried about you, alright?"

"Because of my episodes?" Jerri asked, frowning. She didn't like her problems to define her to anyone, and certainly not Tara. "You know, Tara, the last time I had a bad episode I got through it just fine by myself. I'm not by myself now. I think that you could pull me right out of any hole I crawled into. There might be some stump throwing." Jerri was pretty sure it wasn't a lie. The truth was that being with Tara seemed to drive any remaining darkness right out of her.

"But I don't want it to be my fault, Jerri," Tara said, sounding miserable.

"It won't be your fault, honey. You can't control the crappy behavior of other people. I'll be just fine."

The doorbell rang.

"No idea," Tara said. "Might be Mom. Lori said Mom 'needed' to talk to me. These are done whenever you want them." Tara took the sausages off the stove and went to answer the door.

When she looked through the peephole she saw it was her father and an entire film crew. "Son of a bitch," she muttered. Then she said out loud. "Go away, Dad, I don't want to talk to you." Thinking that would give Jerri time to hide.

To her surprise, Georgia just walked right in followed by the film crew and of course Jerri was still sitting at the bar in her robe.

"Crap!" Tara looked at Jerri, a helpless expression on her face.

It took Georgia a minute to realize what she was seeing. When she did, Tara realized that part of her father was still very much alive.

"Jerri Blue you fucking piece of shit! Are you sleeping with my daughter!" Georgia boomed.

"Only after we have sex," Jerri said. She stood up, no doubt because she knew Georgia was going to attack her. As Georgia lunged forward Jerri ran behind the sofa Tara had bought to shut her mother up. Jerri kept running back and forth as Georgia matched her step for step on the other side of the couch. "Now, now Georgia it isn't lady-like to fight," Jerri said.

If she wanted Georgia to quit coming after her she should probably quit goading her.

"I'm going to kill you, Jerri! I'm going to kill you!"

It would have been funny if it was on TV—which it would be—but it wasn't funny at all in that moment because her dad might be a woman now, but she had still been the greatest quarterback to run the grid iron, and she was super mad and huge.

Jerri ran down the length of the couch one way and then Georgia ran down it on the other. Then Georgia was chasing Jerri round and round the couch till she tried to jump over it, which crushed the couch but Jerri jumped clear. And Tara? Well Tara jumped on Georgia's back, grabbed her arm, and pulled it between her shoulder blades. She then held it there just like her Dad had taught her.

"For the love of God, calm down, Dad. Calm the fuck down," Tara said.

Jerri fixed the tie on her robe, caught her breath, and just looked at her.

Tara looked back.

"How did he get the key?" Jerri asked. She grabbed her phone off the counter and dialed someone. Tara hoped it wasn't the cops, though frankly she didn't know how long she could sit on her father and didn't know what else they could do if

Georgia was hell bent on killing Jerri.

"That's right, Mom had the film crew hand the key back in," Tara said, and twisted her father's arm a little more just because she was pissed off at this ultimate invasion of her privacy.

"Tara, you're hurting me," Georgia protested.

"You were going to kill Jerri."

"You piece of crap, Jerri Blue!" Georgia yelled. "Do you hate me so much you have to make my daughter a queer?"

"Strong words from a six-foot four-inch two-hundred-pound transwoman," Jerri said, clicking her tongue.

Tara realized Jerri hadn't been exaggerating. Her dad and her girlfriend really couldn't stand each other.

"I'll kill you. I swear to God I will kill you! Let me up Tara," Georgia ordered.

"No. Why would I let you up when you're threatening to kill Jerri? You need to calm down, and," then Tara started to cry. "You just called me a queer."

"Honey, queer isn't a bad word." Jerri walked over and patted her back, still waiting for whoever she was calling to answer the phone.

"It is the way he said it."

"She does have you there, butch," Jerri said.

Then she was talking on the phone, but still patting Tara's back. "Yeah, Janice, I've got good news and bad news. The good news is I know just how to find your rat. The bad news is Georgia is over here."

She could hear her mother yelling "Son of a bitch "

"Yeah, that's what Tara said... Never say that; it's just inviting trouble... How do I know the rat is here? Because Georgia let herself in with a key, and that means one of them had made their own copy of the key. Nine will get you ten it's the same one who calls the press every ten seconds."

Then Jerri left her and walked into the bedroom.

"Let me go, Tara," Georgia boomed and tried to get free, but by now Tara not only had Georgia's arm twisted but she also had a knee in each of her kidneys.

"No, you're going to hurt Jerri, so no."

"It's not bad enough that you're a queer, but you have to screw Jerri Blue?"

"And this is exactly why I'm not talking to you. You want us all to accept that you're a woman, but I knew I knew all along that you weren't going to accept that I'm gay because you never have."

Beneath her Georgia seemed to relax, but Tara didn't because it might just be a trick. After all her father had been the king of the fake pass.

"Well damn," Georgia said. "You're right; I didn't. I thought it was just a phase, which is exactly what my family did to me. I'm sorry, Tara, but... For the love of God, Tara, why Jerri Blue?!"

"I've been with Jerri longer than you've been a woman," Tara countered.

Jerri walked out of the bedroom dressed in jeans and a blue t shirt, Tara's gun in her hand.

"What's that have to do with anything? Honey, let your dad up. Georgia, I swear to God if you come after me again I will shoot you."

Tara let her dad go.

"You sit right there on what's left of our couch, Georgia. Which one of these fuck sticks gave you the key to our house?"

"That one." Georgia pointed, now seemingly as mad at him as she was either of them. Why? *Because he wouldn't know I was sleeping with Jerri if it wasn't for this guy, and she was happier not knowing.*

"Give Tara your phone," Jerri ordered, pointing the gun at the man's chest. He looked reluctant, but Jerri caught his eyes and held them. "Georgia, you want to tell this guy why he should do what I tell him?"

"Because she has a gun and she *will* shoot you. Second amendment rights are the only thing she and I agree on," Georgia said.

Which was true because for all her dad's other conservative bull crap he believed in the right to bear arms, but just like Jerri he didn't think that needed to include armor-piercing bullets, thirty-round banana clips, or automatic weapons, though unlike Jerri he still thought it was alright for him to have them in his collection. Tara wondered if she was ever going to be able to think of her dad in female pronouns, and decided probably not.

"I told you, Jerri. I told you it was the skinny guy," Tara said.

The guy handed Tara his phone. It only took her a second to see where he had sent a text to dozens of different tabloid rags. Tara read the text out loud, "'Just caught Tara Darting in a love nest with Pulitzer Prize-winning author Jerri Blue'. He's sent our address."

Jerri looked at the camera man, and it was clear that she was seriously considering shooting him.

"Jerri, we don't have time for you to kill him. We need to get the hell out before they get here," Tara said. "I don't care about the contract with the network. I don't care if they sue me; we'll just pay the fine whatever it is. I don't want this for you, and I don't want this for us. I just want to go."

"Tara, we really need to talk. I can't stand having you so mad at me," Georgia said. Then as if she had Tourette's she suddenly yelled out, "Fucking Jerri Blue!" Georgia took a deep breath and calmed herself. "I didn't know you were sleeping with Jerri. I sure as hell didn't know I had the leak with me. I'm sorry for this, Tara."

As they pulled out of the driveway, Jerri shot a hole in the tire of the van Georgia and the crew had come in. Tara jumped and almost landed in her lap. The small truck wasn't built for three passengers—at least not if one of them was Georgia Darting.

"I don't understand why we brought her with us."

"You guys need to talk…" Jerri said. "…at least enough so she isn't trying to kill me."

"Why Jerri Blue, Tara? I get it you are gay; you've always been gay. But of all the women in the world…" Now Georgia was crying, and she started banging her head into the side glass of the car. "Why, why, why?"

Tara glared at Jerri and hissed, "If I was by a window I'd bang my head, too, and beg to know why, why, why we brought my dad with us. Don't you dare say we need to talk. I told you I don't want to talk to him/ her."

"Why are you so mad at me?

"I already told you, but mostly right now I'm mad because upon learning that I'm gay you immediately try to kill the woman I love. Do you even realize why you hate Jerri so much?"

"Because she's a know-it-all, an intellectual snob…"

"She's neither of those things. You hate her because she never lied about what she was, because she always lived her truth while you hid. You used all of us—and our mother—to hide everything that you were then you tossed us all out when you decided to live the life you wanted. It wasn't Mother's fault or ours that you were afraid to be who you are. You could never stand Jerri because Jerri never hid what she was. She had every reason to run and hide; she never did. I love Jerri, Dad. And you... I don't even know you. Jerri tells me you have his memories, but even though I'm calling you Dad, I'm not feeling it."

"She's damn near a Communist," Georgia said.

"I am not... I am damn near a Socialist, but not a Communist—not even close," Jerri said with a laugh. To the confused look on Tara's face she said, "She didn't hear anything you said after you said she was wrong. She spent the whole time you were talking trying to think of a way to prove that YOU were wrong. She's ultra-competitive. That's why she's so mad that we're sleeping together because in her mind she sees it as her losing the pissing contest we've been having for years. But the truth is she lost that long ago because I never cared what Gary Darting thought of me, and I sure as hell don't care one bit more about what Georgia Darting thinks. She tuned you out the minute you said something she didn't agree with, and... Well isn't that just like your dad, honey?"

"It is." Tara hugged Georgia, and Georgia hugged Tara. They cried, sobbed, said things no one could have understood, and made it really hard for Jerri to drive the truck.

She called Judy and when Judy said she was home Jerri told her they were on their way. Judy was on the front porch when they pulled up in the driveway. When the three of them peeled themselves out of the small cab she took one look at them and said, "What the hell happened?"

"Georgia caught Tara and I together and tried to kill me," Jerri said nonchalantly.

"You knew Jerri was sleeping with Tara?" Georgia thundered at Judy.

"Oh, honey, there is your big male voice again," Judy warned. "Come on in before anyone sees.... Well any of you."

In Judy's house Cyndy brought them all coffee, for which Jerri was very thankful. Judy kept watching Jerri even as she tried to calm Georgia down. Jerri knew why; Judy was expecting her to have a melt-down, but she really didn't think she was going to.

Tara had been pacing back and forth not knowing where

to sit. Finally she just walked over and sat next to Jerri.

Jerri patted her leg and Georgia gave her a dirty look that would peel paint.

"Back off, old woman," Jerri mumbled, taking strength from the gun holstered in the top of her pants behind her back.

Tara no longer seemed to care that her father was there. She rested her head on Jerri's shoulder.

"So basically everyone knew but me," Georgia said, obviously trying to calm down. "My wife…"

"Ex-wife," Judy corrected.

"My daughters…"

"No, just Lori," Tara filled in. "Irva doesn't know yet."

"Why didn't you tell me?" Georgia asked Judy.

"In our community we do not out each other. You just don't. I didn't out you to her or to Jerri even when I figured out who Tara was, and Jerri is my best friend."

"But you knew, Jerri," Georgia said, staring daggers at her. "You knew I couldn't stand you."

"Yes, and thanks for reminding me." Jerri shook her head. "For the record, you aren't exactly my favorite person either, but with all undue respect I'm not banging you; I'm banging your daughter. Or is that the real problem, that I'm not banging you?"

"I'm going to fucking kill you, Jerri," Georgia hissed and started to stand up, but Judy, who was standing behind her no doubt for this purpose, put her hand on Georgia's shoulder and held her in her seat.

Georgia sighed hopelessly and said, "Christ, Tara. She's such a fucking smart ass."

"Her?" Tara moved her head off Jerri's shoulder. "You keep saying awful things to and about her. She can't help it if she's quicker witted so her comebacks are better. She will quit being a smart ass with you the minute you quit trying to kill her and talking crap about her. She will stop verbally tearing you to shreds the minute she believes you respect the fact that I'm a lesbian."

"Did she tell you not to talk to me?" Georgia demanded of Tara.

"No. As stupid as it seems now, she kept trying to get me to talk to you just like she did today. You know, on the day you chased her around like an idiot threatening to kill her!"

Tara yelled, then looked quickly at Jerri.

It was obvious that she was as afraid Jerri was going to flip out as Judy was. And why wasn't Jerri just losing her cookies? I mean this was her trigger in spades... a male voice screaming disparaging things at her, even threatening violence.

I think... I think I'm finally really over it, not just saying the things I want to believe over and over to myself. In this moment my go-to isn't to blame myself. All I want in this moment is to help Tara walk out of it feeling better. Georgia can scream at me, even try to kill me, and I'm not even close to having an episode because I know I'm enough, that I deserve Tara. Not only is it not my fault, but I know Tara belongs with me; I know I make her happy.

She leaned in and whispered in Tara's ear, "Baby, don't worry about me. I'm fine. This isn't my thing; it isn't even yours. It's hers."

Tara turned and gave her a skeptical look.

Jerri shrugged, looked at Judy and said, "I'm fine."

Judy nodded and smiled an indication that she believed Jerri.

Jerri looked at Georgia. "Tara isn't comfortable with the choices you've made, and you aren't comfortable with the ones she has made, so that is your common ground. I think all the reasons you so hated me make very little sense since you are a transwoman. Tara is gay. I didn't make her that way anymore than I made you a woman. I love her, but this is her problem because you're her father not mine. I will support her in whatever she decides. I suggest you try to be a little less rigid and meet her somewhere in the middle. And now I'm going to take my best friend, get another cup of coffee, and go onto the back deck to talk."

She stood up and Tara gave her a panicked look. "You'll be fine." She bent down, kissed her on the forehead, and walked out of the living room into the kitchen.

Judy followed her. "You really are alright."

"Well you don't have to sound so surprised." Jerri kissed her on the cheek then poured herself a cup of coffee and headed for the back deck.

Judy's house was modest but nice. It sat on the side of a hill, so from the deck they had a really nice view of the ocean in the distance. Judy followed her out, but as Jerri sat down on an old metal glider Cyndy had refurbished, Judy stood, undecided.

"Should I go in and referee?" Judy asked.

"You're the shrink, not me."

"Yes, but you wouldn't have said I was going with you if you didn't think they needed to be alone, and you aren't a shrink but you are a witch." Judy sat down across from her so Judy was missing the view.

Cyndy joined them sitting on the glider next to Jerri.

"So... I made a big stinky mess of things between us, didn't I?"

"You drug me into the middle of your project, Judy, even though I wanted no part of it. But it isn't the first time, and if we're honest we both know it won't be the last. This was just very personal for obvious reasons. In your defense you didn't know I was with Tara. Sometimes you could be a better friend..."

"And wife," Cyndy added.

"Yes, you could be a better friend... and wife," Jerri said with a smile, "but you couldn't be a better person. The fact that you are willing to step on the heads of the people who love you for the chance of greater good isn't endearing..."

"Amen," Cyndy said.

"But we know where we stand. You know somewhere below..."

"Way below..." Cyndy helped.

"Your other priorities," Jerri ended.

"Alright I suppose I deserved that. I have been a bad friend... and wife," Judy said. "I know I get tunnel vision when I'm focused on a cause. I don't think we have to worry about this same thing happening in the future because... What are the odds that you'll be banging the daughter of an ex-football player that I'm trying to use to pull transgendered issues out of the darkest of closets, ever again?"

"Very slim," Jerri agreed.

Tara still didn't want to talk to the woman her dad had become, and she didn't really know how. She couldn't even look at her for more than a few seconds much less look into her eyes. The truth was she didn't feel like she owed this virtual stranger any explanation at all. After all where was her explanation as to why her father had done this to all of them?

He had just sprung it on them only moments before telling the world on TV. Then Tara knew just what she wanted to talk about.

"What do you have to say for yourself? You are acting like I did something to you, and I absolutely didn't. The only thing I did was turn off that voice in my head that sounded just like you that said what I wanted for myself was sick and wrong." Then Tara didn't have to worry about not being able to look Georgia in the eyes because Georgia looked at the floor.

"I was just so tired of being Gary." When she said it she didn't even sound like her father anymore. "I never asked to be this way..."

"And I didn't ask to be this way."

Georgia nodded. "I was just trying to do what I thought I was supposed to do. I didn't want to hurt anyone, not your mother and certainly not you girls. I didn't want to be different. Dammit, I wanted to be like everyone else and I worked so hard at it..."

"And so did I. I even married that dumbass. I thought I could do it..."

"The problem is you couldn't live a lie and be happy. Neither could I. Maybe it was very selfish, but you girls are grown and your mother will land on her feet. Tara, if I had to keep looking in the mirror and seeing him I was just going to die. I was either going to find the courage to do what I've done or put a bullet in my head. There wasn't anything in the middle, not anymore."

"I don't know what you want from me, Dad. I understand what you're saying, I do, because it's how I felt when I was with Fred. But doesn't everything you've just said make me, Lori, and Irva collateral damage? A mistake you wish you didn't make?"

"No. I don't want to undo my old life, honey. I'm glad I had you girls. There was a time when I did really love your mother, and part of me always will. I don't want to lose you, especially not you, Tara, and... For the love of God why Jerri? How the hell did you wind up with Jerri Blue?"

"When my soul came to earth I started looking for her, and once I found her I wasn't ever going to let go. I am completely, amazingly in love with her. That's all you need to know. I think if I can handle you being a woman, you ought to be able to deal with the fact that I'm with Jerri," Tara said. Now when

Georgia looked up she was able to hold Georgia's gaze. Tara even managed a smile. "It's not that much to ask, all things considered."

"Judy says we look a lot alike now," Georgia said.

"Yes, and that isn't strange for me at all."

Jerri came running in then flopped on the couch beside her and ordered, "Take a selfie of us."

The last time Tara had even suggested such a thing she had practically had to twist Jerri's arm the way she had Georgia's that morning to get her to allow it.

"Alright." Tara pulled her phone from her jean pocket.

Her dad was giving Jerri a weird look, too, like she didn't understand any more than Tara did why all of the sudden it was a Kodak moment.

"About now a bunch of very disappointed paparazzi are stomping around the beach house, ruining the landscaping, finding nothing even as your mother is having that douche-bag camera man served papers for breach of contract. If you Instagram a picture of us together to your millions of followers..."

"We are no longer a prize," Tara said. She kissed Jerri's cheek. Of course she took three selfies before she found one she was happy with. She posted it with the caption, "So in love with Jerri Blue and don't care who knows."

"Oh, I like that," Jerri said, reading over her shoulder. "See? You're a good writer. That's so much better than the 'suck it' I wanted you to post."

"Can we go home?" Tara asked, feeling as worn out as if it was late night instead of still morning.

"You live together!" Georgia boomed.

"They have been living together for months," Judy said, walking in the living room. "Why does that matter? They do it several times a day. They'd have time for nothing but driving and sex if they didn't live together."

"I don't think you're helping, Judy," Jerri said.

Judy shrugged. "I told the dumbass not to go to Tara's house, but she didn't listen to me any more than she did when I told her not to go to the funeral."

"I miss you," Georgia said to Tara. "I'm sorry I brought the camera crew, and I'm sorry I caused all this, and..."

"It sort of sucked, but now I don't have to worry about it happening," Tara said.

Then she asked Jerri again, "Can we please just go home now?"

"Did you and your dad sort things out?" Jerri asked.

Tara looked at Georgia.

Georgia looked confused for a second and then said, "I'm not going to kill Jerri."

Then she said to Jerri, "You'd better treat her right."

"I do, and I will."

Chapter 18

Irva came sliding into the room, her cell phone in hand. "Mom! Tara just put a picture on Instagram, and..."

"Let me guess; she's gay..." Janice said with a sigh. It wasn't noon yet, and it had already been a hell of a day. Irva showed her the picture and the caption, and Janice actually smiled. "What a simple way to defuse the situation. Not much of a prize to try to catch them together if she's posting pictures herself."

"You knew, Mom?"

"So did I," Lori said smugly as she walked in the room with Tylor on her hip. "Is Tara alright?"

Irva turned to show her the picture and caption.

Lori smiled. "I'm guessing that's a yes."

"Apparently Daddy went over to their house, just walked in and he... dammit she had a meltdown. Tara and Georgia have 'talked it out' whatever that means. Tara is on her way to Jerri's. She wanted me to send someone to get the groceries out of her house so they don't spoil. Only your sister in the middle of all this would worry about leaving a mess." Janice smiled wryly.

"What the hell's going on?" Irva demanded.

"Daddy brought the camera crew with him. One of them had a key, so he just walked in and caught Jerri and Tara together. No, I don't know how 'together' they were. The good news is we found the leak and that little bastard will never work in this town again. The bad news is that before they caught him he had already told every tabloid in this country about Tara and Jerri."

"Is no one even a little freaked out that Tara is gay!" Irva yelled.

"Apparently you are," Janice said. She and Lori looked at each other and shrugged.

Irva seemed to find her sense of humor which she had lost the night before when she'd been caught up in the near riot and her boyfriend had nearly been carted off to jail. She laughed. "I should have known the minute I saw Tara talking to Jerri after her lecture. Remember I even said I thought she had a girl crush. At least this time she's with someone nearly as smart as she is. Tara and Fred made no sense at all."

"Especially since she's a lesbian," Lori said, shaking her head and rolling her eyes.

"We're all just going to lay low for a few days. Try to fly under the radar, and yes, Irva, that includes you. Let's let all this crap blow over," Janice said. To the look on Irva's she face added, "I mean it. I realize Fatty…"

"Fats, Mom; his name is Fats," Irva corrected.

"Yes, how could I mess up something that makes so much sense? A bottle-butted black rapper who never saw a horn, named Fats. I mean it makes perfect sense. I know he's a big hundred-and-twenty-pound bad ass, but we don't need him to go to jail. It won't kill you to just stay home for a couple of days."

"It might," Irva mumbled.

Channing came walking in carrying a plant he had no doubt pulled out of one of the pots they had all over the house. It was dripping water and dirt everywhere. "Channing, what the hell!" Lori yelled.

"This plant wants to go to Harry's," Channing said.

"Shit!" Irva said. "He means Jerri. Even the baby knew before I did."

"Yeah, he can't say J's," Lori said. "Tara said he speaks Hebrew."

"Have to take this plant to Harry's," Channing said with a shrug.

"You'll take that plant and put it right back where you found it," Lori ordered, which Janice figured meant Lori had no more idea than Janice did where he had found the plant.

House full of crap and I seriously don't give a shit about any of it. On any given day if I had to describe a room in this house and the things in that room I couldn't do it. He's making a huge mess and none of us really gives a shit because Rosetta or Margaret will clean it up; we won't. We won't teach them to clean up their own messes and… They'll grow up and be just like Irva expecting that whatever mess they make will magically be cleaned up by someone else.

"Put the plant back and clean the mess up," Janice said.

They all, even Tylor, looked at her like she'd gone mad. "I'm serious. He needs to put the plant back and clean his mess up. What are we teaching them? Nothing! We are teaching them nothing!"

Channing started throwing a wall-eyed fit, demanding to go to Jerri's.

Janice tried to stomp out of the room hoping to lock herself in her bed room and... She ran right into the film crew. She tried to step around or through them; they kept trying to get out of her way but managed to get more in it. Janice just lost it.

"I'm so sick of all this shit!"

"Calm down, Mom," Lori said, even as she was trying to pry the plant out of Channing's grubby little fingers.

"Calm down! Really? Today of all days calm down!" Janice laughed, and hearing it was quite sure her cable had snapped. "I've had no sleep in days. I don't even remember the last time I ate. Since last night it has been one thing after another and... Do you know why these babies don't act like this for your sister and her girlfriend? Because when they are with them they eat real food, not bottled, processed crap, but real food. They don't play with fucking IPads and electronic bullshit that talks back to them, burning seventy-billion points of light through their eyes and into their brains. They play outside in the sunlight in the fresh air. That new-age hippie your sister is shacked up with isn't the one who's crazy; it's us and everyone who lives like us. *This* is what's nuts."

Janice was stomping around talking with her hands, and as her fit became louder than Channing's he quit yelling and handed the plant to his mother as if that was somehow going to fix things.

"Everything we have and everything we are is like a bad made-for-TV movie. Do you think it helps to know *that*..." She pointed at the camera men. "...is all my fault? That I did that to us?" She walked over and picked up Tylor from where Lori had set him down. He was playing in a pile of dirt that had fallen off the plant.

"Grab that plant, Channing. We're going to Harry's," she said.

She turned to face the camera crew. "If anyone at all follows us, I will fire every single one of you, everyone. Hell, why stop there? I will hire a hit man and have you all killed!"

"Mom... I don't think you are safe to drive," Lori said, obviously worried about her kids. The look on Irva's face said she was five seconds from calling the funny farm.

"Todd!" Janice yelled.

He appeared in seconds, which meant he'd been hiding close by just listening.

"Yeah, Mom."

"You're driving," Janice ordered.

Because of course no one ever followed Todd.

From where they were lying crouched in the floor boards of the SUV, Irva was singing. "So long, farewell, Auf Wiedersehen, adieu. Adieu, adieu, To you and you and you…"

"What the hell, Irva," Lori said.

It was clear she thought Janice had lost her mind, and maybe Lori was right. Janice didn't care; she had the sudden need to get them all out of there.

"I feel like that family that ran from the Nazi's at the end of *The Sound Of Music*," Irva said. Clearly Irva was excited.

So was Todd, who kept looking all around covertly in a way that would let anyone who didn't know that he was up to something be sure that he was.

Channing and Tylor who were in their car seats hadn't stopped laughing.

So what did Janice do? She started singing the same song Irva was that neither of them knew. Even as Todd roared out of the driveway past the paparazzi, before she thought it was safe for them to get out of the floorboards, Janice felt a wave of calm rush over her.

Tara and Jerri had just picked the garden. They were heading back to the house, Jerri pushing a wheelbarrow full of produce, when the gate opened and a huge SUV pulled in. Tara recognized the vehicle.

"Dammit, Mother isn't going to be happy till she brings the whole fucking state to our door."

"She's got most of them with her now," Jerri said with a grin.

As Tara watched them peel out of the car she knew just what Jerri meant. "At least they didn't bring the rap star with them," Tara said with a sigh. "I just want to be alone with you, Jerri. Why can't they let us be alone for a minute?"

"They ran away from home," Jerri told her.

"What?"

Oddly it was Todd who was the first one to meet them. He had Tylor on his hip and Channing trailing behind him at a near run. "This is fucking awesome," Todd said. He walked right up and offered Jerri his hand.

Jerri put the wheel barrow down and shook Todd's offered hand.

"I'm Todd; you must be Harry."

"Jerri," she said, looking at Channing then back at Todd. "I have met your children and your clothes before," she said with a grin.

Tylor wanted to go to Tara, so she took him from Todd.

"Your mom sort of wigged out. She insisted we all leave and we were all sort of afraid to tell her no." He pointed back towards the SUV. "She's mostly passed out in there now."

"Why did she come here, Todd?" Tara asked, trying to keep the whiny tone out of her voice.

"She feels exposed and scared and she wants all her chicks in one place. She brought them all here because you're here," Jerri said.

Todd nodded, at least pretending to understand what Jerri had just said.

"But why?" This time Tara was unable to keep the unattractive whine out of her voice.

Jerri laughed and kissed her cheek then took the handles of the wheel barrow and started back for the house.

"It's Channing's fault I think," Todd said. "Something about a plant."

"I brought you a plant, Harry," Channing said from where he was hanging onto one of the wheel barrow handles, mostly making Jerri carry him as he hung there, Tara was sure he thought he was helping.

"Is it a good one?" Jerri asked him.

Channing nodded. "Nana got so mad."

"Did you grow all that stuff?" Todd asked Jerri.

"No, Todd," Tara snapped. "There is a super market in the woods run by woodland creatures and we just came back from shopping. Of course we grew it."

Todd shot her a look. She ignored him and said to Jerri, "I'm sorry."

"Honey, it's alright. I don't mind company at all. It will sort of be nice for me to get to meet the rest of your family without cameras and bullshit. We have plenty of room."

"No we absolutely do not," Tara said, because she knew if they were all there her mother expected them to stay at least the night and there wasn't enough room for all of them. Hell, they fought all the time in that huge house. How were they going to get along all shoved in their super-tiny house with the one bathroom downstairs? They were all going to be at each other's throats. What if all that made Jerri realize she'd made a horrible mistake getting involved with Tara in the first place? Just that morning her father was trying to kill Jerri— all caught on film—and now this. What if it was more than Jerri could handle? After all, Jerri wouldn't have to put up with any of this crap if she wasn't with Tara.

"We do, because I have a really cool tepee I rarely get to set up. Todd and I will pull it down out of the shop, go to The Burn area and set it up. You and I will stay there while they are here. Lori and Todd and the boys can have our room, Your mom can have the guest room and share with Irva, or Irva can sleep on the couch."

"They're all going to bitch about everything, Jerri," Tara said.

"I not bitch, Aunt Tara," Channing said.

"Me either, Aunt Tara," Todd promised with a grin.

Jerri had left the wheel barrow by the back door. Jerri, Todd and the two boys had headed for the shop to get the tepee to load it into the trailer behind the golf cart.

"Where'd all the men folk go?" Irva asked with her best Southern drawl.

"That's not funny, shithead," Tara said.

"It sort of is when your woman is more butch than Lori's husband," Irva said.

"Hey," Lori protested.

Tara sighed and moved to look into the van where her mother was sitting in the back seat with her head against the window, her mouth open and drooling. "Is she alright?"

"If by alright you mean bum-fuck crazy, then yes," Irva said.

"She's exhausted and pissed off at the world," Lori said, glaring at Irva. "But I think she's alright."

Tara smiled an all-knowing smile. "But you all did exactly what she told you to do because you were afraid not to."

"Well yeah," her sisters said in unison. Tara found her

sense of humor again.

She reached in the van and shook her mother, whc didn't wake up. "Mom," she said. Then getting really concerned said louder, "Mom!"

Janice woke up slinging her arms around.

Tara jumped back to keep from being hit. "Mom. come on. Let's take you in the house and you can lie down.'

Her mom nodded and allowed her and Lori to half-carry, half-guide her to the recliner where they sat her down and put her feet up. She was instantly out again—if she had ever been fully awake in the first place.

"What's all this?" Irva asked, pointing to the quotes on the wall.

"Don't start, Irva," Tara said.

"I'm not starting anything. I didn't say I didn't like it, I just..." She flipped her hand in the air in front of herself, dismissing her question and said, "Duh, your girlfriend's a famous author, all smart and stuff."

They aren't being confrontational; I am. Jerri and I have already had a hell of a day, and it pisses me off they are in our space. I'm so afraid they're going to judge me that I'm hearing insults where there aren't any. I need to relax, but... "I'm sorry guys, but the crew caught us together, and Dad tried to kill Jerri. I'm a little on edge."

"Dad really tried to kill Jerri or you're just being dramatic?" Lori asked.

"Yes he—dammit *she*—really did. She chased her all around the beach house screaming that she was going to kill her. He broke our couch, and I jumped on him and twisted her arm behind his back. Jerri went and got the gun. It was a whole huge mess."

Irva laughed. "So somewhere under all the cosmetic surgery and makeup the part of our dad that wanted us to remain virgins for our whole lives is still very much alive."

"Yes and he... dammit *she* hates Jerri. As in Dad hated Jerri before she knew I was sleeping with her. But she's promised not to try to kill her."

"Man, what a fucking day." Irva sat down on the couch. When Tara took a good look at Irva—her sister the model who never had a hair out of place—looked like she had been through the wringer, and there was a bad bruise on Irva's right wrist.

"Are you alright, Irva?"

Irva started to say something flip because... Well, it was Irva. Then she stopped and without saying a word shook her head no. Tara sat down next to her and held her. Irva cried on her shoulder for a minute, then Tara took her sisters into the kitchen and introduced them to Jerri's wine.

They had loaded the teepee, all the poles, and all the bedding onto the trailer—which was way too big a load for it. Then Todd basically lay on top of the load to hold it down. Jerri admitted that she must have more testosterone than estrogen coursing through her body because it was for sure a guy thing to do—trying to take in one trip what would more easily be taken in two.

Channing started to cry that he wanted to ride in the trailer with his dad, but Jerri told him no and that she would let him drive. She drove slowly, but there were still a couple of times when she was afraid she was going to lose the whole load—including Todd. But they got out to the burn site unscathed.

Todd didn't actually know how to *do* anything, but he wanted to help. If she told him just exactly what to do and did a lot of pointing, he was actually not bad help. He was asking about a billion questions as they put the structure together while the boys played on the burn stage.

"And there is a bathroom right there?" he said as he helped her carry the futon mattress into the teepee to put it on the frame.

"Yep, toilets, sinks, showers... the works. We have a few big parties here every year, and I have friends who come out to camp all the time. Sometimes we have huge camp outs, so... I built all this mostly to keep people from stomping my plants to pieces and scaring my livestock. "

"And the lights come on when it gets dark?"

"Yep I flipped them to 'on' so they will come on as soon as it gets dark and go off again when it gets light. It's all solar powered. so Tara and I will be just fine out here."

"Lori, the boys and I could stay out here. I don't want to kick you out of your own room."

"I don't mind; I'd sort of like to stay in it." Then she saw the look on his face and grinned. "And so would you."

He nodded.

"I know Tara wouldn't mind staying out here at all. What

about Lori?"

"I've never been able to get her to go camping, but this... This is pretty swank, so not really like camping. All we have to do is get the boys to want to do it; then she'll have to or listen to them cry and whine. I know it looks like we fight like cats and dogs..."

"I've never seen the show," Jerri said. "Just because people fight doesn't mean they don't get along." He gave her a confused look and she shrugged. "At a scream is how some people communicate. It was the way my ex communicated. You can fight with someone and still love them. I don't like it, and I won't have it because I put up with it for years. Please don't yell at each other on my place. In fact, that's the only real rule; don't yell at each other."

He nodded. "There are no other women here except her mom and her sisters. Most of our fights are because Lori's super jealous..."

"So is Tara. What the hell is up with that?" Jerri asked in disbelief.

"Dude, you used to sleep with Rhonda Heart, and you're like a super famous, rich writer. I get why Tara would be jealous of you. But me? I'm not bad looking, but certainly there are better-looking guys around, and do you know what I was doing when I met Lori?"

Jerri shook her head.

"I was DJ-ing at a crap club. Not a swank club, a crap one. I paid my bills, but that was about it. Lori and her sisters came there slumming. From the moment I saw her..." He smiled and shrugged. "I mean she's hot, and funny and smart. Not Tara-smart, thank God, because I already spend way too much time pretending I know what Lori's saying. We just had chemistry right away and her whole family just hated me— which you and I both know was why she just had to have me. When we first started dating I had several girlfriends, but she knew that, and as soon as we got serious I stop seeing any of them, but... She is still insanely jealous. If I'm honest, it's a little bit of a turn on."

Jerri gave him a startled look and he laughed. "It is isn't it?"

"Yes, and if you tell Tara I said so I'll kill you. So what do you do now?"

"I let them film me. I mostly watch the boys, play video

games and light Twitter up. It's not like we need the money, and every time I try to DJ in a club—and now of course I can get the best gigs—Lori has a complete jealous meltdown... the kind that isn't fun at all if you know what I mean."

Turned out Todd had come from a lower-middle-class background, the same but different from hers. He grew up camping and fishing. He liked to play basketball and drink beer. He hated to watch sports and liked to play guitar, but said he wasn't very good at it. He hadn't minded the cameras in the beginning, but now he wasn't crazy about his kids being on camera all the time and he blamed them for most of the fights he and Lori had. He felt like he was a pretty good dad and Lori was a pretty good mom, and that her family judged them both pretty harshly when it came to their parenting style.

Tara had said he hardly spoke and then only in one to three word sentences, but as they finished setting up the camp and she took him around the homestead he liked to talked her leg off her body. When they got back to the house he stayed on the porch to watch the boys who were playing in the front yard.

She found Tara in the kitchen with her sisters, making dinner. "Harold and Peter and Julie all came by. They took stuff and left stuff. I trusted that they knew what they were doing," Tara told her.

Jerri went to look where Tara pointed and she had three loafs of bread, three quarts of peach preserves, and a box of homemade laundry detergent.

"It's perfect." Jerri walked up behind Tara where she was working at the counter, wrapped her arms around her waist and kissed the side of her neck.

Tara stiffened and Jerri wondered why. Then realized Tara's sisters were in the room. Jerri didn't let her go or move, though because by God this was her house, and she'd hug her woman if she wanted to.

"Looks like we're staying in our room. The boys begged Todd to stay in the teepee, and he said he'd ask Lori."

"Teepee! I'm not staying in a teepee in the woods. Is he nuts? Where is that dumbass?" Lori asked.

"On the porch, and no yelling on our place," Jerri said as Lori left the room. She released Tara went to the fridge and pulled out a beer. "I'd ask if either one of you want one, but it's clear you have been hitting the vino."

"It's really good," Irva said, and from the glassy look in her eyes she'd had more than a little. "I'm Irva." She held out her hand and Jerri shook it.

"Pleasure to meet you," Jerri said.

Tara turned around. "What an ass I am. I forgot you haven't actually met either of them have you?"

"Not since you were kids. I saw them both at the party we fled from, but didn't actually meet them," Jerri said. She grinned. "I answered her question during my lecture."

Lori walked back in and looked at Jerri, and now Jerri could see that Lori had also been drinking quite a bit of wine.

"Is it really more like a house than a tent?"

"Yes..."

"Jerri, this is Lori; Lori this is Jerri," Tara said quickly.

Lori grinned wildly at her sister and then back at Jerri.

"This is Jerri? And yet there isn't a bright light shining on her tongue or anything."

Irva and Jerri both laughed.

Apparently Tara wasn't amused. "You are such an asshole, Lori."

Tara went back to doing whatever she was doing at the sink.

"Jerri, I sort of want to stay in the teepee."

"Honey, we can do it any time. The boys..."

"Is it really nice like Todd says, or is he full of shit?"

Jerri dug the keys to her golf cart out of her pocket, walked over and handed them to Lori. "Have Todd take you and show you himself. If you don't want to stay there, Tara and I will happily stay in the teepee."

"I can't believe you two are fighting over who sleeps in a damn tent. And my choices are sleeping with mother or on the couch."

"The couch makes into a bed," Jerri said, not seeing the problem.

"It does? Hell, I didn't know that," Tara mumbled.

"Yeah, it's one of the old flip style couches. You pick the front up till it unlatches and then the back and the seat are even and it makes a full-sized bed," Jerri said.

Lori left with the key.

"What do you want me to do, baby?" Jerri asked.

"I was just going to make some of those pizza things you

make, pan fry a bunch of the squash and make a big salad. Lori and Irva and I have done most of the prep work, so now it's just putting stuff together. Why don't you go see if you can maybe wake mother up?"

Jerri poured a glass of wine and started for the living room, her beer in one hand the wine glass in the other.

Irva giggled and said, "You can tell she knows mother."

Jerri walked in and put the wine glass under Janice's nose.

Janice sniffed at the air a couple of times and finally opened an eye. She took the glass of wine from Jerri's hand before she had even fully opened both eyes and took a sip before she was fully awake.

"What happened?"

"You went to sleep in the car on the way here. The girls brought you in and you mostly didn't wake up. How are you doing, Janice?"

"Is everyone here at your house, Jerri?"

Jerri nodded.

"Then I'm sorry for imposing on you and Tara again, but so glad to be here, to have them all here. Bet you didn't know you were getting a whole crazy-assed family did you?"

"Actually I did, and it's more than alright. Hell, I got to put my teepee up. I haven't had an excuse to do that for over a year."

"I'm so shocked that Jerri Blue has a teepee."

"Authentic actually, one of the fans made it for me."

"It's a horrible burden to be a mother, Jerri. A blessing and a curse."

"I wouldn't know, nor do I wish to find out."

"What about the kid, Jerri?" Janice asked in a whisper.

Jerri could feel the color leave her face and her stomach knot up. She took a deep breath and let it out.

"Fucking Rhonda," Jerri cursed in a whisper. "I don't have a kid, Janice. I don't. You understand me? I *never* had a kid."

And how did Rhonda know? Because the kid had some kind of health issue and Amy called to ask for Jerri's family medical history, but Rhonda had answered her phone. Amy had told Rhonda way too much before she knew she wasn't talking to Jerri.

"I'm sorry, Jerri. I just thought..."

Jerri took a deep breath and let it out. Janice didn't bring it up to be a bitch. Jerri took another deep breath and let it out even more slowly. "I don't know what it's like to be a mother, Janice, because I never was one. I didn't want her. I never held her. I gave her to people who did want her. So, no, I don't know your pain, and you don't know mine. I don't want Tara to know."

"I won't tell her."

Jerri headed for the door.

"I'm sorry Jerri."

Jerri walked outside, walked between the two boys, grabbed her stump and headed for the darkest part of the woods. She certainly couldn't be slinging her stump around in front of the house with Tara's whole family there.

From the door Janice got her attention and called Tara into the living room.

"You alright, Mom?"

"Mostly, but I said something without fully thinking it through that really upset Jerri, and she took off."

"What did you say, Mom?" Tara said, and she was really pissed off because the fact that Jerri hadn't had a meltdown yet today was a small miracle. Why couldn't her mother have picked her words more carefully?

"I said I felt like I'd been raped," Janice said.

"Great, Mom, really sensitive. Can you help Irva finish dinner?" Janice nodded and Tara walked out the front door. She saw Jerri's bottle of beer sitting on the rail and noticed real quick that the stump was gone. She grabbed the beer bottle and headed for the darkest part of the woods.

Jerri slung the stump as hard and as far as she could, yelling a long list of obscenities. She was crying uncontrollably. Why wasn't this working?

She felt Tara, looked up, and Tara was standing in the shadows with Jerri's beer in her hand, waiting.

What is she waiting for? For me to calm down so that she can try to make me feel even a little bit better.

Jerri had the stump over her head ready to throw it, but then she just set it down, sat on it, put her head in her hands and kept crying.

Tara walked slowly over and handed her the beer. Jerri dried her eyes on her fist and took a long drink.

"I'm sorry for what my mom said."

"What did she say she said?"

"That she felt like she'd been raped..."

"That's a lie, and I'm not that fragile." Jerri wiped the copious snot from her face with her hand because she had nothing else, then rubbed her hands in the pine needles at her feet which made a God-awful mess.

"I don't want to tell you because it's another horrible thing, Tara. I didn't tell Rhonda, but she found out and apparently she told your mother. Your mother didn't mean to upset me; she thought I might understand what she's going through because I gave birth."

She didn't give Tara even a second to process it, she just kept talking because she knew she had to tell her now and the only way she was going to was if she did it fast.

"I gave birth but I was never a mother. It's not the same at all. Don't be mad at your mother because if she was in her right mind she would have known that. And please don't be mad at me."

She took another long drink of the beer trying to wash the tears out of her throat.

"It was before the morning-after pill, Tara. I got pregnant from the rape. I got pregnant."

Tara sat down hard on the ground in front of her.

"I was going to have an abortion, but I worked with this really nice guy Tim. He and his wife Amy helped me out a lot right after the attack. Hell they gave me and Bob a place to live when I couldn't work and couldn't make my rent. They had been trying to have a kid for years; they couldn't get pregnant and had been turned down flat for a traditional adoption because Tim was diabetic. They said maybe something good could come out of what I'd been through. If I had the baby and gave it to them they would pay all my medical expenses and give me enough money to get to LA. Three thousand bucks. I went through nine months of hell and gave birth for three thousand dollars. Now I make five times that for a one-hour lecture. So there is this young woman who has a life now, and Tim and Amy got to have the child they wanted because I didn't have an abortion. In spite of all that there are still times I wonder if I did the right thing because that baby grew in a toxic stew of hate and anger in my belly. That was the worst time of my life. The pregnancy was a constant reminder of what had happened to me, and I was still healing from my physical injuries, too. I wrote *Burning Rain* during that time, and if I think about it Judy is right; that's the real reason I hate that fucking book." She didn't want to start crying again, but she did.

"Have you ever seen her?" Tara asked, and she was crying too now. Seemed that it was the day for crying, screaming and throwing fits... *And not all of it was on camera, so that's a first for most of them.*

"Once, right before you came out here for the first time as a matter of fact. It's why I was such a mess. She always knew she was adopted, and I had agreed to see her if ever wanted or needed to see me but it was never something I wanted or needed. She doesn't know who I am. We—her parents and I— used my given name, and before you ask I lied to her about how she was conceived. I felt no connection to her at all, none. All meeting her did was open some nasty wounds I had to work extra hard to close. Are you mad at me?"

"No. I'm mad at my mother because that was much more insensitive than the lie she told about what she had said. Jerri... I don't know anyone who would have had the strength to do what you did. I wouldn't have. There are so many ass holes in this world, and they all have lame-ass excuses for the fucked-up shit they do because they don't feel good. Then there is you; you have every reason in the world to be bitter and hateful, to just take it out on the whole world, but you don't. No, you pull a heavy stump to the middle of the woods, heave it around and cuss. You don't put it on anyone else. I just wish... I wish I could take any part of it off of you."

"You do, Tara."

"No I don't." Tara sniffled and dried her face on the back of her hand.

Jerri was happy to see they were equally snotty because then she didn't have to be so embarrassed about her nose running like a faucet.

"None of what happened today would have happened to you if you weren't with me. This morning the camera crew stomped into our house, my Dad tried to kill you, and now my whole damn family—except Georgia—is here, and Mother just had to pick at your worst wound till she made it bleed. All that crap in one day is too much for me, and I don't have PTSD. I want to help you, but all this crap is just making everything worse for you."

But when Jerri sat there and searched herself—before she said things just to make Tara feel better that were lies—she realized she was agitated and upset, but she wasn't at the bottom of the dark pit of despair. It wasn't playing in a loop in her brain. It tried to, but the minute she told Tara and she said exactly what she most needed to hear, it lost all its power.

"If we weren't both covered in our own snot I'd kiss you."

"Why?" Tara laughed and sniffled at the same time. "It is annoying. I wish I'd thought to grab a box of tissues."

"Hey, at least you grabbed my beer," Jerri said, holding it up. She took another swig then handed it to Tara who took a drink and handed it right back.

"I swear, Tara, the truth is I don't know how you do it, but you always make me feel better. You can stop being worried right now because I'm not even close to having an episode."

"I love you, Jerri. I never meant to bring all this crazy-assed shit into your life."

"If I get to be with you, Tara, I'll take the crazy-assed shit any day. Come on."

She got up put down her hand and helped Tara to her feet. Then she handed Tara her beer, bent down and picked up her stump. "Let's go clean up in the creek so that we can then pretend that no one can tell we've been crying. Then let's go back to the house."

Jerri pulled out a card table, stuck it against their table and pulled out a bunch of folding chairs. It was tight, but they were all sitting at the table in the kitchen. Tara was sitting next to Jerri keeping an eye on her. She seemed to be alright, but seriously Tara felt like her brain was going to melt and she didn't know how Jerri was doing it.

"So how was the teepee?" Irva asked Lori.

"Bigger than the house." Lori laughed. "And there is a bathroom, but it's a good twenty feet away." She looked at Todd. "You have to go with me if I get up at night."

He just nodded.

"These are really good, Tara," Todd said of the pizza-like things.

"It's Jerri's recipe and she made the cheese," Tara said.

"Why is it called evil-goat pizza?" Irva asked.

"Don't ask," her mother said.

Tara was trying not to be, but she was still mad at her mother. Why on earth would Janice ever in a million years think it was alright to ask Jerri about the baby she had given away? It hurt Tara's heart that Jerri had to relive it for even a minute. Jerri obviously didn't want to tell Tara about it, why would she? The truth was Tara sort of wished she didn't know, but she knew why Jerri felt like she had to tell her; if Rhonda had told her mother, she had told other people as well. Now that the world knew Tara and Jerri were together they would dig up everything about Jerri. If Tara had to hear it, she was glad she'd heard it from Jerri, but she still wished she didn't know. Tara really had no idea where to put the knowledge that somewhere out there was a twenty-year-old woman with half of Jerri's DNA.

Jerri leaned over and whispered in her ear. "I'm alright. Are you?"

Tara nodded then moved and whispered in Jerri's ear. "I'm just... what do you call it... feeling pretty raw. You have had a seriously crappy life."

Jerri chuckled and whispered in her ear. "I've really had an extraordinary life. I had a crappy childhood, a really rough nine months, and a horrible break up with an awful bitch, but most of my life has really been pretty good with some bad moments just like everyone else's. And right now it's perfect."

Tara then whispered in her ear. "And now I'm worried you ARE insane because this was a horrible, crazy-assed day."

Jerri then whispered in her ear. "That is the only gift of having one really bad day; it puts everything else in perspective. We're alright. Everyone we love is alright. I didn't want to tell you, but I think maybe I needed to and we're alright... We are alright, aren't we?"

"Yes, we're alright." Tara kissed her cheek.

Then Tara realized that her family, who were normally so loud you couldn't hear yourself think, were all very quiet. When she looked up they all got really interested in dinner which meant they'd been trying to hear what she and Jerri were talking about.

"What a bunch of ass hats."

"Mom always said it's rude to whisper at the dinner table," Irva reminded her.

"Yes, well it's mother's fault we were whispering, so I think that cancels out her rule," Tara said. "Besides it's our house. Our house, our rules. That's also something Mom always says."

"I wonder how fattening this squash is. I think I could eat like a giant plate of it," Lori said.

"You already have," Irva informed.

"More," Tylor said, and shoved his empty plate at Tara. She gave him another slice of the pizza and he clapped and took his plate from her.

"Normally I can't get them to eat anything but crap," Lori mumbled.

"Is there more wine?" Irva asked, holding up the empty bottle.

"In the basement." Jerri got up and started for the door in the corner that led to the stairs to the root cellar and Tara got up and nearly ran after her. Jerri didn't ask why, just took her hand and lead her down the stairs.

Tara closed the door behind them. At the bottom of the stairs Jerri took her in her arms and kissed her. Tara wondered how she knew just what she needed.

"What were they whispering about?" Irva asked Lori who was closer to them.

"I'm not sure," Lori said. "I couldn't hear them."

"Maybe they wanted to have a private conversation," Janice said.

"If I think Jerri's a little hot does that make me queer, too?" Irva asked.

"Christ, Irva." Lori shook her head.

"I read somewhere that all women are gay or bisexual," Todd said conversationally.

"It ain't ever gonna happen, Todd," Lori hissed.

"They all think they want that," Irva told her sister. "But I bet they wouldn't think it was cool at all if they wound up standing alone in the corner."

"More!" Tylor said. He pushed his plate at Lori.

She looked at him in disbelief then looked under the table to see if he was maybe dropping it.

"You want to try some squash?" she said. He nodded and she put some on his plate and handed it to him. He took an experimental bite then she watched as he all but inhaled the food on his plate and then shoved it towards her again.

"More."

"He never eats," Todd said in disbelief.

"Nothing that doesn't come in a plastic package with a picture of a clown at least. I wonder if he would eat till he made himself sick. That's a lot of food, isn't it?" Lori asked her mother.

"Give him some more milk," Janice said. "A kid will eat themselves sick, but I doubt this food will do it."

"Which is good because Channing has eaten more than I have," Irva pointed out.

When Janice looked at her grandson his plate was empty and he was reaching for—of all things—the salad. Irva helped him put a bunch on his plate and then he was just eating. Not getting up and running around screaming. They were both hungry and they were eating whatever they were given.

"They played outside all afternoon and now they're hungry." Janice smiled. She couldn't remember a more hectic, bullshit day, but she couldn't remember the last time her family had really sat down and enjoyed a meal without some kind of explosion or the kids acting like escaped inmates from a mental institution. She hadn't seen either Todd or Lori argue or touch their smart phones all day. Irva had a couple of times, but the last time Janice saw Irva's phone it was sitting on an end table in the living room.

It's not just because there is no camera crew—though that's the biggest difference. People were never meant to live in boxes away from nature. It's not healthy, not mentally or spiritually or physically. Pretty sure I read that off Jerri's wall somewhere, but it's true.

"Listen up," Janice said. "I don't care how long it takes your sister and Jerri to get back with that wine; I don't want you to give them any shit…"

"Ahh, Mom…" Irva started.

"I mean it. They have had a seriously screwed up day, much worse than any of ours. Part of that was my fault, and us all being here isn't helping them. This is their place so don't ride them high about taking a half hour to get a bottle of wine or it taking both of them—maybe especially if they get back without the wine. I need to be here right now, I think we all do. So don't ask what the food is or how it's made, just eat it and say thank you. Don't bitch about the one bathroom that is downstairs or anything else. Try to be gracious and give them their space."

They all nodded silently and when thirty minutes later Tara and Jerri returned without the wine they didn't say a word as Jerri mumbled and went back after it herself.

Chapter 19

Janice had slept hard. She didn't appreciate her phone ringing and waking her up. When she looked at the clock it was ten; she had slept twelve hours, so it wouldn't be fair to cuss out whoever was calling. But when she picked up the phone and saw it was Georgia she almost answered just to tell her to go to hell. Then she nearly just shut her phone off without answering at all.

Instead she sat up in bed and answered the phone. "What?"

"I was afraid you wouldn't answer."

"I almost didn't."

"I need to talk to you. Have you seen the crap they are saying about Tara on the internet? On TV?"

Janice took a deep breath and let it out. "I have not nor do I want to."

"Most people have been really supportive of her, sort of like they have been with me but, just like it has been with me the bad stuff is really bad... That ass hat Sam Parker..."

"You mean your good buddy, right-wing US senator Sam Parker who you spent a small fortune of our money to get into office?"

"He called a fucking press conference, Janice. He called a press conference to say that what's wrong with America's youth is that they watch our girls on TV. He said that our girls need to understand that they are role models. He called Tara an abomination, Janice. He said Tara was an abomination, and what could anyone expect when her father was an obvious sexual deviant, a freak. He asked the cable network to cancel all our shows and for our sponsors to pull their support."

"Well that ought to get everyone who doesn't watch us now to tune in," Janice mumbled. "I told you a long time ago he was a bastard. You and I haven't agreed on politics for years, but how on earth can you support that party being what you are now?"

"I can't. Not anymore and I won't. I'm done trying to defend my politics to you, my kids, or my new friends. It was alright when they were taking pot shots at me, but how dare they say anything like that about Tara."

Janice wasn't really shocked about Georgia's turn around. After all Gary had been the classic Dad; he could say anything he wanted to or about his kids, but no one else was allowed to. And Tara had always had a special place in his heart. That hadn't changed because he became a woman.

"Does this mean you accept that Tara is a lesbian?"

"Fucking Jerri Blue," her ex hissed, so apparently he still wasn't over his mad at Jerri.

"The same fucking Jerri Blue who has given you the words that have kept the world from attacking you? Or the Jerri Blue that has made our daughter so happy she glows?"

Georgia laughed. "You know I think I'm maddest at her right now because I know she's going to get that smug-ass look on her face when I have to admit that she was right and I was wrong." There was a long pause and then she said, "I miss you, Janice."

"As much as I hate to admit it, I miss you, too."

"I know I have been really hard to deal with. I know what I did blindsided you and especially the girls. It was selfish; I realize that now. I should have found a better way. I never wanted to hurt you, Janice. I just couldn't be him anymore. I know I said some mean-assed things, but it wasn't your fault. I don't need my wife back, but I do need my best friend. I know it's hard for you to see me..."

"But I will learn. I can't promise to get your name or the pronouns right, but I'll try. We still have a family; we need to try to pull it back together if we can."

"Can I come by and see you Janice, just to talk?"

"No, because we're all hiding at Jerri's. Though I know your friend knows where Jerri is, I do not want you to come up here. Someone will follow you, and then everyone will know where we are. We all need not to be in the public eye right now, but especially Tara doesn't need or want it."

"You're right. The film crew has been up my ass ever since Judy brought me home and there are paparazzi everywhere. Could you do me a favor?"

Janice laughed. "Now you're pushing it."

"Could you ask Jerri to call me? I want to call a press conference, and I need her help."

"Why don't you just call her? I know you have her number."

"I tried to kill her yesterday," Georgia reminded.

"Yes, that's what I heard."

"I was just so mad when I saw them together…"

"Were they…"

"Don't even say it. They were just in the kitchen together, but it was pretty obvious what they'd been up to."

"What do you want me to say to Jerri to make her want to help you yet again… you know after you tried to kill her?"

"If I knew what to say I'd call her myself, but I doubt either she or Tara would answer the phone."

"I thought you and Tara talked things out."

"We did sort of, but we're a long way from in a good place… fucking Jerri."

"You're still mad at Jerri, so you are assuming she won't talk to you but Gar… Georgia you have to know…"

There was a knock on the door then Tara walked in.

"I heard you up; we saved you some breakfast." She saw Janice was on the phone. "Sorry, Mom."

"It's alright. It's just your dad. Here, talk to her while I rush downstairs. I'm about to pee myself."

Janice handed her the phone then took off. Tara sighed and put the phone to her ear. "Hello Dad."

"Are you alright, Tara?"

"Yes, because Jerri took my smart phone and won't let anyone turn the TV or a radio on. When Irva started to show me something on her phone this morning, Lori threatened to hit her. We knew what it was going to be like when people found out, and we made a pact to just not read or see or hear any of it—which is easy to do here."

"Judy said Jerri has a wonderful farm. That you love it there."

"I do," Tara said, and realized it was easier to talk to her dad on the phone because she couldn't see "her", just hear her dad.

"You always did love to be outside. You were our nature girl for sure. When we went camping I had to watch you like a hawk or you just wandered off into the woods. Your mother used to love to garden, and you were always in the dirt up to your elbows helping her… Tara, I was wrong about a lot of things. Mostly right now I have to admit my politics were wrong, and I want to make a statement…"

"You need Jerri's help." Tara smiled "But you don't want

Jerri to gloat."

"Yes."

"I can't make any promises." Tara laughed. "She and Todd took the boys fishing. I'll have her call you when she gets back."

"I really am sorry about yesterday, everything about yesterday, Tara, except talking to you."

"It's alright, Dad. I'm kind of glad everyone knows now. There are always haters in the world that are going to talk crap. I'm just not going to listen to them—any of them — anymore. I'm not the fat one or the boring one, and I'm not going to let them make me the gay one. I'm just me and I'm alright with that. I trust myself—for the first time in my life I trust what I think over what other people think about me."

"You know what, Tara, you and I are at a very similar place in our lives. Thank God you had the courage to stand in your truth before I did."

"You need to not listen to or read or see any of the crap too, Dad. Just enjoy being you; that's what I'm going to do. I love you, Dad. Don't really know what to call or how to think about you yet, but I love you."

"I love you, Tara."

Janice watched as Jerri plugged the TV back in. Jerri turned and looked at Janice and her daughters as if she were scolding a roomful of willful children.

"Your dad's press conference, and that's it."

Jerri reluctantly turned the TV on then, never relinquishing the remote, moved and sat beside Tara. Tara wrapped her arms around Jerri's neck and put her head on her shoulder. Jerri put one arm around her while having her finger on the off button of the remote with the other. Jerri wanted to shelter Tara from the ugly tide of public opinion, and why did Jerri know how ugly that could be? Because Rhonda had come out fifteen minutes after sleeping with Jerri, and since at the time Jerri Blue was "nobody" everything from the perversity of lesbians to gold-digging had come into play. None of it was aimed at the pretty, petite blond goddess. All of it was directed at the dark, brooding, lumbering dyke she was bedding. And while LBGT issues weren't as hot button an issue as they were fifteen years ago, they didn't have to be because you could be drawn and quartered by every tom Dick and Harry with access to the internet.

Things the media would never dare say, some ass hat Baptist chicken-plucker in Bum-fuck Nowhere could post, and the ignorant hate they spewed would go viral. Everyone would see it whether they wanted to or not just because everyone who agreed would repost it, but everyone who didn't would be just as quick to do so. How hard was it to figure out that reposting anything with the tag line, "Look what this hateful bastard just posted," meant you were posting it, too? That people who otherwise would have never seen it were seeing it now.

There would be no stopping the tide of public opinion. The Dartings were used to it because they had been Twitter popcorn for years, and it was still hard when people were saying really horrid things and passing judgement on you. Jerri had been hiding in the woods for ten years and Janice wasn't so sure Jerri knew what she'd gotten herself into. Then she actually thought about it.

Jerri HAS been hiding in the woods for ten years. She doesn't need any money. If she had to stay right here and live on her farm for the rest of her life to avoid nasty people saying horrid things she would. It won't last long. It won't take but a few weeks or someone else doing something ever more scandalous for all of this to be yesterday's news.

Georgia cleared her throat as the camera zoomed in on her, and Janice watched her children and found that not one of them could really look at the TV any more than she could. It was going to take a while for any of them to look at Georgia and not think about Gary. *Longer than it will take people to stop talking crap about Tara and Jerri.*

"Mean people suck," Georgia said.

They all laughed and Janice looked at Jerri to see if Jerri was wigging out which she was sure Jerri would do if Georgia got off script.

Jerri seemed fine.

"State Senator Sam Parker is a douche bag." Now they ALL looked at Jerri.

Jerri shrugged. "Yep, I wrote that, too."

"...I have supported Sam Parker for over ten years. I've given him money, helped with his campaigns, and now... He doesn't care about my politics at all. He wants to attack me because of who and what I am and that... that I could take. I wouldn't golf with him anymore, but I would have accepted it. But for him to attack my children, to call Tara an abomination of all things... I am not the only Republican who has had sexual reassignment surgery, and I can assure you I am not by far the only Republican who has a gay child. However I think I very well may be the last member of the LBGT community to actively support a repressive conservative agenda. Why? Why would I continue to argue with all my friends, with my daughters, and my ex-wife—who have never agreed with my politics? Why did I continue to support Republican candidates?

"Because I thought they wanted the same kind of America I wanted, but I was wrong. You see I like my guns, I don't want to pay taxes, and I don't really approve of the welfare system. I don't want big government. But you know what I most don't want my government to do? To discriminate against people, *any* people. Their definition of big government is people passing laws they don't like. As long as they are the ones passing laws they have no problem with big government... big brother... at all. I don't want them to pass laws to keep people like me from having the rights we deserve as working, law-abiding, tax-paying members of this country. It's not easy to be LBGT in America; I'm just now figuring that out. Being who we are is no more a choice for us than it is for anyone else. Our choices are clear, be miserable or be your true self.

"As a party they consistently try to stifle human expression, to repress those people who are different. Let me tell you something you already know—a world full of people Sam Parker would approve of—now that would be a sick world indeed.

"He called my child an abomination not because of anything she has done but because of who she loves. He judged me because I make him uncomfortable. But mostly he said all the hideous things he said about me and mine because he and the ultra-right wing of the Republican Party have taken very large contributions from me over many years and they now want to distance themselves from me because I am an embarrassment to them.

"Now for a lot of you that is just going to strengthen your conviction to blindly follow the party line. But for those of you unafraid to use your intellect, to *see* people instead of judging them, ask yourselves if this is a party you can continue to support. Today they hate me and my daughter and all people like us. Who will be next on their hit parade? They are playing on people's ignorance and their fear. They pull your attention towards our community for one reason and one reason only: they think it is easy for them to make you hate us and in doing so unite America in a common cause. Us against them—history shows us that 'us against them' is the maker of death and war and abuse of all kinds. I'm sure all my former friends will rejoice, but as of this day I am no longer a registered Republican. It is my hope that if you care at all about human rights and dignity and you are a Republican as I was, you will walk away or—better yet—take your party back. Thank you."

They all turned to look at Jerri and she smiled. "Every word." Then she turned the TV off, walked over and unplugged it. She even fiddled with the dish stuff no doubt so they couldn't turn it back on if they tried. Jerri then left the house and Tara followed.

Irva smiled and looked at her mom. "So now that they aren't here can we make fun of the way Tara has to follow Jerri everywhere she goes, that she constantly has to have her hands on her, and that Tara screams like a banshee when she gets off?"

"We were in the teepee, so I didn't hear," Lori said with a laugh. "I did hear her last night when they were in the basement and we were all pretending to be idiots. I'm pretty sure she was working at being quiet, so I can imagine."

"I slept fine on the antique bed-couch thing. How did you do in the teepee?" Irva teased.

Janice watched as Lori winked at her sister then said, "It was amazing. The boys went to sleep as soon as their heads hit their pillows and slept through the night without waking up once. Todd and I..." She winked at her sister again as if Janice couldn't handle the knowledge that they got a little in the teepee. "...went to sleep. I didn't even get up to pee till the sun was way up. The boys were still asleep so I went out and just kind of walked around the camp. I felt so at peace, and I thought, *Wow! Maybe mom was right when she was having her screaming hissy fit yesterday.*"

"The magic hippie cocoa Jerri makes puts me right to sleep," Janice said. Then grinning wildly at Lori added, "I hope you and Todd didn't scare all the farm animals so that they don't produce, because for you to even think to make fun of how loud your sister is during orgasm is a riot all by itself."

"She's got you there." Irva laughed.

They were... They were enjoying each other's company. They weren't at each other's throats. If Todd and Lori had fought at all since they got there they had done so quietly. Why? *We're relaxed, yesterday was a huge, tense, mind-numbing mess, and today we realize that we all lived through it so it wasn't that bad and we're relaxed. All our skeletons are out of the closet. What can they do to us that they haven't already done hundreds of times over the last ten years?*

"How long do we have to stay at Jerri's secret fortress of solitude?" Irva asked.

Janice shrugged. She wasn't ready to even think about leaving.

"You know at Pat's party I thought Tara was being super obvious, but now that I see Tara without the cameras, the crowds and at home with Jerri she was actually playing it really cool," Lori said. "Especially since Rhonda was there."

"Oh crap!" Janice said as sudden realization slid into her brain.

"What now?" Irva asked.

"I'd bet money that Rhonda is having a complete mental break down about now."

"Why?" Irva asked.

"Why do you think, Irva? Rhonda still has the hots for Jerri," Lori said. She rolled her eyes and looked at Janice. "Just don't answer your phone, Mom. Rhonda isn't going to find you up here."

"You know what? You are absolutely right." Janice got up and started for the front door.

"Where are you going?" Irva asked.

"Out to find where Todd took the boys and go play with my grandsons."

Tara looked up from where she was feeding the kid a bottle. "Are you sure you're alright, Jerri?"

Jerri looked down at her from the hole that led into the hay loft where she was hanging herbs from the rafters to dry.

"My only problem right now is that my fiancé won't stop asking me if I'm alright every ten seconds, which is mildly annoying."

Tara laughed. "Okay, point taken... What did you just say?"

Jerri jumped out of the hayloft, landing nearly on her.

Tara jumped and the bottle went flying which pissed the kid right off. He took off running in the direction of the bottle then tried to drink it where it sat on the floor. Tara looked up at Jerri from where she sat on the milk stanchion.

Jerri smiled down at her. "You aren't going to make me do something as gauche as asking if you will marry me, are you?"

For a second she couldn't find her voice, couldn't even think.

"It's alright, Tara. It's too soon and you just got divorced a few months ago. I'm rushing you..."

"Give me a second, Jerri," Tara said quickly. She stood up and looked into Jerri's eyes. "You want to get married?"

"Not if you don't...

"After yesterday... What do you want, Jerri?"

"After yesterday we aren't hiding from anyone and there are no secrets between us. I wouldn't ask if I didn't want to marry you."

"It... it just doesn't seem like something you'd want to do, the whole establishment thing and..."

"I fought long and hard for us to have the same rights as everyone else to marry. People don't get married for some religious bullshit or even just because they are in love. We don't need a stupid-ass piece of paper to prove we love each other and in a perfect world where there wasn't a bunch of legal shit to worry about we wouldn't need to be married. I fought for us to have marriage equality for legal reasons. We should get married so that no one can question who makes decisions for us if we can't when we're in the hospital, for tax and insurance purposes. So that no one can contest my will which I have already changed, and no..." She held her hand up as Tara started to speak. "I don't want to have a conversation where you say you don't want to think about my death because you know that to me death is just part of life. If anything happens to me I want you to have this place and whatever money I have. We should get married because we love each other and because if we aren't legally married we won't be able to take care of each other the way we want to.

"I know that lacks a certain romantic flavor and I could... should be able to do better than spout a bunch of legal reasons in my attempt to sway you to marry me, but the truth is this is something I really want in a 'I think I'm as shocked as anyone else will be' way. I am, believe it or not, super nervous

Tara, because I want you to want to do it, too, or I don't want to do it at all. You don't complete me because if you did then I'd be too broken to be good for you or anyone else, but you make it easier to be me. I love you so deeply in my soul that it shocks me. If you don't want to get married or if you want to think about it or have a long engagement that's fine, but I know exactly what I want. I am completely committed to you and I want it to be legal. I even..." She reached in her pocket and pulled out a ring. Her hand was shaking. "...had this made."

Tara looked at it and smiled. It was hand-twisted silver with a bright orange carnelian stone. Hanna's—one of the homesteaders—specialty was jewelry. One day she had shown Tara a ring just like this one that Tara fell in love with, but it was way too small. Obviously Jerri had one made in Tara's size which meant this wasn't sudden. Jerri had been thinking about this awhile.

Tara quickly plucked the ring out of Jerri's hand and slid it on her finger. She smiled at Jerri.

"So... I guess we're getting married."

Jerri grabbed her, hugged her, then they were kissing and... That poor kid was getting madder and madder that he couldn't get the rest of the milk out of that damn bottle.

Chapter 20

At first they both thought it was best to wait to get married. Tara wanted to be divorced for at least a year before remarrying. They both thought it would be better to wait for things on the media front to die down a little. But as soon as they got back to the house and told her family what they were doing her mother pointed out that it was stupid to wait for things to calm down just to stir them up again.

Janice had a point. Tara's sisters and her mother had been stoked that they were getting married, but Tara was pretty sure they were mostly excited about marrying into the Blue homestead.

"We should rent the..."

"Stop right there, Mother. I did that shit once. I just want to marry Jerri. I don't want to invite anyone but family, and I don't want a fucking film crew. Jerri said Judy has a minister's license and can legally marry us, so I want to do it here quick and simple."

"Are you going to wear clothes?" Irva asked, making a face.

"Why wouldn't we wear clothes?" Tara asked with a chuckle.

"Hello, you guys are crunchy-granola people. Don't new-agers always get married naked?"

"God I hope not," Tara muttered.

Jerri wasn't exactly the most modest person on the planet so she hated to think her stupid sister was right but she might be. If Jerri thought it was spiritually significant, it just might be exactly what she wanted to do.

Jerri and Todd came walking through the kitchen the boys trailing after them and heading for the back door.

"Jerri, I don't want to get married naked."

"Of course not." Jerri laughed. "Now why would we do that?"

"Because you're hippies," her mother said, rolling her eyes and looking at Irva.

"If you really just want to see me naked we can do that and

get it over with," Jerri told Irva.

Todd cracked up and Irva glared at him.

"You are such an asshole, Todd!"

Jerri, Todd and the boys left to do... what... Tara could only guess. It was a farm; there was always something to do, and even if there wasn't Jerri would have made something up. She couldn't imagine why Jerri had said what she did or why Irva had yelled at Todd.

She must have looked as confused as she felt because Lori said, "Last night Irva said she thought Jerri was hot."

"Fuck you, Lori!" Irva yelled.

"No, she asked if thinking Jerri was a little hot meant she might be gay," her mother told Tara helpfully.

When Tara looked at her, Irva was obviously nearly as embarrassed as she was angry.

"It's alright, Irva. Jerri *is* hot and frankly if you think she's only a *little* hot you aren't a lesbian because she is *smoking* hot."

Irva seemed to calm down. Then she got an evil grin on her face. "Dad should be the flower girl. After all it's usually the youngest girl in the family, and he hasn't been a girl nearly as long as the rest of us."

They all laughed and continued to laugh off and on as they planned the wedding by deciding *not* to do every single thing they came up with that would have complicated it at all. Tara realized that they were all in that moment on the same page. They were tired of drama, they were tired of pretense, and they were *way* tired of doing anything for anyone but themselves.

They sat there talking. Tara was making a list that had more things crossed out on it than not. Lori had gone to the fridge to get the bottle of wine the four of them were working on, and as she walked back to the table she looked over Tara's shoulder at the "list" and said, "Isn't this the first time Jerri's getting married?"

"It's the *only* time Jerri's getting married," Tara grinned.

"Maybe... maybe she'd like something a little, well..." Lori looked at the list. "Maybe she would like something besides nothing."

"Hey, we're wearing clothes," Tara said with a shrug. "Pretty sure Jerri would be happy with just signing papers and..." Then she really heard what Jerri had said about her will and mostly heard what Jerri didn't say. *Jerri's picture is everywhere in entertainment news because she's linked to me. It's only a matter of time till that kid figures out who her biological mother really is, if she hasn't already.*

"Are you alright, Tara?" Janice asked.

"Yeah." She was, too. She wasn't going to blame herself, why should she? Till yesterday she hadn't even known there was a kid, so it wasn't her fault, and it wasn't Jerri's, either. "You know what? I'm going to marry Jerri. I'm going to have the life I want to have... It's all good."

Judy watched as Georgia continued to cry about her daughter marrying Jerri, though it was hard to say how much of it was actual despair and how much was just hormones. Either way Judy was really tired of it. For one thing she couldn't understand a word Georgia was saying. She was about to tell her—in not so kind terms—that enough was enough when Georgia finally said something intelligible.

"Are they going to let me give her away?"

Judy laughed. "I know you might find this hard to believe, but Jerri's really not all that traditional. No feminist likes the whole idea of a woman being 'given away' even to another woman. But I imagine if you aren't trying to kill her Jerri will let you walk with Tara and stand with her. She's pretty forgiving; what about you?"

"I just don't know, Judy. Tara's wedding when she married Fred—that was the only wedding I will ever get to be her dad at, and the whole time... The whole time I was wishing the whole thing away. I won't get to walk any of them down the aisle now as their dad. I'm not their dad anymore. Tara said she was calling me that but she wasn't feeling it."

"And how do you feel?" Judy asked carefully.

"What?"

It was always harder to have a patient who just wasn't very bright. Judy took in a deep breath and let it out. "Do you feel like you're still her dad?"

"I don't know. I guess if I'm honest I really don't. I feel like they are my kids but... It's not just what I feel but what I am. I'm not a man. The man I looked like was their dad, and I don't even really feel connected to him anymore. When I look in the mirror now I see me, and I'm happy with who I am now. Sometimes I feel like the rest of my life... the *whole* rest of my life was just a dream I had."

Judy knew just exactly what she meant. Jason didn't feel like her past at all because the whole time she had been Jason she had felt like she was hovering somewhere overhead watching Jason have a life that she could never participate in. She had never for even a moment felt comfortable in that skin, so she just didn't really live in it. It wasn't until she'd been Judy for a while that she even knew what it meant to be actually "present". She smiled at the memory of that moment.

But Judy hadn't been married forever, wasn't in her sixties, and didn't have three grown daughters. Judy easily walked away from being Jason because she'd had no commitments to anyone who would be collateral damage. She had no one to stand in the way of her effort to become the woman whose turn it was to use that body—the one that was all wrong for the soul and brain it carried. Her mother had a meltdown, but she and her mother had bigger problems than Judy's sexual reassignment.

Judy tried to think of just the right words then just told the truth. "You have a lot of baggage from a lifetime of being a man. Since some of those things you are carrying are children you chose to bring into the world, you can't just leave them behind and start over as if they don't exist. I have no idea how to tell you to go about building a relationship with your children. I never had children, but I am someone's child, and I know what it's like to have a parent who turns their back on you because you don't live up to their expectations. There aren't books or TV shows that tell you how to do what any of us have done much less what you are doing—and fully in the public eye. You're breaking new ground, so you and they are going to have to figure out what your new relationship is going to be. I hate to say this, but I doubt seriously that you will ever be as important in their lives now as you were. They already have a mother and now... they don't really have a father. They do, however, have two parents that love them. This isn't any easier for them than it is for you. Give it time; let the relationships grow organically. Don't try to force it. Feel what you feel and let them know what that is. Then listen and be understanding when they tell you how they feel."

Georgia nodded silently.

"What's really wrong?"

"Do you think a time will come when transgendered people...

They'll be able to fix them in the womb or know when they're born and fix everything before they ever know?"

"Honestly I hope not," Judy said. "My experience is unique; so is yours. I don't think I'd want to have never taken that journey. It has shaped who I am and how I live. Give it another year, maybe two, and I think you're going to realize that you aren't unhappy with your life's journey. My goal is not to fix transgendered people before people realize they are 'broken', my goal is to have a world were people accept each other's differences without judging because they realize we are really all the same. Where they let us decide what we need to do and or not do to be who we are."

Georgia laughed and shook her head. "I can see why you and Jerri are best friends. You both spout the same crap."

Tara watched Jerri as she spoke on the phone in their bedroom. "That's right Bob, I'm getting married... Yes the Darting girl, Tara."

Jerri looked at her and grinned.

"Yes she is gorgeous... No she isn't a kid... Ten years but I'm in really good shape.... Can you guys come or not? I would get you all plane tickets." Jerri sighed. "I don't want her here, Bob. I respect that you have a relationship with her, but I don't want or need one... I have forgiven her, but since she hasn't changed at all if I am around her I may unforgive her... If you guys would like to be here I'd love to have you come... Tell her the truth, Bob. That I'm getting married and I don't want her here... She'd have to have feelings for them to be hurt... Bob, be honest. Do you give her money all the time?... That's yes, Bob, so why do you think she wants to have a relationship with me? Because I have more money than you do... The love you have to buy will never be worth what you paid for it... Look, Bob, I love you. I'm super happy right now, and I don't want to have this argument with you again... It's less than a week, Bob, so I need to know if you guys are coming so I can get tickets... If you come you may have to arm wrestle Tara's sister and her boyfriend for the teepee, but I have another tent and we have a house on the beach about a forty minute drive from here if you'd rather stay there. The couch is broken but there is a huge bed and I could have a couple of beds delivered to the guest room for the kids, if you can come... Yeah, sure..."

She removed the receiver from her ear and pointed it at Tara. "He wants to talk to you."

Tara took the phone reluctantly.

Jerri whispered in her ear, "Do NOT let him talk you into letting Mother come even if it means *he* won't come." Then she walked across the room and left.

Tara put the phone to her ear. "Hello."

"Hello," he said, and laughed no doubt because she sounded so nervous which she kind of was since she was talking to him for the first time. "Is my sister still there?"

"No, she handed me the phone and took off. She can't sit still for more than a few minutes. She has to always be doing something."

"I know. So my wife watches your show and of course when I heard my sister was dating you I got on line and looked you up. My wife tells me you're the smart one."

Tara smiled. "That's nice. Most people call me the fat one."

"Oh, honey, me and my wife are both heavy feeders. You don't look fat to either of us. I don't know you, have never met you, and... I already like you sooo much better than Rhonda Heart. Though I hate to say it, and I know my sister knows it already and has done the therapy—Rhonda... Just like our mother, and that is why Jerri doesn't want mother there. I love my mother, but she is everything my sister says she is. I'm sure she told you to say Mom can't come, but I wouldn't ask you because the truth is I just needed to ask so that I could tell Mother that Jerri was the one that said she couldn't come so that she'd be mad at Jerri instead of me. I know makes me a chicken shit. You might tell Jerri, though, that giving me money to help me with my bills—that I wouldn't need help with if our mother wasn't constantly hitting me up for money—is sort of the same as giving Mother money."

"I will never tell her that, and neither should you," Tara said with a smile. "You laugh just like Jerri." She realized that was why she had gone from feeling really nervous to feeling like she was just talking to... her brother-in-law.

"Our loving father used to call us the hyenas," Bob said. In that instance Tara knew that Bob had as much resentment for their father as Jerri had for their mother. "So... you're going to marry my sister."

"I am."

"And no one has a gun to your head"

"No."

"Then tell her to get us the plane tickets; I wouldn't miss it for the world."

Georgia had stayed the night with them. They got up at five in the morning before the film crew could get there and Cyndy drove while Judy and Georgia messed with their makeup in the car.

"The wedding isn't till two this afternoon. there will be plenty of time for you to preen once we get there," Cyndy said, as Judy nearly elbowed her in the face while trying to apply her base coat.

"My beautiful rose you wake every morning looking more amazing than the morning before..."

"Judy... you are so full of crap."

"Oh." Judy fell silent and continued to put on her makeup, being more careful not to hit Cyndy while she was trying to drive.

Cyndy elbowed her in the ribs. "I didn't say you should stop."

Judy laughed and so did Georgia. Judy was glad because she was hoping that Georgia was going to be able to get her nerves to calm down enough for her to enjoy the day. "My dearest love, your breath is like sweet gardenias, your skin smooth as the finest silk, and your eyes are the blue of the depths of the ocean. Every breath I take I take only for you." As stupid and sappy as she knew that sounded, it was true, and exactly what she forgot when she got stuck on something.

"You forgot my hair," Cyndy said with a smile.

"It glistens with the light of a thousand stars."

Georgia laughed again and put her makeup away. "She's right; it will be easier to do it there. I... I want to go, but I don't want to make everyone nervous."

"You can't control how other people feel; you can only try to put them at ease to the best of your ability. If you aren't there it will break your daughter's heart. After all, you were there for the wedding she did just to please you and everyone else, so if you aren't there for the one she wants that would be a little hard to swallow."

Georgia nodded. "I was mostly thinking about Janice, about making her uncomfortable."

"But she said she wants to have a relationship with you.

You are going to have to build new relationships with Janice and your kids. Personally, I think today will be the perfect time to start. This is a joyous occasion. Jerri and Tara are in love, and they want to commit themselves to each other in every way. Their two lives are coming together, and they will be happy."

"Do you think so?"

"I know so. Jerri said they glowed with the same aura."

"What a bunch of..."

"Wonderful, amazing blessings," Judy said, cutting Georgia off.

Georgia grinned. "Yes, that's exactly what I was going to say."

As they pulled into the driveway, Georgia watched Todd close the gate behind them. It was the most effort she'd ever seen Todd put into anything.

Channing and Tylor were playing with some old stump, rolling it around. She hadn't seen them in months and they had grown so much. She stepped out of the van and an immediate wave of calm enveloped her.

Judy got out looked at her and said, "Welcome to the Blue Homestead."

"It's... wonderful." Georgia no longer wondered at all about whether or not Tara was making another horrible mistake. If she could have built a place that said "Tara" it would have been this place, and this place was Jerri. She realized that Gary Darting hadn't known Jerri Blue at all. Gary Darting had a limited view of all things, and Georgia finally heard what Tara had said in the truck.

I hated Jerri because Jerri knew how to be herself. There was never pretense with Jerri. She didn't believe things she was told; she believed in what she knew. I never hated Jerri I hated the way Jerri made me feel because I was living a lie.

The boys saw her then and they came running over.

"Grandma!" Channing said in a language that could actually be understood, and then he was hugging her around her knees.

Then Tylor was hugging her just because his brother was.

Georgia reached down and grabbed one of them in each arm and picked them up. They hugged her neck and she hugged them.

Tylor laughed and patted her cheek. "Pretty," he said.

She couldn't help it; she started to cry.

At her shoulder Todd said, "Everyone else is still asleep, so jump in the golf cart and I'll take you all down to the camp."

Georgia got in the cart still holding the boys and Judy and Cyndy got in as well. "The Burn site?" Judy asked.

"Yeah," Todd said.

He started driving and Georgia realized something. Todd wasn't snubbing her or really uncomfortable around her. Todd wasn't talking to her because now she was a woman.

Judy was sitting beside her and she leaned over and whispered in Georgia's ear, "Children don't have gender issues. They tend to see what people are instead of what they look like. They have probably always seen you like you are."

Georgia nodded and stopped crying.

The baby was talking a mile a minute.

"Thanks for getting up early for us," Cyndy said to Todd.

"Yes thank you Todd," Georgia echoed.

"No problem," Todd said. He wasn't going to elaborate because it was Todd, and to him they were a golf cart full of women. In his own way this WAS Todd accepting her as a woman.

"We get up with Daddy," Channing told her. "We live in a teepee. Harry marry Aunt Tara today."

"He means Jerri," Todd said.

"I can't believe how well he's talking, and the baby well he's talking better than Channing was the last time I saw them."

"Yep."

They pulled into the camp which was very nice but that wasn't what made her gasp.

Lori was standing over a campfire cooking. She looked up at Georgia smiled and... Lori was happy to see her.

As if reading her mind Judy whispered in her ear, "This place is as magic as Jerri Blue. But mostly Lori has gotten past her grief over losing her father and is ready to embrace you as the person who takes his place."

Todd stopped the cart and Georgia got out still carrying the boys.

Lori pulled the frying pan over to the edge of the grate off the fire and walked over. She kissed Georgia on the cheek and then said, "So, what do you have there?"

"Boys who have grown like bad weeds and who *talk*."

They wanted down then, so she set them down and they ran off into the woods of all things. She looked from the teepee to her daughter and back.

Lori smiled and patted her on the shoulder. "I blame you. Mother made us all run into the woods to escape the media storm over Tara sleeping with Jerri," she said.

From the smile on her face Georgia got the idea that she was more than happy to be right where she was.

"Come on, I'm still figuring out this camp-fire cooking thing, but I've made some coffee and I'm making some sausage and eggs that should be ready in a second."

They... they all got up early for us. They did this so that everyone else could sleep as long as they wanted. She made breakfast for us and... Lori has never gone out of her way for anyone, not even her kids. My decision to live in my truth, Tara's decision to live in hers, has shifted everyone. I don't know if that makes me feel better or worse.

Lori had met Judy at Georgia's house, but she hadn't met Cyndy, and neither of them had met Todd, so Georgia introduced them all.

"Your makeup's a mess. Come on." Judy led her to a bathroom with two sinks, two shower stalls and two toilets in stalls.

Lori's stuff was everywhere and Georgia smiled; some things never changed.

"Is this Jerri's yard or a state park?"

"I think you're forgetting who Jerri is," Judy said with a laugh. "This place runs completely on solar and wind power, and Jerri rarely eats something she didn't grow or trade for, but never forget that she has nearly as much money as you do. That if she wants to do something she has the money to do it right. Cyndy and I actually helped her build this."

"Well it's a beautiful place and just what I'd want for Tara." Georgia looked in the mirror. Her makeup really was a mess; crying had it running all over. She washed her face.

"I told you to get the water-proof mascara. Here use mine." Judy handed her a tube as she was drying her face.

They finished, did their business, and when they walked out Lori announced that breakfast was done. She was setting the pans on a picnic table right outside the Teepee. Before they could reach the table the boys had come running out of the woods. They were already seated and basically shoveling food into their mouths before Georgia and Judy could even get to the table. Georgia was shocked.

"They will eat anything up here," Lori said, reading the expression on her face. "They go right to bed without fusing, and they sleep all night. Seriously, Todd and I are talking about buying the place down the road that's for sale."

"We've looked at it twice," Todd said, filling his plate.

"It's only two bedrooms, but the master bedroom is huge and I think we could split it into two bedrooms for the boys and we could take the smaller one," Lori said.

Todd just nodded.

"It's five acres, mostly wooded, but there is a small garden area and a chicken pen."

Georgia looked to make sure she had the right daughter. That Tara wanted to live up here didn't really surprise her, but Lori was another matter altogether. Then Georgia looked over at the boys sitting and eating—not running all over yelling and crying, but eating. Todd and Lori weren't fighting and they were actually enjoying their children. Of course Todd and Lori screaming was always Lori bitching loudly over crap that never made much sense and Todd giving her dirty looks, slamming stuff around, and grunting as each of them tweeted something about what a shithead the other one was to millions of strangers every three seconds. When he looked at them now none of them—not the kids, not Todd, not Lori—had their hand-held devices that connected them to the world. And Georgia had always been sure Tylor was born with an IPad in his hand.

Stress—that's what being plugged in all the time did It caused a raging, cascading river of stress to ball up in your belly.

In that moment Georgia felt herself completely relax, and a peace about who she was and the decisions she'd made fell over her. They were all going to be alright; she hadn't ruined them. They were all going to be fine, and so was she.

"We have a rabbit," Tylor told Georgia around a mouth full of food.

"You do?" Georgia said.

He nodded.

"We call it Mr. Hops," Channing supplied. "He lives in a cage down at the rabbit building. Harry lets us play with him, and he's really nice. Harry swears we won't eat him. You want to see him, Grandma?"

That was the second time he had called her that. Georgia looked at Lori.

"Jerri said since they called Mother Nana they should call you Grandma. That way it wouldn't be confusing for anyone," she explained.

"Thank you, and I guess I should thank Jerri, too," Georgia said, grudgingly.

"I think it will be enough if you get through the day without trying to kill her." Lori laughed.

"She pulled a gun on me," Georgia defended.

"Yes well you *are* three times bigger than she is, and she knew Tara would have to let you go at some point," Judy said.

"I'm alright with Jerri," Georgia said.

"Geez, Georgia, if you say that a hundred more times you might actually be able to sound like you mean it." Lori laughed.

"Yeah, that's what I'm hoping." Georgia sighed.

"Were they doing it when you caught them?" Lori asked, and there was that mischievous grin Georgia loved so much.

"No."

"Well that's actually pretty shocking because your oldest daughter is a complete slut. Poor Jerri can't get a minute's peace."

"I haven't heard Jerri complaining," Judy said.

"How could she? Tara's always got her tongue in her mouth," Cyndy added.

Lori cracked up pointed at Cyndy and said, "You're my kind of gal."

"You really aren't helping," Georgia said.

Jerri had let Tara tell her what to wear, but now she was sort of wishing she hadn't because the suit coat was hot and she felt more like she was going to give a lecture than getting married. Though she wasn't sure what that was supposed to feel like because she'd never done it before.

Tara looked amazing in a short off-white dress she'd had in her closet. She caught Jerri's eye and smiled at her, and when she did Jerri didn't mind sweating in the suit coat at all if it made Tara happy.

Georgia had been waiting on their front porch when they woke up. She and Janice had gone on a walk that lasted a couple of hours. The whole time it was obvious that Tara was tense. As Janice and Georgia were returning Tara saw them walking down the road laughing, and for the first time that day she relaxed—which in turn let Jerri relax.

Bob his wife and two kids had decided to fly the day of the wedding. Their flight had been delayed and they hadn't gotten there till one-thirty. Even that hadn't freaked Jerri out. After all it was just the family and they could wait for him. So it didn't matter if they started late. She was stoked about the whole getting married thing because from the minute Tara saw her parents weren't going to be either avoiding each other or fighting, she had gone from being a nervous wreck to just enjoying every single process of the day. Tara was happy, excited, and not the least bit nervous, which just encouraged Jerri to believe this was the best decision she had ever made.

She and Bob had walked to the stage together. She looked over at her three-hundred pound brother in his made-for-a-two-hundred-and-fifty-pound man suit that he had put on in five minutes. Jerri smiled; he was sweating more than she was. Jerri reached over and unbuttoned all the buttons on his suit coat and loosened his tie; he started to breathe again.

Lori turned on the IPad to play a traditional wedding march.

Jerri frowned and started to wish she'd blown this whole thing out, invited all her friends, all Tara's friends, had her musical friends play something loud and joyful and not traditional at all. Let her homesteader friends bring on the feed bag. Then her sister-in-law, Shirley, snapped a picture and when she did Jerri remembered all the reasons they were doing this so small and simple.

Jerri turned and saw Tara walking towards her with Georgia on one arm and Janice on the other. Tara was near glowing she was so happy, and Jerri decided nothing could be more perfect than that.

"She is gorgeous," Bob whispered in her ear. Because of course his lateness meant this was the first time he was seeing Tara.

Jerri just nodded, finding that she had a little catch in her throat she wasn't expecting to have.

"More importantly," Judy said, "...she is completely and totally in love with you. It's what I always wanted for you, Jerri."

"Judy, please don't make me cry. My plan is to get through

this without crying."

"Good luck with that," Judy said with a sniffle.

The ceremony only lasted a few minutes, and Jerri only actually shed a tear once. She wouldn't have cried at all if the vows she had written hadn't made Tara, every other woman there, her brother Bob, and Todd—so everyone but the kids—cry. That wasn't her intention at all, so she wondered if maybe she hadn't lost her literary touch.

After the ceremony she was holding on to Tara's hand and found she couldn't even begin to think about letting go. Tara started to go to talk to her mother and sisters at one point, but Jerri just held on and wouldn't let her go. Tara gave her an odd look. Jerri smiled shrugged silently then followed Tara to where she was going, apparently to talk about food. They had all been cooking for most of three days, though why they needed so much food Jerri had no idea. There certainly weren't that many of them.

Lori looked at Jerri, grinned and shook her head, but it was Tara that asked, "What?"

"Irva's right; she is a little hot," Lori said.

"Jerri, come here!"

Bob hollered at her from the vicinity of the bathroom, reminding her of when he was little and she had to take him to the john. She looked from her brother to Tara, wondering why she didn't want to let go of her.

"Go on," Irva said. "We aren't going to let anything happen to her. And you are legally married, so she ain't going anywhere."

Janice laughed no doubt at the goofy-assed way Jerri was acting.

Jerri nodded and reluctantly let go of Tara's hand.

"What was that all about?" Janice asked with a grin.

"I'm sure I don't know. I'm the one who's usually clingy, not Jerri," Tara said with a grin.

"Those vows she wrote for you..." Janice sighed wistfully. "She laid her soul out for you and everyone else to see. I imagine she feels a little vulnerable right now."

"That's very insightful, Mom but I think it has a lot more to do with the way Tara looks right now." Lori turned to look at her. "You look amazing."

"Yes you do," Georgia said at her shoulder. "I'm so very

happy for you, Tara."

Tara would have said she couldn't have been any happier than she had been, but she was. Logically nothing had really changed, yet it just felt different. The minute she had said "I do" when she had married Fred she had felt trapped, but when she said nearly the same thing to Jerri, she felt free.

"I'm breaking up with Fats," Irva announced. "It's a sure bet that he will never write vows like that for me. It would be all 'put a cap' in this and 'slapping his thang' in that." She walked away pulling her smart phone out of her purse

"Every time she hears Jerri speak she gets rid of a boyfriend," Lori said with a shrug.

"What?" Jerri asked her brother.

He grabbed her arm, pulled her over and pointed down at his pants. The zipper had broken in the "up" position. "I'm stuck in my fucking pants, Jerri. I hate to ask on your wedding day and all..."

"At least I don't have to wipe your ass." Jerri mumbled, took his hand and led him into the bathroom. She pulled her pocket knife out of her pocket and her brother backed away a bit.

"Be careful with that thing, Jerri and... This is my only suit."

"I will buy you a new one. I hate to be the one to tell you, but this one doesn't really fit you." She took the pocket knife and cut through the waistband. Bob immediately ran into one of the stalls and when he stepped back out a few minutes later he looked relieved and was wearing jeans.

Jerri took off her suit coat and tie and put them on a hanger.

Bob was washing his hands a lot longer than it should take.

"What's wrong Bob?"

"I was kind of surprised you wanted me at your wedding."

"Why?"

"You haven't come to visit in a year and a half and you hardly ever call. I had to find out about Tara on the TV." He quit drying his hands and turned to face her. "I thought... well I thought you were mad at me."

"About mother?"

"Yes."

"I'm not mad, Bob. I just don't need her," Jerri said gently. "And neither do you. What does she add to your life?"

"Nothing," he admitted. "I thought when she wanted to see us that maybe she felt sorry for abandoning us. But she's not; in fact she has fifty different excuses for why it absolutely wasn't her fault. You know, just like you told me she would. She found you because you were easy to find." He meant on the net not in person. She had communicated with her mother in Emails. "She contacted you because it was obvious you had money. You told me I shouldn't get in touch with her, and of course you were right. There is no part of her that owns any of the choices she made that affected us."

"I was never mad at you, Bob. I didn't stop calling you. If you will think about it you'll realize that I call as much as I ever have. *You* stopped calling *me*. I used to fly out to spend holidays with you, but now you spend them with her and... It's hard for me to enjoy a 'holiday' anyway, much less have to sit in someone else's space and bite my tongue out of my mouth as I listen to her passive-aggressive bullshit. Face it, since you moved to Phoenix the only time we really saw each other was over holidays. I'm not going to tell you how to run your life or who you should or shouldn't let into your space. I told you how I felt about it. I'm not going to lie, Bob, at first I was really pissed off. It seemed like you were choosing her over me, and who was always there for you? Not her, me. But I knew that was wrong thinking. You were trying to do the right thing and trying to have something you always wanted. But being with you got harder because of what I have already told you over and over—I don't *want* and surely don't *need* her in my life."

"You have to know I would never choose her over you, Jerri. I hate that your life was always so hard and know that at least in part it was because you did have to take care of me. I'm glad you have such a great life and someone wonderful to share it with and... How do I get rid of Mother, Jerri? She's bleeding me dry, causing problems between you and me, and me and Shirley."

"Please tell me she is not living with you," Jerri said with a sigh. "That's the one thing I asked of you, Bob, that you not let her move in."

He looked at the floor.

"Dammit, Bob." She walked out of the bathroom and he

followed her. "Kick her out, Bob."

"How?"

"Tell the fucking truth, Bob." Jerri was starting to get mad, so she looked around till she saw Tara and when she did, as expected, her mad just left her. "Tell her she is ruining the life you made not because of, but in spite of her. Tell her she has to go. It will hurt a lot at first, but then you will realize that if she really cares about you at all she will still talk to you. If she doesn't talk to you because you will no longer let her leech off of you, then she never cared about you in the first place which... If you're honest, you already know that."

He nodded.

"Be an adult, Bob. Put yourself and your family first. Mother always put herself first, so she ought to understand that. You've grown out of your suit because you're eating the stress she causes you. I'm not going to do it for you because I didn't make this mess, you did."

This time when she looked at Tara, Tara was looking at her.

Jerri patted his cheek. "You'll be fine, Bob, and now I'm going to go back to my wife."

My wife! How huge and monumental and how simple was that? Five years ago I never would have thought we'd have the right to do that much less that I would ever find someone I'd want to be connected to in every possible way.

She walked up and slung her arm around Tara and said to Tara's parents and sisters, "If you will excuse me, ladies, I'm going to borrow my wife. I'm sure the food is all fine and the less complicated you can make it the better. We'll meet you back at the house."

Tara was obviously more than willing to walk back to the house with her.

Irva walked back just as Tara and Jerri left. "So are they going for the record in consummating a marriage? I mean they've only been married about ten minutes." She looked at her mother with meaning. "Or are we still supposed to pretend that we don't know what they are doing?"

"I wish you would," Georgia said, making a face.

Janice found that after their talk she could finally look at Georgia without cringing. It seemed that when Janice allowed herself to release responsibility for her ex-husband's issues and choices, she felt neither like a victim nor a villain, which made it easier not to blame anyone else. It was the past; Gary had already moved forward and now she would, too.

Tara was leaving the show. In fact, Janice had been online negotiating with the network trying to keep them from suing Tara. The problem was that they wanted to use all the footage they had of Tara and Jerri already as well as anything they got in the future as a trade, and Janice didn't know if that was going to fly with either Tara or Jerri.

Lori and Todd had agreed to fulfil their contract, but then they also wanted out, which had shocked Janice more than a little. You know, that they could actually agree on something.

Janice was also sure she wanted out of most of it if not all. Irva was more than happy to have her own show since all of the attention would be focused on her, and Georgia thought her show was important, so she was hoping to keep doing it if the ratings were high enough. Janice wasn't worried at all about the ratings.

"So?" Lori asked Irva.

"So what?"

"Did you break up with Fats?" Lori asked.

"I'm not going to break up with him over the phone," Irva said, in a shocked tone.

"Because that isn't how you broke up with the last fifty guys you dated?" Lori sighed and shook her head. "Then what were you doing?"

"Instagramming pictures of the wedding, and check this out." She turned the phone around. "Joan Night already sent her congratulations, and so…" She turned her phone towards Janice. "…did Auntie Rhonda. Well, maybe not her congratulations."

Janice read it out loud. "I feel like all the wind has been sucked from my lungs, my blood has turned to water, and my soul has left my body. There was ever only one person for me, and now she is gone forever. I have nothing to live for. I wish Jerri well and sadly say good bye." Janice sighed. "Crap!"

"She's just being her super-dramatic self," Irva said.

"That doesn't mean she won't do something really stupid if it will get her the attention she wants," Janice said. She got out her phone, walked away from them, and called Rhonda. It took only a second for Rhonda to answer.

"You traitor!" Rhonda screamed in her ear.

As soon as she both answered the phone and said something that stupid, Janice knew Rhonda wasn't going to even pretend to try to kill herself. Further, Janice was pretty sure that not only did she no longer want to be on TV but she also didn't want to be an agent anymore. She sure as hell didn't want Rhonda, "I'm a flaming bitch on good days", Heart for a client.

"You know what, Rhonda? I am so sick to death of your fucking bullshit. Could you just not stop yourself from posting such insane crap on the day my daughter married a woman you were done with years ago?"

"I was never done with Jerri. I will never be done with Jerri."

And then she heard it in her voice Rhonda was drunk, high or both.

"You knew, you knew everything Jerri had been through and you used it to your advantage the whole time you were together. Hell Rhonda, are Jerri and I the only ones that remember that you were the one that kicked her out? She was willing to put up with your lying, cheating, abusive crap off into the sunset and YOU kicked HER out. That isn't love, Rhonda. Love isn't twisted, and it doesn't hurt people. She loved you, but you never loved her, and that's why you have just kept chasing her—you know whenever you aren't 'in love' with someone else. What you miss is having someone around who actually loves you, someone who loves you even when you don't deserve it."

"You're fired!" Rhonda screamed for the thousandth time since she had first taken her as a client.

"No, I'm firing you, Rhonda. *I* fire *you!* I'm Janice Darting. Good luck finding another agent as good as I am. My daughter-in-law is your ex-girlfriend, so I don't think we should work together anymore." And then Janice hung up on Rhonda Heart.

Everyone was clapping. Her new in-laws, her daughters, her ex-husband, Jerri's best friend, and… she didn't just *feel* like a hero she *was* one.

Back at the house they ate too much and most of them drank too much. They danced in the front yard and on the porch till it was nearly one in the morning. Jerri pulled down a second tent and Bob and Shirley set it up right after the wedding. They were camping in it with their kids since they were too toasted to drive to the beach house. Judy and Cyndy had brought their own tent, and Georgia was going to bunk with them.

Tara was pretty tipsy. Jerri had a hell of a time getting her upstairs, and when she did Tara just sort of flopped onto the bed.

"Best day ever," she announced.

Of course Jerri wasn't drunk. Still, no one had been so drunk they annoyed her. She smiled back at Tara. "It was pretty special."

"It's not over yet."

Jerri started to help Tara out of her clothes and when she did Tara started unbuttoning the buttons on Jerri's shirt.

"I'm mostly trying to get you out of your clothes so that you can go to sleep." Jerri bent down and kissed her on the forehead.

"That is not why I am taking your clothes off," Tara said, then she laughed the way only a drunk will.

"I sort of guessed that."

"We need to consumé our marriage," Tara slurred out.

"First off, honey, I think what you have described would include using soup as lube. Second, we already consummated our marriage hours ago."

"We could do it again," Tara said. "I mean this is our honeymoon."

"Yes with your mother in the next room and our family spread out all over the farm."

"Thank God they are all leaving tomorrow. It will just be you and me. I'm so happy. Are you happy?"

"Yes."

Jerri pulled Tara's pants off. It wasn't easy; in fact it had been lots easier to get her out of the dress earlier. It didn't help that Tara was trying to undress her the whole time and actually doing a pretty good job. There wasn't a button on her shirt or her pants that wasn't undone. In fact, Tara had managed to pull Jerri's pants down far enough that if she wasn't careful she was going to trip. She sat down on the side of the bed and pulled her pants the rest of the way off. When she did, Tara ripped—probably literally—her shirt off, and had her hands all over her.

Jerri laughed. "Honey, aren't you way to drunk and too tired…"

"Drunk people have been having sex since the beginning of time, and you know I have never been so tired that I don't want you." She didn't slur at all.

Chapter 21

They had been married a little over four months, so they were now old news. While they turned heads whenever they were in public, and a few pictures were shot, they just didn't go out in public very much. When they did she found she didn't mind being Tara Darting Blue at all.

Her dad's show *Being Georgia* was a ratings cash cow. Irva's show *Just Irva* was doing even better. Occasionally they found themselves on one of those shows, but even Jerri sort of ignored the cameras on those rare occasions.

The farm was mostly dormant in the late winter, so it turned out this was when Jerri did anything book related that had to do with travel. The publisher always wanted her to do more; she always did less. Jerri would do a book signing only if it was attached to a lecture. She charged big bucks to speak at college campuses, but did at least as many lectures in smaller non-paying venues, which seemed to piss off everyone who got a chunk of Jerri's money. Jerri told Tara she took great pleasure from not giving rich people what they wanted, especially when they were gaining from her work.

They were at KCU in Missouri. Jerri had just given the last of two talks on "The Spiritual Aspects of Creativity". Jerri was right; she did always do a better job with the second lecture. Jerri was now sitting in a huge common area doing a signing.

Tara was sitting off to the side behind the same table where Jerri was sitting. Tara doing some sketching and mostly trying to ignore the security people turning people who wanted Tara's autograph away saying she wasn't signing—which she wasn't. This was Jerri's thing; not hers.

As soon as things had started to calm down in their lives, Tara felt her own creativity come back. She found that she couldn't go back to the novel she had been working on because she was no longer in the same place she had been in when she had been writing it and had no desire to go back there. Tara had been working on a children's book and finding the work very fulfilling. She should have been working on the art for that project but instead at that moment she was sketching Jerri.

"It's a very good likeness," a girl said, nearly at her shoulder.

"Thanks," Tara said, not really looking up.

Security started to move in, so she looked up, saw it was just a single girl with nothing in her hand for Tara to sign, and nodded her head at security basically telling them to stand down. She didn't want to be bombarded with people at Jerri's signing, but she also didn't want to be one of those people who froze everyone out.

"She's brilliant, isn't she?" the girl said.

"Yes, but I might be a little biased."

The girl started to walk away.

"If you get in line she will talk to you. She's not scary at all, and you don't have to have a book for her to sign to just shake her hand and talk to her; however, I'm not about to push you up in the line and risk starting a riot."

"That... That wasn't what I was trying to do."

There were a couple of other empty chairs behind the table. To her surprise the girl grabbed one, pulled it over in front of Tara and sat down. Tara had been reading her wrong; the girl wasn't shy.

Security started to move in again, and this time she looked the girl over hard. She not only didn't have anything in her hand, she didn't have a purse or a backpack. The jacket she wore would only be good for getting from one building on campus to another, not to stay in the cold outside for any length of time, and surely not to conceal a weapon. She was sort of plain looking; she felt troubled not dangerous, and of course Tara had lived with Jerri just long enough to start trusting her gut.

Tara waved security off again.

"Can I help you?"

The girl looked around, obviously to see if Jerri was looking their way, which lead Tara to believe she was one of her fans and not Jerri's at all. Maybe Tara wasn't yet evolved enough to go with her gut. She was about to call for security when the girl caught her eyes and held them.

"Please, I don't want to cause trouble. She knows me. I've met her." The girl was nervous way too nervous for it to be about meeting her favorite writer or to even be one of Tara's fans. "They told me they would tell me if I wanted to know and then... Well they all lied to me, didn't they?"

Tara took in a breath as she realized she might as well have been looking into Jerri's eyes. Tara released the breath she was holding.

"So you do know about me."

Tara nodded, and a lot of the girl's nervousness left her.

"I really don't want to cause her or you any trouble. I'd just like to know why they all lied."

"Not telling isn't the same as lying," Tara said defensively.

"She's a world-famous writer and they told me she was a farmer."

"She is."

"She told me I was the product of a one-night stand, and that's a lie too isn't it?"

Jerri seemed to show up out of thin air. She sat on the table facing them, her back to the fans that were lined up for most of a city block. She looked down at them with a frown.

"Stupid TV, stupid internet," she muttered.

She looked at the girl and shook her head. "What are you doing here, Connie?"

"I go to school here, and I'm pretty sure I know where the money for my tuition comes from," she said. It was hard to tell what the girl was feeling. "You were all over the news."

She looked at Tara and said, "She told me her name was Anne Borough."

"It's her birth name," Tara said.

The girl was pissed off and so was Jerri, though no doubt for very different reasons.

"You're my birth mother," she said to Jerri. "I didn't expect that we would be best friends or spend bunches of time together, but I did think we might be friends on Facebook—at least have some contact. When I realized who you were, well then I knew where the money for my college came from. I can tell looking at your wife that she didn't know you were paying for my education, but I'm sure you are because I don't for one minute believe the crap Mom and Dad told me about some secret charity for adopted kids. Why can you pay for my college but you can't talk to me?"

Tara knew why. Except for the eyes, this girl looked nothing like Jerri, which meant she looked just like one of Jerri's attackers. Tara couldn't for one minute even pretend to know how that must make Jerri feel.

"I asked if they needed help with your tuition. They said they could do it in that way that told me they really couldn't. I have more money than I can ever spend; it's not a big deal."

But it was. It was a huge deal because this kid was only alive because her parents had begged Jerri to have her for them. They had given Jerri barely enough money to move her and her brother to the west coast and now she was putting their kid through collage. Tara knew why Jerri was doing it even if Jerri didn't. Jerri felt responsible for bringing this kid onto the planet, and she wanted to make sure a kid she brought to the world didn't put a hole in it. She wanted this kid to have the best shot for a productive life. The money was nothing to Jerri now. Hell, she was always giving money away.

"It's no big deal to pay my way through school, but I traveled all the way out there and you couldn't talk to me for more than fifteen minutes or tell me who you really were? What was the point of making the trip if you were all going to lie to me, if you weren't really going to talk to me?"

The crowd was getting restless, and Jerri looked like she was about to lose her shit.

"Jerri, I can talk to her. I can tell her anything she wants to know. Why don't you go finish your signing?"

"Could you do that, Tara?"

Tara nodded and Jerri seemed immediately relieved. Without another word to the girl, Jerri went and sat back down.

"Let's go to the cafeteria," Tara said, standing up. She put her sketch pad down and picked her purse up. The girl followed her, closely followed by Tara's security. She got them some coffee oblivious to whether the girl drank the shit or not and sat down at a table away from everyone else. The girl... Connie... sat across from her.

"I know she was sexually assaulted; she said so in her talk. I really can't think of any other reason for my parents to lie to me or let her do so. So is my father a rapist?" She looked close to tears.

Before Tara could answer Jerri showed up as if she had appeared out of the ether. She sat beside Tara; she was shaking.

"I can't be a chicken shit, Tara. I trust you, but I can't be this big a chicken shit. I told them I had to deal with something. They can wait till I get back, but I don't really care if they do or not."

She looked at Connie. "Alright, kid, what do you want to know? Let's get this over with."

"Why did you lie about who you are?"

"Because who I am isn't important. You seem like a nice enough kid, but I never wanted you; your parents did," Jerri said.

"Because I'm the product of your rape?"

Jerri looked at Tara and Tara said, "I didn't get that far. She was at your talk today."

"I don't go into the gory details, but every time I give any talk I mention my assault. Do you know why?" Jerri asked.

The girl shook her head.

"Because sexual assault is an all-too-frequent crime that leaves its victims feeling broken and worthless. When a survivor stands up and says, 'Look I made it', it makes every person in that room that has lived through it feel a little less alone, a little more like a survivor and a little less like a victim. As odd as this may sound it gives them hope. When people who have never been victims see someone like me who looks strong and healthy say they were sexually assaulted then maybe they are a little more careful about where they go and who they trust. Do you know why I don't tell them that I got pregnant by one of my three rapists?" She didn't wait for an answer. "Because that is an all-together too depressing story. The fact that there is a kid that I gave birth to in the world is like a loose end that I would never put in a book. It's too sad. What do you know about post-traumatic stress disorder?"

"A little, not much."

"I have it; look it up. It's nothing to do with you, kid. Tim and Amy are good people. I'm sure they raised you to be a great person, and maybe it's like they said—you are the good thing that has come from my trauma. It's not your fault, but when I see you a hundred terrors flood my mind."

She held her hands so that Connie could see her palms. Her hands were shaking and covered in sweat.

"I'm sweating; it's not hot. I'm shaking; I feel like I'm going to puke. I'm getting a headache, and mostly right now I do not feel safe."

"What's that make me?" Connie's voice cracked, and a few tears leaked from her eyes. "Someone's nightmare?"

She was obviously upset, and Tara couldn't really blame

her. Finding out your father was a rapist had to be a damn sight worse than finding out your father was a woman, and that wasn't an easy pill to swallow by a long shot. Tara remembered a quote from one of Jerri's books and their bedroom wall. *Life would be so much easier if people just wouldn't ask the questions they don't really want the answers to.*

"It doesn't have anything to do with you, Connie. Your parents are Tim and Amy, not me and some violent asshole. Besides, who knows that he wasn't just some dumbass who got caught up with his friends in the moment and has beaten himself up all these years for his part in it? Peer pressure can make people do the most hideous things. If you add drugs or alcohol... well, you'd be surprised what even the most seemingly-normal person will do. Maybe even now he works and gives all his money to rape crisis centers." Seeing the look Connie gave her she said, "Give me a break, kid, I make up things for a living and I hate unhappy endings. Listen to me, if it was all about genes or all about environment, few people would do much more than exist. I sure as hell wouldn't be what and who I am if I let who and where I came from dictate who I was going to be. We are at our core the essence that is our soul. There is nothing at all wrong with you; I can tell you have good energy. I can't help it if seeing you, even thinking about you, makes me have an episode any more than you can help being upset. It's not a plan."

"If you could go back and change time, would you still have me?"

Tara cringed a little because Jerri had as much as said she wasn't sure because it was the worst time of her life, but Tara should have known she didn't have to worry about Jerri saying something to cause the kid to feel any worse than she already did.

"I would. Mostly because now I know for sure that it wasn't going to kill me. More than that, I couldn't have gotten out of that horrid place without your parents' help. You wouldn't be here, and Amy and Tim would have remained childless. They are good parents, aren't they?"

"The best." Connie managed a smile.

"I would do it again because everything has worked out just the way it was supposed to work out. And that is what you learn with age. Anything you can live through isn't that big a deal. It just becomes your back story... except for the crazy."

"Why are you paying for my college?"

"I have lots of money, and you aren't in my will. If Amy and Tim didn't give me the money to get to LA I wouldn't have anything I have, not the great career, not the hot wife, not even the fully-functional off-the-grid lifestyle. At the end of the day I don't really feel responsible for you, but even though your parents could have sent you themselves it would have been hard for them. You know, you might have worked harder to get some scholarships."

"Yeah, that's what Dad said," Connie said with a laugh. Then she got all serious again, and when she set her mouth like that Tara saw a little bit of Jerri in her again. "Do you hate me?"

"Fuck, kid. Why on earth would I hate you? You didn't ask to be born. None of us ask to be born. Why did you have to pry? We gave you a perfectly good lie. Why couldn't you be happy having an ordinary lesbian birthmother and a random idiot she picked up in a bar for a Daddy? Why were you not happy till you figured it all out?"

"Like you, she's never happy with anything but the whole truth," Tara said. She turned looked at Jerri and smiled. "She can't be happy with a lie because she's like you, Jerri."

"What a horrible thing to say about a child," Jerri said.

Connie sniffled and laughed.

Tara dug in her purse and handed the girl a pack of tissues which she quickly used.

"Look, I really do have to get back to that line. Tara can finish answering any questions you have. I just couldn't have let her answer those and not been really ashamed of myself later."

She kissed Tara on the cheek and then she took off.

"I didn't mean to cause her any trouble," Connie said.

"She doesn't come with a warning label. She mostly has a handle on her PTSD."

Tara didn't really want to stay and talk to this grown kid. She wanted to go with Jerri and make sure she wasn't going to have an absolute complete meltdown because Tara hadn't seen a good stump all day. But Jerri wanted her to stay there and do... what she didn't exactly know.

"So how on earth did you wind up with Jerri Blue?"

I guess just what she said. I'm here to answer the girl's questions, well duh.

"My mother was Rhonda Heart's agent. Mom and Jerri have been friends for years. I was having some trouble with... well life really, and I wanted to be a writer so Mother took me to study with her friend the famous writer. Our souls sort of ran smack into each other and we've been mostly together ever since."

"Who is Rhonda Heart?" Connie asked in confusion.

Tara laughed. "Girl, you just made my whole day. Rhonda Heart is the very famous, slutty bitch rock star your birth mother lived with for years."

"When I showed my mom and dad a picture of her and asked if my birthmother was really Jerri Blue, they said yes. I couldn't really imagine why they wouldn't want me to know. Believe me, I've bragged to friends since that she's my birth mother; I'm proud of it. I love my parents, so I'm glad she gave me up. I came up with a whole list of reasons why they didn't want me to know and purposely avoided the one that I guess I knew all along was the answer. *She* wasn't the thing they didn't want me to know. None of them wanted me to know how I came to be. But if it really doesn't matter, why wouldn't they just tell me?"

"Because we often want things not to matter. Our logical mind knows it doesn't, but at the end of the day knowing that you're the end product of a rape... It will change the way you see yourself. It shouldn't, but it will."

"But you know what will create the balance? My birth father was a creep, but my birth mother is Jerri Blue. I had read a couple of her books before I figured it all out and three more after I found out. I heard her talk today and she is eloquent and extremely charismatic. If I have even a little piece of that in me, I would feel blessed."

"Have you read *Burning Rain*?"

Connie shook her head.

"Read it. She wrote that one while she was pregnant with you. I think it will answer a lot of questions for you." She didn't tell her Jerri hated the book or why.

"What's her favorite color?"

"Blue, closely followed by yellow."

"So is that why she changed her name to Blue?"

"Yes and no. She changed her name because she wanted

to kill the person she had been and become someone new. On the flight from Memphis to LA she sat next to a man named Jerry who was some sort of spiritual guru. He told Jerri that he could see that she was in a state of flux. Then he told her that in order to leave all her problems behind her she would have to leave the person she was behind and build a new identity. That her soul felt trapped by who she was and that she had to kill that person. So she decided to change her name. She feminized his name and picked her favorite color for a last name. His name so that she would always remember that she was leaving her old life behind, and her favorite color so that any time she or someone else said it, it would make her happy."

"What about her family?"

Connie asked questions and Tara answered them, occasionally pulling up pictures to show her. Surprisingly, she didn't feel weird at all.

Jerri walked away at a near run, mumbling to herself, "Seriously I look up to see what my wife is doing and she's talking to the kid I gave up. What the hell! Stupid kid just wants to know. Who can blame her? But damn I have a line of fans backed up to the next town. I have to go sign their books, make small talk, and I'm sweating like a bitch, and rattled..."

She wasn't watching where she was going, so when she rounded the corner she almost ran into a seeing-eye dog. Of course it barked at her to warn her she was about to run into its master. She jumped, then without thinking looked heavenwards and yelled, "Seriously God! Are you serious?"

She ran her sweaty palms down her equally-sweaty face.

"I'm sorry," she said to the blind guy. "But I was here doing a signing, and the kid I gave away twenty some years ago showed up, and dogs barking is a trigger."

"Ah, that's fine," he said, and walked away quickly—no doubt so that the crazy didn't get all over him.

Jerri started walking again, and... she was really nervous and felt a little sick, but she wasn't having an episode. *Every time I say it out loud it loses a little more of its power. I already knew that about the rape. That kid is alright; she seems like a good kid. Telling her didn't open an old wound; it closed an old door. I'm... I'm going to be alright. Why?* It only took her a second to have an answer. *I didn't have to tell her. If I didn't*

Tara would have handled it just fine. I could stand in my vulnerability and do what I needed to do because Tara had my back.

She reached the table and her line had not diminished which meant they all trusted that she would return. She took a deep breath, took off her jacket and announced to anyone in hearing distance, "I'm sorry for the delay, but a woman I gave birth to twenty-some years ago and gave away just showed up with a lot of questions she needed answered."

She sat down, started signing books and making small talk, and her nausea went away. She even stopped sweating. After thirty minutes of it she put up her hand and said, "Give me just a minute."

She pulled out her phone and called Tara. "Honey, are you still talking to Connie?"

"Yes."

"Ask her if she wants to go to dinner when I get done here."

"Are you sure...?"

"Tara, I think I'm better than fine right now. If she really wants to get to know me, I think maybe that is going to close more wounds than it will open for both of us."

Chapter 22

Tara watched as Jerri and Judy walked onto The Burn stage.

Jerri caught Tara's eyes, held them and smiled. "The time has come to burn the things we hate most."

"A purifying ritual to purge our souls," Judy said. "I will start, and then we will go around in a circle." She walked to the fire's edge, "The pre-surgery picture of me my mother refuses to take off her wall." She threw it in and it burst into flames.

Jerri got off the stage and walked not towards the fire but into the woods.

Tara noticed there was no book in her hand.

When Jerri walked out of the woods she was carrying the stump. She stopped beside the fire and said, "Many years ago when I first cleared a spot for my garden, I easily pulled all of the stumps but this one. This one broke the plow on my tractor. I chopped it and tried to burn it and dug at it and chopped some more. I tore the bumper off my truck trying to pull it out. By the time I finally got it out I was so filled with rage that I threw it around and cussed it for nearly an hour. Then I sat down and... My rage was just gone. For years I have poured my anger and frustration into this thing till it almost has a life of its own. I hate all the energy and time I wasted being mad about things I couldn't do anything about." She threw the stump into the fire.

"So what's she going to do when she gets mad now?" Cyndy asked, turning to look at Tara.

"There are lots of other stumps lying around," Tara said with a grin. "Honestly, I haven't seen her throw the stump around in months. She said a couple of weeks ago that every time she saw it she remembered how much time she had wasted on rage." Tara shrugged. "Still I'm as shocked as everyone else that she didn't throw a copy of *Burning Rain* into the fire."

"It's like nothing means anything anymore," Cyndy said with mock despair.

People started making their offerings. Her mother was there with a man she "wasn't dating" in that she was but they were all supposed to pretend they didn't know way. He was some yoga instructor nearly as flakey spiritually as Jerri. He talked of gem energy and realigning chakras, and Tara was pretty sure he was realigning her mother's on a fairly regular basis because Janice was calm in a way Tara couldn't remember her ever being.

Of course Janice was also doing her own gardening again. Since Tara had moved out, Lori and Todd had moved into a house about five miles down the road from her and Jerri, and Irva was mostly gone—as she was now—Janice had sold the family home. She wound up buying the beach house Tara and Jerri had been renting. She just fell in love with the place, and the yoga guy Janice hadn't gotten the nerve to tell them she was actually dating seemed to like it, too. The one time her mother had actually let Tara talk to him to say more than hi, he had gone on and on about the energy of the beach in front of the house.

Tara didn't know who her mother thought she was fooling. She probably was well aware they all knew, just didn't want to be teased about it, and that Tara understood.

Georgia's show was been a huge ratings smash, so that the fact that not just Tara but Janice, Lori, and Todd jumped ship as well hadn't so much as pissed off the cable network their show aired on. Irva's new show was doing better than theirs had, so they could all get really depressed about not being as interesting as their transsexual father and model sister or just admit they were all just glad to be out from under the microscope of public opinion that had been held over them.

Georgia moved up beside Tara and looked across the fire to where Janice and the yoga guy were standing talking. "So are your mom and the hippie..."

"If you want to know don't ask Tara, ask Janice," Judy said. She had walked over and now sat down beside Cyndy.

"You know they are, Dad," Lori said.

She and Todd were both pretty wasted, but it didn't make Tara nervous the way it used to because they rarely fought at all anymore. When they did Tara no longer feared that the cops were going to cart one or both of them off or that Tara was going to wind up raising their kids when they split up.

After hearing all the legal reasons Tara and Jerri had gotten married, Todd and Lori decided they should, too. They had done so in fifteen minutes in Vegas, so splitting up now would be a lot harder for them to do. Plus they seemed to be pretty happy living in the country and raising their kids.

One of the homesteaders pulled a knotted ball of twine out of a bag. "See this? I found this by the side of the road years ago and decided to recycle it. For years every time I needed a piece of twine I farted around with this piece of shit till I got enough to do what I needed to, and... I hate this knotted ball of shit. My time and sanity are worth more than a ball of twine, and so..." He threw it in. "Burn you bastard burn."

Jerri was across the fire still talking to Joan Night. No one wanted their spouse to be talking to Joan Night. Tara hated to say it, but she was glad when Jerri started moving back around the fire in her direction. Of course she couldn't walk five feet that someone didn't stop her.

She started to go meet Jerri in the middle, but Georgia grabbed her arm. "You are with her twenty-four/seven. I hardly get to see you at all."

Tara nodded; Georgia was right. Tara shied away from the cameras these days, and Georgia had to move heaven and hell to get up there for The Burn without them.

"I brought a copy of that picture that someone took of me on the beach at Mom's that went viral where my ass looks like a small planet," Lori said.

"Jerri always says you can tell a lot about a person by what they bring to the burn," Judy said.

Lori laughed wildly. "Then I guess it's obvious I'm still a vain little shit."

"Mostly you hate that other people are so shallow that's all they see," Tara said.

Soon it was Georgia's turn. She walked up to the fire, grinned, reached into her jeans pocket and pulled it out. "I have two things; my last driver's license from when I was Gary, and my Republican voter registration card."

They all laughed, and she got a round of applause.

Tara reached into her pocket and stepped up to the fire. She pulled the small item out and held it high. "I came across this when Mother moved and I had to finally clean out my room. It's a four-leaf clover I pressed in a book when I was just a kid. You see I made a wish on this clover; I wished I wasn't queer. I wished that I wasn't different." She looked at Jerri across the fire and their eyes locked. "And now everything I have and am that I love, is only because I am so different. So I hate that I ever for a minute wished to be anything but what I am." Then she threw it into the fire.

About the Author

I started writing at twelve as an escape. The situations I have lived through are the stuff of which my fiction is born. My relationships with the many and varied people I have come into contact with over the years is a catalogue of characters from which I pull.

I am Jewish but consider myself spiritual not religious. I have studied every form of spirituality and try to live a spiritual life. I don't always succeed, but I do try.

My wife of nearly twenty-six years and I own a small farm where I raise milk goats, rabbits, chickens and a garden. I raise—depending on the weather and bugs—between forty and sixty percent of our food mostly organically. By "mostly" I mean if it looks like I will lose an animal I will do what I think is necessary. We make no trash; we use or recycle everything.

I lived for fourteen years of my life without electricity or running water. I had my only son naturally with no drugs. Though I was married off at sixteen (in an attempt to keep me from being gay) to a thirty-four-year-old man who immediately took me to New York and stuck me in a drug den for a month, I have smoked a total of five joints in my life. I have never done any other drugs. My son was a prescription drug addict for nine years.

I have worked every shit job you can imagine from pulling car parts in a junk yard and cleaning rich people's houses to home health care. I ran an industrial plane and have logged timber using a team of mules. I have worked at saw mills, framed houses, and poured slabs. I am a carpenter and a rock mason. I can run (install) electricity, and I can plumb (I hate plumbing). I have also built more than one house using only hand tools and a chain saw. I like to hike and cave, and I love the ocean.

I fought heavy weapons (and trained other fighters) with the SCA for about twelve years. During that time I broke several bones, and I have a seven-inch plate and eight screws in my left arm as a result of a bastard sword blow. Elizabeth Moon talked me into fencing many years ago and I still do that, but I sold all my armor and heavy weapons last year. Erin Grey talked me into trying Tai Chi to help with my CFS, so I have now been doing do a mixture of Tai Chi and Chi Gung every day for the last five years.

Mercedes Lackey helped me get my first short story sale in Marion Zimmer Bradley's magazine. That sale opened the door for others to MZB, one of which was included in a German-language anthology, and the royalties came in steadily for many years.

CJ Cherryh line edited the first two chapters of *Chains of Freedom* and taught me more about writing doing that than I had learned to that point.

I'm not just name-dropping here; I'm giving credit to people who helped me who certainly didn't have to. Over the years I've come to know many very famous people, and here's what I know for sure—we are ALL the same.

In the writing community the person who is the most famous and makes the most money is often the least talented or deserving—not always, but often. In our business who makes it and who doesn't is often determined by nothing in the world but dumb-ass luck. That being the case, the near worship we see of the "famous" is something I just don't get at all.

The truth is I always think bios are sort of a waste. Anyone who reads my work knows more about the real me than I could ever put in a bio. If you want to talk to me, find me on Facebook. If you see me somewhere, come right up and talk to me. I am just like you. Luckily, I have a job I love, and the reason I have this great job is that people like you let me.

About the Cover Artist

Melanie Fletcher is an expatriate Chicagoan who currently lives in North Dallas with her husband the Bodacious Brit™ and their five fabulous furbags JJ, Jessica, Jeremy, Jemma, and Jasmine (yes, they were following a theme, moving along now). When not herding cats, she turns into SF Writer Girl, and has the SFWA membership card to prove it. Her recent SF sales include "The Groom Wore Wings" (*Debris and Detritus: The Lesser Greek Gods Running Amok*, Story Spring Publishing). She also writes speculative fiction romance under the name Nicola M. Cameron, and her latest novel *Degree of Resistance (Pacifica Rising 1)* was just released in February from Belaurient Press.

Yard Dog Press Titles As Of This Print Date

Fantasy Writers Asylum (A YDP Imprint):

Blood Songs
Julia Mandala
Gateway to Corimar
Julia Mandala & Linda L Donahue
Tale of the Black Heart
Linda L. Donahue

Non-YDP titles we distribute:

Chains of Freedom
Chains of Destruction
Jabone's Sword
Queen of Denial
Recycled
Strange Robby
Sword Masters
Selina Rosen

Three Ways to Order:

1. Write us a letter telling us what you want, then send it along with your check or money order (made payable to Yard Dog Press) to: Yard Dog Press, 710 W. Redbud Lane, Alma, AR 72921-7247

2. Use selinarosen@cox.net or lynnstran@cox.net to contact us and place your order. Then send your check or money order to the address above. *This has the advantage of allowing you to check on the availability of short-stock items such as T-shirts and back-issues of Yard Dog Comics.*

3. Contact us as in #1 or #2 above and pay with a credit card or by debit from your checking account. Either give us the credit card information in your letter/Email/phone call, or go to our website and use our shopping carts. If you send us your information, please include your name as it appears on the card, your credit card number, the expiration date, and the 3 or 4-digit security code after your signature on the back (CVV). Please remember that we will include media rate (minimum $3.00) S/H for mailing in the lower 48 states.

Watch our website at
www.yarddogpress.com
for news of upcoming projects
and new titles!!

A Note to Our Readers

We at Yard Dog Press understand that many people buy used books because they simply can't afford new ones. That said, and understanding that not everyone is made of money, we'd like you to know something that you may not have realized. Writers only make money on new books that sell. At the big houses a writer's entire future can hinge on the number of books they sell. While this isn't the case at Yard Dog Press, the honest truth is that when you sell or trade your book or let many people read it, the writer and the publishing house aren't making any money.

As much as we'd all like to believe that we can exist on love and sweet potato pie, the truth is we all need money to buy the things essential to our daily lives. Writers and publishers are no different.

We realize that these "freebies" and cheap books often turn people on to new writers and books that they wouldn't otherwise read. However we hope that you will reconsider selling your copy, and that if you trade it or let your friends borrow it, you also pass on the information that if they really like the author's work they should consider buying one of their books at full price sometime so that the writer can afford to continue to write work that entertains you.

We appreciate all our readers and *depend* upon their support.

Thanks,
The Editorial Staff
Yard Dog Press

PS – Please note that "used" books without covers have, in most cases, been stolen. Neither the author nor the publisher has made any money on these books because they were supposed to be pulped for lack of sales.

Please do not purchase books without covers.